****

ABSORBING WHITE

An erotic novel
The third part of The White Trilogy
Copyright ©2015 by Charlotte E Hart
Cover Design by MAD
Formatting by MAD

1

Charlotte E Hart
ABSORBING WHITE

License Notes

Table of Contents

To Absorb

English definition of "Absorb".
-To take in or soak up (energy or a liquid or other substance)
-To fully understand (information, ideas, experiences)
-To take control of (a smaller less powerful entity) and make it part of a more powerful one

To Comprehend

English definition of "Comprehend".
- The ability to understand something, in its entirety
"Some won't have the least comprehension of what I'm trying to do"

To Assimilate

English definition of "Assimilate".
-The process of making new ideas or pieces of information part of your knowledge so that you can use them effectively
-The process of becoming part of a community or culture

Belligerent

English definition of Belligerent
Line breaks: bel/li/ger/ent

Adjective:
1, Hostile and aggressive
2, Engaged in War or Conflict
Origin
Late 16th century: from Latin *belligerent*-"waging war", from the verb *belligerare*, from *bellum* "war".

ABSORBING WHITE

By
Charlotte E Hart

2015

"A belligerent state permits itself every such misdeed, every such act of violence, as would disgrace the individual."
Sigmund Freud

Charlotte E Hart
ABSORBING WHITE

Chapter 1

Elizabeth

"**E**lizabeth, we're not done yet."

That's what he said five minutes ago, and I've been lying here ever since, still curled up in a ball, and still trying to will him away because I have no idea what I'm supposed to say or do. He's just admitted to murder, to killing a man – actually two men – with a knife and his hands. I mean, I knew he was a fighter. I'd worked that much out and seen it in action, but an actual murderer? Is this what he didn't want me to know? I hope to god it is, because I can't imagine much more horrific than killing a man. Why did he kill a man? *Two* men? I can't think straight. Christ, I wish he'd go away and just give me some time to process this, to think about it and get some order to my brain.

Alexander White – killer. Or was it Nicholas Adlin who killed, and Alexander White is who he is now?

I haven't got a fucking clue who he is. I was confused before, but now I'm an utter mess about who I'm in love with. Why has he gone all cold on me, and what is this kidnapping me and taking me off to New York all about? I don't know who I'm dealing with anymore. Why the hell was he holding a knife at my throat – his throat? Oh, I don't know whose throat belongs to whom anymore.

I'm so tired. I'm almost dulled of emotion. There's no pain, no real sense of surprise. If I'm honest, there's just a strange sense of disappointment, or maybe disenchantment. The man I love is a murderer. He's also a sadist, which I know I haven't met the measure of yet. Is that what Pascal meant with his, *"He's more than I could ever be when he embraces himself,"* comment?

No, surely not. That couldn't possibly have meant that he needs to kill people to have a good time, could it? What the hell am I supposed to say about all of this?

I wish it made me love him less, but the fact is I'm still lying here thinking about reaching my hand out to him and feeling his skin. Of pulling him down here so that he can make love to me and show me that none of it matters, and that it hasn't changed anything between us, but it has, hasn't it? The beautiful man who's standing there looking at me is someone I never knew existed. And if I open my eyes again at any point, I'll be able to see it in him now. I'll be able to look into those eyes and see a murderer, a killing machine, a man with no sense of right or wrong.

"Hands made for butchery" – the statement couldn't be more true. How little we knew when we sat in the coffee shop and looked a picture of him on a screen. How the hell were any of us supposed to see the man behind the image he portrayed? I should have seen this in him by now. I should have noticed the ambivalent swipe of blood from his face when he damn near killed that guy for what it really was. Only I didn't. I knew it wasn't quite right, but I didn't ever believe he could actually kill. Well, I don't think I did… Maybe I did?

I can hear him breathing next to me. He's feet away from me, with those hands that are, quite literally, made for butchery. I can smell his aftershave, still feel his touch on me and feel those eyes of his penetrating me, even though I can't see them. Why is he just standing there? Why doesn't he just go away? I'm not even sure I can take this silence much longer myself. I just want to go to sleep, or home, or anywhere other than here.

Damn him.

Time stretches on again, and I'm almost at the point of opening my eyes when a chuckle leaves his mouth. *A bloody chuckle!* Is something funny? I think not. My eyelids squeeze themselves together tighter in the hope of containing the bubbling anger that is beginning to surface again. I thought I was over that, devoid of any emotion whatsoever other than tiredness. Apparently I'm not.

"We can do this the easy way or the hard way, Elizabeth, but one way or another, I will make you see this."

What the sodding hell does that mean?

My eyes open slowly to see him staring down at me. There's no amusement in his eyes, so it clearly wasn't an amused chuckle that left his lips. He looks glazed over, lost in his own twilight world that is completely normal for him. That place that brings out the monster in

8

him, the one who has no regard for anything other than his own needs or thoughts. He's still infuriatingly beautiful, regardless of the fact that he's just admitted what he is, what he's done. That black hair of his is ruffled and messy, and those damned lips are still moving around each inhalation of breath with stunning results. And I so wish his strong jaw didn't still make me want to nibble my way along it and kiss his pulsing throat to soothe us both.

I gaze up at him, and once again, I wonder who it is that I've been with all this time and whether I've got a hope of getting my head around what he's done. Sudden images of blood on his hands race through my mind, so I glance down at his fingers and feel my stomach churn at the thought. Those wonderful hands, those hands that used to hold me and tell me that he loved me, that he'd stay with me forever, have killed someone, twice. Well, not one person twice, but two people, twice. Oh god, I can't think again, so I do the only thing available to me. I close my eyes again and curl tighter into the foetal position in the hope of forgetting, or at least not seeing him.

"Just leave me alone, Alex. I can't do this now," I mumble into the pillow.

"Remember, I did give you a choice," he says as I hear him walk away from me. The door opens, so I exhale a breath and try to relax my body a little. He's left me alone. I can think. I can have some time to consider, maybe find the reasons why in my own brain and try to process what the fuck I'm going to do about any of this.

Suddenly, there's a clinking of bottles and glasses coming from the main cabin, followed by the irritating giggling of what sounds like Tara the bitch. He's having a fucking drink? My eyes fly open again, not at the fact that he's drinking, but at the fact that I can hear him laughing, too. With her. My stomach instantly turns again as my legs pull up into my stomach, and I yank at the sheets furiously. What the hell is going on out there?

More giggling ensues and now whispering. I can hear his velvety voice has moved into seductive mode, although why he's bothering, I don't know, because the whore will clearly spread her legs for anything. Oh my god. I can't believe I just thought that. What the hell is wrong with me? Or him? What on earth is going on out there? And why the hell am I still in here?

I rapidly search the room for some clothes then realise I haven't got any because he sliced – yes fucking sliced – them off me, with a damn knife. I haven't got anything here – no suitcase, no clothes, nothing. He really has kidnapped me. Where's my bag? At least I've got my phone. Who can I call to get me the hell out of this? I need to tell Belle what's happening. What she can do, I have no idea, but maybe Conner can do something. Throwing the sheet out of the way, I sit up to search for it and realise all to quickly that it's in the main room. I threw it on the bloody floor when Neanderthal come MI5 arsehole dragged me onto the plane. He is absolutely not in my good books. He wasn't before, but he certainly isn't now. Who the hell does he think he is, assisting in this, whatever the fuck it is?

"Yes, Sir," I hear being said, which is followed by another giggle and the ruffling of clothes. My eyes swing to the door again. Has he just asked her to take her clothes off? Oh my god, what the hell am I going to do about this? What the hell is he trying to do to me? That burning anger suddenly comes rushing back with a vengeance. Clothes? Fuck it.

Scrabbling off the bed as quickly as I can, I yank the top sheet off and tie it around myself. The thought suddenly occurs that maybe I should go out there naked.

"Do maintain your dominance over him, my dear. He needs it to be honest."

Honest? I think the shit is being perfectly honest, for once. And what that freak is doing spinning around in my brain is anyone's guess. The man is quite clearly deranged. As is the murderer in the main cabin, who is now apparently chuckling to himself again, probably at the squeal of exuberance coming from Tara the slut. I can't contain it any longer. Not that I have a clue what I'm about to walk in on, but I'm going in. Tucking my hair behind my ears, I try for one last moment of decorum before stomping towards the door to find out what the hell is happening.

Frozen – that's a good description of what happens when I reach the hall. My feet abruptly come to a halt as I stand in shock and stare at what's in front of me. A perfectly naked Tara is beaming at me as the eyes of the man I love gaze at me over her shoulder. There's a small hint of amusement in the lifted corner of his mouth as he trails his fingers along her stomach and rests the other hand on her hipbone. Thank god he's still fully dressed in the remnants of his tux, although why that matters to me I'm really not sure. My body's damned reaction to the fact that he's rolled his sleeves up to highlight those hands and forearms is worrisome. Put that together with his open collar showing me his throat, and I'm thinking all sorts of inappropriate things I really shouldn't be thinking, given the situation in front of me.

My muddled mind reels over a few different responses to this scenario. I could go at him in style, I suppose, let loose all this bubbling anger and fly in for the kill. I could whimper and crumble into a pile of wet tears and snot. Unfortunately, or maybe fortunately, Pascal is still floating around in my head, and before I know what I'm doing, my feet are carrying me nonchalantly towards the bar with a flick of my hair, because that's where my bag is, and that means my phone. Also, there's alcohol there. I'm not completely sure what I'm doing, but the fact is I know he's doing this to wind me up for some reason. I'm still confused as to why, and while that inner slut of mine doesn't seem to care much for logical thought, my brain's trying to keep me calm. I'm not entirely up for whatever game this is, but I'm also not prepared to show him, in any way, that it's affecting me. And given that she is, in fact, a slut – a slut that he doesn't care about in the slightest – I have no reason to be worried that anything else is going to happen. Other than the fact that he's currently got his hands all over her. Arsehole.

Snatching a tumbler from the unit, I reach towards the decanter of brown liquid and pour a large shot of whatever it might be. I don't even care. It could be turpentine and I'd still drink it because the vision behind me is very disturbing, regardless of my grace in dealing with him.

"Put the drink down, Elizabeth," he says firmly. My head wants to turn at the authority there. To be honest, my eyes want to look at the floor, but I carry on with my ambivalence and lift the glass to my lips. Before I know what's happened, the glass has been knocked from my mouth and smashes on the floor ten feet away.

"What the hell are you doing?" I very nearly scream as I jump backwards, away from him.

"I fucking meant it. Do as you're damn well told."

I'm open-mouthed gaping because there's not a hint of anything nice in those eyes. Not one inch of love or connection of any sort is

11

being shown to me, just what I'm beginning to realise is the Alexander White I don't know, the one who's told me he's going to teach me something. Or rather, *show* me someone.

"Alex, I don't know what-"

"Look at the floor."

"What?"

"Are you struggling with English? In fact, get on your knees."

"I..."

"Do you want me to put you there? Look, I'll show you how simple it is. Tara, down."

Of course the bitch drops to the floor like a stone, knees spread and head lowered as he continues to stare at me. Nonchalance has left me completely, it seems, because I'm actually shaking. I'm not sure if it's from fear or anger, but I get the distinct impression I'm going to have to use it wisely.

"No, this game isn't one I'm prepared to play," is my eventual calm response.

This isn't what we're about. It never has been, and given whatever the hell is currently happening, I refuse to be on the back foot. He said this was about him being honest? Well, he can have it back if that's the way he wants it. "And I don't know what the hell you're trying to do but it's not working. After what you've just told me, now you're out here doing this? What is wrong with you? Are you going to fuck her while I watch? Is that the plan? Piss me off or something? Don't you think what I've just heard is enough to confuse me?" Suddenly I'm on a roll. I can't even begin to stop my mouth, so I don't even try. "Well please do. Crack on, but I'm not having any part of it. I thought this was about you telling me the truth, about us getting closer or something, but ... Well, I haven't got the faintest idea what you're trying to achieve here, and-"

I am abruptly cut off as his hand clamps over my mouth, and he begins to drag me across the floor towards the bitch. I wrench around in his grip but I haven't got a hope and I know it. One last final shove at him is enough to send the damn sheet skimming away from me and onto the floor.

With a clearly practiced manoeuvre of my body, he has somehow managed to get me on the floor and on my knees next to her. My eyes swing to the left to find her still calmly resting there as if nothing else is going on in the room, so just as his hand begins to leave my arm, I try to scramble back up onto my feet again. I am not being naked in this room with the bitch from hell and Alex the dickhead.

"Don't push me, Elizabeth. Stay there."

It's venomous, deadly even. Just like in that room in the Lake District, there is not one ounce of warmth, and he seems to be becoming even more devoid of emotion, if that's possible. What the hell is going on here?

I look back up into his eyes as he stands there, looking far too fucking attractive for the situation, and I try to hold his darkening blue gaze as best as I can.

"Alex, I ... I don't want this, whatever it is. I just want to go back to the bedroom. Just let me-"

"You do want this, Elizabeth. You told me you did."

My eyes widen in surprise as his brow raises a touch. Is he suggesting I've asked for this behaviour in some way? I haven't, or not that I'm aware of. I just wanted to understand the man I love a little better, to be a part of him and help him battle his demons.

"Not like this," I reply quietly as I try my best to cover my boobs and decide to not listen to the slight snicker that's just left the bitch's mouth.

"Tara, lower," he grates out without removing his eyes from mine. She instantly moves and places her forehead on the floor in front of her knees. She's clearly a professional sub then, although why he's chastising her for being rude to me is completely unknown. It's not like he's being particularly friendly at the moment. It suddenly strikes me that I understood that exchange – that I knew what he was trying to do to her. She was rude to me, and he didn't like it, so he told her off. Wow, I get this shit. I understand. When did I learn to understand that? Has all this time in his company taught me things I hadn't even thought of? Has the time with Pascal enlightened me to stuff I wasn't aware had sunk in? It's not like we've ever really had that type of relationship. I've never really had to deal with this type of behaviour before, but clearly I do understand it somehow. It doesn't mean the current situation has changed, but maybe I can use it to my advantage, because regardless of his malevolence, he's clearly still here with me, otherwise he wouldn't have just done that, would he?

"I don't know what you want from me," I say quietly, as I continue to look at him. Those dead blue eyes just keep staring back. There's nothing for me to work with. If we were alone, I'd reach out for him, try to bring him back a little, maybe even give him what he needs, but we're not. In fact, I'm pretty sure it should be him making me feel better, shouldn't it? It should be him telling me why he killed people, him explaining himself and trying to make me understand his reasons so that we can move on.

"I want you to endure, Elizabeth. Learn," he replies, almost reticently as he licks his lips, lets go of my gaze and moves towards Tara again. Unfortunately, I'm one part interested and two parts irritated. I haven't got a clue what he's about to do, and I'm pretty certain I'm not going to want to watch it, so I've only got a few choices left. Run, storm off, or close my eyes and lower my head. Unfortunately, my curiosity seems to be getting the better of me, because try as I might, I can't seem to get my feet to move me anywhere. Regardless of whatever strange emotion is unsettling my stomach at the thought of those butchering hands, I still want him. I want to reach inside that soul and drag him back to me, knit us back together somehow and force him to tell me more. Why? Who? Where? Why do I need to know this crap? It's ridiculous of me. I should be running for the fucking hills, screaming about the murderer in the room, not kneeling here waiting for whatever snippet of information he's about to deliver like I'm some love-struck puppy. I should get a bloody grip of myself.

His hand suddenly grabs hold of the back of Tara's hair and pulls her upwards. It's harsh even by his standards. She winces at the pressure but lifts herself up until she's standing in front of him, still completely fucking naked, not unlike myself, obviously.

"I want you to show Elizabeth what I like to see you do to other women."

What the hell does that mean? My throat can't stop the unconscious gasp that slips out at his words. I told him I wouldn't do that – that I didn't want another woman involved.

"Yes, Sir," she replies as she drops her head again and turns towards me. Yes, me, because I'm the only other damn woman in the room. The slight sneer she allows to creep over her face once her back is to him doesn't go unnoticed. Bitch. Am I not worth her fucking time or something? What the hell did I just think that for? Jesus, I'm confused.

Her hand reaches for my shoulder. Oh my god, what am I going to do? My body freezes again at the thought as she gently lands her fingers on my skin. They're warm. I'm not sure why, but I expected them to be cold, like her, but they're not. They're soft, tender even. My eyes shoot back to him again.

"Alex, I..." I can't even finish what I want to say, because for whatever reason, her touch is somehow soothing, and his intense stare does not make me feel like I've got much choice in the matter anyway. Safeword... I should use that, shouldn't I? I should just say it now. Then all of this will stop and I can go back to the bedroom. Yes, *Chess*. I need to say it. The word lingers, but I can't seem to make it come out of my mouth. I can't find speech anymore, and her lips moving towards mine as she kneels in front of me really aren't helping my cause.

"First time?" she whispers, surprising me with a far more friendly smile on her still very beautiful face than I was expecting.

"Umm..." It's all I've got, because she's now moved her hand to my face. One long finger moves along my cheekbone and down towards my mouth with a feather light touch. I'm sure my mouth is open, and I know my body has become a rigid fortress of closed gates, but I can't move because her eyes have changed. They've become liquid, or some other unusual thing that can't be described. I'm being drawn into them so acutely that I'm not even in control of my breathing anymore.

"Relax, honey," she says. "You'll be fine."

And then she's there, her unfairly full lips on mine, tenderly, quietly, and my first reaction is to pull away so my head snaps back to look at her again. She's doing that smile still, the one that makes me want to trust her, and her tousled blonde hair around her face seems to bring on visions of fairytales and dreams for some odd reason. My eyes flick across to Alex. He's standing at the bar now, leaning on it with a glass of something dark in his palm, still no flicker of emotion to tell me why he's doing this.

"Don't think about him," she says seductively. "Think about what you need."

I have no damn clue what I need, but I'm positive it had nothing to do with kissing a woman ten minutes ago. I wish I could say the same thing now, but the core clenching that's currently going on means I'm clearly no longer commanding my faculties. My inner slut is very much in control, and now Tara's mouth is moving in again. I'm positive this is the moment I should get up and leave, but I don't really want to. Those lips are suddenly tempting me, inviting me to try yet another new version of Alex that I've never met before. So I move forward into them, and before I know what's hit me, her tongue is there, too, gently teasing my mouth open and asking for more. There's absolutely nothing aggressive about it, not one hint of power or force, just sweet delicious licks of enticement.

My body's humming, and then her hands wrap into the back of my hair and I do everything I can to not enjoy the experience, but I'm lying to myself because the fact is, I'm revelling in it. Feeling her moving around my body is like soft winds caressing silk, and her touch on my skin sends exquisite shivers of uncertainty coursing across me in a way I've never experienced before.

"Lie down, Elizabeth." His velvety voice comes crashing into the moment. I'd almost forgotten he was here, lost in the arms of another woman, but the strength of his tone reminds me exactly what's going on here. My hackles come racing back from God knows where. Who the hell does he think he is, making me do this? Manipulative bastard.

"No," I mumble in response through her lips as I begin to pull away again. She instantly tightens her hold on the back of my head and tries to keep the kiss going, so I push on her shoulders to get away from her and shift myself away. "No, I won't do this. I'm not playing with you, or her."

Something flashes in his eyes. It's so quick that I can't begin to understand it, and before I can even get to my feet, he's crossed the space between us and is pulling Tara by the hair again. His frame moving in that manner has me remembering every second of his power over me, every bruising touch that has me yearning for more. Tara groans at the pressure and manoeuvres herself around perfectly to accommodate his every move. Within seconds, she's on her back with him in between her legs. Those long fucking legs are wrapping themselves around the man I love as he hovers on his haunches in front of her and moves his hands to his belt with a sneer.

16

"You want to do this the hard way? Fine," he clips as he flicks the buckle and then the top button of his trousers. My mouth is gaping again. Is he really going to do this? In front of me? What the hell am I supposed to do about this? My hands itch with the need to slap seven bales of shit out of him, but still I can't move. I can hardly close my mouth from its ridiculous gaping, and now even my ability to speak seems to have left me again. Her hands travel down between her legs, and unfortunately, I can't stop my bloody eyes from following them as her fingers find the tops of her thighs. I'm so mesmerized by them that I don't even notice that he's got himself out and is ready and waiting to dive into her until it's almost too late. That's mine. What the hell is he doing? No, I can't see that. I don't want that. I'll do anything to avoid that, and as her fingers grasp at his thigh and pull him toward her, I feel speech come rushing back to me.

"No, Alex, stop. Don't..."

He doesn't stop. He just lets her touch his thighs, lets her carry on with her moaning and writhing, and then moves lower over her until his face is inches from her lips and his body is aligned perfectly.

"What do you want, whore?" he says to her as he drags his tongue across her lips. She nips lustfully at them and looks even more glorious for it. Oh my god! My stomach churns again at the thought, but I can't fucking move. I can't move my fucking hands or any other body part to try and save myself from whatever the hell it is that's going on.

"You, Sir," she replies breathily as she moves her hands to the back of his head and tries to pull him down to her mouth. And he fucking lets her, right there in front of me. Their lips begin rolling across one another, and the sound of desire echoes in the room as his body presses onto her and she twines herself in tighter. Bitch. Bastard. Why can't I speak?

Her fingers find their way to the back of his neck, then his throat – *my* throat. That's my damn throat. Suddenly, my body fires back to life and I'm pushing at his frame with all my might – anything to get him off her and to gain some sense of control again. Slapping happens, and then more shoving, but before I can do anything with his weight, he has me pinned by both wrists at the side of him, that expert pressure of his grasping more firmly than normal as he chuckles and moves back slightly. Tara continues her groaning beneath him, her naked form continually trying to entice him back to the task at hand, and I have no damn clue how, but he somehow manages to get me on my back beside her. My arms are still pinned beneath my back as he dips his head and runs his tongue along the entire length of my stomach until his face comes to a standstill in front of me. Why do his eyes have to be so damned consuming?

"Joining in, Elizabeth? Here, have a taste." I have no idea what that means until his finger is in front of my mouth. It's glistening with what must be Tara's wetness. That's all I've got to describe it. Does he expect me to put that in my mouth? "Open up."

Clearly he does, and while fifty percent of me is running for the hills, there's another part that's being held captive by his gaze, those darkened eyes that once again hold an element of amusement. The monster, it seems, has retreated for a while, but his mouth is still stern, serious. He means it, and for whatever reason, my damn body is traitorously yielding to his request. Thankfully, my lips aren't as I clamp them closed.

"Are you going to do what you're told?" My head shakes slowly in his face. I'm not doing it. I'm not having that woman in my mouth. I can't. I don't even know why this is happening, let alone understand the reason why my inner slut is licking her lips and running full throttle into the breach. He shifts his body weight around on top of me until he's lying between my legs. He releases my hands with yet another smirk and dips his fingers into his own fucking mouth. Jealousy rages through me at the way his lips move around them, tasting her, savouring it, and then he finally pulls them out and gazes down at me with another chuckle. "Someone is going to come, Elizabeth. Choose who."

What does he mean by that? Does he mean him? I have no idea. I'm completely lost, and it only seems to heighten the need to have him grind into me, which he isn't doing. My body instantly starts to ache, and I just suppress the need to push myself up to him so that I can feel that muscle and rid myself of this fucking nightmare. What the hell is this all about? He's a murderer. What am I even doing lying here beneath him? I have to get out of here and stop this ridiculous game. I need to get myself back into that bedroom, where I can avoid all of this craziness and call someone to help.

"Alex, let me get up. I don't want this," I say quietly. His head tilts a little, and then he's off me and pushing Tara back down again until his mouth hovers around her breast.

"Seems it's going to be you," he says to her as his tongue flicks at her nipple. She instantly begins her moaning again, writhing and grinding into him as he swirls that delicious tongue around her and reaches for his drink. I can't believe what I'm watching. My mouth is gaping, again. It's not possible he really means this, is it?

"Alex, please don't do this. What the hell do you want from me? I don't want any of this. Why are you doing this? You said you didn't want another woman. Just stop, please."

He doesn't stop anything at all, just continues with his mouth on tit action and smiles at Tara the slut as she forces her chest up into his face. The fact that I've suddenly noticed how incredible her breasts actually are is neither here nor there.

"I gave you a choice, Elizabeth. You chose to not do anything with it. So just run along and let me enjoy myself."

What the fuck? He really is going to do this. What an arsehole. I'm leaving. I'm on my feet and making my way to the bedroom when I suddenly remember how fucking angry I am. Furious doesn't even begin to cover how damned irritated I am. Of course, Pascal flits into my mind again. Well, he can just take a running jump with his "*stay in control*" speech. They're both fucking insane. This whole thing is insane. How can anybody put up with this sort of shit? This is so not normal. I'm not surprised, given his upbringing, but does he have to be such a fucking bastard for no reason whatsoever? He's the one in the wrong, not me. How fucking dare he do any of this?

My feet have turned me back towards him before I've even considered what I'm doing. I have absolutely no control over what my body's about to do, but I'm pretty sure it has a lot to do with hitting him, because I can feel my fists tightening and my nails digging into my palms. Fucking arsehole. Why? Why me? Why did I fall for him, and why is that fucking slut still moaning and groaning? I hate that sound. I hate her. I fucking hate him.

"Alex?" I say as I reach the pair of them, his perfect backside in my line of view as I try to let go of my fingers so I can slap the shit out of him the moment he turns around.

"What?" he replies without removing his face from her fucking faultless body.

"Look at me."

"I'm bored with looking at you." Tara giggles. It's not fucking funny.

"Turn the hell around and look at me."

My hands have found my hips. I'm not having this at all. I can feel my eyes searching for something to pick up and throw at him. There must be something I can use to stop this shit. I suppose I could just jump on him or something... That could work. Or I could use that rage thing he somehow found in me. In fact, I think it's beginning to wind its way up my spine quite effortlessly already. I can feel every thought turning into some sort of explosion of fury. My limbs are shaking again, and that blindness seems to be coming at me from somewhere.

"Alex, I'm warning you." What the hell I think I'm warning him about is inconsequential at the moment. I'll make a decision when he answers me or turns himself round. Yet again, he doesn't, and Tara keeps giggling, which just increases my rage to new heights. My eyes fly around for something again, and then I remember the knife. That'll damn well stop him. I stomp off towards it with no rational thought at all, and on eventually reaching it, I bend down to swipe it off the floor with such ease I can't even believe my own actions. It suddenly feels comfortable in my hand, an extension of my thoughts and fears, and he did tell me to use it, didn't he? So I'm damn well going to use it. To rip his fucking head off.

Swinging back around, I launch back up the hallway, still listening to the bitch who has now lowered her giggling to some sort of erotic mewling sound. Presumably Alex, the fucking god, has started his deviant fingers on their mind-bending course that should be reserved for only me. What a wanker.

Before I know it, I've grabbed the back of his hair viciously and tilted his head back towards me. Then, without any further thought on the matter, the bloody knife is at his throat.

My hands are still shaking, and I can see the fear jumping from Tara's eyes at me as I lean over the pair of them. She's clearly in shock. So am I, if I'm honest, but the fact is this suddenly feels completely okay. It's as if I've done it a thousand times. So why isn't Alex fighting me, or at the very least trying to get the blade away from his neck? I can feel the texture of his hair in my hand. I can smell his aftershave assaulting me. I can't stop myself from inhaling it into my lungs and taking a snippet of that calmness to try and get myself together. My thighs are trembling around his back as I yet again increase my grasp of his hair and let all that rage twist my fingers until his jaw is tilting up towards me. What the hell am I doing? My teeth are grinding on themselves in a bid to tell me I'm doing something wrong, but the rubber in my hand feels so right, so natural, so vengeful. How dare he do this to me, to us? What the hell is he trying to achieve with his little game?

"Do it, Elizabeth." What the fuck does that mean?

Tara gasps and recoils away from him, feet scrabbling against the floor as she backs away hurriedly and casts her eyes to the floor in fear. I must look like a wild fucking banshee because she's now cowering in the corner of the room. At least she's not bloody moaning or giggling anymore, thank God. I might be able to think without that crap going on. God, I just want some time to think, and a fucking drink.

"Put your sodding clothes on, Tara," comes out of my mouth. Christ knows where it comes from, but I'm fed up with looking at her flawless body, with her endless legs. Anyway, she hasn't really done anything wrong, has she? It's the murdering bastard in my hands that has, the one who is now completely still between my thighs as I tighten my hold on him just in case he moves. I'm not even sure I'm processing what's going on until I feel him flinch a little while my gaze follows Tara as she scuttles over to her uniform.

"Are you going to use it, or shall I show you how?" he says. I feel the words rumbling through his back as a throaty chuckle leaves his mouth, his muscles shaking as if something amuses him again. "You'll never know it, will you? Never feel it as I do... You're still thinking too much, Elizabeth."

I'm utterly confused as to what the hell he's talking about, and Tara's still crawling around, trying to do up her shirt and pretend she's bloody innocent in all of this, which she sort of is. I'm still fucking irritated with her, nonetheless. So I continue my watchful gaze of her, just in case she decides to do something ridiculously stupid like try to get me off him. That would be incredibly stupid of her, given the odd sensation that's currently keeping me attached to him like some feral cat. I haven't got a clue what any of this is, but I'm not letting go of him in a hurry. I can keep him here, keep him safe, keep *me* safe from him touching her again. I'm in control here, holding the blade to his throat. I've got the power, haven't I? Well, I think I have.

Oh my god, I can't think again. I really need a drink.

"I just want this to stop," I say quietly as he turns his head around towards me. Those dark blue eyes hit me like a battering ram, and all thoughts of hatred and anger are suddenly replaced with that rush of love that always hits me so hard when he gazes at me. The rubber in my hand falters as logical thought seems to wind its way back into my brain. What am I doing? My fingers in his hair relax just for a second, and he uses the instant to his own advantage so successfully that before I'm aware what's happened, I'm on the floor again beneath him. One of his strong hands is holding down the wrist that's still grasping the knife in some sort of death grip.

"Drop it," he says as he continues with his detached stare.

My arms are not complying in the slightest with any thought I have, of dropping the damn thing or not. I'm just lost in those eyes and that face again, just barely holding on to coherent thought of what's going on around me. The floor abruptly jolts beneath me, which reminds me we're in an aeroplane – *his* aeroplane. Alexander White's aeroplane – the businessman, the murderer, the sadist. The love of my fucking life. Oh my god, what am I doing?

Chapter 2

Alexander

"Drop it or fucking use it," he said again as he gazed down on her. Christ, she looked good, all wild eyes and frustration as she stared back up at him in confusion. He eased the pressure off her wrist and allowed her a chance to take a swipe at him. She was the only one who would ever deserve a shot at it, and if that was what she wanted then so be it. His damaged soul was hers to keep, and if she chose to kill it completely then it was probably for the best.

She continued to stare as he moved back a little and released his hold of her until she was lying on the floor beneath him. Her body still trembled, and her hair fanned out around her head as she lifted the blade towards him and then looked back at it in puzzlement for a second or two. Her body suddenly shifted as she scuttled backwards away from him and opened her grasp until the knife landed on the floor with a dull thud.

"What the hell are you doing to me?" she hissed as her wide eyes glanced down at the offending object and then back at him.

"Teaching you," he replied indifferently as he put his cock away and stared back at her.

"Teaching me what, Alex? How to bloody hate you?" she replied with her eyes shifting towards the slut at the back of the room. It had been an interesting choice of manipulation, but it had definitely worked. Elizabeth Scott was unquestionably a jealous woman, and regardless of the situation, she'd reacted just as a woman in love would. Viciously. "What is all this? I don't understand what you're trying to achieve, Alex."

Would she ever? Christ, he hoped so.

He stood back up and looked down on her as he kicked the blade across the floor to her again. She just sneered at it and shuffled her sexy arse away.

"Who did you want to kill more, Elizabeth?" She frowned and glared up at him, probably in disgust.

"I didn't want to *kill* anybody. I'm not a butcher. You, however, might want to check the mirror."

He smirked at her as Tara did some fucking stupid gasp behind him. *Whore*. Her opinion wasn't welcome in the slightest.

"It felt good though, didn't it? Hmm? That sudden feeling of control, that feeling of absolute power and hatred?"

She screwed her beautiful face up and stared down at the knife again in repulsion. She could deny it as much as she liked, but she'd felt it. That moral decency of hers may have brought her back from the brink, but she'd had a snippet of the sensation he'd craved every day since the first time it found him. Or since he found it.

She shook her head and grabbed onto the table to pull herself up, then stood there in all her stunning beauty and placed a hand on her hip. He tilted his head at the move. She was either about to launch herself at him again or make him feel something he wasn't prepared to tolerate at the moment. He watched as her fingers flicked on her hipbone, presumably thinking of some emotional response to even the score to some degree.

"Regardless of who you are, or what you have done, I will never hate you, Alex. So I suggest you just try real honesty and we'll see where that goes, shall we?"

No, she wouldn't, would she? And real honesty was what he was trying to give her. He shook his head slightly and looked back down at the blade on the floor with a snort of amusement.

"Pick it up again, Elizabeth," he said. Tara gasped again.

"Mr. White, shouldn't we tie her up or something? She's clearly delusional. Why would you ask her to do that?" He flicked a quick sneer over his shoulder at her and raised a brow. Had the whore just dared to speak? She bowed her head slightly and shut her mouth, so he turned back to the real woman in the room. Elizabeth just stood there staring at him, her brow mirroring his own as she slowly turned her head towards the back of the room, her face full of contempt, and opened her lips.

"You can keep your bloody mouth closed," she scathed as she briefly glanced at the knife again and continued to tap her fingers against her hip.

"I wasn't talking to you, psycho," came racing back as Tara arrived beside him and offered him some rope. When the fuck she'd got it was anyone's guess.

"Alex, can you at least remove this bitch before I do something I'll regret?"

Definitely not. That could be the first interesting moment of the night. To see her purposely let that demon loose might be the best thing for all of them.

"Who the hell do you think you-"

"Oh, piss off! I'm the only woman who means a damn thing in this room, honey, so get your arse out of my face before I grab that knife and cause some real damage."

His other brow shot up as he watched the woman he loved sneer and land both hands on her hips. It appeared rage was working efficiently again. His cock instantly leapt to attention at the venom that was beginning to drip from her tongue as he studied her body with intense interest. Tara, quite stupidly, took a step towards her.

"You're a fucking nutter. I'll rip the hair from your head, and-"

That was enough. Nobody called the love of his life a psycho and a nutter, and certainly not a common slut. In one swift move, he'd pushed the whore to the floor and had her head pinned to the carpet.

"Quite appropriately proven, I think. You should know your place, Tara," Elizabeth said from above him. His head shot up to look at her as she crossed her arms and licked her lips with a wry smile. Clever bitch. Had she just goaded him into that? Who the fuck was in control here?

It wasn't her.

"Elizabeth, pick the knife up," he said again.

"No," she replied instantly, still with her brow raised.

"Pick it up or I'll make you."

"Why? And we've talked about this forcing rubbish. It doesn't work with me."

"Just pick it up."

She hesitated for a second before glancing at the knife and moving a step towards it. Her arm reached forward, but something stopped her again as she slowly swivelled her head back towards him.

"How will you make me? Hurting me won't work, Alex, and you wouldn't do that anyway."

His fingers gripped the back of Tara's head tighter. If there was one thing he could count on here it was Miss Scott's sense of right and wrong, so he lifted the blonde hair until Elizabeth could see her face.

"You're right, Elizabeth, but hurting *her* will."

He heard the gulp of panic as Tara stiffened in his hand. She never had been one for any real sense of pain. Mildly amusing and reasonably decent entertainment, but a serious masochist she was not. Hi angel's face didn't change in the slightest as she continued to gaze at him quietly. She'd now resumed her cross-armed stance and seemed to be contemplating her next move, so he stood and dragged Tara to her feet sharply. The yelp of pain coming from her mouth instantly tore straight through his love's apparent calm. She couldn't stop the flinch that followed, or the look of care that took over her face.

"Alex, you can't be serious. Let her go," she said cautiously as she carefully unwrapped her arms and took a small step towards them. He wrenched Tara's head to the side and downward until she was balanced at an awkward angle, which had her damn near screaming in pain and scrabbling her hands around for something to hold on to.

"Mr. White, please. I can't..."

"Alex, let her go for God's sake. Just stop it. You're hurting her."

"I'm not going to ask you again, Elizabeth."

Nonchalance seemed to return to her face after a small staring contest. That may have worked before, but it really wasn't going to help her now. If she tried to reason with him at the moment, it simply wasn't going to go her way. The whole point of this was that she learned to hate. She thought she knew him, but she didn't know this version.

"Oh, screw you and your threats. You can't do it, can you? I can see you, Alex. You made me see you. So if you're trying to manipulate me, you shouldn't bother. I know all your little games, and you're not really going to hurt her."

Two quick strides and he was dragging a screaming Tara to the bedroom, her feet tumbling around beneath her as she tried to keep herself upright and hold onto his wrist to ease the pressure on her hair. Adrenalin flooded his already eager system as he listened to the gasps of panic and the moans of pain coming from behind him.

"Alex, stop it," Elizabeth's voice shouted as he rounded the corner and kicked open the bolt on the floor.

"Get down, Tara," he said as he released her head and sensed he kneel at his feet. Two swift latches later and the pole slid from its concealment and locked into place on the floor.

Elizabeth crashed into the room and glared at him. Before she could open her beautiful mouth, he grabbed at her and reached for the sheet on the bed. Her face screwed up in confusion, but she apparently got the idea because she began shoving at him as he wound the cloth around her arms and manoeuvred her backwards towards the pole. This seemed to bring all sort of venom to the forefront as she realised what he was doing.

"Fuck off. You're not tying me up in this mood." Too late, because three twists later, she was encased by the arms and restrained against the pole. He slowly walked behind her and pulled the sheet ends together to cross them in front of her body, then returned to stand in front of her. Clearly she wasn't amused. His dick was.

"Open your legs, Elizabeth. It's for your benefit." She scowled at him and looked down at Tara. He'd forgotten she was there, to be honest. There was only one thing his mind was currently focused on, and it had nothing to do with the slut at his feet. Seeing Elizabeth here again, wrapped with makeshift bindings and ready to fight him, was almost more than he could stand. That blue satin swirling up and down her pale skin was enough to send any man insane, let alone one as fucked up as he was. She shook her head and stared him down. "Fine. When you're ready to do as you're told, let me know."

With that said, he tied the end of sheet around her knees to hold them closed and started to take off his shirt.

"Alex, just stop this. If you want to talk then we'll talk, but this is ridiculous. Tara, just get up and leave the room, will you?"

He pulled the remainder of his shirt off and stared at her. There was no need to look at Tara. She wouldn't be moving anywhere; she knew better. And of course, those beautiful eyes just kept drilling into him. Elizabeth had learnt well to not look away. Standing up to him was becoming second nature to her, not a flicker on her face as she held that chin up and bored holes right through him all over again. He ran his tongue over his teeth and pushed the need to kiss her lips away.

"Tara, stand up and take your clothes off."

Elizabeth's eyes flicked to Tara as she instantly stood and began peeling her skirt away. He never removed his gaze from her face. He didn't want to look away from it at all, didn't want one other female form to ever get in between them, but this had to be done. It would be enough to repulse her, and that would be the beginning of true hatred.

"Carry on with what I asked of you earlier," he said. Elizabeth's eyes widened but still remained transfixed on his. "She can't fight back this time."

"You dick," Elizabeth snarled as she tugged at her restraints. "How dare you? Have I not given you everything? You're the psycho here. And, Tara, don't you fucking touch me."

He glanced down at the diamonds sparkling on her wrist as she wrenched at the sheet and chuckled to himself. She definitely wouldn't ever be owned by anyone. With a few strides, he reached inside his jacket pocket and removed the matching necklace. He'd said he'd never leave her, and he meant it.

Tara scuttled out of his way as he lifted the choker to Elizabeth's throat and wrapped it around her skin. She twisted her head in every available direction to dislodge it but it was no use. He latched it together and took a step away again. She stared back at him, this time in disbelief.

"Oh my god, you are delusional, aren't you? Do you think I want this around my neck? Fuck off. I don't want any of this. Let me out of this." He smiled and made himself comfortable on the bed.

"You told me I could make the decisions about what we need. You need this."

"What? You think this is morally acceptable? I've just found out you're a... well, you know..." She stuttered as she shot a look at Tara. "And you think you still have the right to tell me what to do? I might still care, Alex, but you're pushing the damn boundaries of reason here."

He smiled again. She was still trying to protect him. After everything she'd been through so far, she still wouldn't say the words directly.

"I'm a what, Elizabeth?" Her eyes shifted again. He couldn't give damn about Tara. She could easily be paid off, or disposed of. He couldn't have cared less. The whore had no proof anyway. Elizabeth's eyes looked towards the floor as her mouth moved around unspoken words. "Louder, Elizabeth. Say it."

She shook her head and continued with her downward gaze, then appeared to mumble something about Phillips beneath her breath. He sneered at the mention of the man. He still didn't understand why she'd been talking to him in the first place. She may not have wanted the man, but why she knew him was irritating as hell. "What did you say?"

She shook her head again and sighed out a breath.

"Alex, please... I just want to go home. I'm so tired," she replied. Good. Hate would descend more rapidly that way. There was no way she'd ever give up completely. He'd seen that fire in her. She just needed to let it back out again.

"Talking of Aiden Phillips, why were you with him? Do you want him as well as Pascal? I'm sure I can arrange it. Three seems a little greedy if I'm honest. However, you know I'll give you anything you want." Her face flew back upwards. Apparently he'd hit a nerve.

"What the fuck sort of question is that? Really?" she said as a scowl of annoyance flashed across her face again.

"Well, do you?"

"I can't believe you're even suggesting... Are you insane? You're the one who wants that, not me. I'm not even discussing this with you, not unless you let me out of this, anyway. I don't know what this odd mood is you've got going on, but you need to let me out of this and then we can try and figure-"

"Tara, start at the floor and work your way up," he cut in.

"No," she near shouted as she glared at Tara. He wasn't entirely sure who she'd aimed the comment at. "Stop! Don't... Alex, please, stop her. You... Stop, I don't want this."

"Aiden Phillips?"

"Okay, okay! No, I don't want him at all. He's evil or something. I don't even really know him," she replied as she inched her feet away from Tara whose head was hovering around them.

"You looked like you knew him, very well, actually."

"Alex, don't be ridiculous. You're clearly doing that *making stuff up in your twilight mind* shit again," she said as she stared him down.

"You were the one cavorting with another man, Elizabeth. How is that my fault?"

"I wasn't cavorting. How dare you? I was trying to not make a scene, for you, and then you went all alpha oddness on me and told me to stay still. Which I did. *For you.* Until he acted like some macho arsehole who thought he owned me. Not unlike you at the moment. Let me out of these fucking binds, will you?"

"What were you talking to him about, and how do you know him?"

"I don't. I told you that. He was just in Tudor's when that Cecily bitch came over and asked if I wanted to have lunch. I didn't even know who he was until she introduced him, then he wouldn't let go of Belle's hand, and it all got a bit bizarre. So we left."

"So out of all the places you could have gone, you purposely went to Tudor's, one the clubs he owns."

"Yes, but it wasn't me. It was Belle, and... I don't even know why I'm telling you this. There is nothing going on between me and Aiden Phillips. You're the one who seems to have dealings with the thug, not me. Care to explain?"

"I think I already did, didn't I?" She instantly opened her beautiful mouth and then closed it again. She repeated the action a few times and her eyes widened as she cottoned on to what he was saying. Presumably, she had thought it had just been the two men, probably in a fight, self-defence of some sort in an unprovoked attack, maybe. That's the only decent reasoning for killing someone, isn't it? The only morally acceptable explanation for taking another's life?

How little she knew. His bastard of a father flashed in front of his eyes as he pictured his mother, holding her son, cradling the promise of love and adoration, of happiness. Of a life taken from him before he even knew it could exist. Why had he killed her? He'd asked himself that a million times over the years and found no justifiable motivation for the bastard destroying her other than control, or maybe lunacy. He needed to ask the man himself. Why hadn't he done that yet? Why hadn't he just forced the man to speak and explain himself? It's not like he was scared of the dick. He knew where he was. He could just walk in and ask, confront him and deal with it all. He could wander into that manor house and make him admit what he had done, and subsequently what he'd created.

A phone rang somewhere, so he shook his head to clear the fog and found her eyes still intently trained on his. He also realised he was rubbing at his throat, so quickly removed his hand and stared at his fingers in confusion.

"What is it? What do you need?" she said quietly, with that look that said she understood every emotion flying through him better than he did. She probably did, and it seemed regardless of her present state, she still wanted to help him. He frowned in response, got up and walked into the main cabin to get his phone.

"Tara, no higher than ankles," he called. Maybe ten minutes panicking would persuade her otherwise.

He swiped at his phone and saw Henry's number flashing. What the hell was that bastard calling for? As if this wasn't difficult enough, now he had yet more deceit to be played with. Christ, a bit of that normalcy was very much needed. He really was getting too old for all these games. He swiped again to answer and wandered to the bar for another drink.

"Henry," he said, as cheerfully as he could.

"Alex, old chap. Where are you? I thought we could celebrate the closure of this deal. It's only a week or so off, and Tate's just told me the legals are going through fine."

Had he? Why the hell was Tate talking to Henry about any of this?

"Sorry, can't. I'm en route to New York for a few days. I need to tie up some loose ends at the office and such like before everyone decides to forget they work for me for a few days."

"Oh, right. I thought you skied with Conner at this time of year?"

"No, not this year. I have some other things to deal with."

"You'll be back for my party though?"

"Of course. I wouldn't miss it."

"Right, well. I'll see you then. Will you be bringing the Scott girl?" The Scott girl? Why couldn't he just say her name? Fucking ridiculous. It wasn't as if he didn't know she might have mentioned him by now.

"I'm not sure yet. She may have family commitments."

"Well, Sarah quite likes her so bring her along if you can. Conner's coming with the other one so it should be a hoot."

Hoot? *Jumped up toff.* What he wouldn't give to go a few rounds with the fucking idiot right now. He wouldn't be surprised if the bastard was planning something at the New Year ball to show him up. Three steps ahead, always. Mind you, the deal wouldn't have closed by then – the deal in Henry's eyes, anyway. The deal would actually be closing three days earlier as long as Tyler Rathbone honoured his side of the agreement and the Chinese didn't have some other problem. Tom Brindley seemed to be handling everything very well, given the covert nature of his current work, so everything was on track to complete on time. At least that side of his life was in order to some degree. What he was actually going to do about Henry was still perplexing him. He'd have another look at that file Jacobs sent when he got to the apartment. Perhaps there was something he'd missed that he could use to destroy the bastard. Hopefully, Andrews would have some information on AP, too by the time they landed. Christ, he really needed to know who sent that fucking photo, and why?

"Alex? Alex, are you still there?" Shit.

"Yes, sorry. Must be a bad line. Listen, let me get to New York and I'll give you a call over the next few days. I'm not sure how long I'll be there but we'll work something out."

"Okay, you alright? You sound a bit... "

A snarling sound suddenly interrupted his musing thoughts, so he turned his head to find Tara kneeling in the doorway, holding her face. It appeared Elizabeth wasn't happy at all about toe stimulation.

"Preoccupied?" He chuckled. "Yes, I am rather. I've got something I need to go and handle."

"Ah, right'o, I'll let you go then. Wouldn't want to stop the fun. How many this time?" Henry asked with his usual dirty cackle.

"Two, and I've got to go. I'll talk to you soon, okay?"

"Cheerio then."

"Mmm."

With that, he ended the call and looked towards the curled up Tara, who clearly didn't know what to do next. Neither did he, to be honest. He poured a glass of Cognac and looked up at the ceiling for inspiration. Why the hell he thought he'd find any up there was unknown. Hate, hate, hate. How could he help her hate him? Continue being a bastard, he supposed. Maybe he needed to ramp it up a gear or two. He clicked his neck around and wandered back toward the snarling sound to find a furiously glaring Elizabeth wrenching at her wrists to try and remove them from the silk.

"I don't know why you're bothering. You should know I never leave them loose enough," he said as he ambled over to the bed again.

"This is not okay, Alex. I will not be manhandled and forced to do something that I haven't agreed to. And from my limited knowledge, this is not the behaviour of a decent dominant," she damn near screamed at him. "And stop fucking smirking at me."

He couldn't help it. It always had wound her up successfully. She had a good point, though. Decency in dominance was never something that appealed to him, until her, anyway.

"Tara, start again. Go as far as you like this time," he said as he caressed his angel's smooth skin again with his eyes. Those legs that went on for an eternity were still a sight to behold, and those graceful arms straining at the silk and reddening her milky skin heightened every nerve in his body.

As always, Tara shuffled back across on her knees and tentatively moved her face to Elizabeth's feet again. Alex stared back up at Elizabeth's eyes and kept his gaze focused there for a few minutes while watching as she fought with herself not to kick Tara in the head again. Her body began squirming against the ties as she tried her hardest to contain the feeling that was more than likely bubbling up inside her. Regardless of her assertion that she didn't want this, she would enjoy it in a roundabout way. Hopefully the after effects would be not so pleasant.

He licked his lips and locked his own hands behind his head as she gasped a little and opened her mouth to say something. Another smirk crossed his mouth. He couldn't help it. She was glorious in her frustration and anger.

Suddenly her face frowned again. He glanced downward and noticed blonde hair not far below her waist.

"Tara, stop. Please," she said as her hips tried to rotate themselves away from the moment. She didn't stop. She wouldn't – not until she was told to, anyway. "Alex, this isn't right. Please, stop this. You said you'd never make me do anything I didn't want to do."

"No, I didn't. I told you how to get out of something. Nothing else."

"I have to safeword you to stop this madness?" The words sprang immediately from her lovely lips as he continued to gaze at her, chuckling at the thought. Much as she might be confused by his actions Elizabeth Scott wasn't about to use her safeword unless desperation set in. She was far from desperate, she had more about her than that.

"Keep going, Tara." He chuckle again as green eyes suddenly swept into his mind, which made him chuckle even more. Why the hell they'd arrived was bewildering to say the least. Perhaps he should ask the man about it later. That was a point. What time was it? And where were they? He glanced at the clock and realised they'd only got an hour of the flight left. Time flew when you were having fun, it seemed.

"What the fuck, Alex? Stop this now. You told me you'd stop if I-"

"But you haven't," he replied as he watched Tara curl her tongue up towards her pussy – *his* pussy. He licked his lips again at the thought and shifted his weight around to accommodate his cock as sudden irritation bit at him inexplicably.

"Alex, please. Stop her. I don't want-" she cut herself off with a small moan of appreciation as Tara did precisely what she had been put there to do. She did have a good tongue, always had had. He reached for his fly and pulled himself out with a grunt as he watched blonde hair try to bury itself between bound legs. Elizabeth squirmed again and started panting slightly as she either tried to get away from the eager moves or grind herself into them. She should have opened her legs when asked. She'd be very close by now if she'd done as she was told.

Slowly sliding his hand up and down, he realised he wasn't enjoying the show as much as he thought he would, so he focused his eyes back on hers. She had them closed, her mouth screwed up as if she were trying her hardest not to enjoy herself.

"Open your eyes, Elizabeth," he said as he continued stroking himself.

"Fuck off," was the mumbled response.

"Tara, I don't think she wants you. Come over here instead." That made her eyes open. Tara immediately left Elizabeth, and was at his side in seconds. "You know what to do," he continued as he watched furious eyes scowling back at him. This was all for her, and if the only way he could tell her that was to keep looking at her throughout, then that's what he'd do. He'd do it and imagine her lips, her tongue, her mouth wrapping itself around him. Fuck, he wanted her tongue. Why the hell was he doing this again? Sudden warmth poured over his cock as furious eyes widened and her lips parted in surprise.

"Don't. Please, Alex, don't make me watch."

"I told you someone was going to come, Elizabeth. You had a choice," he cut in as she closed her eyes again and shook her head. "Open them," he continued. She shook her head again and dropped her face towards the floor.

"I don't know why you're doing this. I haven't done anything wrong. Please, just stop this."

Tara's tongue swirled, sucked and licked, over and over again. His hands tightened in his own hair as he watched a tear roll down the face of the woman he loved. "I can't do this, Alex. Please, stop her..." Her breath caught as she choked on a sob that was beginning to consume her at the same moment as his stomach tightened in sensation. "Alex, please. I don't... I can't..."

He grabbed Tara's hair and plunged her down on him as fast as he could. He needed to get closer, and looking at tears wasn't helping him for once in his life. He felt the back of Tara's throat banging on the end of him and focused all his thoughts on Elizabeth – on her love, on her mouth, on her eyes – and only then did he feel his balls rise.

"Open your eyes, Elizabeth, and I'll stop this," he grated out. She shook her head again and sniffed as Tara's moaning and groaning echoed in the room. "Open them, and I'll do as you've asked," he said again as he tried to stave off the inevitable. Her head twisted to the side, and she slowly began to open her eyes. "Look at me," he growled.

She sniffed again and turned her head, and those eyes were all he needed to let go. He grasped Tara by the hair, yanked her over his cock and let himself flow into her mouth, probably all over her face. He didn't give a fuck because it wasn't her face he was looking at, or her mouth he was imagining. It was the woman in front of him, and that was all he could see as she gazed back at him in defeat and sobbed back another tear.

He grunted out the last of his come and stared back at her as Tara's tongue flicked over him again. He could hardly feel it, because all he could see was the pain he'd just caused. It was coursing across every inch of her. He took in her reddened eyes, wet cheeks and trembling bottom lip as she tried to look anywhere but at him. He sneered at himself and felt the dry hair in his fingers for the first time – peroxide, fake, untrue. Indecent.

Fuck.

Taking in a long breath, he continued to watch her, as she stood perfectly still and mumbled to herself, her head occasionally shaking, and then her eyes closed and she was still again. Now what? Even he didn't know. He noticed her legs shaking a little just as Tara's pathetic face tried to get in front of his, so he pushed her head away and stood up to take the steps towards the only person in the room that actually mattered. She stiffened instantly.

"You should have chosen more wisely, Elizabeth."

"Fuck you," she replied quietly. He frowned and put his cock away again. That "*fuck you*" wasn't quite so endearing.

"Tara, untie her and get me a drink," he said as he walked out of the door. He needed some time to think about what to do next, about how to handle the next scenario.

"I hate you," he heard her mumble behind him. He turned and headed back towards her with swift strides and picked up her chin to look into her eyes. There was no real hate looking back at him, no fire, no venom, just disappointment still filled with love for some unknown fucking reason.

He chuckled and licked his lips again.

"Not yet you don't, Elizabeth."

Chapter 3

Elizabeth

Having this bitch untie me is beyond frustrating. It would help if she did it faster, although why I'm in such a hurry I have no idea, because the moment I can move I'm probably going to do nothing more than sink to the floor and cry my eyes out. I can smell him on her. In fact, even though I'm trying my hardest to look away, I can't help but notice the smear of him on her cheek. And if she keeps licking her sodding lips, I'm quite possibly going to slice them off her irritatingly beautiful face. My legs feel like jelly, and I'm sure I'm going crazy, because did that seriously just happen? Did he honestly just purposely make me watch him having a fucking blowjob from her? Why? Why would you do that to someone you say you love?

"If it helps, honey, he didn't enjoy it. I've felt him enjoy it. That wasn't it. Still, he does taste good," she says as she licks her lips again.

What the hell am I supposed to say to that? My mouth opens but nothing is forthcoming, so I focus on the unwrapping of my arms and try to recall the anger that's threatening again. I don't even know what's going on. Her telling me that he didn't enjoy his little fucking experience really isn't helping matters. I certainly didn't need to know how he tastes. Funnily enough, I already know.

I sense the moment the last of the silk leaves my skin, and for the life of me I don't know what to do. I'm part exhausted, part furious and part ready to kill. There's some kind of heat seeping into my cold bones that wasn't there before he started whatever the hell this was. He told me he killed two people and I stared in a strange sense of shock and wanted nothing more than to hold him or be left alone to deal with it. Now he's done this I don't know what to think. What sort of game is he playing here? Does he want me to push him away? Is this his way of telling me we're over? No, it can't be. He would have just left me like he did the last time. Then why is he forcing me to do things I don't want to do, and see things I don't want to see? Jesus, I'm confused. And why the hell don't I hate him? Why can't I just mean it when I say it? I sodding well mumbled the words, knowing I didn't feel them. Regardless of the bastard and what he made me witness, I felt nothing but despair and loss when he looked straight into my eyes.

I suddenly remember Tara standing in front of me and find her looking over at me. She still has no clothes on, and unfortunately, neither do I. I need some clothes.

"What are you looking at? Go get him a damn drink like a good little girl," is the first thing that falls from my lips. Bitch. I hate her at the moment. Oh my god, why can I hate her and not him? And what did he mean by that, anyway?

She giggles – yes *giggles* – in my face and points her talon-like finger at me.

"You should have seen your face. What did you think, that you were special to him? Elizabeth, no woman will ever be special to someone like him."

"It wasn't me that had her head pinned to the floor," I spit out as my hand finds its semi-permanent new place on my hip.

"It wasn't you who had his cock in their mouth either, was it?" she replies as she spins her hips away from me, and heads towards the door. "You should just forget about him and move on. There's no way you'll ever be enough for him."

Bitch. As if that thought hasn't crossed my mind a million times before. Irritatingly, I was just beginning to truly believe I might be enough for him. I mean, he's given me buildings, for God's sake, and his memories, both of which I know he hasn't done for anybody else. He's cried on me, let me hold him in his darkest moments and give him the comfort he's never even dreamed of allowing before. What the fuck is he playing at? I don't believe for one minute that he doesn't love me in his own deluded way, but why is he doing any of this?

Three thoughts cross my mind, suddenly, before I know it. I still hate her, Alex is an utter bastard, and unfortunately, I still need some clothes, which she may have some of. My arm reaches for her as my brain tries to install sensible mode. Regardless of my utter contempt for the bitch, I could use a little female help.

"Tara, I'm sorry. Look, I just need some clothes. Do you have any I could borrow?"

"What, and give him a chance to get angry? Not likely. I'm sure he has you naked because that's the way he wants you," she says with another one of those infuriating little giggles.

Helpful. I'm really feeling the sisterly love of womanhood there. Perhaps I could drug him or something. Actually, maybe I could make Phillip fly this damn plane all the way home again if I just storm up there stark naked and demand he turn the plane round because I've been kidnapped. And then, of course, I remember that he knows that very well, because he saw the MI5 arsehole drag me on board.

"Right, thanks," I eventually reply as she sashays out of the door and away from me, wiggling her sodding fingers in a wave.

I sit my backside down on the bed and stare at the floor. It's the only option I've got. I wish I knew what else I could do to make this nightmare unhappen, but I don't. I only know I'm absolutely not in control of anything that's happening to me, and I'm also completely at his mercy because I haven't got a chance of overpowering or outmanoeuvring him at the moment. I don't even know how I feel.

Was this his plan all along? I should go and ask him, shouldn't I? Just storm in there now and demand that he tells me what the hell he's playing at. Oh god, I'm repeating my own bloody thoughts to myself. And why on earth does he want me to have that knife so much? Given the now obvious Mafia zone that's part of him, maybe he thinks I'm unsafe with him. Oh shit, I almost forgot that part in my random head mess. He's killed people purposefully. It wasn't an accident or self-defence; he's just told me he worked, or maybe still does work, for Aiden Phillips. Was that why we did that odd lesson in his safe room at home? His home, that is – not mine, because I'm never stepping back inside it again.

Think, Beth, think.

What does that mean for me, for us? I'm sitting here on the way to New York, with no way of changing course, with no fucking clothes, and I have no idea who that man out there is, or what is going on. If that's what he is, a murderer, then why didn't he just tell me and maybe we could have found some way of dealing with it. Maybe I could have somehow forgotten about it and just been in love with the man I knew, or thought I knew, anyway.

I let out a long sigh and find myself more tempted to climb into the bed than to even try to pick my feet up again. I've tried too many

39

times to work out who he is, and now I have to deal with him being a murderer as well. *A murderer.* Why would anyone do that? Why would he? I can't even fathom the thought. Being a brutal fighter is enough of a concern, let alone someone who actually takes life away completely, on purpose. The scene at the club springs into my head as I stare at the wardrobe. The blood, the awkward angle of that mans thigh, Alex repeatedly kicking and punching with little more than a slight frown crossing his face. Entirely in control of every vicious, purposeful hit, fluid movements, precise, direct, specific, he knew every area to attack in order to cause maximum damage. He wasn't out of control at all; he was absolutely in control, utterly ready to demolish.

To kill.

I'm in love with a fucking hitman of some sort – a sadistic, absurdly wealthy murderer.

Who has me on his plane, and where is that man that tried to rape me? Did he kill him, too?

Oh, what fucking planet have I been living on?

I need a drink and my phone. I'm sure I should be panicking. I'm sure I should be running around screaming or something, but I either haven't got the energy or I'm simply not scared for some reason. Tara might be, but I'm not. He won't hurt me. I know that because he wouldn't have shown me his tears if he was going to do that; he wouldn't have put this collar around my neck, his collar. He certainly wouldn't have asked me to move in with him, love him, accept him with all his issues and promise to never leave him. My fingers skim the necklace around my throat and tingle at the cold stones – icy, just like him to everybody else. But not to me.

Fuck this shit.

"Alex, give me some fucking clothes," I scream as my feet quite unexpectedly lead me straight into the main cabin. Tara's head swivels from his lap as he simply raises a brow at me. "I fucking mean it. I've had enough of this crap."

Christ, does he have to look so bloody hot all the time? He's sitting there with his shirtless body on display, looking glorious, arsehole.

"And what exactly are you going to do, Elizabeth?" My eyes flick to the knife again. That could work. He raises the other brow... Maybe not.

"I just want some damn clothes. If I'm going to deal with your shit, I want at least some sense of decency while doing it."

"Tara doesn't need any. Why should you?"

"Tara's a slut. I am not."

"That is a fair point," he says as he shoves her off him and ambles over without the slightest emotion crossing his face, raising a hand towards me.

"Do not even think about touching me," is my snapped warning.

"You know I'll do whatever I want, Elizabeth." He's got a point, but I'm not making it easy for him. Regardless of the fact that he's a killer, which appals me, I can't stop that damn trembling thing that's beginning to occur again down below.

"Not if you still love me, you won't, not if you've got any thoughts of this moving forward from here. I don't care what you think you're doing. I will only take so much before I can't forgive you anymore."

He halts abruptly in front of me, and pockets those damn hands with an arrogant smirk plastered across his face. What the hell he thinks he's got to be arrogant about, I don't know. My body appears to agree, because before I know what I've done, the cabin space echoes with the slap that I've just delivered to his face. He doesn't move an inch. Not even a shocked expression appears. Those icy blue eyes don't waver from their intensity at all, which just pisses me off beyond belief.

"Feisty. Better," he says slowly in response. He wants me angry? Clearly. "You want another go? Go get the knife, Elizabeth. There will be two of us to deal with soon."

What the hell does that mean? I can't be bothered, and I'm certainly not picking up that damn knife again. He's not manipulating me into becoming some sort of sidekick in his little adventures.

"Clothes, Alex. That's all I want, and then I'll be able to make my own way back from New York. This is not going on any longer."

He chuckles and wanders back to the bar again.

I'm just about to go in for the kill again when Phillip announces that we'll be landing in 20 minutes. Thank God for that. I'll be able to get my stuff together and leave. My eyes stare directly at my bag as I realise, yet again, that that is really all I've got with me – that and a diamond necklace and bracelet, both of which I should probably launch out of the window. Actually, we'd die if I did that, so I won't bother just yet. What I need to do is call Belle and get her to sort me a ticket home so I can get myself off this plane and straight onto the next, via a quick stop at a shop for some bloody clothes.

"I need to phone Belle. She will be worried sick about me."

"No."

"Alex, please, I need to tell her I'm okay, and I need some damn clothes."

"You've said that already, and the answer to that is also no."

"What the hell is your problem? I'm not doing this anymore. Fuck your slut senseless for all I care. Just leave me out of this. I don't want any part of it, or you."

"Yes, you do," he replies with another smirk.

"Do not," I reply childishly, and actually stamp my foot.

"This is all for you." What? Fucking insane.

"You come in another woman's mouth in front of me to satisfy your own sick fantasy, and then tell me it's all for me? You are quite clearly a lunatic. Give me my fucking bag."

"Better. Keep it up."

"I have no idea-"

"Tara, buckle in please. Preparing for descent." Phillip's voice comes drifting softly through the intercom. Great, we're landing soon.

"Strap in," Alex says as he casually wanders over to the chairs, and Tara disappears around a corner somewhere after emptying and stowing glasses in the bar. She's also still wearing nothing. Apparently she's still quite good at her job, though.

My feet eventually stomp over to the seat behind him that also happens to be facing away from him, thankfully, and I try to strap myself in. Unfortunately, my damn hands are shaking so much that the metal won't go in the sodding hole. Over and over again, I try to clip all the right bits into the right orifices, but it just won't do up, and I can't even begin to fathom why I can't do a fucking seatbelt up because there's some shithead chuckling away to himself in the background – more than likely at my ineptitude. He bloody won't be in a minute because that knife is looking more and more friendly at the moment. How dare he laugh at me?

"Need some help, Elizabeth?"

"Piss off," comes snarling out. He is so not touching me again. Thankfully, just as the words leave my mouth, all the bits finally slot in together beautifully. I stare out of the window and try for a moment of rationality in all this mess as I suck in a long breath. This plane just needs to land and then I can get myself home.

Happy Christmas, me.

It's less than a week away and I've invited my parents and sister over to have lunch at his house. I need to sort that out. We are obviously not going to be having a cosy Christmas dinner together around roaring wood fires and glinting candle light. And Conner? Does Conner know about this? Is Belle safe with him? Oh god, is he part of all this, too? My mind is suddenly racing again with all sorts of imagery involving him holding Alex back and "talking him down". He knows about this, doesn't he? I know he does. That means Belle could be in danger. He could be mixed up with the wrong people, too. She said that Conner had told her things about himself that she didn't like or understand. Maybe this is what she was talking about.

I shift around in my seat, trying to get rid of the metal buckle that's pressing into my bare stomach and reminding me of that damned icy cold again. I can't even see him, and I can still feel those blue eyes piercing me from behind. It's almost like they're part of me, constantly there when I close my eyes or try to think of something else.

"Is Belle safe?" I ask quietly. There's a pause, so long it seems to stretch for an eternity, and it instantly worries me.

"Why would she not be safe?" he replies in that monotone voice of his that has me thinking he's hiding something. To the rest of the population it may seem honest, but to me it seems devoid of emotion, and therefore it's probably a lie.

"Conner knows about you, doesn't he? Is he part of all this, too?" He chuckles a little and I hear the chair creaking behind me as the plane pitches a little.

"Conner's a good man, Elizabeth. Your sister is very safe with him," is all he gives me in response. Well, at least that calms my fears a little. I know Conner's a good man, but I don't know how much he's been involved in over the years.

"Is he like you? Has he... you know...?" My words trail off as I try to form the actual words around my lips. Why I can't just say them out loud is a mystery.

"Say it, Elizabeth. Get the words out of your mouth. They're true, and as uncomfortable as they might be for you to hear, you did say you wanted to know."

My eyes close again at the thought because regardless of my pain, he's right. I did. I asked and pushed and tried to get so close that he would have no choice but to be honest. That's what I asked for, complete honesty – to know him and to be part of him, regardless of what the issue was. I told him I wouldn't go any further if I didn't get the whole truth about who he was when we were in Pascal's office, and he knew I meant it then. So this is what I have to deal with, isn't it? The truth. Fabulous. I so wish I could stop my fingers from wanting to reach backwards and touch him. Regardless of all that is happening, I still want to feel his skin, drag him closer and find some sort of way of making us whole again.

"Why are you being such an arsehole to me?" There's yet another pause long enough to eclipse the sun as I hear a sigh and picture his face in my mind.

"Stop deluding yourself with the belief that this isn't who I am, Elizabeth. You wanted the real man. You've got him."

"You're lying. I know the real man, Alex. This is not the man I fell in love with. This is the monster that you promised not to be anymore. You said you'd be better."

"I'm a murderer, Elizabeth. I have killed, several times, and with little regard for why. I am not a good man, and the sooner you start to accept that, the better."

"But why? Why did you do that with her? And why are you putting me through all of this. I don't understand why you're purposely trying to hurt me when all I've ever tried to do is love you and be part of you."

"I have my reasons," he replies quietly, just as we start the descent to land. My stomach recoils at the movement as my fingers grab onto the armrests for some sort of support, probably emotional, frankly.

"There is no reason good enough for what you're doing. You're destroying everything."

"Stop acting like a fucking child, Elizabeth. This is the real world, not some fairytale you've created for yourself. You wanted honesty. I'm giving it to you."

My eyes fly open at the statement. A damn fairytale? Is that what he thinks I've been imagining we are? Hardly. It's not like I haven't already had to deal with varying amounts of new and unimaginable things since we've been together. How fucking dare he?

"You think hurting me is going to help me accept what you've done? This has not been a fucking fairytale, Alex, not by a long shot."

The screeching sound of the tyres hitting the runway assaults my ears as the brakes engage heavily and pull me back to the fact that we've touched the ground, and I still have no clothes. At this point, I'm pretty close to running straight out of it naked. Presumably, if I leapt onto the tarmac starkers and bolted for the nearest building, someone would have something for me to wear.

Unfortunately, he's standing in front of me before I can even unclip the bloody seatbelt.

"Are you going to behave?" he asks, without an ounce of warmth on his face.

What sort of question is that? My eyes stare out of the window again as my nose twitches in irritation, just as Tara sashays back into the cabin from the front fully dressed, which means she still has another set of clothes in the bedroom. Much as the thought grates, I really need them now. Perhaps I should try sweet and pouty. That works for him normally, and perhaps if I go along with whatever this is for a while, I can get myself out of it when I get a chance and he thinks he's winning. So I put on my best *come play with me face* and slowly turn to look at him. My inner slut throbs away at me at the thought and causes the trembling to start again.

"Alex, I need some clothes. If this is something you think you need then I'll do whatever it is, but please, just let me get dressed."

His eyes travel the length of me as I slowly unbuckle the belt. He takes his time, and it makes me feel just a little bit nervous, like the first time he did it. I suck in a breath and lift myself up to stand in front of him. If there's one thing I will not be its intimidated by him. He told me to fight him, and I intend to until the end if I have to.

"Make yourself come," he says.

What?

"Why the hell would I do that?"

"Because you want to, Elizabeth, and because you want some clothes. You're wet, aren't you? I bet you're dying to be fucked. Legs trembling slightly, face faintly blushed. Did you enjoy watching Tara's lips around me? Perhaps I should just dry you out, lick that right off for you. What do you think?"

Damn him.

"Clothes, Alex?"

"Negotiations, Elizabeth."

My mouth is gaping again. Tara's giggling. Damn her, too. Is he seriously suggesting I should make myself come in front of him in return for having something to wear? What an arsehole. What pisses me off even more is that he's right. I am aching, much as I hate to admit it. But I will not be doing anything of the sort.

"Alex, this is ridiculous. I just want..." His brow arches slowly, and within seconds, there's a darker shade of blue threatening. My foot gingerly takes a step backwards, away from him. "Alex, don't even think about it."

"I've already thought about it. The taste of you on my tongue is firmly imbedded," he replies as he licks his lips and puts his hands in his pocket. "So, before I put a shirt on, make your choice. Orgasms for clothes seems fair to me. I'll give you to the count of five. One."

Oh my god, he is serious.

"Alex, just-"

"Two." He's amused again. *Bastard.*

What the hell do I do now? I need clothes. And I know he'll happily let me walk out of here wearing nothing. He'd probably enjoy it, too. *Manipulative arsehole.* I should so hate him now. "Three. Tick tock, Elizabeth." *Wanker.*

"You have to be kidding me, Alex. This is not reasonable. Come on, please?" It's probably my last plea, because I know there's only one decision to make here. If I'm going to make a run for it when I step foot outside that door, I'm going to need to be wearing something.

"I could just force you, you know? But where's the fun in that? I thought you'd like the choice. Four." Tara is giggling again. My eyes swing to hers with a death glare attached. She's one messed up cookie. An hour ago, he was dragging her around and scaring her, and now she thinks he's funny? Utterly deranged.

"Five." My hands shoot up in front of my body to stop him. I have no idea what he's about to do, and while my inner slut might be widening her legs for him, rational thought is interfering extremely well.

"Alex, no. This is not normal. You cannot negotiate for clothes. You've kidnapped me, for God's sake.

And now you won't allow me the freedom to wear clothes outside? What is going on in your head?"

"I have given you a choice. I'd make one if I were you before I change my mind. And you're not welcome in my head anymore. No one is."

The gasp that leaves my mouth echoes because that hurts more than a slap round the face, and I can tell by the look he's giving me that he's deadly serious. My arms fold gently around myself as I stare across at a man I am no longer in contact with. I may be standing with him. I may be mere feet from him, and I may be speaking to him, but he's not hearing me anymore. The man I love has apparently left, and the realisation sinks in that I'm now dealing with someone I hardly know at all. I'm dealing with someone who has little or no regard for my thoughts or feelings, and who will do as he sees fit or entertaining, regardless of the consequences to my heart. I thought I knew him. I thought I could find a way through this for us and try to understand. I even thought I could fight him about this, but I can't. I know that now. He won't let me.

"Why?" It's all I've got left. Not the clothes, not Tara, not the kidnapping, just why would you destroy something so wonderful? Why would you ruin love for no good reason at all.

"Still thinking too much," he says as he removes his hands from his pockets and walks away from me to the bedroom. My eyes fall to the floor in defeat. I'm utterly lost, three thousand miles away from home, and naked with no idea what he's doing or why. "Here," he says, suddenly in front of me again, doing up a blue shirt and now wearing jeans. I look up at his face, desperately hoping to see some emotion etched into it. There isn't any that I can see. "Take it, Elizabeth." Take what? I shake the mist of defeat off and look towards his hands to see the knife there. What is it with this bloody knife?

"I don't want the knife, Alex. I want to go home," I reply quietly as I try to move away from him. He grabs my arm, and I can't even find the strength to pull it away. "Please, just let me go. I haven't got anything left. You win." He physically turns me towards him and opens my palm.

"You keep this with you all the time. Use it if you need to," he says as he wraps my fingers around it firmly and turns to walk away again.

Tara is by his side in seconds, applying a new coat of lipstick and pouting stupidly. I watch as he grabs her hand and leads her out of the cabin towards the opening door. Phillip arrives beside them, so I rapidly try to cover myself with my hands before bolting for the bedroom to snatch Tara's clothes. Whatever was happening with the orgasm negotiation has passed it seems, so sod it. I'll just put her clothes on and deal with whatever temper tantrum he might have. Besides, if I give them a bit of time to get into the car, hopefully I can just leg it from the steps and head for a building.

Throwing the bloody knife down onto the bed, I do some quick shuffling and buttoning and I've at last got some clothes on. I grab my shoes and head back into the main cabin to get my bag. Phone! I need to call Belle. One look at it has me rolling my eyes in exasperation. Of course it would be dead, wouldn't it? Helpful. Digging around, I find fifty pounds and then realise that that's not going to be very useful in America, either. Jesus, could I be in a worse position?

I look over at the door and wonder what the hell I'm going to do. Just run for it... That's all I've got, isn't it? I just have to get myself down those steps as nonchalantly as possible and then run as fast as I can towards the nearest people. I scan my shoes in my hand. Four-inch heels are not going to be helpful in the slightest. Well, not until I can stop running anyway. I quickly cross the space to the window to check which way I should be heading, and I can thankfully see a small building with what appears to be a tower or something sticking up off the top of it. That'll do. It's not too far, and once I'm there, I can call Belle and she can sort tickets, and maybe she'll send Conner over to kill bastard Alex, or at the very least find my version of him. Right, I can do this. I'm ready. My head spins back to the bedroom as I remember the knife. Do I need that? No. Why would any rational human being need to carry a weapon? Mind you, we are in the States. Don't they all carry guns? Maybe I do need the knife.

My feet are carrying me toward the offending item before I've thought anymore about it, so I grab it by the blunt end and slip it into my bag. I won't be using it anytime soon, but I've got it nonetheless. Oddly enough, as I walk past the space where I had it at his throat, I smile to myself because regardless of my confusion after the event, he was right. I did feel in control for a few minutes. That power he was talking about was very definitely etched into my thoughts. It was clearly a moment of complete lunacy, but it was there. *Arsehole*. Why does he have to be so fucking superior all the time?

Three more steps have me rounding the corner to the exit and planning my running strategy. The freezing air hits me as I look down towards the car that's waiting at the bottom and see a burly man standing by the back door, presumably waiting for me to arrive. Phillip suddenly bumps into me, so I spin around, wondering if he might actually be helpful to me if I plead my case. I'm met with a small smile but nothing else that shows he might give me a hand.

"Miss Scott, I think it's time for you to leave now," he says as he glances towards the car.

"Phillip, I don't want to go with him. Can't you help me?"

"I'm afraid not," he replies with another smile. Clearly he's not about to piss his boss off any time soon.

I swing myself back around to face the car again and just put one foot in front of the other until I'm hovering at the bottom step, trying to assess the best route. There's only one, and it's pretty straightforward. The door of the car opens just as I'm preparing to run, and out he steps, that sodding hair ruffling about and a frown of irritation marring his brow. We stare at each other for precisely thirty seconds, and I know this because I can feel my heart pounding at the exact same rate. I can hear it rattling in my ears, and that pitched thudding causes all sorts of memories to come flying back to me. His heat on me, his arms around me, his weight on top of me, his hands holding me, his love, his grip. My fingers grasp the rail tighter as if somehow trying to tell me not to run for some inexplicable reason, and yet I can't stop my foot from picking up, ready to run for it.

"You know I'll catch you," he calls across to me with a slight lift of his mouth. He's right. He probably will, but as my other foot leaves the step and I let go of the rail, I know I've got to try. I have to at least try and find some level of sanity again. My bare feet hit the tarmac just as I rip my eyes away from his, and I head for the building as fast as I can. It's not far. I just need to keep this pace up and I might even make it. My thighs scream at me as the cold air rushes across the thin silk of Tara's blouse, and my feet hammer into the floor, hoping to propel me just that bit faster. I'm so focused on my target that I feel my shoes leaving my hand in a bid to increase my pace because I can hear him gaining on me. I can almost feel his hands on me, in me, holding me and refusing to let me get away, just like he always does. Oh god, I can't even run away from him successfully because there's a small part of me that wants him to catch me, to touch me again, to make all this crap go away. And then an utter miracle happens as I see a man leaving the building in front of me.

"Help me!" I scream. "Help, please."

The man looks over and stares at me in shock. He starts to move towards me, so I find the last of my strength to get to him. Just as I've got about twenty metres to go, I hear his agitated voice at my side as his hand grabs my wrist from behind.

"Don't make me hurt him, Elizabeth." My feet start to slow at the thought. He wouldn't, would he? His grip tightens as he comes around to my side and grabs hold of the back of my neck to stop me. "Amusing as it might be, I know how you hate the sight of blood," he continues as he twists my neck so that I'm looking directly into those eyes again. I shift my gaze to the man and try to calculate my situation. There's a building full of people in there. Surely he wouldn't be so stupid as to beat someone up when anybody could be watching? No. Brutal he might be, but an idiot he is not.

"You alright, Miss?" the man says, as he gets closer. This is it. I've got one chance to leave him, and if I'm going to do it, now is my opportunity. Alex's eyes narrow at me as I heave in a breath and yank my neck away from him.

"No, I'm really not. This man is trying to take me with him and I don't want to go," I reply as I pull my wrist out of his grasp and take a step backwards. The man moves closer and holds an arm out to separate me from Alex, so I keep my gaze trained on him in the hope that it will stop him from going off into some uncontrollable rage. "I just want to leave, and he won't let me. Could you help me phone my sister please, so I can get back to the UK?"

Alex's face doesn't change as he watches me like a hawk. There still isn't any emotion, and I'm sure he's not in the least bit bothered about the man standing between us. He isn't, however, doing anything other than staring for now. I take another step away and reach for the man's arm to drag him away from the potential threat, who has now pocketed his butchering hands.

"This won't work," he says as he continues to stare. I tug again on the man and keep retreating one step at a time. "I told you I'd never leave you, Elizabeth. I meant it."

Oh, I'm sure he did, but that isn't going to stop me getting the hell away from him for the time being so I can find some normal people to rationalise with. He takes a few paces towards us, so I speed up our movement by pulling the man even harder. Thankfully, at just the right moment, another man appears from the building and calls over to his friend, whose name is apparently John. Alex stops and watches the other guy with a sneer, raising a brow at me as his hands come back out of their confines. Oh my god, he is going to do it.

My body is in front of the man before I know it, and my hands shoot up in defence of some sort. I will not be the cause of this poor man's demise.

"Let me go, Alex," I say as I keep moving us all backwards and hear a door opening. "Please, if there is any love left in you then you have to let me go now."

John grabs me by the arm and moves me into the doorway behind him as his friend follows and twists the bolt to secure us all inside. All I can do is keep staring at the man I still love as he turns his head away from me and walks back toward the car.

That's it. I've made it. I can go home.

Chapter 4

Elizabeth

"**W**hy the fuck are you at JFK?" That's what Belle is screeching in my ear as I try to explain where I am over her ranting. She's clearly not best pleased with Alex, and given the twenty-four missed calls from her on my phone, I'm not surprised. Thankfully, John has the same phone charger as me so I've been able to plug in and call home. John has also been out and rescued my shoes from floor, although he waited until Alex's car had disappeared. I wouldn't let him go until they'd all driven off and danger had gone with them. "Are you saying he kidnapped you? I mean, Conner said he thought it all seemed a bit strange, but I assumed you'd just gone home, and what the hell happened with that Aiden Phillips chap?"

"Belle, can you just get the ticket sorted and we'll talk about it when I get home? I just can't explain it over the phone," I reply as John drapes a blanket over my shoulders and passes me some much-needed coffee. I smile up at my saviour and huddle into the comfy chair. I'm apparently in mission control's lunch area.

"I'm doing that as we speak. You're on the next flight out but it doesn't leave for another seven hours so you'll have to find something to do for a while," she says. "Anything worth doing there?"

Probably. I've always wanted to come to New York, just not under these circumstances. I scan the area around me and realise that no, there is absolutely nothing to do here.

"Doubt it... I don't care. I'll just hang around and then go over to the main airport to catch the flight."

"Do you want me to check you into a hotel for a bit? There are a few here that you could go and relax in?" The thought is very appealing to say the least, and I'm sure John could get me there safely.

"Is it far?"

"No, there's one just around the corner. I'm booking it now."

"Thanks, honey,"

"Listen, just go and get yourself a hot bath and I'll try and organise some clothes for you. I can't believe you've got nothing with you. I'm sending you the details of the hotel via text now."

"Okay, I'll give you a call when I've checked in and got settled."

"Okay, love you. I'll let Conner know what's going on. He was worried about both of you, not that I'm worried about Mr. Dickface White. I hope he rots in a fucking hole somewhere."

"Belle, don't, okay? I can't listen to that right now."

"Alright, I know. I haven't got a clue why you put up with his shit. Honestly, Beth, what the hell is his problem? Is he a psycho or something?"

Very probably. And a murderer.

"Thanks for the help. Chat later," I mutter, then end the call and drain the remainder of my coffee to go in search of John. The sooner I'm in that hotel room, the better as far as I'm concerned.

Two hours later, having been safely delivered to the hotel, I'm sitting on the bed wrapped in a towel, staring blankly at the wall in the hope that some sort of logic will present itself to me. Unfortunately, nothing is forthcoming. I suppose I'm just going to have to admit to myself that this is over, that for whatever reason, him telling me about his past has created something we can't get past. I don't know why he's doing any of this, but I do know that I can't put up with it. I also know, without a shadow of a doubt, that the thought is very nearly killing me, again. He left me before and we found a way back together. This time I walked away from him. Not because he's a murderer, but because I wasn't prepared to tolerate his behaviour, because I just needed some space. And now I can do nothing but think about the look on his face when he told me he meant what he said about not leaving me. Resolute is the best word I've got for it. He may have held himself back from just grabbing me again, but I'm not stupid enough to think that he won't be coming for me again. There's not a cat's chance in hell that I'm never going to see him again, because he's just not going to give up that easily. But, if that's the case, why all the bloody strange behaviour? And why did he appear to want me angry with him? He was doing things to make me angry, or maybe upset me, hurt me. I can't even begin to process why, though. Why isn't he just talking to me and seeing if I can find a way to accept what he's done in the past.

Regardless of all of this, I do still love him. Doesn't he know that? Doesn't he know that when all's said and done, I'll probably still follow him to the ends of the earth because I love him?

Stupid Beth. What idiot would do that for a man like him?

Me. I would, because I can't imagine him not next to me every day, every night. I already miss his smile, his cadence, his very rhythm of being near me. It doesn't matter to me what those hands have done before now. That's not the man he is to me, and this odd behaviour may be who he was once, but it isn't the beautiful man I know now. It isn't the man who gives me his thoughts, his memories, his love. It isn't the man who chuckles sweetly when I try make light of something serious, and it isn't the man who lay in my lap and had tears running from his eyes.

God, I'm so tired of all this. Actually, I'm just plain tired to be honest.

I look over to my bracelet and necklace lying on the bedside drawer and wonder what the hell I'm supposed to do with them now. A bracelet that means I'm his and a necklace that means he's mine. Mine... Is he still mine? Do I even want him to be mine anymore?

Confused is not enough of a word for what I'm feeling right now. I've had to deal with so much from him that I can't think straight anymore. You hear about these types of relationships – the ones where one of the parties is just plain weird – but I never believed I'd actually be in one. I always assumed that plain old me would just find a nice quiet man who made me laugh and pottered through life reasonably happily. Maybe have some children, live in a normal sized house and socialise with other normal couples who talk about gardening, and holidays in the Med. Perhaps strive for the slightly unattainable in some hope of creating a better life for my children while watching the world go by and wishing for something a little more. And that's what he offered me in a roundabout sort of way, wasn't it?

"I will give you every piece of the damaged soul you ask for in return for your acceptance of it. That is all I ask of you – that you do not condemn me because of it."

The words ring in my ears as I reach my hand across to the bracelet and finger the stones lightly. Accept him for it, not condemn him because of it. He knew then, didn't he? All that time ago in the back of the car, he knew he was going to have to tell me this at some point and hope that I could deal with it all, that I could forget the man he may have been and concentrate on the one he is for me. Can I? Can I let all this go and become part of some conspiracy in his twilight zone of Mafia come MI5 stuff that I have no idea about. It's not exactly the quiet life I was hoping for, is it?

And I'm still not accepting the strange behaviour, either. *Bastard.*

I pull my fingers away from the bracelet and glance across at the clock to realise that I've only got a couple of hours left before check in so I need to get myself dressed and ready. Belle has performed a minor miracle by somehow managing to get some clothes sent here. A lovely woman appeared about thirty minutes after I arrived with some jeans and a navy jumper that looks about the right size. There's also a brown wool jacket and scarf included in the bundle, and thankfully some underwear. Lord knows how she managed it but at least I have something of my own to wear now and not just Tara the slut's cast offs. I don't have any make-up but sod it. That's the least of my concerns at the moment. Scraping my hair back into a messy bun, I pin the grips in that I have left from last night's up-do and pinch my cheeks in the hope of making it look something like blusher. It may also make the tiredness disappear. It doesn't work, so I just stare at myself in the mirror and wonder who is staring back at me. She's not who she used to be. There's another, more balanced, individual looking at me now. She's stronger, wiser, less insecure and more dominant in nature. She knows what she wants to some degree, can manage herself with more authority than the girl before and I know without any hesitation that he did this to me. The woman staring back at me now is a product of Alexander White. She is a new version of the old, less confident individual. I have spent so much time trying to understand who he is that I have somehow managed to understand myself a little better, or at least expand myself to accept things I simply wouldn't have before.

A sudden sharp knock at the door has me spinning in confusion. Who would be knocking on this door? Nobody knows I'm here, and it's not time for the taxi back to the airport yet, so who the hell is it? My eyes narrow at the handle as I wander back into the main room and grab my jeans and jumper. Maybe it's housekeeping or something. Unfortunately, my random sixth sense begins to kick in because I'm clearly part of his world now and this could possibly be him, or one of his employees.

"Who is it?" I call as I zip my jeans and pull on the jumper until it's over my head.

"It's the manager, ma'am. There's been a problem with payment," an American accent replies. Well, it's not Alex. It could still be someone else connected to him, though.

"I'll sort it out when I check out," I shout back. How, I don't know, but I'm not leaving this room yet, and I'm not talking to anybody until I get firmly back on British soil.

"I'm afraid I need to deal with it now, ma'am," he says. Oh, shitting hell.

"Okay, hold on a minute," I reply as I start the process of unlocking the various bolts and latches on the door. Americans are tight on their security, it seems. Not surprising given the guns they carry about casually. "What's the problem?" I ask as I twist the handle and open the door a crack.

"You are, my dear," he says as the door is damn near booted in and I go flying backwards towards the bed, trying to keep my balance.

Those intoxicating green eyes pierce me so quickly that I haven't got a hope of moving away from them. A sneer of disgust is firmly imprinted on his irritated face as he moves closer and opens his mouth again. My hackles get the better of me, so I move a step towards him and glare back at him. What the fuck Pascal is doing here is anybody's guess, but I'm in no mood for his games either, regardless of the shaking thing that's going on all over me.

"Why am I always coming for you, my Rose? Hmm? Intolerable. I am no longer finding this amusing, and I am not known for my patience. You will put your shoes on and come with me, immediately."

I think not.

"Oh, sod off, Pascal. This is none of your business. I don't even know why you're here. Go away, and take your fake American accent with you. I don't have the time for your games, and I can assure you I'm not damn well amused either. How did you even fucking find me, for God's sake?" I plant my feet as steadily as I can and hold my chin up.

His brow rises at my stance, and one of those breath-taking smiles lights up the bloody room around him. As much as I don't want them to, I can't stop my eyes from travelling to his body as he licks his lips and taps his cane in his hand. He's fully dressed in a three-piece grey tweed suit with a silk cravat. Sodding royalty couldn't look more regal if it tried. I catch the breathy moan in my throat before it actually releases itself into the air. Damn him for looking so hot all the time.

"It appears you are finding yourself at last," he eventually says as he closes the space between us and wanders behind me. I keep looking forward. He can look at my arse all he wants. "You look disgraceful in this ensemble, though. We shall have to go to *Saks*. This will not do at all."

What the hell does that mean?

"Pascal, please get out. I need to get ready to travel home. I *am* going home."

"Really? How? For such a beautiful woman, you are remarkably foolish sometimes. You should work on this. It is unbecoming on you," he says as he bangs his cane on the floor behind me with a loud crack. My body instantly jumps at the noise and takes a step away. So in control...

"Umm... in an aeroplane? You know, those things with wings that fly us all over the world." My sarcasm is thankfully still in full swing as I flap my hands at my side.

"And you think the Americans will just let you walk on, do you?" he replies with a smirk as he comes around in front of me again.

"Of course. I have a ticket." What the hell is he talking about now? Infuriating man.

"Passport, my Rose. I assume for your rather hurried escape plan you do have one of those, too, yes?"

Fuck.

"Oh..." My body shrinks from its positive position and lands me flat on my backside on the bed in defeat. He's right. I haven't got a bloody passport with me and therefore I have no way of getting home at all. My eyes are filling with tears before I know what's happening. I'm completely stuck in New York and now the only friend I have is Pascal, who I don't trust for a second.

"Wipe your eyes," he says as a handkerchief is waved around in front of my face. "This is also unflattering and of no intrinsic use to the situation whatsoever."

I grab it from him and try my best to resolve my apparently inappropriate reaction to my situation, although why I'm bothered about how he feels, I don't know. He wanders off towards the mini bar and grabs a glass then removes a hipflask from his pocket and proceeds to fill it up.

"I daresay he will refuse you a drink, my rose. I would suggest you have a large one or two while you have the chance," he says as he comes back to me and holds it out.

"I don't want to be here. Can't you help me get home? Please, Pascal. I'm not ready. I can't do this. I thought maybe I could, that maybe I could be who he needed, but I can't. Well, maybe I can, but I need time to think about it all, to try and find some..." I cut my ridiculous rambling off as I glance across at him, sitting there at the desk, looking far too attractive with a cigarette in his hand and an amused grin plastered on his face. He clearly finds something funny. There is nothing funny happening here. My hackles shoot back up again as I gulp down what appears to be neat gin and launch the glass across the room at him. It misses, and he just watches it fly past him as he blows out smoke. "Why are you here, anyway? Did he send you?"

"Mmm, yes, he did this time. He thought I might be a little more persuasive."

"You're not. Go away."

"Tsk. Elizabeth, stop being so unintelligent. It doesn't suit you. You have very few choices available to you, and I'm afraid I am one of those choices. It would be quite unwise of you to deliberately antagonise me."

I pull in a large sigh and try my hardest for calm of some sort because he's right. I've either got to do as he says or find my way to an embassy to get them to organise my way home. What a bloody mess.

"I'm not sorry for leaving him, Pascal. He told me about stuff. I can't just erase that and pretend it didn't happen. I don't even know if I can accept it. And he was an arsehole to me. Did he tell you what he did on the way over here? Or explain why? Watching him have a fucking blowjob was not very-" He stands up abruptly and pulls at his cufflinks to straighten his already perfect suit, a slight frown gracing his face as he picks up his cane again and turns for the door.

"I told you he had demons, Elizabeth. You are aware of his nature and needs. If you do not wish to help him or comfort him then I will not force you to do so. I am becoming tired of your weakness in this. There are a plethora of others who will give him his solace if you refuse him."

I'm off the bed in an instant, my finger waggling about in the hope of getting my point across. This is not all about Mr. White.

"His solace? His needs? What about me? What about what I need? This is not-" He swings around on me so quickly I tumble backwards onto the bed and stare up at him in shock.

"What about you? I am not concerned with you. You know exactly where you need to be to find your solace. It is waiting for you, in his arms," he says with a snarl as he towers over me and flicks his hand around in annoyance. "He offers it only to you, has only ever offered it to you, and you are sitting here weeping like a child over some rotting corpses who had very little reason to exist. I have done far worse things with my existence, and yet you were ready to let me fuck you with no thought on the matter. Taking life is easy, Elizabeth. Asking for forgiveness, for acceptance or understanding, is not. He is only what he is, and despite his infuriating behaviour, he is in pain, and unfortunately, he needs you. If you wish to be part of him, you will meet me in the car in ten minutes. If not, I will do your job for you."

And with that, he swivels on his heel and storms out of the room. I have a feeling I just pissed him off beyond belief. I stare at the open door with a gaping mouth, not knowing what the hell I'm supposed to do with that information.

He needs me? If he needs me, why has he been acting like he doesn't give a shit about me? And forgiveness? Really?

I'm up and pacing about while watching the clock ticking by, trying to work out what I'm supposed to do next. I can't get home. Well, I can if I go to the embassy, but I certainly can't get on a plane yet. Pascal has just called me a weeping child because I happen to care that people are dead. I have no money, no other clothes or luggage, and the only option I seem to have is to go and get in a car with another killing machine, who will then take me back to the crux of all my problems, who apparently needs me. For what? He had me. He just needed to talk to me, for God's sake. And if I don't go, I'm pretty sure I know what Pascal means by doing my job for me. That's definitely not okay.

With very little thought for anything other than making sure Pascal doesn't get himself beaten to death, I grab my bag and slip on my shoes. Who knows? Maybe I'll be able to get some damn sleep on the journey to wherever we're going. My hand reaches for the door handle, and before I'm aware of where I am, I'm wrapping my scarf around my neck and crossing the lobby's marbled floor to get to the car. The glint of the morning sun reflects off the spinning doors in front of me and halts me in my tracks as I try to refocus on where I'm going. Time seems to stop for a second or two as my eyes find balance again, and I notice Pascal leaning against the side of a limousine, waiting for me. His legs are crossed as he raises his cane at me and tips back his trilby hat just so that he can make his smirking face more apparent to me, I'm sure. He damn well knew I'd follow him out here, didn't he? He probably didn't give the possibility of me refusing to join him a second thought. When the fuck will I actually be in control of anything? I need to work on this. He's right. I need to be the one in charge of myself. I need to let both these men know exactly who they're dealing with and ensure they're both aware that I won't put up with their little games any longer. I feel myself cracking my neck from side to side and realise how similar a move it is to Alex. When he's deciding something or making a statement in his own head, he does exactly the same thing. My chin lifts as I tighten my leg muscles and stride towards the door in the most authoritative manner I possess. I am Elizabeth Scott, and I will no longer be dominated by anyone. I will no longer be the one who bounces between everyone else's feelings. I will make my own damn decisions. I am feisty, I am capable and I am a serious business owner. I am no longer Alex's plaything, regardless of whether he needs me or not. He will be honest with me, even if I have to beat it out of him. My heels hit the first step on my way down to Pascal as he holds the door open for me and continues to smirk.

"He isn't terribly partial to a whip, my rose. I would not attempt it," he says as I slide my backside into the leather seat. Mind reader he may be, but I'm not even responding to that. I'm not even sure if I like him much at the moment, the condescending, arrogant bastard.

He climbs in beside me, and knocks his cane on the privacy screen so the car pulls away, and now we're heading to God knows where. I keep my gaze fixed on the outside of the car. Quite frankly, if I wasn't so pissed, tired and confused, I'd be gaping like a bloody idiot. The New York skyline is glinting back at me, and I so want to sigh at it in delight. It's positively beautiful and more than likely full of treasures that I want to explore.

"Where are we going?" I snap without removing my eyes from the view.

"The where should not concern you, more the why," he replies softly. My head turns toward his to find him tapping his lips and looking, quite bizarrely, a little nervous, if that's even possible.

"What does that mean? Why do you look worried?"

"I am not worried. I am a little perplexed. He is confusing me for once, and I am not entirely sure how to respond to him."

"Well, thank fuck it's not just me."

"Language! Really, my rose, do try to keep your composure. You looked positively magnificent ten minutes ago. Fuck is a beautiful word. However, keep it for use when it's intended to prove a point only. One should be either soft with it – breathy moans of desire etcetera – or venomously deadly."

Now I'm having a sodding English lesson from a Dutchman. I roll my eyes at him and stare back out the window in irritation, while I take a deep breath and hope I know what I'm letting myself in for.

"I've never been here. It's quite wonderful," I say as I watch the skyscrapers lounging gracefully in the air.

"It would be if it were not for a-" He cuts himself off and coughs a little. "However, I find it all too new, too polished. It holds none of our European charm. "

"Really, Pascal? Did I sense some emotion there?"

"None whatsoever, my Rose," he replies as I feel the end of his cane touch my chin and draw me round to face him. "What is your plan to alleviate his tension?"

No fucking clue.

"I am going to tell him what I think of his behaviour, possibly hit him a few times, probably show him how much I hate him at the moment, and then demand that he takes me home. I have had enough of whatever this is, and I won't put up with any of this bullshit anymore."

There. That's exactly what I'm going to do. I don't care what greets me when we get there, wherever there is. I don't care what den of iniquity I'm faced with. I shall hold my head up, look as if I own the space around me and dictate the outcome. Alex would be laughing his face off if it weren't him I was going to deal with. I couldn't sound any more like Mr. White if I tried.

"I feel your plan may be floored somewhat."

Whatever. Even he doesn't know what to do with the bastard, which is a little worrisome.

"Pascal, if I knew what I was doing, I wouldn't have gotten on the plane with him in the first place. It's like he's suddenly deranged or something. I'm completely lost, to be honest, but as you said, weakness is not going to do me any favours with him so I might as well try for this 'dominance' you keep banging on about. It does appear to have worked on occasion."

"Dominance is good, my rose. However, I think it may be the 'hate' that he wants from you. I can only assume that he believes if you understand hatred literally then you will be able to come to terms with the whys."

Well, fuck me. That's insightful. Really? What sort of screwed up brain thinks like that?

Alexander White's, clearly.

"Did you know Alexander White isn't his real name?"

"It is to me," he replies with a smirk, the smarmy bastard. "And it should be to you, too. That which has passed should not be used to determine the man in front of you today." My mouth gapes in response as my brain rapidly catches up. It's cloud sodding cuckoo land around here.

"What a load of rubbish. What we were does exactly that. It determines who we are now and why we have become this way. And you yourself obviously spend far too much time trying to analyse who he was and why."

"No, my dear. I spend time helping him comprehend his worth now. I persuade him to embrace all that he is, to do nothing other than dredge positivity from his past, regardless of the negativity that consumes him."

I'm really too tired for this shit. I'm not even sure I understand what that means, and why does he have to have an answer for everything all of a sudden instead of being his normal vague self.

"I..."

"Elizabeth, why would you spend time foolishly trying to weed his past from him when all you need to do is encourage his persona today? Love is a wonderful thing, exquisite in nature sometimes, in fact. However, if you allow what was to consume what is because of your own insecurities, you will never have him entirely. He will spend all his time concerned with how you perceive his past. You said you wanted him. Now is the time to show him that."

My mouth is still gaping. Have I not told him I want him enough? Have I not told him and shown him that I'll give him everything? How much more does he want from me?

"Is that what you do? Just let him do exactly what he wants?" I eventually reply as I look at my shoes and try to summon up the courage to accept an uncontrolled Alex. He chuckles and reaches for his hipflask and a two glasses.

"There would be no fun in that, and he cannot have his own way all the time. He would die of boredom, no doubt. However, you should know by now that when he needs his own way, it is always prudent to let him have it. It cleanses him. You must choose your timing cautiously."

How the hell am I supposed to know? I'm still not sure if I want any further interaction with him anyway, other than getting me home and telling him what a twat he is.

Pascal passes me a drink and waves his hand at me, indicating that I should down it. I feel a little sick if I'm honest, and the thought isn't all that appealing.

"Drink it," he demands, with a tone he's only ever directed at me a few times. Funnily enough, I find myself relaxing a bit at it, not jumping ten foot in the air like I used to. Perhaps I've really got a hold on this dominance thing now. The corner of his mouth twitches as I giggle quietly to myself at him. Tyrant, he may appear to everyone else, but not to me. Loveable rogue, maybe – distinguished, charming and somewhat deviant gentleman, definitely. But he's beautiful in his own unique way, and still trying to help me understand the man I'm unfortunately still very much in love with. I must be because I wouldn't be in this car if I wasn't, would I?

I blow out another long sigh and lean my head back against the seat.

"Why me?" I mumble as I close my eyes for the first time in over twenty-four hours and try to relax.

"Because you are the one he chose, my rose, and because it is your position to choose the rest of his life for him."

Chapter 5

Alexander

Where was she?

He'd been waiting for over eight hours and was getting beyond pissed off with the irritating man. Why he'd allowed Pascal to persuade him into letting him go after her was still a mystery. He should have just turned the damn car around and sent it back towards the airport. The current floorshow of debauchery wasn't helping his mood in the slightest.

Sitting there, watching varying women in slutty attire parading themselves about for their significant others was becoming tiresome and bland. He had no idea where Tara had gone. He didn't fucking care either.

The room reeked of that old-school elegance that Pascal managed in all his clubs. They were basically the same in every city, with just slight changes to layout and format to accommodate the individual needs of the natives. Alex had never been to this one before. For some reason, Pascal had left the old venue and moved Eden here. Christ knew why. The other place was fine, but this New York version of Eden was slightly more polished than the last – slightly more chrome orientated and modern. It didn't quite have the same graceful, dirty feeling that all his European venues had. That air of age and distinction was lacking, to say the least, although the clientele were certainly no less high-class.

"Sir, would you like another cognac?" some random waitress asked him as she sashayed past in little more than a French maid's outfit. What the hell was that all about? Was it some sort of dress up night he wasn't aware of? Ridiculous. He nodded at her and scanned the doorway again for Elizabeth. Pascal said he would bring her here straight away. He clearly hadn't, and that was getting beyond frustrating.

"Alexander," a woman's voice called chirpily from over his shoulder. He was in no mood for chirpy behaviour, so he slowly turned his head to see who it was. He found Vixon stalking towards him – a

Domme of the highest repute who was, quite literally, dragging two large men along behind her on leads.

"Vixon," he replied with a nod of his head as he noticed the thigh-high red boots and smiled a little. She still had very good legs. "Still using two?"

"Always. New ones, though, from the last time, I reckon. Where did I see you last? Berlin? Stop checking out my thighs. You know you couldn't handle them."

"Mmm, we both know we'll never know the answer to that, don't we? And yes, Berlin."

She pointed her finger at the floor, which caused one of the men to drop to all fours and the other to crouch across him. She then sat down on them and reached for his drink.

"You don't mind, do you? I'm quite exhausted," she said as she picked it up anyway and drank some. Luckily, the French maid returned with his next drink at the correct moment. "So why are you here? I can't remember ever seeing you in here before."

"I'm waiting for Pascal," he replied. He had little else to add to the subject and couldn't be bothered with niceties.

"Someone's grumpy. My boys here can help if you need something?"

"No, thank you."

"Where's the fun in you gone?" she said as she slid a crop across his leg. "You used to be a right giggle, Alexander." He'd grabbed it and thrown it over his shoulder before she had a chance to blink.

"I'm not in the mood for fun. I just need Pascal to get here so I can deal with some issues that have cropped up." He'd have pardoned the pun if he could be bothered...

"I think he has a room here for you. I know he changed the layout from the old place, but I'm pretty sure it's up on the third floor. Why don't you go on up and I'll get some food sent up for you? You're clearly not comfortable here."

Comfortable? What a fucking thought. The only time he was even vaguely comfortable anymore was when she had her arms wrapped around him, and for the briefest of seconds, he could forget his true nature. Just a few minutes of those legs entwining with his own seemed to somehow create just enough peace for him to hope for more of it. He scanned the area with the exits to the upper floors.

Vixon was right. He did need to go and find some silence for a while. He needed to be ready for when she arrived. He needed to try and rid himself of all this anger and frustration so he could be in control of the man he wanted her to see. He couldn't find the doorways and turned back towards the woman for some sort of guidance.

"I never could manage that eyebrow thing," she said in response. "Look." She wiggled them about, presumably trying to lift one of them. She couldn't achieve it in the slightest. He felt the corners of his mouth lift in amusement and blew out a much-needed breath. "That's better," she said. "I'm not sure what you're fixing to do, but you'll get it wrong if you go at it in that mood. And I quite like Pascal." Clever bitch.

"Are you trying to play with me, Clarissa?" he asked, chuckling a little at her screwed up face.

"Do not call me that in front of these imbeciles," she replied as she hit big chap number one on the head and stamped on number two's hand. "You know I don't like it, and master or not, I won't be humiliated by you at any point. I was just trying to help."

"Well, could you help a little more by pointing out the door?"

"It's over there," she replied as she stood and took his arm to lead the way over. On reaching a quiet corner, he noticed the thumb pads encased in the wall and nodded at her again. She smiled in response and smacked number one around the head again. "I'll get some steak sent up. Enjoy the peace for a while," she said as she wandered away and leant across the bar area. Imbecile number two seemed to have found his tongue attached to her legs all of a sudden.

He drew in a long breath and reached his fingers towards the pad. Two bright red flashes and the heavy, dark wood doors swung open to reveal a long, green corridor. It was typically Pascal, all low lighting, with some sort of chanting type music drifting along the passageway. He smiled a little and continued towards the end of the walkway where it seemed an elevator awaited him. Once again, he pressed his thumb against it and the doors instantly opened to reveal a mirrored space and no other buttons whatsoever. He stepped in, and as soon as he turned around, the elevator rose. Pascal really had gone to town on this outfit.

The doors swung open again after very little time, and a small foyer greeted him with fresh, white lilies in tall, crystal cut vases either side of two more heavy, dark wood doors. Which one was his? He moved to the right and noticed a small card on the table. He picked it up and turned it over.

The choice is yours, dear boy, as it always will be.

He smirked to himself, knowing full well that Pascal would be taking the room next to his. Whichever one he chose would be his, but his friend, his mentor, would be within arm's reach if needed – still there to help him through his turmoil, or at least to feed his own masochistic needs.

He moved to the right and pushed his thumb against the door. The lock clicked and opened into a large suite decorated in dark blues, with hues of pale grey adorning the windows. Chandeliers separated the space into three distinct areas. Start, beginning, end: the start being a simple grey rug on the floor and a set of drawers off to the right; the middle being a cross, a bench and, yes, suspension hooks above his head; and the end being a king size four poster, which matched the one in his suite in Rome. It was covered in appropriate tie holes and ropes, as usual. In fact, on further examination, the room was entirely set up like his suite in Rome. Apart from the colour scheme, there wasn't any difference at all. He sighed and scanned the area again. It felt comfortable to some degree, homely, if that was a word he could use to describe the lair of a sadist. The very thought had him picturing Elizabeth's eyes again when he sliced the dress off her, a move so easy, so comfortable for him, and yet shame had held him back again.

The room would do. Pascal could have the other one. There wasn't going to be anything else in there that he needed or wanted. At the moment, given that all he needed or wanted was for her to be there, he couldn't see any point in venturing into the space next door. Wherever Pascal was with her, he wasn't there. The room would do.

Before he had time to close the door behind him, a young man knocked on it and dropped to his knees beside a trolley of food. He widened the door again and watched as the moron scrambled to his feet and pushed it inside. He then hovered about, looking a little sheepish about something.

"Are you waiting for something?" Alex asked as he damn near collapsed into a leather armchair and stretched his head back.

"Um, no, Sir. It's just that I wondered if you knew." What was the little shit talking about? And how the fuck did he know who he was anyway?

"I'm assuming you know who I am, somehow. Well done, you. But what the hell are you talking about? I'm in no mood for conversation."

"No, Sir. No. I'll just leave then," he said as he began to back his way out of the room, bowing and scraping as he went. Definitely a Pascal sub – overdramatic to say the least.

"Wait. What were you going to tell me?"

"I shouldn't have said anything. I'm sorry, Sir. It wasn't my position to say anything, and-"

"Speak, for fuck's sake," Alex shouted as he heaved himself up again and wandered toward the bathroom. He needed a shower and a change of clothes before he ate anything. The boy shuffled from foot to foot a bit and then hovered again.

"It's just, well, he told me not to tell you. And then he used that wink that he does, and now I'm not sure if that means I should tell you or not. He's very confusing, and I don't want him angry with me for not doing the right thing. It's just, I'm new here and I don't really understand how I'm supposed to know everything."

Alex continued to undo his shirt as he turned on the shower and then wandered back out to face the boy. He looked scared, and it didn't take a genius to know whom he was scared of.

"What is it he told you not to tell me?" he asked as he unclasped his cufflinks and pulled the shirt from his body. The boy shuffled again. "If he told you not to tell me, it means that he doesn't trust you enough yet, and therefore presumes you'll probably tell me anyway. More than likely because you don't know what you're doing and will be as scared of me as you are of him. So in reality, he told you to tell me. It's the way he is. You'll get used to it, eventually."

"Oh," the boy said. "He doesn't trust me? I've given him everything and he still doesn't trust me?"

He sighed again and put his hands on his hips, then smirked to himself at the position as her face raced into his brain. The poor boy shrank away from him, and he watched as his face began to turn white

69

with fear. Lessons in Pascal were difficult to say the least. How he managed it with apparent ease most of the time was still beyond him.

"How long have you been here?" he asked as he noticed the bruises around the boy's throat.

"Three months."

"You've given him nothing then. He will play with you for at least another year if you interest him long enough, and then maybe he'll be a little more open with you. At the moment, you're nothing but a passing fad."

"But, but, I love him," he stuttered with a look of sheer terror. Alex shook his head and turned again for the bathroom.

"I would suggest you stop then. He doesn't do love. Love complicates everything," he replied, hearing Pascal's own words ringing in his ears. How right he'd been. "Now, tell me what he asked you not to tell me."

"He said he didn't want you to know that she was here." Alex's steps stopped instantly as his body swung back around to face the boy.

"Who?"

"I don't know. He carried her in. I think she was asleep, maybe drugged," the boy replied, still shuffling and fidgeting from side to side.

"What did she look like?"

"Long, red hair. She looked very-" He was past him and out of the door before the boy could finish his sentence. Had that bastard had her here all along? There must have been a way in that he couldn't see from inside the club.

Three strides and he was at the other door, wondering how the fuck to get in. The choice was his? He pressed his thumb to the pad and the door opened to reveal the room. Pascal sat there in an armchair with a cup of coffee, smirking like a fucking arsehole at him. He was just about to bellow several expletives at him when the shit raised his finger to his lips and nodded towards the other end of the room.

There she was, lying on the bed, fast asleep, that red hair spilling all around her as her languid, barely covered body lounged gracefully underneath deep red satin sheets. He flicked his eyes back to Pascal. Had the bastard undressed her, too?

"Did you touch her?" he seethed quietly. Someone had clearly undressed her.

"No more than I had to, dear boy. It was quite a hardship to behave myself, though. As you said, her skin feels just like silk. Would you like some coffee?" *Wanker.*

"I should kill you for this," he said as he walked over towards her to see that she was okay. "Did you drug her?"

"Dear boy, really, what do you take me for? She is simply exhausted, and very much in need of slumber. The poor thing is very confused, interestingly still extremely spirited, though."

"Mmm," was all he could force from his mouth as he stared down at her, picked up a piece of her hair and rubbed it between his fingers. Her mouth opened and a whisper of his name left her lips before she rolled away from him to reveal her glorious backside. He gazed like a love-struck teenager until he eventually sighed out some of his tension and drew the curtain along the side of the bed to give her some privacy. The shit had probably been leering at her for far too long already. He wandered across to sit in the chair opposite Pascal and picked up the already poured coffee.

"You look thoroughly exhausted yourself. Still beautiful, thankfully. However, did you have to come in here half dressed? You know how it unnerves me," he asked, another sinful smirk plastered on his face.

"Why didn't you bring her to me?"

"I did. She has been here all along."

"You could have told me." He would have been in here hours ago.

"I left a note. The choice was yours." *Scheming bastard.*

"I didn't know she was in here, though, and you knew I didn't. Had I known, I would have come to her."

"Obviously, but she needed rest, and you're right handed." What?

"What the hell does that have to do with anything?"

"I brought her to the left hand room. You always favour your right. Right handed predictability, and as I said, she needed rest. Also, you are not thinking clearly enough to be with her yet. Have you eaten the food that Reubin brought for you, cleansed yourself? Hmm? Slept, even?"

"I am not predictable." The thought disturbed the fuck out of him.

"You are to me, very predictable indeed, actually. In the most volatile of ways, of course."

"That makes no sense at all."

"To me, it makes perfect sense. You have always made perfect sense. Now, what do you need?"

"I just need to…" He didn't know what he needed, and Pascal's raised brow as he stared across his coffee cup at him and smiled indicated that he was very aware of it. The man still said nothing to interrupt or give any direction whatsoever as they looked at each other, which was unlike him. She did that, too, lately, didn't help him find the emotion or word he was after, almost pushed him harder to find it himself. He sighed again and looked across his shoulder at the bed. What the hell was he doing? What did he need? Sleep was probably a good idea. "I need her to understand."

"Ah, yes," Pascal replied as he placed his cup on the table, loosened his green tie and stripped himself of his tweed jacket. "This comprehension of a murderer… I assume that you feel if she learns what true hatred feels like then she'll understand your ability to kill with no remorse, yes?" He didn't move or speak in response. What was the point? Pascal clearly understood him better than he did himself most of the time. It was irritatingly comforting. "It is an interesting technique, not one I have ever used before. One can only try, I suppose."

"What other choice do I have? She will never forgive this, nor should she. She has always been too pure for the likes of me. We both know that. She does, too," he replied quietly.

Pascal sat for a long time, just staring at him, no emotion on his face, arms resting on the armchair as he presumably thought of his next burst of intellect. The silence stretched on as those green eyes bore into his until the point where he actually looked downwards for a split second to get away from the intensity.

"Why did you tell her?" Pascal immediately asked.

"I had to. Aiden Phillips was going to tell her if I didn't." Pascal's chuckled response clearly meant that was not a good enough explanation.

"I doubt that is true. The man may be a psychopath but he is not a moron. You told her because you wanted her to know, did you not? Hmm? You wanted her deeper inside you than anyone has been before. Are you not man enough to admit that, Alexander?"

"Fuck you."

"Lovely, shall we get started? How would you like me? Is this why you came half dressed? We have all we might need in this room. Let me just-"

"Pascal."

"Well, really, dear boy, just answer the question."

"Yes, then, I suppose you're right."

"Wonderful. True love... How delightful, if not brainless. However, how do you hope to achieve the continuation of true love if you make her despise you? I am struggling with your concept somewhat. This theory of yours is flawed."

"Flawed? Aren't we all? Her dreams of a happily ever after will never be achieved if I continue to lie to her about what and who I am. I promised her she would know me entirely, that I would let her in. She needs to see the bad as well as the good she is somehow managing to pull from me."

"Do you want to hurt her as you do me?" How was that relevant?

"This isn't about you, Pascal."

"Of course it is, to some degree. You use me for your needs. Do you want her to take it all from you?"

"No."

"Then please enlighten me as to why you believe she needs to hate you to understand your past. It is beyond confounding. I understand your past, and you feel the need to beat me, yet you do not need me to hate you for that to happen,"

"You are a masochist, and a psychopath."

"I think that is a little harsh."

"Okay, you've killed. You understand that as she never will."

"We could have her kill someone. I have several lined up."

"Pascal."

"You're not enamoured with this idea. I can tell."

"No."

"Mmm. I think you are underestimating her ability to see you for what you are. I have watched you dismiss countless wondrous women over the years, and many of them would have accepted you without any need for this chivalrous if not deluded behaviour."

"You think I should hide this from her?"

"No, but I fear you are being too – how should I say? – devious about it? She is not a fool, Alexander. She is quite astonishing really, and if you pursue this, I think you will push her too far. She is more capable of handling you than you give her credit for. She reminds me somewhat of myself in my younger years."

"She is nothing like you." The thought was alarming, regardless of the fact that he could hear truth in the words.

"We were all innocent once, Alexander. We may have become broken over the years, but we are still the same person inside, and while we may choose to suppress our natures, we still have the same loyalties to those who we care for, do we not?"

"Your idea of 'care' is not the same as hers."

"You tarnish me with the brushes of others. Have I not always been here for you?"

"I have seen your sense of morality, Pascal. I've lived it, breathed it, and revelled in it. Elizabeth is more than that, more..."

"Angelic? Mmm, however, she now needs to be less so to accept you, yes? And so you must show her. I understand that, but you must love her, too, dear boy. She will not entertain this unless you allow her to absorb your nature and become part of it. She will not sit on the side lines and watch you destroy all she has worked hard to achieve because you believe playing a game will help her comprehend your deviances. You have to let her in, let her in deeper, Alexander. Give her every memory of your father if you wish. Give her every tear you choose to shed. If you are ready to hand yourself over to someone entirely then you should do it honestly, declare it with your soul."

Alex sat and watched as the man's eyes softened a note and drifted to place he'd only seen a few times before. His body was almost relaxed, instead of the constant façade of perfection that was usual for him. He was clearly thinking of someone else. Whoever that someone had been, they had known the real Pascal – a Pascal of long ago.

"You're talking about yourself, aren't you?"

Pascal was up and pressing the bell for service again before he could blink. Clearly more coffee was required, as well as a normal distraction technique.

"I don't know what you are talking about," he replied as he started to strip his waistcoat and shirt off.

"You know I can read you better than that. Why won't you discuss it?"

"Alexander, I have no need to revisit my past, nor the people in it. They are ghosts to me, and that is where they shall remain."

"Has it got something to do with Roxanne?" Pascal just stood there, stock still, his back facing Alex as he watched the faint rise of his back muscles and smiled at the scars he'd put there. All on the right hand side of his body. Nothing but silence and the quiet ticking of a clock echoed in the room, along with the occasional deep breath from Pascal. Eventually, he moved to the wardrobe and pulled out a deep blue Edwardian style ensemble of clothing. "You don't need to hide this from me. You can talk about it if you need to. Haven't you been pushing me for my feelings all this time? I can return the favour."

"I have never pushed you for feelings, nor will I ever. That is for her to do. I have simply allowed you to be greater than you were when we first met, to be more," he replied as he pulled on his rather more 'Pascal' look and moved toward the mirror. "Now, can I suggest you go and get some food and then sleep? I have work to do and an abundance of deviance to fulfil. We are not all so restricted by this love you insist upon."

"For someone so intelligent, you can sometimes be far too closed off, Pascal. You know where I am when you do need to talk about it," Alex said as he moved towards the door.

"I will order you more food. Eat it, and then sleep. I will come for you when she has awakened."

"No, I just need a few hours sleep. I'm not hungry yet. I'll come and find you downstairs later."

"Where you will be honest, yes?"

"You should try some of that yourself, Pascal. You never know where it might lead you."

No response, just a raised brow as he turned his back again and walked toward the bathroom. The subject was still very much in the 'we're not talking about this' phase, which, for now, was fine by him.

He glanced across at Elizabeth one last time to see nothing but a sheer curtain greeting him with a faint outline of her body etched across it. She'd be fine in here. No one else could get into the room other than himself and Pascal, and frankly, if the man wanted to, he could have done anything before he got here. Still...

"Don't touch her again," he called quietly as he opened the door. "Not until I tell you to." The bark of laughter that came from the bathroom didn't fill him with quite as much comfort as he'd hoped for. So, swinging back around, he stared at the door and waited for the man to materialize again.

"Go, Alexander. I will wait for instruction. I am not totally untrustworthy," his European accent said from the depths of the room somewhere. And then his body reappeared out of the darkness, not a scrap of submissive on display, not the slightest hint of masochist to be seen. One mention of a certain woman's name and Pascal Van Der Braack had become the epitome of arrogance and dominance again, dressed in his finest regalia and probably ready to wage his version of war on something. "Besides, I suddenly feel the ache for something more substantial, and I wouldn't want to break your little thing."

He needed to find out more about who Roxanne was, and what she had over the man. Pascal certainly knew.

Chapter 6

Elizabeth

Okay, why am I nearly naked, and where the hell am I? Much as I might feel rested, the sudden realisation that I'm not in my own bed has just hit me. Where was I before this happened? Oh, yes... In Pascal's car, on my way to Alex. Then why am I in a bed?

I gingerly tighten my thighs in the hope that I'm not going to feel the tell-tale ache there that lets me know I've had sex. I'm positive that if I had, with either of them, I wouldn't have been able to sleep through it, but you never know. Thankfully, I swiftly realise that I do have underwear on – well, at least panties. Thank God for that. Nothing is aching in the slightest, apart from my head.

I heave myself upright and grab at the red curtain on the side of the bed to see what I'm dealing with, then rapidly halt my progress because there could be anybody out there. Including either or both of them. My eyes narrow at the thought.

"Alex?" I call out. Nothing.

"Pascal?" Again, nothing. Apparently I'm alone. Thank God for that, too.

Tentatively poking my head out around the curtain, I scan the room for enemies. There's nobody there, only a darkened room. My eyes suddenly widen at the array of paraphernalia dotted about. This is definitely a dungeon of sorts, very similar to Alex's suite in Rome. Is this his room? Did he undress me? I need some clothes. Why the hell do I always seem to need clothes at the moment?

Another quick recce of the room proves, without a shadow of a doubt, there are no clothes here, again. Sodding hell. Maybe some kind soul has left some in the wardrobe. I wander over to it, and as I open the door, aftershave assaults my senses, and it's not Alex's. I'm in Pascal's room. This is confirmed by the array of crushed velvet and fine silk shirts staring back at me. Unfortunately, there's not much in the way of female clothing to use. I sigh out a breath and wander back over to the bed. What the hell am I supposed to do now? Digging through my bag, I find my phone and check for missed calls. Nothing... only a few texts from Belle saying she'll pick me up from the airport. Well, that isn't going to happen. How she even booked flights without my passport number is beyond me. I quickly send a text back to her trying to explain my situation, not that I know what it is, but there seems little point worrying her any more.

A soft knock at the door has me jumping up from the bed and grabbing at my boobs for protection. Who the hell is that? I've only just woken up, for God's sake.

"Yes?" I call out while scrabbling around with the sheets for some cover.

"Lovey, come and open the door, would you? I've got rather an armful here," a woman's voice replies. At least it's better than a man.

"Of what?" I ask as I make my way over to the door and unlock it.

I'm met with what can only be described as a whirling dervish of fake bright red hair, very long red thigh high boots and several items of women's clothing. She shoves them towards my arms, instantly causing me to drop my sheet to grab them, and then proceeds to wander her way around the room, leaving me standing there like a prat.

"Ooh, I like it in here. Very posh. Why didn't he let me have one of these?" she says as she meanders her fingers over various things I have no idea about.

"Umm, who are you?" I ask, still standing here like a prat, now with an armful of clothes.

"Vixon. Clarissa, if you must, but not in front of anyone else, please. That man of yours used it once already tonight, and I had to beat seven bales of shite out of my boys because of it."

"You're English." It's a statement, not a question. She's a true Londoner, I'd say, with a good twang of American here and there.

"Yes, residing in New York most of the time. The men are more pliable over here, up for more punishment, if you know what I mean."

"Oh..." I have no fucking clue what I'm supposed to say to that. I try politeness. "Do you come here often?"

"Are you asking me out? 'Cause, honey, I know you like pain to be messing with those men. Or maybe you like giving it? Have you had a woman yet? Nice tits, by the way."

"What? No, I haven't, don't... Umm, sorry, I didn't mean that. I just..." Yep, words fail me. My mouth is gaping. What the hell am I talking about?

"Honey, calm down. I was joking. Sort of, anyway. He just asked me to bring you some clothes is all. I suppose they want to see you dressed before they rip it all off you."

"They will not be doing anything of the sort."

"Ooh, you're a wild one, aren't you? Not normally his type at all. No wonder he's gone all boring. You've killed all his spirit. How have you done that? Didn't think I'd ever see him break for a woman. Pascal, maybe, but not a woman. What's the secret?"

"What do you mean by that?" I'm still standing here like an idiot, now also getting a touch defensive about the fact that Pascal could break Alex but I couldn't. Who the hell does she think she is? And why would Pascal be breaking him at all? He's not gay. My hand finds its place on my hip as I flick my arse out to increase my dominant posture. I will not be belittled in this place – wherever this place is. I am in control of myself and the situation. If I keep chanting this to myself, maybe it'll work. Why is she unbuttoning her corset? "Umm, what are you doing?"

"We're trying on clothes, girly things." We are so not. I may be, but I don't need her help.

"I think I can manage on my own, thanks."

"I'm sure you can, but I quite like the look of that purple number, and you'll need help with the buttons on that green PVC outfit. My hands quickly drop the bundle of clothes on the chair as I scan what I'm actually holding. There's not a normal thing amongst them.

"What the sodding hell is all this crap?"

"Very expensive crap, lovey, and quite fitting for what's going on downstairs."

"Where am I?"

"Eden. Did he drug you? I keep telling him he can't drug people and bring them here, but he won't listen. You know what he's like. I mean, all that stuff going on with selling chicks into the third world

really isn't cricket, but hey, I suppose if he's good at what he does..."
My dominant posture has drooped very slightly as I try to hold eye
contact with the woman, because seriously? She must be joking, and I
will not shake in my boots at the thought. She scans me again as she
puts a toothpick in her mouth and crosses her arms. "So, what's your
story anyway?"

"There's no story to tell. I just need to see Alex and I'll be on my
way. Once he lets me go home, that is." That last bit is mumbled. I
don't even know why I let it slip out. *Ridiculous, Beth.*

"Alex? Wow. I've never heard a soul call him that. You must be
one special bitch. Why is Pascal all protective of you? He told me not
to touch you. What have you got that's so intriguing?"

"Nothing. I don't know, and quite frankly, I don't care. If you can
just leave, I'll get dressed and be on my way."

"Nah, not buying it. Anyway, it's not my business. I just work for
him, do as I'm told, only by him, obviously. So let's get you dressed."

"I can do that on my own."

"Lovey, don't go all alpha on me. It only suits you when you
mean it, and I can tell you don't, yet. Just let me help and then we'll
form a plan."

"A plan for what?"

"To get you out of here. That is what you want I assume?"

"Oh, well yes." How does she know that?
"Good. Now, let's see. The only vaguely normal gear is this," she says
as she holds what can only be described as a black, leather, eighties
style LBD with orange bands running around it. I do nothing more than
tilt my head in recognition of its existence, and then she opens a
suitcase and holds the matching heels up. They are possibly the most
beautiful things I have ever seen. High? Yes. Elegant? Absolutely.
Going to break my neck in them? More than likely. "You're a classy
type, aren't you?"

Well, I'm not sure about that, but if not wanting to look like a
common slut all the time is categorised as classy, I'll nod my head in
agreement. So I do.

"Where are they?" I ask.

"Downstairs. Pascal has gone all ferocious for some reason, and
Alexander is being his normal, non-readable self. Last I saw of him, he
was fiddling with some puppy's ear."

"What?" Jealousy courses through me instantly. I know I should stop it, or not even feel it, but it's there, snarly and biting its way around me like the devil.

"It's dress up night – happens once a month. The staff wear stupid outfits and act like whores. That bit's pretty normal actually, but the clothes are not normally so comical," she says as she strides across to a mirror and re-applies even heavier dark eye make-up.

"What time is it?"

"About ten," she mutters through another layer of bright red lipstick. Ten? Shit. Where's the day gone?

"Okay," I reply quietly as I try to think about what it is that I'm hoping to achieve. I still haven't got a clue if I'm honest. I just know I want to feel in control of something for once, and also that I want to slap Alex so hard he falls over. That's clearly not going to happen, but I'll be damn well trying.

"Look, lovey, just put the shit on. Either that or we can have some fun for a while. That bed looks amazing." The burst of giggles that leaves my mouth breaks all the tension in the room. "You're cute. Enjoy it. You should try making them beg."

Well that's an interesting idea. Pascal does keep telling me to do the dominant thing, which does work with Alex. I'm not sure about Pascal, though, not that I care quite as much about that. Actually, it would be quite entertaining to watch Alex beg. He said he'd do it for me. Maybe it's time to make that happen. He can stick his games up his arse. I shall be feistier. He made me this way, so now he can have me.

"You think I could?" Why I'm suddenly asking her advice is utterly beyond me, but she certainly seems like she knows what she's doing.

"Nah, afraid not if I'm honest. Likelihood is, if you try, he'll hang you from the ceiling until you scream, and then keep going until you can't anymore. That's his normal MO. Actually, when the right mood sets in, sometimes that doesn't even stop him. Have you seen it yet? They're quite a sight when they get going together. I wouldn't like to be on the receiving end of it myself, to be honest. That's why we've never fucked. But then, I'm clearly not a pain slut, which I can only assume you are. 'Cause you definitely shouldn't be playing with boys like that if you're not."

"Umm..." Yep, that's all I've got. The widening of my eyes must show my naivety in these matters because she's suddenly narrowing her eyes and staring quite strangely at me.

"You do know what you're messing with here, don't you?"

It appears not. Well, I thought I did. He told me, and I've certainly seen small pieces of that side of him, but whether I've scratched the surface of his true nature, I don't know. I believed I'd thought about it enough, but now, standing here in Pascal's room with its instruments of doom and gazing across at a woman who has clearly witnessed it all, I'm suddenly not sure at all.

My eyes scan the room again and land on what can only be described as a black dentist's chair – a dentist's chair that appears to have straps and buckles, loops and ropes. It also appears to have a seat that separates. My mind races with all kinds of thoughts and visions as I lift my head to look at the bench close to it, which is padded with nails. Nails? I wander across to it and find myself pricking my finger on the top of it, then look at the locked cabinet beside it.

"What's in there?" I mumble to myself as my eyes scan more Interesting – if not quite as scary looking – gadgets and leather implements hanging next to the bench. Alex's room in Rome was different somehow. Maybe it was the lighting, or the mood, or the fact that I'd been drinking and was so intent on giving him what he wanted that I didn't really stop to think about what I was doing. But this all looks worrying, strange. Is it because he's not here to make me feel at ease about it? He whipped me and I loved it, for God's sake. Why am I so shocked by these things all of a sudden?

"I'd say knives, maybe other blood play things, needles etcetera. Pascal may be abnormally vicious in our world, and he's not known for any sort of rules, but he's actually damn squeamish about infections and stuff. As we all should be really."

Knives... The vision of Alex slicing my dress off is immediate. The shiver that follows along my spine can only be described as chilling. Unfortunately, my thighs clamp at the thought. Not the knife, but his eyes when he was doing it – almost gone, but just managing to hold onto reality somehow. To me, maybe?

"Is Alex into that?"

"What? Cutting? Never seen it first-hand but I've seen the results of his handiwork. Talented boy, if you like that sort of thing."

She's staring at me again, and I know this because the thought of 'the results' had me spinning with a gaping mouth to face her so quickly I almost fell over. Okay, he may have amused himself with frightening me on the plane. I get that, sort of, but actually enjoying slicing skin? "You haven't got a clue, have you, lovey? These fucking morons and their vagina toys. Come on. Get dressed. I'm getting you out of here," she snaps as she storms around the room and picks up various clothes. "You're not ready for this sort of stuff, and both of them should know better. He can't do this sort of thing any more. It's starting to give us all a bad name. He should be teaching the newbies the right way and protecting them, not scaring the living shite out of them every ten minutes. I mean, poor Reubin is bad enough." Does she mean Alex? Is this normal for him? Surely not. And who the hell is Reubin? "I've told him time and time again, fucking with children is not acceptable." What? Children?

"Stop, Vixon, Clarissa, whatever your name is. Who exactly are you talking about? And what have children got to do with anything?" I interject into her irritated babbling as she continues to slam things around the room. It's starting to become a little on the scary side if I'm honest, but the thought of children being involved in any of this bizarre world is damn disturbing, enough so that my hackles stand to attention.

"Come on, clothes on. I've just got to make a phone call and we'll be sorted."

"What the fuck do children have to do with this?" She spins to face me and stops her whirling dervish movements.

"Turn of phrase, lovey. You, you're a child. Naïve, immature, not yet developed," she says smoothly as she puts her phone to her ear and points at the clothes. It's clear from her dominant pose that she must be a dominatrix. I've never met one of those before. Another notch on my bedpost. Well, not literally.

My body automatically finds its way into the scrap of leather that's considered a dress of sorts at her command. I cross the room to the mirror, trying to make it more presentable somehow and sigh out a breath. I slip my feet into the sky-high shoes and gaze at myself. Sex goddess is probably appropriate for the reflected result. My inner slut is putting me in all sorts of poses, regardless of the fact that we're apparently leaving, and at the moment, I couldn't give a damn how either of them thinks I look. I'm still angry with both of them, but obviously more so with Alex. I roll my eyes at myself and try to tie my hair up. Christ knows where my clip has gone, and frankly, I don't care.

I watch her reflection in the mirror and wonder what the hell is going on. I don't even know where it is that she says she's taking me, or why, and I don't know if I want to go. I need Alex to get me home. It's that simple. What the hell am I doing? I may still be on the furious side of irritated, but nothing she's said has scared me – surprised me maybe, but I'm actually quite calm about his preferences. I'm still moving around and contemplating what I should do next, and still thinking about the fact that I miss those hands, his smell, his size, his very presence near me.

She closes her phone after a few moments of talking to someone in the background and comes across to stand behind me.

"You ready, lovey? Looking hot by the way. You could be either this way. You know the term switch? Mean anything to you? I can smell it on you. He must, too. Wonder if that bothers him as much as it would me?" Another new expression to deal with.

"Okay, what the hell is going on here? Why am I going anywhere with you? Who the hell are you? And is Alex a fucking monster of some sort that I should be worried about? I know he's a sadist. He's told me that, and other stuff, which is none of your concern. But he's also a normal man who's told me he loves me, on several occasions actually, regardless of this weird sodding game he's trying to play with me. I just want to go fucking home. Do you hear me? I'm tired of all this bullshit, and all these new terms and words that I have no idea about." My hands find my hips as I stare her down and watch her eyes widen a little at my venom. "Enough is enough, for Christ's sake. Is it too much to ask for some normalcy around here? Unless you can get me on a plane back to the UK without a passport then I just need to get to him, not go somewhere else to be put under more pressure."

"Woohoo, watch you go. All hair and talons. There's the reason Pascal's so interested in you, lovey. Has he had you yet, or has Alexander stopped him?" she says as she steps closer. My feet stay planted and I even feel my lip curl at her. Lord knows where that's come from, but screw her. It's none of her business anyway. "He's never not shared anything with Pascal before. Usually he enjoys watching it happen, lets him play first before he finishes them off."

I haven't got a clue how I'm supposed to react to that. My eyes are like slits as I stare at her and refuse to show any emotion at all other than contempt. Should I be surprised, sad, upset at the carnage they may have caused together? Probably, but I'm not. Funnily enough, I recognise instantly the familiarity of this happening for both of them, the reassurance that they both must get in that type of scenario. I even smile a little at the thought of them being together and enjoying something, using something together to rid themselves of their demons. I can see it so clearly in my mind. I can still feel Pascal's hands on me, his lips, his breath against my neck. I can still see the intensity in Alex's eyes as he watched and tried to stay in control of the situation in front of him. Yet, in reality, it was all for Alex because we both love him. And Pascal's feelings for him, while odd and still not entirely comfortable, are in no way doubted by me. He will probably always do whatever he needs to in order to keep Alex safe and contented, just as I would have done, still would if I'm honest. That's why he's brought me here, isn't it? To help him in his pain, and that's why I came. Arsehole.

"Roxanne can get you home without a passport, lovey. Roxanne can do anything. So can Pascal, which tells me he's under Alexander's control at the moment, otherwise he would have helped you," she says as she buttons up her corset thingy again and licks her lips. "So, you can either go down there and take them both on – happy to watch that by the way – or we can meet Rox at the door and she'll have you back on a plane within two hours. The choice is yours. She's coming either way."

My mouth falls open as my eyebrows shoot up.

I can get home? Without Alex? Utter confusion swallows every corner of my mind as I try to find some sense to my decision. Regardless of Pascal saying Alex needs me, he has been a bastard, treated me appallingly, kidnapped me for fuck's sake, and then made me watch whatever that was on the plane with Tara the slut. And now she tells me I can get away from him if I want. Who the hell Roxanne is, I don't know, but the woman sounds completely fabulous at the moment. I could have that time to think, find a way past this without having to actually deal with Alex again. I'm sure he'll come after me, but at least I'll be home by then, where I can feel safe to some degree.

But if he sees me, he won't let me go, will he? Especially not to some random woman. My head falls again at the thought.

"He won't let me go. You know that. There's no way I'll get out of this club."

"Trust me, neither of them will mess with her. If she says you're leaving, then that's exactly what you'll be doing. I may also have to leave for a while, which is a shame, but hey ho, there's plenty of other places for me to have fun."

"Why are you doing this for me? Won't you get in trouble?"

"Sometimes, and only sometimes, Pascal needs standing up to, and you clearly need time to prepare yourself for them. Whatever it is that's going on, it's not normal playtime. And if you want to leave, you should be given a chance to do just that," she replies as she grabs a bullwhip from the wall. "Besides, it'll be funny to watch him squirm."

"Oh," I respond as she expertly cracks it at a lamp and sends it tumbling to the floor. "And the whip is for what, exactly?" She glances me up and down then opens the door and extends a hand to me.

"We have to get past them first. Rox won't go any further than the lobby so we need to get to her."

I grab hold of her offered hand and follow the sea of red hair into the lift, which opens the moment we close the suite door. A very quick few seconds later and we're walking along a green corridor, which has some kind of chanting music going on. It instantly reminds me of the atrium at Alex's house when we fought. It's not quite as aggressive but definitely hypnotic it its rhythm. My feisty Beth comes racing back to me at the memory of fighting with him. He made that happen, turned that switch on in me and allowed it free. And it appears I might need some of it right now to help me get to the door of this establishment. I crack my neck from side to side as we approach a set of dark wood doors, and involuntarily squeeze Vixon's hand, probably more for my benefit than hers because she certainly knows how to handle herself. She smiles over her shoulder at me. It's disturbingly evil, somewhat like Pascal's in certain moments.

"You're going to be fine, lovey. Stay close behind me unless I tell you to run, and do that disgusted look you did upstairs. It could be useful for his henchmen."

"Umm, okay," I reply with a pant as my heartbeat increases and I try to find my disgusted face. I only have to picture Alex with his damn cock anywhere near Tara the slut's mouth and it comes rushing back.

"Perfect. You ready?" she says as she presses the door forward and doesn't give me a chance to reply.

The heat and noise hit me instantly, lights flashing everywhere to illuminate the very nearly pitch black space. Vixon keeps moving forward so I stride my best to keep up and keep my disgusted face firmly planted on. I am strong. I am in control. She flicks the whip casually in my direction and two men appear and flank me at her order. I have no fucking clue who they are but they're both big enough to eclipse the bloody sun so I keep my chin up and storm onwards. I can't stop my eyes from looking everywhere for both of them, and I also can't stop myself from noticing all the sex that's happening around me. The space is filled with bodies in various positions, nearly all naked or at least half naked. Why they have rooms here is completely unknown, but this is definitely Pascal's world, full of depravity with that 'nothing's off limits' type of feeling going on. It's very similar to Rome, albeit slightly more polished, shiny even, somehow not managing that old European feeling. We continue down a small staircase where I'm suddenly squirted with something. My head spins at the same moment as Vixon reaches for the culprit and quite literally throws him down the stairs.

"Fucking cum whore." She sneers as she walks straight over his cock in her heels and he winces in pain beneath her. "Open your mouth wider next time." I can only assume the wet patch on my arm is someone's semen, so I rapidly go to brush it off, only to have big chap number one lick it off my arm for me. I stop and stare at him as he smiles at me shyly and dips his head into a bow before extending an arm to point me forward again. Who would lick unknown semen off someone else's arm? I'm not even sure I'm happy with the cleanliness of his mouth. "Lovey, come. I'll get you a fucking wet wipe when we get out," Vixon snarls at me.

Oh, yes, leaving. Quite right.

I quickly catch up to her as she turns another corner, which appears to bypass a small pool full of yet more debauchery. I can't help my small gasp as I watch a woman being lowered under the water by her throat while a gang of men watch on. I'm so consumed by the vision that I don't realise Vixon has stopped until I nearly slam into her back, and big chap two grabs my arm. My head comes up to find her halted with her legs two feet apart, staring straight at the one person we really didn't want to bump into. And, damn it, why does he have to look so sodding intoxicating?

He's standing there, cane in hand, full-on Edwardian suit with white frilly shirt completely open, chest on display for the whole bloody world to see. My thighs do that ridiculous clenching thing before I've even had a chance to pull myself together. Apart from the length of his hair, he's exactly like the man I met in Rome for the first time – eyes lifeless and devoid of compassion or kindness as he glances at me across her shoulder and then returns his amused glare to her.

"Clarissa, I believe you have something there that does not belong to you. What exactly do you think you are doing with it?" he asks as he leans against the glass window beside him and crosses his legs. Vixon widens her stance slightly and raises the whip until only the end dangles on the floor.

"She's leaving. We're leaving," she replies. That's it, no other explanation. He smirks at the whip and then back at her.

"Are you planning on using that to defend yourselves? You should know I'll have it around your throat in a matter of seconds. It will give me the greatest pleasure to show you how it feels."

To be fair on Vixon, she doesn't even budge, not even a flicker of movement.

"Possibly, Pascal, but she will get away while you're trying. And a very special person is coming to pick her up. Also, there are three of us to defend her. Even you're not that good."

"You misplace your trust too easily, Clarissa," he says as he flicks his hands in the direction of the two big men behind me and then waves them away as if they should go, and they do. Both of them instantly drop to the floor and crawl off down the corridor, arses wiggling. I watch them crawl away and wonder what the hell to do now. I'm certainly not going to put her in danger because of whatever is happening here.

She backs up to me and pushes me towards the wall, then begins to sidestep us along it with her arm outstretched. I can see a pair of doors in the distance, about twenty metres away, and assume that's where she's heading for. I quicken my steps somewhat in the hope that we can get there before Pascal pounces. He, of course, is watching us like a hawk and casually following us as if he doesn't have a care in the world. He probably doesn't, and I'm under no illusions that we'll actually make it, but I'm giving it my best shot as she steadily walks backwards away from him.

"Do you think this will end because you run from him again, my rose? Hmm? He will not let you go. You know this. Why would you leave him in pain?" My feet stop at the thought of Alex in pain. I so want to make him happy again. I don't even know why, given his behaviour.

"Don't listen to him," Vixon says as she keeps backing into me. "He's trying to confuse you, manipulate you." The word manipulate has my heels moving again in seconds as I shake my head to clear the fog that's descending and make for the door again.

"Elizabeth, this will only anger him further. He loves you. Breathe his name in your heart and come back to him. He needs you, loves you. You know how he feels," he says as he drops his cane on the floor, smiles and reaches a hand out for me. My eyes shoot to the discarded cane and then back to him as he gets closer, and my body halts again. He needs me, loves me, can't breathe without me. I love him. What am I doing, running from him? I can't think anymore. Those damned intoxicating eyes and that soft smile have me confused. Where the hell did that come from? I just know I need some time to think, to be away from them both.

"Keep moving," Vixon shouts again as she holds the whip higher and pushes against me.

"I... I can't. I have to go back. I have to..." I can't speak again. I don't even know who I'm speaking to anymore, and those sets of eyes just keep pulling me – green, blue – and those hands just won't let me go. Either of them.

In a flash of blue, the whip is suddenly grabbed from her hands and wrapped around my wrist in seconds. I can't even comprehend what's happening until I notice Vixon on the floor, nursing the side of her face and Pascal turning me in a circle until the whip is also wrapped around my body in some sort of knot.

"Child," he snarls at Vixon as he picks up his cane again and glares down at her. "How dare you defy me in my own home? Do you suppose you have the right to question me in this? I would have thought better of you. Stay there while I deal with this abomination."

By abomination, I assume he means me. I turn in his hold to try and look at him, but he grabs the back of my head and pushes me down to the floor with such force that I squeal in surprise until my arse is in the air and my lips are on the carpet.

"And you, you will lick the ground he walks on until we get back to him. Perhaps you'll have learnt some fucking manners by the time we arrive."

I don't even know where I am now. I do know that he means every word, judging by his vicious tone. Gone is the Pascal I know and like, love even. This man is clearly the one everyone fears. I twist my head towards Vixon to see if she's okay, or maybe see if she's got any advice on the matter at hand. She just continues to look at the floor, refusing to acknowledge me in any way. She looks scared and completely apologetic as she sits perfectly still, and we both listen to irritated ramblings in a foreign language that I've never heard before. Maybe it's Dutch.

His hand is suddenly on my backside, and his fingers seem disturbingly close to sliding my panties to the side. My whole body stiffens in response, as yet again, those confused feelings conflict with each other in every possible way. I want it. I don't want it. I need it. I don't need it. Hit me. Please don't hit me. Not without my permission. Take it from me... Each thought flashes through my mind as his fingers just linger there as if waiting for some sort of response that I don't have a clue about.

"I should fuck this insolence out of you," he snarls down at me. I'm actually trembling at the tone. It's just the same as in the back of the limo, frightening. "Why he hesitates so is beyond me. When will you learn? Hmm? Perhaps an hour with me before we reach him might loosen you up, help you appreciate who this is all for. You disgust me with your weakness. You deserve neither my patience nor my consent in this any longer." Now what the hell is he talking about? My face tries to turn again to look at him but he just increases his leverage on the whip, which lifts my arse higher and sends my weight down onto my face again. I'm not even sure what I want to say if I'm honest, because for whatever reason, my brain seems to want to give in to this, wants to let him do what he thinks is the right thing to do. God knows I don't know what it is. Perhaps I should just let him take the reins and stop trying to figure out what it is that I actually want. Run, hide, stay here, do whatever they want, he wants. Alex...

His name spins through my mind and then seems to skim across my skin, a whisper of those fingers caressing me, those eyes boring into me and showing me love, commitment, honesty. Where's he gone? Why? Christ, if I could shake my head at the moment, I would. Instead, I just close my eyes and wait. The feelings that hit me are instant and powerful. I want *his* weight on me at the moment, want him to be holding this whip, want him to be hovering his hands over me instead of Pascal, readying me, showing me more. I may want to leave, but I can't deny this need I have to be beneath him, in whatever form, to give him everything he wants, regardless of his behaviour.

"Mmm, still so confused, my rose," Pascal says above me in a slightly softer voice. He removes his hand and loosens the whip so I can move again, then tuts at me. I can only get one hand to the floor so heave myself up with it and begin to pull myself forward a little as he walks a step away from the door, from my freedom. "Well, this should be amusing. My mood should improve greatly by the time we find him." Arsehole. "Do remember to lick the floor on the way, my dear. I'd hate to have to keep reminding you."

We're about five feet from where we started when I hear the doors open behind me.

Chapter 7

Elizabeth

"Put her down, Pascal." The softest, most feminine voice I've ever heard comes drifting over the air, almost angelic in quality as it somehow lingers all around and drowns out all the depravity of the situation. Pascal instantly stops and drops the weight of my body, so I sink to the floor again and sigh in relief. I watch his boots slowly turn and try to twist my body round to see where the voice has come from. "Elizabeth, can you get to me or do you need untying first?" she says as I finally see her.

I can't even speak. Her very aura is like nothing I've ever experienced – peaceful, serene, yet so utterly in control of everything around her. Her long, jet black hair and slim, six-foot frame seem to almost shimmer as she stands there, glistening like some kind of divine force. And she's obviously completely in control of Pascal somehow because as I flick my eyes up to him, he's actually looking at the floor a little, almost refusing to look into her eyes for some reason. "Vixon, are you harmed?"

"No, Rox. I'll be okay," she says as she gets up and gingerly makes her way across to me, constantly looking at Pascal. "Do you still want to leave, lovey? Now's your chance."

Do I? Yes. No. I don't know. Actually, I think maybe I do. If only for some sodding peace and to get away from Mr. Arsehole, who I don't like very much at the moment, regardless of my irritating trembling and confusing thoughts.

I nod over at her and then look back to the woman in the structured white dress and fedora in the doorway, who smiles at me as Vixon tugs and finally undoes the whip. Pascal still hasn't moved, but as I get to my feet and glance at him, he has lifted his eyes to meet hers. There's a strange look on his face, as if she's the only woman in the world that he can see in that moment. He seems transfixed on her, and as I glance back at her, she seems the same. It's almost like everything is intruding on something incredibly private, and I find myself looking away from them and towards the floor because I feel like I'm watching something no one should be seeing. Vixon shoves me towards her until we're almost through the open door behind her, and that's when I see my own vision of an angel coming along the corridor towards us. He drowns out the corridor with his stature, like he owns every inch of the space around him, and he directs all of his focus at me. Oh god, he looks good. I feel like I haven't seen him for weeks. There's not an inch of a smile on his face, just that same beautiful frown and irritated sneer, as he gets closer. My feet freeze, mid-step as my body hums at his impending proximity. It takes everything I've got to fight the need to go to him, run into his arms and fall at his feet. Arsehole. How does he do that? Why? His hair's all messy, he's got a black shirt on, and those icy blue eyes still pierce mine with commands, somehow forcing me to move back in his direction. It's like there's a devil on one side of me, and a rescuing angel at the other, in the form of Rox, whoever she is.

"Elizabeth, come here," he says, an order not a request, however nicely he puts it. My thigh twitches to move my feet before I've even thought about my actions. Roxanne steps in front of me and blocks him from my view.

"You get your own way too much, Alexander," she says sharply in reply, seemingly for me because I can't think at all, or speak, apparently.

"Roxanne, what do you think you're doing?" he says in his smooth, velvety voice. I peek over her shoulder to see him stop beside Pascal and then step a foot in front of him, almost protectively, quite oddly. "She's not yours to take away from me."

"Alexander, given your behaviour a short while ago, I'm very sure she's not yours to keep either, unless she tells me otherwise. I've never known you fall apart for a woman before, and I won't let you tear her down now unless she wants it that way. I am only concerned for her wellbeing and that she knows the truth. So she can come with me if she wishes, and maybe she'll call you when she's ready to deal with your arrogance."

"I am not Pascal, Roxanne. You have no right to-"

"No, you are not. You have none of his beauty, nor his forethought or intelligence. You are supposed to be less maniacal since Pascal's involvement with you, more measured in your skill.

This," she snaps angrily as she glares at both of them and flicks her hand in our direction, "is not what I would expect from any dominant, let alone a master of stature or consequence. Tyrannical behaviour is reserved for idiots and fools. You remember those, don't you, Pascal, the foolish times?"

She sucks in a breath and is suddenly dreamlike again as she clasps her hands behind her back and continues to stare at Alex, as if she's perfectly happy to take him on at any level he chooses. He clearly isn't aware of any reason why he shouldn't be looking straight at her, because he doesn't remove his gaze from her and manages to achieve that growing thing that he's quite good at. She eventually murmurs something to herself and nods her head toward Pascal again. "He will tell you what you need to do if you listen carefully enough. He knows it only too well himself, don't you, my love?"

I can't believe what I'm hearing. I'm hovering behind this strange conversation in my semi slutty dress, trying to fathom what the hell they're all talking about.

Who is this woman? Whoever she is, she seems to have some influence over the two most powerful men I've ever met. And why does she smell so good? Random, I know, but it's exotic, potent and heady. It's making me feel somehow calmer. Alex actually seems to be snarling a bit now. Pascal is still standing there looking very serious while trying not to crack a small smile. I can see the corners of his mouth twitching at her compliment, and his eyes are as bright as I've ever seen them, almost glowing.

"Let her go, dear boy," he says as he eventually steps in front of Alex and walks towards the vision in white, still not removing his eyes from hers. "She will come back in time. She loves you."

I will, will I? Who the hell does he think he is? He's probably right, but that's entirely beside the point.

"You should not be here. I warned you what might happen should you ever frequent my floor again," Pascal says as he advances towards her, cane tapping as he goes, his devilish smirk now firmly attached to his lips as he rubs his fingers around his chin. She simply laughs and continues to keep her frame serenely in place.

"I'm bored, and I was called for help. She's not thinking clearly enough, and you are taking too long, which is quite unlike you. Did you think I wouldn't want to join in at some point?" she replies as she takes a step toward him and reaches a finger for his face. I swear I see him flinch. It's the first time I've ever seen him look even slightly nervous. No, that's not the right word. Apprehensive, maybe, as if he has no idea what's going to happen next. She drags her white painted fingernail along his cheek and lets it drift down his chest and out towards the cane, until they're both holding onto the silver top of it. They stand there for what feels like minutes, just staring, completely focused on each other and seemingly having silent dialogue of some sort. Given his ability to read minds, I'm not surprised, but he's not relaxed like he is with Alex. There is nothing calm about his demeanour this time. He looks primed and ready to explode at any moment, and she just seems utterly relaxed and composed, as if none of this is causing her any concern whatsoever.

"No," he eventually says, nothing else, just that, with a slight sneer of his lip. She stares a moment longer and then mouths something at him, some words that the rest of us aren't allowed to hear, but he gets it. It's clear he understands it with acute clarity because his eyes widen a little as he rips the cane away from her hand with a frown and spits that language at her that I don't understand. She still simply stands and chuckles her way through his tirade of what I assume is Dutch.

"Still not ready? Shame," she says as she turns her back on him and walks back towards us, winking at me as she does. I can't stop the smirk that shoots across my face. Watching Pascal get put down is highly amusing, if that's what it was. She spins her finger at me, indicating that I should turn and leave, so I begin to move.

"You said you wouldn't leave," Alex growls. I turn back to see him raising a hand out for me. I flick my eyes to his fingers and halt my progress away from him. "No matter what, you said you wouldn't leave, Elizabeth."

"You said you loved me. I haven't seen any love from you lately," is my immediate response. I don't even think about the answer. It falls from my lips as if it's the only thing that's been troubling me. And when I don't over think it, that's exactly what the problem is here. It's not the depravity, not the murderous tendencies, not the Mafia ties, not the unknown quantities that he keeps hidden. It's his lack of love. I could cope with it all when he loved me, when he showed me he loved me.

95

"Come, Elizabeth. It is time for us to leave. Let him have some time to think about his actions," she says softly as she puts her hand on my shoulder and gently nudges me towards the exit. "He needs time, as do you."

I have no idea what I need anymore. I'm so damn tired, but for whatever reason, her very presence is more calming than even his. Vixon wraps an arm around my waist and leads me towards the main door as I notice Roxanne stop and turn back towards Pascal again.

"Whenever you are ready," she almost whispers at him.

He raises a brow in response and snarls at her again. I watch him hold his hand up at Alex to stop his movement to get to me, and I realise I'm in the company of Pascal's past, possibly his one try for real love and a happy home. My eyes find hers as she glides past me.

"I will tell you when you're ready to accept that life cannot always be made perfect, Elizabeth. Sometimes we have to just accept that only time can close the holes that drive us apart."

~

We are sitting in another one of New York's finest kinky establishments, this one owned by Roxanne. The Parlour, so far, is everything I would expect of the woman. Sensuous, sophisticated, lathered in swathes of gold fabric, creating an evocative atmosphere that resembles something out of the thirties era. Decadent hints of Art Deco glamour hint at an air of naughty Charleston behaviour, and the clean lines and angles only declare her love for structure even more. I'm lounging on a black leather sofa in a small room, which, it seems, is her private sanctuary, and drinking a large glass of champagne as she continues to study some paperwork in her hand. She's been doing that for about an hour now, never looking at me, just tutting to herself occasionally and writing notes on the paper. Where Vixon has gone, I don't know. She just shuffled me in here when Roxanne pointed this way, disappeared, then brought me a white fluffy bathrobe and disappeared again. I instantly removed the offending dress and slipped into my new comfy outfit, and here I still sit, drinking champagne and eating a bacon sandwich that I requested when offered something to eat.

I have no idea what the hell I'm supposed to do next. Make small talk? Ask her what I'm supposed to do? She does seem to be the fount of all knowledge all of a sudden. Belle would so love this woman. She's clearly American, but her facial features are almost Asian. Given her height, she can't be truly Asian, but her beautiful, cat-like hazel eyes just remind me of that part of the world.

"Are you going to speak, Elizabeth, or just make up your own mind about what is happening around you?" she says, still not looking at me. "Either is fine with me, but if you require any answers, I'll need to talk now as I have work to get on with shortly." Oh.

"Umm..." She laughs and then drops her paperwork onto the floor near her exquisite heels – zebra print no less.

"You must amuse him, both of them, actually. You really are quite a distraction from the norm," she says as she picks up her champagne and leans back onto the sofa.

"How do you know anything about me? And why are you helping me?"

"You are of significance to Pascal, and therefore to me. I don't care much for your Alexander, but Pascal does so I have to tolerate him. And I'm helping because it serves a purpose. Please don't think I'm your friend. I'm not."

"Oh..." Yes, it's pretty much all I've got. I'm not even sure I should say anything else. So I don't. I just stare over at her and shrivel up into a ball. I thought she liked me. She obviously doesn't.

"Don't look so scared. Poor little thing, he's done quite a number on you, hasn't he? Do you have any power over him at all, or are you too timid to try your hand at it? I thought you might be the one to change this all around, hoped anyway. There has been no one until you."

More stupid, never talking directly crap. Who the hell does she think she is? Obviously another Pascal type, which I have no patience for at the moment.

"Look, I really don't know what you're talking about. I think it's best if I just leave. Vixon said you might be able to get me back to the UK without a passport. Can you do that? I need some time away from him. Even if I do still love him, he's behaved appallingly and I don't know if I can forgive it. I don't see him changing back to who he was any time soon, so I think it's probably best if I just let all this go and move the hell on." Suddenly I'm up on my feet and pacing. "I can't cope with him, you see, no matter how much Pascal tells me I can. It's like a split personality all the time – me, that is, not him." I'm rambling, watching my bare feet wandering around beneath me towards the window. "Well, actually, him too, but that's not the point at the moment, I suppose. It's just, one minute I'm quiet and happy, the next I have to be all feisty and kick his arse or something, which he told me to do because of morals by the way, whatever that means. I don't even know what I'm doing most of the time – all the time actually. There's no logic or sense to it. He's all over the place. I guess he's as bad as he said he was. I don't know." I turn back towards her, shaking my head in confusion once more, and try to find some order to my chaotic thoughts. "I've got a business waiting for me, and Christmas with a family I love and a mum who's just been diagnosed with cancer. I just need to get home. I..." There's nothing left. I can't find any other things to say. Either that or I can't get them out of my throat, which is still longing for his fingers around it, so I look down at my bracelet and rub my fingers across it.

"Well, that was quite a speech. Why haven't you walked away from him yet?"

"He won't let me. He kidnapped me and brought me here to do God knows what, and I don't have my passport, and-"

"What utter rubbish. You could have gone to the embassy. Why did you go with Pascal instead?"

"I don't know. He's got this way with words. It's sodding magic or something. I'm beginning to wonder if the pesky fairies are his and not Alex's at all."

"Fairies?"

"Yes, they're there to... Oh, it doesn't matter. It's silly really." She looks at me thoughtfully for a while, probably considering how ridiculous I am. Given my current situation, sitting in a kink club dressed in a fluffy white bathrobe and spouting rambled rubbish from my mouth, I'm not surprised. Best to at least try and defend myself. "It's just, he..." She holds a hand up to silence me. It works.

"He kidnapped you, as you call it, because he loves you, Elizabeth, and Aiden Phillips was possibly about to tell you everything about him. Your Alexander is, or rather has been, a very wicked man. He is also a sadistic beauty who enjoys torturing woman and beating the hell out of the only man I have ever loved. Unfortunately, he seems to enjoy being the recipient, too. It's very arousing to watch. I daresay that is what he was about to introduce you to, had you not run from him."

My mouth's gaping again. She really is the fount of all knowledge.

"How do you know all this? What about... Why was he such a bastard to me on the plane?"

"I don't know what he did on the plane, but being a bastard is who he is, or was, depending on your preference in accepting reality. I should think he just wants you to see the real him and accept it. Do you think you can? Because if you can, I suggest you go back over there and tell him you can so that all of this can move forward. I'm quite bored with it all now."

"What do you mean, you're bored?"

"I have plans, and this little 'thing' of yours is getting in the way of them." I don't know what that means, and to be honest I don't think I care either. I have enough going on in my head without having to deal with another person's plans, whatever they might be.

"I'm no longer sure what accepting it all entails – women, men, murderers, Mafia zones, twisted preferences that mess with my thoughts and cause more problems? I didn't sign up for all this. I knew he was different, but I don't think I can do all the other stuff."

"Is Pascal the only one who's touched you?"

"What?" Where did that come from? "Umm, yes, a little, but it was under Alex's control. How do you..." This is actually a little embarrassing now. Why does she know everything about this? How?

"As it should be, and if you want nothing else than that then you tell him and that will be all you will be involved in. Don't you see, Elizabeth? You have all the power here, not him, for the first time in his life. And yet you are giving it to him on every occasion by fearing him and suffering your own feelings. If you want him, tell him how it's going to be. Stand up for yourself. What's the worst that can happen?"

"Is that what you've done with Pascal? Because it doesn't seem to be working out too well for you."

"I won't share him, with anyone, and he's not ready for that yet because of your Alexander and this tedious little situation you've all got going on. But he'll come back to me when he's ready, and I have everything I need until he returns."

I can't even begin to process what the hell that means, although my eyes can't help but widen at the thought that she's waiting for Pascal, as if anyone could ever own him and be at peace. I dare say she'll be waiting quite a while for that party to happen.

"Well, great for you. I, however, don't know how to stand up for myself, apparently, because I tried that on the plane. I tried to stand up for myself, be feisty Beth and stay in control of him, but he just ignored me, kept playing his games and humiliated me. I don't know what to do. I can't keep taking his strange punishments, if that's what this is. I haven't done anything wrong, for God's sake. He's the one who told me he's a murderer. You'd think that would mean asking for forgiveness from the woman he loves, not turning on her and showing her how much of an arsehole he can be. This is not normal behaviour. He is not normal."

"Did he ever say he was? Did he ever imply to you that he would be easy? Elizabeth, he has chosen you, has shown you and will continue to show you as long as you have the strength to take it. Do you think it has been easy for Pascal to understand him? Love him? Do not think you are the only one who has to handle him. Pascal has spent years teaching him to absolve himself, enjoy himself, be at one with who he is. Do not assume you don't know how to handle his behaviour. If you didn't, Pascal would have made you go away long ago. It is within his power to do just that."

"Pascal is not in control of Alex. No one is. That's pretty clear to everyone, including Pascal."

"Really? You need to be cleverer than this, Elizabeth. Think about the situation you found them in in his office. Who was in control of that? Who came to get you when you ran from them? Who told you what you'd need to do to make this work? Where is your man at this very moment? Your Alexander is only in control of his thoughts for a while before Pascal shows him how to behave again. Conner Avery may be his conscience, but Pascal is his confidante, and Pascal is his peace. It's a gift reserved for only him, a gift Alexander gives without even knowing he's doing it. Pascal is trying to hand him over to you. I gave him this time, gave him the space he needed to punish himself, discover himself more, and help his beloved Alexander, but you are going to have to catch onto the plan. It's my turn now."

What the hell? I don't even...

My mouth is hanging open as I try to figure out what the hell the woman is talking about. Is she trying to suggest that Pascal is in control of all of this? That I need to be some sort of female carbon copy of the man to have Alex completely? I suppose he has been trying to teach me how to handle his varying moods, how to recognise behaviour patterns and dictate the outcomes of them, how to be submissive sometimes and dominant others. Is that what he meant by his *'There will be times when he needs me'* speech? When he needs to go too far for me to be able to handle then Pascal will be there for me, for us?

Oh my god. I finally get it, I think. It's starting to make sense. Pascal doesn't want to be part of us. He wants to be with the woman sitting in front of me, but it is reasonable to assume that he wants to give Alex over to someone he trusts to look after him, to understand him, to accept him and make him happy. So he's able to walk away from him with a clear conscience, knowing that he has given him everything he can and that he can leave him in the hands of another. I knew he was a good man in his own way, but he's just trying to show me what to do, how to handle Alex. I look across to find her studying my shocked face with a small smile crossing her lips. Christ, they must be the two most intelligent people on the planet.

"He doesn't want Alex?"

"Very much. But your Alexander is not bisexual. If he was, it may be different. Pascal has simply tried to show him the way and give him an experienced outlet for his needs. It's not easy to be at peace with yourself, Elizabeth, until you understand what you truly need, so these men have been playing with what it is that they both require."

"And you fit into this how?" Because honestly, I hadn't even met the woman three hours ago, and now it seems I'm learning all about a background story I wasn't aware of. Yet another layer of intrigue to tread my way around, which is obviously incredible helpful to my situation...

"I will not share his scars and bruises with anyone else. Your man has marked him enough since he left. Once he returns, they will be for me alone, unless I choose otherwise. It was not something he was willing to accept until you came along."

"You love him?" Random question, I know, but sudden protective instincts are kicking in from somewhere, as if I have any right to be questioning whatever this is.

"Elizabeth, I don't need your permission. We have been a part of each other for a long time now. I just need you to do what's inside you. He can see it, and so can Alexander. He just doesn't know what to do with it yet."

"Well, insightful as all this is, I still don't know how to handle him. It's a fucking maze that has catastrophe written all over it most of the time. I'm just not strong enough."

"Stop trying then. If he wants you then make him do it your way. Is that not what Pascal has been telling you all along? He was right when he told me you over think everything. You need to stop that and go with your gut feeling every time. You will never outmanoeuvre him anyway, and you shouldn't have to, not where love is involved. Pascal plays games with him because he needs to. You do not. He really does know your man very well. You should trust his judgement on whether you're capable of handling him."

I'm sure my eyes are slits. They're not supposed to be daggers of any kind, more complete concentration on trying to understand what she means. I'm just not a dominant. I can't control Alex. I don't even want to. I like being at his mercy. I like being under his influence, apart from when he's being an arsehole, then clearly I don't. And I don't get this switching about thing – backwards and forwards, up and down, loud then quiet. Switch, that's the word Vixon used earlier. What does that mean?

"Am I a switch? Whatever that is."

"I don't think so, not in the true sense of the word, but you will need to be for him in a roundabout way. It's quite an oddity in our world, to be submissive only in the sexual sense of the word. Most subs are just that, with no discussion on the topic other than terms. But to have to fight a dominant man in the real world, to choose your own way with no yielding to orders will be quite a challenge, something my love seems to believe you are capable of. That's what Pascal is trying to teach you, while trying to show Alexander it's what he needs. I don't envy him the task," she says as she gets up and pours another glass of champagne. "Now, I have a client in a minute. Do you still want to go home? I only have to make a few calls. I'm happy to do it."

"Other than that, fight me." He said that, didn't he? That I should fight him when those lines blurred, when morality and immorality confused each other. Is this one of those situations? I suppose it is, and Pascal seems to think he's been trying to make me hate him so I understand how it feels to hate, so I can appreciate why he would have committed those acts in the first place. I still can't see how that would work, but I can see a little logic in it. I'd still rather he just talked to me. Maybe I should just make him get on with it and see how far he'll go. Is that the way I should prove that none of it matters to me, that I'll take him whatever he's done as long as he loves me? Should I just walk over there and say 'Go on then. Show me what you've got. None of it matters. I'll still love you. You can't make me hate you, Alex'?

"No, I don't want to leave."

"Good girl. If you go through that door, you'll find my wardrobe. Some of the clothes should fit you, and they will look a damn sight better than whatever that was that you walked over here in. I'll send my girl in for make-up and hair. Prepare yourself for them."

"Thank you." I think that's the best response here. I'm not even sure what 'prepare yourself' means if I'm honest. Prepare myself for what exactly? Am I supposed to go over there all *in control* again? I don't know who is *in control*. She seems to think it should be me. Pascal also seems to think it should be me, but he clearly doesn't think I should be in control of *him* after his little 'you will crawl' moment. Is there any way of making this simple? "Roxanne?"

"Yes?"

"I don't understand who's in charge?"

"Elizabeth, really? Are you dense? Did Pascal ask for your permission?"

"Well, yes, but you know how you found me an hour ago, and-"

"You were confused." Damn right I was. "And he was trying to teach you to accept your situation." *What?* "Did Alexander ask permission?"

"Well, I suppose so. We've done the safe word thing, and apart from the random Tara thing on the way over when he didn't stop even though I screamed it, which I don't understand at all, he's never pushed me into anything I didn't want."

"Then you are, my dear." She sounds scarily like Pascal. "It's really very simple. Stop over thinking everything. You are more than aware of what is going to happen when the three of you engage properly. Embrace it. Let Alexander show you who he is, let Pascal take what he needs from him, and let yourself be a part of it. Relish it. I can promise you will enjoy it, but set the limits yourself. Don't let him ask you to hate him. Accept him wholly, killer and all."

Wandering away from me, she closes the door behind her and leaves me in the room, still with a slightly gaping mouth. I'm really not entirely sure I understand everything she said, and I'm also not entirely sure I know what I'm doing, but what I do know is that I'm damned if I'm going to be the weak one in this situation anymore. Pascal knows that's not who I am. Alex must know that's not who I am because that's what he's asked me for. Why am I the only one who seems to think I can't do this?

If this is going to have any chance of survival then I need to forget what happened on the plane, whatever that was. I need to slap that down as a Mr. White fuck up, or an Alex oddity that I could use to my advantage if I thought about it. I wonder what he would think if I told him I didn't care about it, really didn't care? I wonder what he'd think if I made him watch Pascal and me and didn't give him a chance to say no. Because I could make that happen, make him feel that same pain he put me through.

I can clearly see the look in his eyes when he told me he'd stop it if I looked at him.

"Elizabeth, look at me and I'll stop."

Elizabeth. He called me Elizabeth.

"The choice is yours, Elizabeth."

All the way through, he kept saying my name, kept reinforcing my name.

"You do want this, Elizabeth. You told me you did."

I did tell him I wanted it. I told him I wouldn't accept anything less than him giving me everything – every thought, every memory, every tear, every twisted, sadistic thing. I told him that no matter what, he had to be honest, had to show me, let me understand him and be a part of him.

"If I say your name, you'll know I'm still with you."

He really was trying to show me how much of a bastard he could be, make me hate him. Oh god, and I should hate him. I should, but I don't. There's not one part of me that could ever hate him.

"Alex..." His name comes from my lips like some unanswered prayer, as if, for the first time, I finally understand him. I'm finally getting a glimpse of how his messed up brain looks at things. That he would try to make me hate him, simply so that I can understand what it feels like to truly hate, is his way of showing me that he wants me to understand him that well, that deeply. Who else would do that? Who else would offer the potential devastation of a ruined relationship to prove how far he's willing to go to give me what I need from him. So that I'll forgive him, so that I'll feel him completely, and so that I'll absolve him.

Most men would hide it, wouldn't they? Most men would go out of their way to avoid any depth on the subject. Alexander White himself would normally hide such things and manipulate the situation so that he doesn't need to answer the questions, let alone tell you the truth. Yet, here he is offering me the option of hating him so that I can, wholeheartedly, love him.

Murderer, sadist, lover.

Mine.

I open my eyes to find myself hovering in the doorway of a large dressing room lined with clothing racks. Clothes, yes, I need some of those. It's a shame they're not my own, but there has to be something here that will make me feel *prepared* for them, for him. Funnily enough, I'm not in the slightest bit bothered about Pascal anymore. Whatever his nasty side is, it's not meant for me. It's only meant for the weak me. I realise that now. Looking back, he's only ever shown me that kind of behaviour when I've run, or when I've been what he would consider disloyal or rude. Alex has clearly been his world, his life's work, his project of sorts – the man he loves. This is his way of putting someone on a new course, of helping them and proving to himself that he can be reasonably good, decent even. Is that what he was before whatever he has with Roxanne?

I slide the door on one of the many cream wardrobes and am assaulted by hundreds of perfectly pressed clothes. It's perfectly lined up, all neatly boxed and tucked with colour coordination going on

everywhere. Instantly, I feel my hand move toward a blue dress –
Alex's eyes, Pascal's suit... I don't know whom I'm thinking of more.
The softness of the fabric reminds me of crushed velvet, which has me
smiling as I remember the first time I saw him in Rome. There was
such a bright light shining as he stood there and urinated on that poor
chap. So full of life, arrogance, verve, and utterly astounding in his own
unique way, why he would feel the need to punish himself, I don't
know. Maybe I never will, but I will be asking him. If he trusts me
enough, perhaps he'll tell me. It would be good to understand him a
little more. The light bounces off the material and glints a paler blue
back at me, which brings me back to those eyes again, those never
ending pools of liquid ice. Cool, distant, detached, but not to me, not
anymore. He's doing all of this for me. In his own screwed up way, he's
trying to show me how much he loves me, wants to protect me. He's
trying to get his point across and pull me closer. Oh, and I want to be
closer again, want to feel those arms around me, his breath on my
face, the weight of him on my body, his hands firmly grasped onto
what he owns. My throat, his throat, it doesn't matter anymore. Skin
on skin, his scent, his force, his voice, his tattoo, his...

"Miss Elizabeth?"

What? Who the hell? My body jumps round at the interruption
and I glare at the owner of the voice that just ruined my thought
process, which was getting very nice indeed. Jesus, can't a girl get a
minute's thinking space anymore?

The small woman immediately throws herself on the floor by
the doorway and presses her forehead to the ground. I'm confused for
a second and look around for a dominant of some sort, then realise
there isn't anyone else in here. I think I just made that happen. Wow.
Fuck me. It seems my glare must be somewhat Alexander White like.

"Please, get up off the floor," I say before I've thought about it
too much. She stays put but does raise her head slightly to look at me.
"Yes, you. Up, please."

Whoever she is, she slowly rises up until she's standing in the
corner again.

"Mistress sent me to do your hair and make-up, ma'am." Oh,
lordy, not another ma'am. Andrews would be proud. I smile to myself
and turn away from the woman. Actually, I'm still pissed at him. I need

to have some very serious conversations with that man. I roll my eyes at the thought, and wave her over to the bedroom.

"I'm going to have a quick shower. Could you have a look to see if there's anything red in there, please? Preferably something that will fit me?" Why I want red, I don't know. Perhaps because it's the colour I was wearing the one time I felt reasonably in control with the two of them, sitting there in Pascal's apartment waiting for Alex to materialise because he had, in Pascal's words, *'come for me'*.

"Yes, ma'am," she replies as I storm off in search of a bathroom. I'm presuming there will actually be one behind one of the many doors.

There better be because I need to prepare myself for them.

I think I need another drink.

Chapter 8

Alexander

Quiet. That's what he needed.

Sitting there, watching and listening to the constant tirade of Dutch, really wasn't helping him understand what he was supposed to be doing about Elizabeth. Why the hell had Roxanne turned up and taken her away from him? Who the fuck did she think she was?

His phone began vibrating on the table in front of him, so he leant forward to answer it and stared across at Pascal as he continued to pace backwards and forwards across the room.

"Louisa?"

"Everything is in place, Sir. The deal is set. Tom Brindley says there should be no problems with the takeover and that you don't need to worry. He also thanks you for the apartment I put him in at your request."

Good, that was one less thing to worry about. He'd stayed in touch with her to some degree and kept his eye on the hundreds of emails that came in daily, but other than that, he couldn't give a fuck. If it all collapsed around him tomorrow, he'd still be a very rich man for the rest of his life. Shit like that happened when someone threatened you. He'd moved money to various locations over the last few months to ensure everything was safe, and when Conner suggested his sister was looking into his bank accounts for some reason, he moved some of those around as well. He still didn't know why she was doing that, and when he could be bothered to think of anything else but the task at hand, he'd phone Conner and find out. Maybe he'd even apologize for the Caroline fuck up at the same time, if his friend was in an amenable mood, but at the moment, his entire focus was on Elizabeth and her thoughts about his past.

"Thank you, Louisa. Are you still keeping your eye on Tate?" That man was still a quandary.

"Yes, Sir. All seems normal."

"Hmmm. Keep me updated. Other than that, carry on."

"Do you know when you'll be back?"

"No." Until he worked out what the hell Roxanne was playing at, why she was talking like that with Pascal, and decided the best course of action to take, he couldn't honestly say.

"Take your time. I've got everything covered," she replied. He nodded his head and ended the call. A quick scan through the notifications showed three missed calls from Conner that he definitely couldn't deal with at the moment, and also a text from an unknown number. He swiped across it and opened the message.

- I need to see you, son.

He stared at the screen in confusion and eventually looked into the room. Why would that bastard send him a message? It wasn't possible that this was real. It had to be a hoax, or something to try and throw him off a scent. Maybe it was something to do with whoever sent his angel that picture. He snarled back at the text and forwarded it on to Jacobs and Andrews. One of them could deal with it, track it down, or do whatever the fuck they did with this sort of thing. He hadn't got the time or the patience.

Quiet, he needed quiet.

He stood up and made for the entrance to the hallway. They'd been in Pascal's suite since whatever the fuck that was in the corridor downstairs. Who the hell did she think she was, talking to him like that? And why was Pascal so irritated about her now? He'd never see the man so furious and mouthy, which was saying something.

"And where the fuck do you think you're going?" The tone shocked him so he swung his eyes back to the man. He was standing there sneering over at him, waving his hands around and falling back into more Dutch again. Christ, he wished he understood that language.

"Pascal, Italian would be preferable, English even better. I can hardly discuss this with you if you're spouting that crap. And I need some space to think."

The man stopped and stormed over to him. He reared back and continued with his glare in the hope that it was warning enough. It wasn't, because before he could defend himself, a punch had landed on his cheekbone, causing him to grab onto the doorframe for support.

"What the hell?" he growled as he felt himself rise up and glower back. This was not the time for the man to piss him off. He was already fuming enough about his missing woman. A fight was not the best course of action. "What the hell was that for?"

Pascal just stood there and glared in return. Whatever he was doing, he meant it, and although that fight might release a little tension, the result might not be in anyone's best interest.

After a few moments, the man simply threw his hands up in the air, turned and walked away to the chair.

"Sit, Alexander."

"I think perhaps it's best if I leave before this gets-"

"SIT DOWN. If you want her then you will sit and listen to what I have to say. There are matters you are not aware of, and that woman has just made her point a little too clearly for my liking. As she always does, witch that she is."

That caught Alex's attention, so rubbing his cheek, he wandered back over to the chair and carefully placed himself in it. It was entirely probable that the arsehole might punch him again at some point in the near future, and he'd be ready for it the next time.

"I don't want to fight with you, but you should know I won't tolerate that again."

The laughter that erupted was quite unexpected, and he stared in confusion at the odd behaviour currently happening in front of him.

"I have been doing this with you for too long, dear boy. Your hands hold very little surprise for me anymore, and beating me does you no good anyway because I enjoy the prospect. But I thank you for withholding yourself from retaliation. My flurry of exuberance was not aimed at you." He didn't reply. There was nothing to say to a man who probably knew him better than he knew himself anyway.

"Do you understand what I have been trying to achieve with you all these years? Hmm? Has it made any sense to you? Do you see how you've changed?"

What the hell had this got to do with anything? He had neither the time nor the inclination to discuss what made him tick, or what the man had done for him.

"What point has Roxanne just made?"

"Do not change the subject. We are talking about you. You need to appreciate the principles of yourself a little more," Pascal replied sharply. "Elizabeth will only be able to do this if you accept yourself, fully."

"What are you talking about?"

"I have been trying to show your Elizabeth how to comprehend the very nature of you, to accept it, to harness it, cherish it, love you for it. However, you are sometimes brutish in your behaviour. You save your finesse for manipulation alone, and she will need you to combine the two."

"I don't understand,"

"No, you wouldn't. Alexander, she is going to come back here a different person. Ten minutes in the company of that woman and she will understand more about what has been happening than you can even comprehend. She will have been told what I have been up to, what I have been trying to do for you. She will also have been told how to behave, possibly incorrectly. Switchy women should not be allowed to linger with her for any amount of time. The result can be quite disruptive."

"What have you been up to?"

"How angry do you get now? When was the last time you had no control over yourself? You are more measured in your skill, but what is the one thing that still sends you over the edge? The one thing you quite stupidly showed her."

"Who?"

"Roxanne." As far as he was aware, the only behaviour he'd shown her was him losing control when he went there last. And given the fact that she'd mentioned it in the corridor, she presumably knew it was because of Elizabeth, but how?

"Are you talking about my reaction to Elizabeth, when we were apart?"

"Yes," the man replied, hanging his head a little. He'd not seen that look often. That was a Pascal in the wrong, and he wanted to know why.

"What have you done?"

"Why did you react like that?"

"I thought she lied to me, which is nothing to do with you. What have you done?"

"No, it wasn't the lie, Alexander. It wasn't even Elizabeth. It was the love, the feeling of needing someone, and the hatred for anything that might destroy a little of that feeling. A small boy who does not know love will grow to be a tyrant, and to find himself again he must reveal it all, fall down on his knees, beg for redemption and hope for the love to be returned. You must be willing to fall, and crumble, disintegrate for it. You are so close to perfection with her, so close I could taste it on her lips, smell it on yours. You tremble near her. Did you know that?"

"You're over complicating things, Pascal. I'm very aware I'm in love with her, and I'm also trying to show her all she needs from me. You were the one who told me I shouldn't do this – still do sometimes. You are as confusing as she is. Stop playing with me and just spit out what you're trying to say, will you?"

"I love you," Pascal said in reply, with no expression other than a slightly raised brow. Alex stiffened instantly and continued to stare back. He'd actually said it, and now what? Did he expect a response? This was not expected. "Do you understand that? How does it make you feel to hear it from another's mouth? Hmm?"

He just continued to look at the rogue in front of him and pondered the thought. How did it make him feel? Surprisingly, he felt the corners of his mouth trying to lift into a smile. The thought was warming somehow. It wasn't like the feelings associated with Elizabeth when she said the same words, but there was no denying that the sentiment attached to Pascal actually saying the words out loud was tugging at the heart she'd pulled from him again. Then there was this strange need to touch the man, hold him close maybe, or comfort him. It wasn't sexual. It never had been, but it was something other than what brotherly love would suggest. He let the corners of his mouth rise and kept his smile in place as he watched Pascal's frown grow.

"You are a conceited bastard, Alexander. Your display of superiority does not become you in this moment. It was not my intention to inflate your ego any further."

"Pascal, anyone who dares to love me, stay with me and harbour me has nothing but my respect. I told her that once, and I will tell you now. Your feelings, now that I'm aware you have some, are more precious to me than you can imagine, but I still want to know what you've done."

"That's it? No come back? No running for the hills in fear of me leaping on you?"

"Why would I run?"

"I may take advantage of your sudden rush of emotion, and because you do not reciprocate those feelings."

"Have you ever asked me how I feel about you? She has. She pushed me to answer questions that you dare not. Why not?"

"I am more than aware that you are not inclined that way. Why would I ask? And your ability to love or respect anything has never been something you're noted for."

"It appears, given your apparent teachings, that you've never tried to harness that side of me. Were you scared to tell me?"

"Not afraid, but the fear of losing you was enough for me to bite my tongue on the matter. And up until she came along, you were not equipped to hear it anyway. I am surprised you are now."

"I've had time to consider it, and I suppose, if she was asked how I feel about you, she would say I loved you, too. I think we all knew something was different in your office, didn't we?"

Pascal just stared back, all expression gone. There was no flicker of anything to give his thoughts away on the question, just a piercing gaze that damn near tore straight through him and made him feel just as exposed as she always managed to.

"Do you?" Clearly the man wasn't going to accept a vague answer, so after a moment's thought, his reply was simply the same. Her thoughts on the matter were probably more appropriate than his own anyway.

"She would say I do."

Pascal continued to gaze for a while longer, his mouth slowly opening and closing. Alex chuckled in response. He'd never really seen the man lost for words before, and while it was a humbling moment, it was still quite entertaining nonetheless. Eventually, those bright green eyes dulled and the normal harder edges of them returned.

"My body is with Lucinda. I belong to her," the man said, looking down and away from him as he picked up a glass of cognac and swallowed the lot. Who the fuck was Lucinda? And why had she even been mentioned in the midst of this conversation?

"Who are you talking about now?"

"Roxanne. I belong to her, much as that grates on my nerves. You have been my playground for a while. However, it is almost time for me to return. You need to cement this relationship with Elizabeth so that she can hold you together. Unfortunately, I will not be able to participate in our games much longer, dear boy. "

"What? You acted like she wasn't that important, and now you're telling me she owns you? When were you going to discuss this with me? Are you collared?"

"Why would I need to discuss it with you? You've never asked to own me yourself, have you?" Pascal replied as he stood and moved across the room to the far wall. He watched carefully as Pascal picked up some rope and wandered back towards him. "You may be a sadist, Alexander, but you do not want me as you do her. Don't confuse yourself now. I am simply telling you the truth because I will have to leave you at some point, and I want you to understand why. Elizabeth should be enough for you, if you are honest."

Fury welled up inside him at the thought. He may not want Pascal in that way, could never be what the man wanted, but he was damned if he was going to let him walk away, not now that an emotional situation had developed. The man was like his home – in a different way to his angel, but he still filled a void that no one else could, or should. Pascal was like an extension of him, a piece of his soul that he didn't own himself, a part of the jigsaw in his fucked up mind, and he wasn't about to let him leave. He gazed across at the rope in Pascal's hands and felt his insides relax a little. Peace – it was suspended there. The rogue gave him peace. It was the same feeling that Elizabeth pulled from him. When the hell had that occurred? He'd never realised it before, never felt the sensation or given it the time it deserved, but it was there nonetheless, that underlying serenity. His hands itched at his side as he watched Pascal pull the end of the rope through the ringlets on the bedpost, almost as if he were setting the room up for the next occupant. He wasn't going anywhere, and no one was coming in either. He had things to say.

"Fuck you. You do this to me and then you try to walk away?"

"I will have to. She owns me, and is becoming impatient with her leash. You also asked for frankness earlier. I am being candid, for once."

Owned him? No one owned Pascal apart from Pascal, and maybe him on certain occasions when the right mood set in and the man offered it. He knew without a shadow of a doubt he had no right to think about what was currently brewing, but couldn't stop it regardless. His muscles began to tense up with irritation at the very thought of never being able to use Pascal again. He thought he didn't need any of this, but it was too strong to deny anymore. His fists clenched as his pulse began to race at that feeling of freedom without any concern for the consequences.

"Where is your collar? Show me."

"I don't see how that is relevant, dear boy. And this is not up for debate, no matter how glorious you become in your rage."

"You will not walk away from me." Every dominant trait was now in full flow, that calm before an impending storm rumbling along beneath his skin for the first time since the office, and this time strengthened with a sense of fear he'd not felt before.

"Temper, temper. Do calm yourself. There is nothing you can do, and your orders are somewhat negligible at this point, beautiful as they are."

Alex was across the room and flooring the man before he could think any more on it, the pit of his stomach dropping with that undiluted sense of power as Pascal immediately relaxed in his grip and rolled in perfect unison to his movements. There was probably nothing either of them wanted more in this moment than to accept nature and let whatever it was that could happen, just happen. All those innuendos over the years, combined with every vision of lust or debauchery, brought on a strange sense of belonging, needing, wanting something other than the normal immoral acts of another time. What was that? Pascal turned in his arms and manoeuvred himself until he was inches from his face, his lips hovering as their breaths mingled. He was so close, so very close to touching him in a way he'd never considered unless a woman was between them. It had happened many times before but never had he even be tempted by the thought, until now. But force and anger at the circumstances overrode as his fingers grasped and hauled the man back to his feet again until he was standing in front of him with an annoyed expression.

"What do you want from me, Alexander? To be your toy for amusement? Hmm? What do you have to offer me? You tell me I cannot leave you, yet you offer nothing more than the occasional beating, perhaps a taste of your woman to share as and when she thinks it acceptable," he spat out at him, hands waving about and sneer firmly in place.

"That's not fair. You made me this way. You always knew I couldn't do what you needed. And you gave her that choice, not me. You've turned her. I would have kept her the way she was, introduced her slowly."

"Made you this way? You are this way. This is all you. Do not dare question yourself. Your sense of decency is as reckless as mine, if not more so, and if you're going to survive with her, she needs to understand that, needs to see it, feel it, absorb you as I want to and let you be the perfection you are."

"I'm trying to show her it all, and you."

"What are you trying to show me? Please, enlighten me. That you're jealous for something you do not want? Jealous of something you cannot give? This has gone on long enough, Alexander. It has been entertaining. However, it is time to-"

Jealousy? Damn right he was jealous. He couldn't even hear the man speaking anymore. That woman wasn't taking his other source of peace away from him, not now he realised he had it. The backhand across Pascal's face sent him reeling towards the bed and landing on his back. How dare he even think this a possibility? He would do as he was fucking told.

"Where is your collar?"

"I don't have it, and this isn't helping, nice as that wa-"

"Where is your fucking collar? Do you want me to beat it out of you?" The thought was fucking appealing at the moment, and the rising agitation combined with the slow calm spreading through his veins was making it damn near impossible to control what was coming next.

"Alexander, there is nothing you can do to-" That resulted in another blow to the face before Alex crawled over him to grab his throat and choke it out of him. He was going to find that collar and destroy it, burn it if necessary, before he let the man leave the room. Pascal's eyes bored back into his as his fingers tightened around his skin, his body melting beneath his own as he watched the bright green come back to life and widen in fear.

"Tell me before I fucking kill you. I won't share you with her. You will not leave me as well."

"It... It makes little difference what you want," Pascal stuttered as he tried to gasp for air. His hands squeezed together, cock hardening at the very vision as Pascal's mouth opened again and began to quiver in his grasp. "You don't want me."

"Once more, where is it?" Tighter, closer, almost to the point of feeling the bones in his neck giving way under his fingers, and as he continued to stare down into those vivid green eyes, his heart pounded with the same feelings he had for his angel. Never had he felt such emotion over an act of violence, overwhelming clarity in the perfection of the moment, as he watched pain etch its way across the man's skin and saw the love reflected back in those eyes. His breathing was disappearing, his jagged breaths rough and panted, and yet not once did Pascal grab onto him to try and stop what was happening. "I won't ask you again. You will fucking answer me," he said with a final squeeze.

"She... She has it," he eventually spluttered out. The release of Alex's hands was immediate as Pascal heaved in a breath, trying to calm himself, and blew it out. Much as Alex's cock was aching at the act, he didn't much like the colour of the man's lips, and he could deal with that pain at another time, preferably when Elizabeth got her fucking arse back here. He leaned back on his haunches and sat astride Pascal, whose face was now returning to a more acceptable colour through his panting for air.

"Why the hell did you make me do that?" he growled as he glowered at the man from above.

"I was quite enjoying the visual of you up there." He coughed. "You know how I like you in full force, and the purchase on my cock was quite indescribable," Pascal replied as he shoved his hips upwards. "Do take your clothes off. Let's just get this out of the way, shall we?" Alex shook his head at the man and began to move off of him. It wasn't happening that way, however oddly he may have just been tempted. "Why do you continue to spoil my fun, Alexander?"

"Get up. We're going," he responded as he got to the floor and reached for his jacket.

"Going where? We have everything we need right here. Elizabeth will be back here soon, and then we can-"

"She is not having a collar around your neck." Alex halted and turned back to face Pascal, sudden thoughts of compassion entering his mind. "Unless you want it there... Do you want it there?"

"I am not entirely sure. I have never had reason enough to beg for its removal." Alex turned and began walking towards the door again with a smile. Whoever this woman was, she was about to feel his wrath.

"You're wrong, you know?" he said as he listened to the grabbing of clothes and mumbled musings behind him, a truly wonderful sound, comforting somehow now he thought about it in a different light. Even in Dutch.

"It is not possible that I'm wrong, Alexander, but pray tell?"

"I do want you." The movement stopped. The mumbling stopped. "It will be on my terms, but if you needed clarification, there it is."

If he'd dared to turn around, he'd more than likely have found an astounded Pascal with his mouth hanging open. Instead, he turned the handle and began to leave the room, trying to work out yet another problem he had to deal with. Not only did he now need to understand what those terms would be, but he needed to understand how he was going to make Elizabeth accept them, too. He supposed he could kill two birds with one stone. He was going there for Pascal, and his angel was there, too. She would just have to hear it as it fell from his lips and hopefully feel as at ease with it as he did. And Roxanne? Well, she would just have to do as she was told, because regardless of her status over Pascal, she wasn't keeping him.

"She also has my wedding band," came as a reply to interrupt his planning. He rolled his eyes in response and kept walking, as if anything was ever fucking easy where Pascal was concerned.

Twenty minutes later and they were sitting in the *Limo*, staring at each other. The car was idling by the side of the red building, and he cracked his neck to ease the tension that was beginning to develop. A collaring was reasonably easy to deal with. A wedding ring was not quite so simple. Pascal was incredibly wealthy, and while he was sure the man was clever enough to have dealt with as much as possible, if they were married, she could take the man to the cleaners if she chose to. She certainly wasn't poor herself, but the term 'a woman scorned' popped into his mind. And she certainly wasn't a woman to be taken lightly. She never had been, but now he knew she had control over Pascal, his respect for her power had tripled.

"Why?" he asked evenly. He wasn't beating around the bush with the man anymore. If Pascal wanted a dominant, he could damn well have one, a real one.

"It's not something you need to-"

"No, Pascal. This stops now. You will not question me. You will just answer me," he cut in before the man had a chance to deflect the conversation. Enough was enough. If he was even going to entertain what he was about to do then he wanted the damn truth.

Pascal stared in response, probably trying to make up his own mind about what was happening between them, what that meant for him, and whether he was prepared to accept what might be coming.

"I am not sure what your terms are," he replied quietly as he removed his stare and looked out towards the building with not a flicker of any emotion other than perhaps a small frown. Alex smiled to himself. He hadn't got a fucking clue what his terms were, either. The only thing he did know was that Pascal would never have his wings clipped, unless he was the one to do it.

"Look at me," he said. Pascal turned back towards him slowly with the same expressionless face, green eyes devoid of colour and seemingly lifeless. "My only terms will be that you yield when I ask. That is all. Other than that, you will be able to do whatever the hell you want. Nothing will change between us."

"Anything?"

"Everything," he replied with a smile. A Pascal who didn't do everything he wanted to do would simply be a ghost parading in his clothing. "You will do everything with no restriction from me other than when I need it."

The slow creeping of a smile over Pascal's face was glorious to watch, his eyes returning to a brighter green as he clearly imagined something that amused him and straightened his body to a more Pascal-like posture.

"Even her?" he asked with a nod of his head towards the building and a devious grin, that brow raised in its most corruptive way. Presumably he was talking about Roxanne, or maybe Elizabeth. He narrowed his eyes in response and thought about it.

"Roxanne will be your choice. Elizabeth will be mine unless I say otherwise." The fucker pouted. Clearly he knew what that response was going to be before Alex had even spoken. "Now, why?"

"It is a long story, dear bo-"

"And that damn well stops, too. Never again will you call me that." Pascal chuckled a little and held his hands up.

"It is a habit I find hard to break. However, you are right. I will stop. Unless it means I'll get a beating," he replied, now with a smirk firmly in place. "Will I get a thrashing if I continue? I do so love your idea of punishment. It's so very limitless, and-"

"Pascal," he growled out. This was getting them nowhere, and he had a story to hear before he went in that room. After another snort of amusement, the man reached for the console and filled two glasses, pretty much to the brim.

"It is a long story so I'll try to condense it for you," Pascal said as he handed a drink over and got down onto the floor between Alex's thighs. He looked down in shock and raised a brow. "It is where I belong now, Sir." Was it? He was fucked if he knew, and that Sir thing didn't feel at all comfortable for some reason, unless it was in the right moment. Pascal turned his back, leant backwards and sighed. "Once upon a time, there was a fair young maiden with jet black hair and a heart as bright as gold. Rather unfortunately for her, a spoilt child came along and sat down beside her, an apple in one hand..." Alex tilted his head back and closed his eyes, the effect of Pascal's voice already creating that familiar sense of peace, comforting him and relaxing that tension out of him once more. Elizabeth should be here for this. She should know, too. He turned his head for the building and scanned the frontage in the hope of seeing her while Pascal continued his story,

"...and his father's cane in the other."

Chapter 9

Elizabeth

Am I ready? I think I'm ready.

I couldn't look any better if I went to some high-end shop and spent millions. The dress the little woman has found for me is simply amazing. I don't even care that it's a little short, anymore. I'm not sure what the material is but it's very nearly see through, with some kind of corseting structural thing holding it all in place. No bra, fabulous, and of course there's even a pair of matching panties, ones which appear to have diamonds encrusted on the back. It's all probably worth more than my apartment. My apartment – the one I don't spend any time in any more. It seems so long since I just sat on the sofa with Belle and Teresa, and just chatted the night away, got drunk, enjoyed myself. You know, all the things normal people do. Unlike me. Instead, I'm sitting in a kink house, staring at myself in the mirror and trying to prepare myself for the onslaught of Alexander White and Pascal Van Der Braack.

The little woman – I'm calling her that because she says she doesn't have a name – is scooping my hair up into one of the most elegant creations I have ever seen, while I put on my final sweep of lip gloss and try desperately to shake the off the fear that has started developing. I don't even know why it's there. I'm not scared of either of them. Whatever happens, I know they won't hurt me physically – not unless I ask for it. But emotionally, I just don't know if I can take anymore. I'm just going to be honest and make him be honest with. No more messing around, and no more hiding from me. I mean, what the fuck else can he have in there that could scare me off, for God's sake. There isn't anything left, is there? He's a sadist and a murderer, who I think still loves me. He doesn't want anything more than to be himself and have me love him for it, does he? And that's what I said I'd do. I promised I wouldn't give up on him, no matter what he threw at me, that I would love him regardless of his past. So I will forgive him for his fuck up on the plane, slap him for it, and find a way to get closer, so close that he can't hide it from me. I won't need to share him with anybody to confuse the situation because Pascal will be going, although for some odd reason that saddens me a little. He's like a second skin for Alex that I didn't quite appreciate until I really thought about it. The thought of the two of them not being a part of each other is disturbing.

"You're finished, ma'am," she says from behind me. I glance up at the truly exquisite styling and smile back at her. It's a little Audrey Hepburn for my liking but the rubies sparkling in it do look fabulous. *Rubies, Belle.* I should call her and explain what's going on before any of this happens, maybe find out if she and Conner are okay. Jesus, I'm a crap sister at the moment. Thank God the business doesn't actually need me because of her fantastic Christmas season planning.

The small woman just stares at my reflection, and the moment I catch her eye, she drops her gaze to the floor. Do I need to say something? I'm utterly shit at this Domme thing. This should never be an option for me.

"Umm, you can go if you like," is all I can find. Thankfully, she nods at me and walks away, backwards with her head still lowered, quite cleverly managing to not bang into anything on the way. I would so fall on my arse if I tried that. Well done, her.

Slipping on my red high heels, I grab my bag, with Alex's knife still firmly inside it, and head back into the lounge area in search of more alcohol. I've already had two glasses of champagne, but the very thought of dealing with the two of them has me reaching for a third before I even think about stopping myself. I gently sip at it and wonder what to do next. Do I wait here for Roxanne to materialise? Or do I go out there and search for her? I can't very well just leave without saying thank you for the clothes and stuff. I should at least tell her I'm going and offer her some money or something. I can't stay here forever, can I? I need to go and find her. Besides, I have no idea where Eden is in relation to here. I'm going to need a taxi or driver, or at least directions.

Slurping down the last of my drink, I take one final glance in the mirror, grab my bag and open the door to go in search of her. Maybe I'll bump into Vixon on the way and she can enlighten me as to where the hell I'm going. The door opens into a brightly lit corridor, so I follow the sound of music until I reach a set of glass doors leading into a foyer of some sort. The heat hits me first as I pass through it towards another set of doors, which appear to lead into the club area. I keep my eyes focused on where I need to get to in the hope that I know what I'm doing. I keep my head up and stride forward, letting the music own my swagger as I try and find feisty Beth and let her lead the way for me. I will feel in control of the situation I'm about to put myself in. If I can feel in control here then I'll hopefully be able to manage the two of them with reasonable success.

My hand pushes the door wide to find a normal club, with normal people drinking and chatting. Well, I say normal, but they can't be that normal or they wouldn't be in here, would they? I don't even know what the definition of normal is anymore if I'm honest. I doubt I could be considered normal myself anymore, not with what I'm about to head into, and the very fact that Alexander White is my other half is far from normal, even to me. I can't even begin to process what these people think of me. Do they know who I am? Or who I'm a part of? Roxanne certainly did.

It quickly becomes clear that some of these people do know who I am or are aware of my connections, if the parting of the walkway as I make my way to the bar area is anything to go by. People I have never met before are smiling and nodding at me as I pass, so I smile a little in response and keep heading for the bar, hoping that someone there can show me where Roxanne is.

A very well dressed young man instantly approaches from behind the bar and smiles.

"Can I help you, ma'am?" I almost roll my eyes, but refrain.

"Yes, please. I need to find Roxanne. Do you know where she is?"

"She's in the suites, ma'am. Just go straight along the bar and take the first door on your left. She's waiting for you, said for you to just go on through."

"Okay, thanks." She's waiting for me, is she? Fantastic. Maybe she's going to give me another round of '*I haven't got a clue what you're talking about*'.

When I eventually find the door, I'm met with a very large, bouncer-like man who I'm sure I recognise from somewhere. It's only when he opens his mouth that I remember him clearly.

"What's your name, ma'am?"

"Gage? I think you've asked me that before, and I believe he said my name wasn't for you to hear," I say firmly. I don't know who I'm trying to kid about this in control thing, but the man pissed me off the last time I saw him at that sex auction we went to. He could do with learning some bloody manners.

"He isn't here this time. What's your name?" That just pisses me off even more. He knows damn well what my name is, arrogant arsehole. Where is the man's respect for a dominant's wishes? Even I know you don't mess around with that sort of stuff.

"I tell you what, why don't I slap that stupid smirk off your face and then give him a call. I'm sure he'd love to hear you say that again." I don't know where that came from, but my hand has found my hip, so can only assume feisty Beth is irritated. My inner slut has also just joined in on the fun, because the thought of Alex knocking three shades of shit out of this mountain is making my knees wobble a bit in excitement again. Ridiculous, I know, but I'm beginning to get used to this odd feeling associated with violence.

"Woman, I don't know what you think you're-" Yes, go on then. Why has he stopped? I'm quite ready for a battle of venom. It'll get me in the mood for whatever I've got to deal with when I actually find the two of them. Why the hell is he suddenly bowing? Have I done enough of an Alex sneer to make him go all submissive on me? Wow, go me.

"Thank you. Now open the bloody door, will you?" I say in my sternest voice. I could get used to this shit.

A hand reaches around my hip and pushes the handle down to swing the door open in front of me. It's not anybody's hand; it's his hand, and I know that because I'd recognise it anywhere. The creases in it instantly remind me of his grip, his strength, his continued hold over me regardless of my current predicament. It doesn't help that his aftershave is now assaulting me and slamming me with visions of an intoxicating nature. Combine that with the trembling that's already occurring because of the violence association and, oh god, I'm in trouble. Alex. Where the hell did he come from? My body freezes. I'm so not ready for this. Every single *in control* thought has just left me, and I can't even turn my body to face him. I don't know what to do, what to say. Every available part of the English language appears to have abandoned me in this moment, as has feisty Beth. Fuck. I just stare at his hand, which is now palm up, as if inviting me to go forward through the doorway and saying *'after you'*. Arsehole. How does he still manage to appear superior, even when he's been a twat?

"Are you going in, Elizabeth?" he asks in his velvety tone as his teeth graze the back of my neck.

Oh my god!

It's taking all my effort just to stay upright, let alone try to deal with a seductive Alex. I can't deal with a nice Alex. I've been getting myself revved up for arsehole Alex, and him delivering warm lips and inviting teeth is doing me no favours at all.

"Is she switched on, Alexander? Maybe her batteries are exhausted. We should perhaps purchase a new one, or maybe two." Oh, and he's here, too. Great. I am so not fucking prepared. Christ, I just needed a few more minutes to get ready. I was on my way, in control, sort of, and now they've come over here and surprised me. Why have they done that? My other hand finds its way to my hip, too. "Oh, look, it is switched on. A delay, maybe, in the circuitry. It will need thorough examination. I should get my tools."

"Pascal," Alex growls sternly behind me, which increases the trembling no end. And no, Pascal, you will not be using any tools on me. Unfortunately, I can't stop the slight smile that's now gracing my lips in amusement. "If you're not going in, Elizabeth, we need to, so you will either wait here or follow Pascal."

What? I thought he was here for me. What the hell is going on now? My body swings around to find them both standing there like cocky bastards, looking every bit as delicious as they have absolutely no right to, given their past behaviour. Pascal is now in a pristine, white suit, and Alex is still in black, entirely in black. My feet wobble immediately in response to his utter manly perfection.

"Why are you both smiling? This is not funny, and you are both fucking arseholes."

Well, that's one way to feel in control, I suppose – go straight in for the kill. Although, I'm not entirely sure this is the right place for it. Alex immediately glowers in disgust at me and grabs my throat. My hands scrabble around to find purchase, but as usual, it's no use and I end up being forced to the floor by his feet. It's the firmest display of dominance I think I've ever seen from him. It simply isn't an option to stay on my feet, and it isn't a question of sexual desire, more an order to be followed simply because that's where he wants me.

"Stay there," he demands. Clearly he isn't best pleased with my remark. Well, screw him. How dare he come over here and try this shit on? I will stay in control. My feet begin to move to get me back up again when Pascal drops to his knees in front of me.

"This is true, my rose, and we will atone. However, in this moment, please, be quiet and let him do as he must," he whispers in the most sincere voice I've ever heard from him, liquid green pools gazing straight at me, almost pleadingly. My eyes shoot up to Alex's to find him staring blankly at me, those icy blues turning darker by the second as I gaze into them and wonder what the hell is going on. There's a slight twitch at the corner of his mouth before he runs a finger over my lips, then simply walks past us through the door and leaves us both kneeling there.

"What's happening? Where is he going? I thought you'd come for me. I'm… I don't know what I am. Confused maybe? Again. And why are you on the bloody floor?" That's damn scary to me. The only time I've seen Pascal on the floor is when Alex was about to beat the hell out of him. Why would he be down here with me now? I don't like it. Something's afoot. My eyes narrow when no response is given, as if I didn't have enough things to try and work out on my own, for God's sake. "Speak, Pascal!" He actually flinches a little. Go me. I still haven't got a response, though.

He slowly gets up and offers me a hand, so continuing with my snake eyes, I grab hold of it and try to dust my dress off on the way.

"You still look astonishing, my dear. He was quite distracted by you. As am I," he says, smooth bastard. He clearly looks completely ravishing himself, but I'm not telling him that regardless of his compliment.

"What's going-"

"You will have to watch. He will show you, but, Elizabeth, do not speak, move or do anything to undermine him. The result will not be pleasant for you." Umm, how about another screw you?

"What the hell? He deserves my venom. Undermine him? I was about to slap the shit out of him, and you. I thought I was supposed to take control. You told me to do that, and now you're telling me not to? For God's sake, Pascal. You see this, this is what I don't understa-"

I'm rapidly cut off by warm lips meeting mine, and no matter how much I want to push him away, I can't stop myself melting into

126

them. My treacherous knees begin buckling beneath me as he grasps me tighter and pushes his thigh in between my legs. Everything I remember from the last time comes rushing back to me in milliseconds – his hands are in different places, his lips warmer, his hold seemingly more ferocious somehow. Our tongues swirl until I feel myself relax into him and push back, asking for more from him. What the hell am I doing?

He abruptly stops and takes a step back, leaving me reaching for him again, just as it happened last time we were on our own.

"Exquisite, still, and quite fuckable in your fury, my Rose." I pant in response, unable to think of anything but that ridiculous need to do it again, soon. *Get a grip, Beth.* He reaches forward and runs a finger across my chest. "Perfect skin, ripe for marking. Are you wet, my rose? Hmm? Dripping?"

And now I'm gaping, too, here? Really? My eyes quickly narrow, as I take a small step away. I'm so not in control of this. He chuckles and closes the gap again. "Do you remember my office, when you conjured the image of submission so precisely?"

"What?" I can hardly remember five seconds ago after that assault.

"When Alexander brought you to me, to teach me a lesson. You claimed to be submissive by your actions, yes?" Arsehole. How did he know that? I thought my performance was quite good, to be honest. "He asked you to behave in that manner so he could prove a point to me. He did. He needs to achieve the same reaction from you again, only more fiercely so. It is real this time, my rose, and you must obey."

Right.... I have no idea what he's talking about at all, but he does suddenly look really serious, and I can do that submissive thing. I may not be entirely comfortable with it, but yes, I can pretend, play the game if I have to. Although, that being placed firmly on the floor thing is actually incredibly nice, and quite freeing, as long as Alex is the one who's doing it, that is. My eyes flick to green ones again, eyes that are now smirking a little, maybe he could, too. I roll my eyes at myself and dust my dress down again. It seems we have some sort of charade to get on with. I'm still not sure why I'm bothering, but it appears to be important to some degree.

"Why should I do anything for either of you?"

"It's your duty to him," Pascal says simply, with no other explanation. My lip curls with the thought of '*my duty*'. What's his duty to me? Where's the love? I suck in a breath and stare at him for a few more moments, trying to convey my lack of comfort with this situation. If he understands, he doesn't show it. He just stands there looking thoroughly fuckable and smirking back at me. Fuckable? Christ, I need to get a hold of this ridiculous trembling thing.

"When this is done, I'm having it out, with both of you," I snap in irritation.

"Yes, indeed you will. Out, in, on, over, up," he says, hand twirling around in that way he does as my eyes widen. "Tied, bound, strapped, held in place, ratcheted." Ratcheted? What the hell does that mean? He clearly seems to enjoy the prospect, whatever it is, while I still stand here, staring at him because he's now licking his lips. "Whipped, broken, bruised, used, abused, anything you'd like eventually, my love. However, it all has the same finale: both of us at his feet, repeatedly," he says, as if it's all mapped out and I'm the only one who was ever in the dark about it, the only one questioning the end goal.

"What?" I can hardly find the words. I'm not even sure what words I'm trying to find anymore.

"He will have you on your knees, begging for hours for just one moment of release. He has shown you nothing but pleasantries, and if you want him, you may as well begin to see him for who he is."

He offers me his hand and nods his head toward the door, where Gage is still bowing. Hand holding, really? I'm not sure I've ever considered Pascal a hand holder – an arm wrapper rounder maybe, arm linker, definitely, but hand holder?

"I'm not sure I want to take your hand," I mumble. Not only am I now concerned about what I'm about to witness, but the thought of this all becoming intimate is confusing me again, too. Why, I don't know. "He told me to stay there." He looks at his hand, then the floor with a frown before gazing back at me.

"I'm insulted. Do you realise what a rare occurrence this is, my rose? You'll take my tongue but not my fingers?" I've already had his fingers, which my immediate thigh clenching only highlights. He laughs. Bastard. "I was referring to guidance, Elizabeth, comfort even.

You are quite immoral, and once this small interlude is concluded, we shall find out how much so, yes?"

Guidance, yes, I need that, I suppose. It's either that or I walk myself straight out of here, and I can't do that because Roxanne is in there, somewhere. So I look down at his hand again and slip mine into it as he smiles genuinely at me, links our fingers and takes a step forward.

"Pascal, who are we going to see?" I ask as we wander slowly past a selection of rooms, all with windows big enough to see into. I sneak a look into one to see a man dressed in a nappy and a large woman in some sort of nurse's uniform. "What the hell is-"

"It doesn't concern you. It is his kink, his fetish. Do you understand the significance of the world you are in, the honesty it takes to admit what you are? I think this is a problem we must address. He has not shown you nearly enough, has he? Hmm? It is the reason why you are struggling with your veracity. Why do you think he has not done so? I can only assume he is being selfish, which is quite unlike him. You must explain that, in your own inimitable way, my dear. I fear this is worrisome and could exacerbate our issues. Have you held a whip yet? Has he allowed it, or is he being-" I cut him off, rather extraordinarily.

"You're rambling, Pascal. Why? Are you nervous of something?" I know he is because his palms are damp. I've never seen him anything other than fully composed or utterly furious, and even in fury, he seems composed somehow. His eyes flick across to mine, and then back on the corridor in front of us. "Who are we going to see?"

"My wife," he says evenly. My feet trip over themselves as I stumble to a stop.

"You're married?" I exclaim. It comes out something like a strangled cat spluttering for air in utter astonishment.

"Mmhmm, and collared," he replies, still walking as if this is no big deal, completely regal again and knocking his cane on the floor as he goes. "You understand what this means, collaring?" My feet launch forward again to catch up.

"Well, yes, sort of. Alex explained about a ceremony he'd witnessed, and my choker is his collar." His brows shoot up as he abruptly spins round on me and halts us both, so of course, I stumble backwards a bit like a fool and wobble on my heels.

129

"He collared you, and you accepted it?" he asks in amazement, watching me trying to regain my balance.

"It's not my collar. It's his," I reply as I rub at my ankle and straighten myself up. "It represents one around his throat. Well, it did, and I assume it still does, if you know what I mean." Did that even make sense to him?

"This situation becomes ever more perplexing," he says as he narrows his eyes and then spins and begins walking again. "Why did you not tell me this? Why did he not? And where is it? You should be wearing it."

"It's in my bag."

"Put it on, now."

"Why?" He frowns back at me, and it's slightly scary to be honest. "Okay…" I glance down at my bracelet and then at the diamonds in the bag, and I know, for the time being at least, it is the right thing. They both need me at the moment, and although I don't really know why, I can't stop the need to help them. We'll deal with the rest later. "It's Roxanne we're talking about, I assume?" I ask as I fumble with the catch. He hands me his cane, takes the choker from me and clips it around my neck.

"Mmm," he replies as he starts on his course once more, leaving me to catch up, still holding his cane.

"Are you going to explain any further, because I think-"

"He will show you," he says as he reaches across and runs a finger over my choker. "This is very you, very him – elegant, graceful, yet thoroughly complex in design. It is just as he would choose. "

Right, we're clearly not having any other conversation on this matter. I guess I'm just going to have to do as I'm told and hope I get a clue about what's going on when we get in there, wherever there is.

Another set of doors later and we're in a large space that's full of people. These are not normal club goers. We have hit the land of debauchery. Several latex suits, masks, whips and chains later, we arrive in front of another window with an audience gathered around it. Uncertainty creeps up my spine as Pascal lets go of my hand and nods at me. I have no idea what the bloody hell that means, but I can only assume it's time for me to perform my submissive duties. But wait… Do I have to be submissive to Pascal, too? What do I do if Pascal gives an order? Do I listen or just do as Alex says? Oh, fucking hell.

More preparation was needed. Why do they always keep me unprepared for this stuff? I don't know what to do. My legs freeze a little as we get closer to the window. Pascal turns slightly and looks me over in interest, one brow raised, as if he's asking what the matter is. I'm about to speak when I notice all the other people have turned to look at us. Some are clapping. It seems they've been waiting for us. I'm positive now is not a good time to question anything and show how completely incompetent I am. Words have obviously failed me anyhow, so I lift my chin a little higher and stride forward again in the hope that I can get close enough to his ear that I can whisper.

Three women drop to the floor in front of Pascal, hotly pursued by two men. I have no idea what that means either so reach my lips towards his ear.

"Do I have to do what you tell me, too." He places a hand in the small of my back to push me towards a door at the side of the window.

"Only him," he says simply as he reaches for the handle. "Head up and eyes on him, my rose. Unless he tells you otherwise, that is. Are you prepared?" Not a bloody hope, but his sentence makes me smile a little nonetheless. He takes a deep breath and opens the door wide, then slaps my arse ferociously. My feet scoot me into the room in the most inelegant fashion possible at the intensity of it. If he was hoping for stupid person who doesn't know what she's doing, he's managed it. I quickly scowl over at him and try to regain some composure as I find a spot on the wooden floor. There isn't any movement from the two people standing in front of us, no acknowledgement whatsoever that we've even entered the room. I just stand here, flicking my eyes to Pascal to see what it is that I should be doing, still holding his damn cane.

He's just staring over at the two most beautiful people in the world, one of whom is Roxanne, who is dressed in a long, black, hooded cloak. I can't quite make out what she's wearing underneath, but I can see shiny black boots poking out of the bottom. Her hair is up in a knot, severely scraped back against her pale skin, and her make-up is extremely heavy with dark red lips glinting in the candlelit room. There's not a hint of the angelic creature I saw earlier today, just another version in her place.

They're just staring at each other. I wish I had a clue, but nothing is being said so I blow out a breath and just keep my eyes up

131

and focus on Alex. It's not hard to do. The last time I had any real time with him, he treated me like dirt, then told me he wouldn't let me go, and yet I'm standing here for him again. I'm still holding on to the hope that this is going to work out okay somehow, that we can make it through this mess and find each other again. He's still completely breath-taking, so masculine, his frame still owning every inch of the space around him and keeping all my attention on him, just him. My mouth is suddenly drooling at the thought as I glance down at his hands – his utterly wicked hands made for butchery, even more so now, given the content of the room around us. Yet he needs none of these objects to make me feel overwhelmed. Not one of these pieces of equipment holds any sense of fear for me because if they were in his fingers, I'd be willing to take them. For him, for me, for us. My knees buckle a little as I notice a brown whip coiled on the table in front of Roxanne. I remember that feeling, the sharp, intoxicating stings on my back, my thighs, and the lingering dulled ache that followed – the ache that was only taken away from me when I begged him to fuck me, to take me and make me come until all the tension was gone. Oh, I miss that. I didn't realise how much until this moment, until I've been put back in a room and shown all the things he could do to me. My eyes flick to Pascal again. He's still looking incredibly serious, and he's waggling his finger by his thigh. Random... Why is he doing that? Is he pointing at the floor? Should I get down there? Alex hasn't told me to. Pascal closes his fist and then points at the floor again, as if signalling about holding something. His cane. Should I put that on the floor? I gently lower it to the floor until the metallic end taps the ground, which instantly causes Roxanne to spin her head towards me.

"Give me that," she snaps. It's harsh and immediate. I haven't got a clue what to do, but Alex hasn't told me to so I think not is probably best. Although the vision of her now swaying towards me can only be described as pure evil as she sneers and stops a foot in front of me. I so want to step backwards, but Alex hasn't told me to do that either, so I direct my gaze back at him and put a death grip on the cane. "I said give it to me." Yep, still not giving it to her, no matter how much she's helped me. The slight lift of Alex's lips is enough to further my intent to hold onto it like it's my air. His beautifully darkened eyes draw me towards him as if there's no one else in the room, just me and him and this connection that holds us together, binds us somehow. It doesn't matter what he did. It doesn't even matter what he's going to do now, because I'm lost in him again. He may be a dominant at the moment, may always be, but to me, he's also the man I love – the man on the stairs in pain, the small boy in the rain, the man who needs me to breathe. Those eyes keep pulling me in, telling me where I need to be. I can almost feel my skin leaving my body to get to him, tugging at my bones to move me across the space between us and force us together once more. He inclines his head to the side, and somehow, it's all I need to understand where he wants me. I move around Roxanne and walk straight across to him, cane tapping on the floor along with my heels just as Pascal would. Alex's eyes leave mine as he inclines his head again, and in milliseconds, I can feel Pascal moving behind me almost in unison. Before I know what's happened, we're both standing at his feet, just where a pair of green eyes told me we would be, like it's our home.

"Alexander, you're not having him. I won't allow it."

Okay, that shocked the shit out of me, enough so that my head swings around to look at Pascal, who is still staring at Alex. He doesn't flinch in the slightest, just smiles slightly and licks his lips. I can only assume she's talking about Pascal, and I'm not entirely sure how I feel about that. There was love between them. I saw it – him and Roxanne. Why would Alex be asking for Pascal, and why would Pascal want that?

"Down," Alex's velvety voice says. It's not harsh or demanding this time. It's a simple request, one almost filled with emotion. It's also one we both yield to, side by side. Pascal grabs my hand again and places it on his thigh, covering it with his own. I peek up to find Alex still looking at Roxanne, but I can see the smile playing on his lips. No one else can, maybe Pascal, I suppose, but she will only see a hard mask of defiance, a sadist's face with a blank stare and a look of devastation embedded behind deadened eyes and a murderer's body. "They're both mine, Roxanne. You have no choice."

"He is both collared and my husband. Pascal, come to me," she says sternly. He flinches beside me this time, and I feel his hand tighten a little over mine so I squeeze his thigh in response, hoping to relax him. I have no idea of the severity of what's happening but the fact that one of the scariest people I know is flinching probably doesn't bode all that well. Is he emotionally struggling or is there a physical threat here I should be aware of? Wow, way to get myself involved in Mafia come war games. Where's my bag? There's a knife in my bag. I could defend us all. My eyes glance at Alex's feet and I almost laugh out loud at myself. A killer, I am not. I have a feeling all three of the other people in here probably are.

"He won't move, Roxanne. I haven't told him to. Your demands are useless now and you know it. So just agree and then we can all leave here unharmed."

Unharmed? What the fuck? I didn't sign up for this. Good lord. There really is an actual threat of danger here. My arse twitches at the thought. I mean, I know I love him, possibly Pascal, too, but come on. No one really owns anyone when they collar them, do they? And marriage is just a piece of paper. It may be an expensive one in Pascal's case, but it's still a piece of paper. Do we really need all these dramatics? I could just stand up and tell them that, couldn't I? Just stand up and protest about whatever this is. Alex takes a step towards me and nonchalantly forces his foot between my knees until my thighs open up. I'm guessing he knew exactly what my thoughts on the matter were. It seems I'm not allowed to move, and I swear I hear Pascal chuckle. The instant quickening of my breath reminds me of my place down here at his feet, ready for whatever he wants. In fact, I'm actually quite horny, which while wonderful is also quite disconcerting given the situation around us.

"Give me the cane, Elizabeth," he says as he lowers his butchering hand in front of my face. I hold it up to him and he takes it off me and removes his foot to walk across the room. Pascal flinches again.

Lord knows what's about to happen.

Chapter 10

Elizabeth

"**Y**ou will give me that fucking cane. How dare you waltz in here and believe you have some right over him? You do not, you arrogant son of a bitch. He is mine. You can keep your little pain slut but you're not having mine," she screeches like a banshee. I can hear her heels stamping around the floor as if she's about to erupt in a fit of rage. I haven't dared turn round, and Pascal's hand has begun tightening on mine again, so I look over nervously to find him looking down at the floor with an expressionless face. It's so unlike him, so quiet, so reserved.

So submissive.

"You okay?" I whisper to him as she carries on with her tirade behind us. He doesn't answer or even move, just blinks and continues to stare downward.

"You disgust me. You will not come into my home and take things from me. It was a game, Alexander. That was all. It isn't real. He is mine. This has all been a game, you fool. Take your little toy and get out. Pascal, get over here, now."

He still doesn't move, but his fingers are actually beginning to cut off my blood supply a little now. I flex them in his grip and pull them away to cover his hand with mine as a sudden rush of emotion for him assaults me. I'm even starting to well up with some undiluted sense of fury as I sit here and listen to her scream about ownership of such a man. Who could own a man like him? Who would want to, for God's sake? He's free, an explosion of sin, vice and lust, and all things that he wants and needs. Who would want to control that? I certainly wouldn't.

"He wants to be with me. The discussion is over," Alex says. Apparently, Alex does. I still can't get my head around that, but it's better than this new bat shit crazy bitch.

"Over? Over? It will never be over. I will drag him from the room myself if he doesn't get his scrawny, disease ridden hide over here now. I will tell you one more time, Pascal, before I make you."

"You will not touch either of them, Roxanne. That would be very unwise."

"Or what, Alexander? Will you beat me? Show the world how out of control you are? Look, they are all watching. Please, by all means let them see your insanity. It will only help someone kill you sooner so I can get on with my own fucking life."

"Roxanne, I am trying to do this correctly, but don't test my patience. I am tired enough and will not need much more to end this incorrectly." He's tired? Poor thing, me too. That would be about me, I assume. Well, he fucking deserved it, perhaps not in this moment but there's a lot of shit he's got to make up for.

Heels are suddenly clicking louder against the floor, and I realise she's heading over here. What the hell do I do now? Pascal doesn't move, but I flick my eyes round to see her storming over with a rope in her outstretched hand. What the fuck is she going to do with that? Self-preservation kicks in at the same time as my hackles rise and my body swings around to protect Pascal. I have no clue what I'm doing but my gaze is fixed and relentless as I stare her down and shield the man behind me. I'm fucked if she's hurting him to get her own way. Oh, shit, that may not have been the right thing to do. I flick my eyes to Alex to find him looking at me with no expression at all, just blank eyes and the stance of a primed man, ready to wage war if needed.

"Get out of my way, you ungrateful little whore," she snaps while coiling the rope around her fist. Should I speak? I don't bloody know. I scoot closer to Pascal until my back is pressed to his and continue with my staring. She reaches her talon-like hand towards me and I flinch away from it at first, but then find my feisty Beth again, and before I know it, I'm up on my feet with my hands up for protection. Rage: I can use that. Why Alex isn't doing anything, I don't know, but the woman is not hurting Pascal, or taking him anywhere he doesn't want to go.

"Get your stupid little thing out of the way, Alexander. She won't look quite so pretty when I've finished with her if this carries on."

"Why? This is becoming interesting. It appears she wants him, too. Perhaps now would be a good time to accept what is happening here, Roxanne," Alex replies with a slightly disturbing chuckle. Chuckles? There is nothing funny going on here. What the hell is he laughing about? I don't even know why we're all bothering with this. He could just say it's over and we could walk out, couldn't we? She sneers again.

"You want to fight me for him, whore?" she asks, still fiddling with that rope. Do I? Christ, protecting him is one thing, having an actual fight? I'm not so sure. And why the fuck is Alex still just standing there? Shouldn't he be doing something? "Poor Elizabeth doesn't understand, do you?"

No, I don't. She takes a step away and undoes her cloak to reveal an unfairly astonishing body encased in black PVC. Another step and she stands tall and arches a perfectly sculpted brow at me.

"This is the way we'll have to play, Elizabeth. I'm refusing, and it wouldn't matter if my slut begged me. I still wouldn't let him go. Your Alexander can't fight me. It wouldn't be fair, would it? So what I will allow is for you to take his place."

Holy fuckballs!

I hope I didn't let that show. One ounce of weakness is going to be the death of me here, I'm sure. Okay, this is worrying to say the least because she means it. She's about to go all out to kill me and show me who Pascal's going home with. Why is she backing up to the wall behind her, all cat like and sleek? Oh shit, she's grabbed a whip off the wall. We're fighting with whips? I swing round to the table and grab the coiled one from it. I have no bloody clue what I'm going to do with it but at least she might think I do. I so wish I hadn't been dragged into this. Yet another thing to have it out with them about when this is over, if I'm alive.

"He's worth death. I assume you're aware of that." I'm not sure if I'm honest, but I turn round and look at him, still perfectly still, still staring at the floor and not moving an inch. There must be another way around this.

"Look, it doesn't have to be this way, Roxanne. Just let him go and then we can all leave. I mean, I know you've collared him, and he's your husband but-"

The first strike across my calf muscle sends me reeling to the floor in agony. The second hits me straight on the middle of my back as I'm trying to deal with the first, and has me howling in pain. My body screams at me to stay down but the dull throb as it begins to subside reminds me of where I am and who I'm with. Dull echoes of pain start to ride across my skin as I feel that slight delirium begin to creep its way up my spine to create that glorious warming sensation. I see Pascal's hand reach for me to pull me out of the way and scuttle out of his grasp as he begins to stand and turn toward the room.

"You stay down there," I shout at him. He stares back at me for a moment in shock and then drops back down to his knees again, this time facing the room. "That fucking hurt, bitch," I snap across at her as I right myself again and look over at her. I should probably kick these heels off, but sod it... I shall look fantastic if I'm going to die. Belle would be proud.

"Just warming up, Elizabeth," she replies as she starts to circle toward me again. I drop the whip in my hand from its coil and glance across at Alex to find him still the same. I see a slight tilt of his head as he looks me up and down and retreats a step away. Where the hell is he going? I could use this on him if I'm honest. If I knew how the hell to use it, that is. It can't be that hard. I let the weight of it hang in my hand and swing it around in the hope that I look like I know what I'm doing. I know I'm going to have to have a crack at it at some point, so without much further thought on the matter, I pull it behind me and then flick it forward as viciously as I can. It goes nowhere near Roxanne but it does leave a rather wonderful cracking sound hanging in the air, and at least shows me I can use it to some degree. She glares back. Apparently I've proved a point.

"Are you ready, Roxanne? We can still do this the easy-" Another stinging lash across my thigh has me raising my arm in retaliation so quickly that I don't even think about it. And far more by luck than judgement, I hear a shriek in response as I see her hand move to her face.

"You fucking whore," she screams at me as she removes her fingers, and I see the red welt on her chin. I smile in response. It feels good to have hit her so effectively, so precisely, even if I didn't mean to. She doesn't know that. The dull ache that's beginning to stretch across my skin only highlights the room around me. My eyes find all sorts of instruments dotted about. Steel, rope, wood – they're all there for me to play with, be a part of, learn and understand. They're all new adventures to encounter, and... Alex. I gaze over at him to find a small smile gracing his mouth as he licks his lips and then looks behind me. I spin my head to see Pascal with the same smile, and before I realise what's happened, my whip lands inches from his side, cracking the floorboards with a loud snap. He doesn't even flinch, doesn't move in the slightest. He just looks up at me with that smirk still in place and his eyes boring back into me. *'Yes, more,'* he seems to say. I'm not even sure what we're talking about here, but the three of us seem to being having our own internal conversation, those conversations I used to look at the two of them having and not understand. I'm part of it now. I can feel them both swirling around in my skin, in my mind. I look back at Alex again. He's still got that lip licking thing going on, a brow now arched as if daring me to challenge him. *"Don't you dare. Only when I say."*

I can feel a new version of him within me – actually inside of me – telling me what to do without any need for words whatsoever. This is a more explicit connection that has nothing to do with audible language, nothing at all to do with the physicality of words, just a reaction to internal noise, almost the ability to hear thoughts somehow.

"Fuck you," she screams again, breaking my moment and causing me to turn toward the threat that appears to be running at me.

My hands go up into brace position for the onslaught, and just as she's about to slam into me, my body is flung out of the way. I skid to a stop just as she reaches her new target and begins throwing her hands at his face, scratching viciously and spitting at him until he grasps at her hands and stops her. Her body writhes and twists in his until she suddenly stops and looks straight at him.

"Leave her alone. Your dispute is not with her, nor Alexander. It is with me," Pascal says quietly.

"Get on the floor," she demands loudly.

"It's over, Lucinda. My heart is not here anymore." Who the hell is Lucinda? I do wish these people would just have one name.

"Get on the fucking floor," she shouts again, louder this time, so much so that the boards beneath my feet shake.

"No, I do not wish for that any longer."

"You will fucking beg then, and I'll still say no. You will do as you're told. It is my right, and..." He grips her harder, squeezing her wrists as she twists them in his hands and tries to pull away again.

"There will be no begging, no servitude, no games. I will no longer allow you to control me. Our time has come to an end."

"You can't say that. You love me. Do as you are fucking told."

"That is quite irrelevant. This is still finished."

He taps his foot on the floor and holds his hand out. I have no idea what that means, but as Alex steps out of the darkness and holds the cane out to me, I can only assume I'm supposed to take it to him. So I carefully take it from Alex, as he nods ever so slightly in the direction of Pascal, and walk across towards them. She scowls at my approach and opens her mouth to shout. I have absolutely no clue why, but I drop my eyes as if something private is going on again between them, some sort of secret code that I'm not to be part of, or witness to for that matter.

He holds the cane up to her face and tips her chin with it towards Alex as she struggles against it.

"This is his now, and then hers. It will never be yours again. Am I making myself clear."

My loud gasp at the comment doesn't go unnoticed as she flings her eyes toward me and sneers again. I have a feeling that while she may be backing down a little, she will never believe that, nor accept it. Her glare is enough for me to take small steps away until I hit the table behind me.

"You will crawl back to me. You know you will. This is all futile. You'll have no choice," she snaps as she grabs onto the cane and tries to wrench it off of him. He holds it firm and eventually breaks her grasp on it until they're just staring at each other again. Are they having their own internal dialogue now? It's like fucking la la loopy land in here – not normal, not normal at all. I can only hope that I fully appreciate this whole thing one day, truly understand what on earth is happening around me.

"Give it to him," Pascal says. She steps away from him instantly and spits on his jacket. I hate spitting. I could slap her face off for that. How dare she? Bitch. My feet are itching to walk over and do something about it, including wiping it off his probably five thousand pound suit. "I will ask you one more time before I remind you of the past. Respect has never been your finest quality, has it, my love? You should follow the rules I slaved to teach you before I am forced to forget the few manners I have."

Oh, that's thrown me... I thought she was in control of him? What the bloody hell is going on now?

She sneers again. She's very clearly not going to do anything of the sort. He gives her about one more minute of staring before picking her up and forcing her over the desk beside me. Her heels kick out at him, and then her nails scratch out at me so I move away slowly to give them the room for whatever is about to happen. I'm so engrossed in it that I don't realise I've bumped into Alex until he grabs me around my waist and snakes a hand onto my stomach.

"Are you wet, Elizabeth? I think you are."

"What?"

"Keep watching," he growls as his hand moves to my thigh and drifts its way up my leg and under my dress. My fingers instantly go to stop him, because however nice it might feel, I am not doing this, not until we've had our conversation anyway. His other hand is on mine, moving it and pinning it behind my back immediately, wrenching it upward slightly to increase the pressure and drive me down towards the ground until I land on my knees. "Wider," he says as he pushes onto my thighs and forces them apart. I try to keep them closed, really I do, but I just haven't got the strength to fight him, and he smells so good, and Pascal is being so aggressive, and... "You know what to say to stop me, don't you?" he whispers in my ear as he drags those damn teeth up my neck and reminds me who he is again. I could at least try to stop him. I don't. I just keep staring at the physical conversation that's happening in front of me and try to stop the sudden onslaught of trembling that's overtaken my body. I haven't got any hope of being in control in here. I should get up and walk out. I should tell them all to go to hell and enjoy their strange little world, but I can't take my eyes off what's happening. Cogs begin clicking into place as I start to comprehend the dynamics around me. This battle between Alex and Roxanne is about ownership of Pascal, and the battle between Roxanne and Pascal is about who is now in charge. The original teacher, it seems, is now beginning to reverse the roles again, maybe to show the former student who is going to control the outcome and allow the situation to change. Manners – he said manners, as if this world has any manners in it at all. But as I watch him pin her and push her around, I can almost feel the order in his complicated brain. This is rude to him and disrespectful to Alex, and she should be put in her place for her reaction. As if she should know better than to not challenge some set of unwritten rules that I have absolutely no clue about. Or maybe I'm starting to, no matter how confusing.

Pascal's suddenly ripping at Roxanne's clothes as she squirms and squeals beneath him. He's mumbling in that language I don't understand again and holding her so fiercely I can actually feel the winces coming from her mouth.

"You will be honourable to him," he suddenly shouts at her, and with one quick movement, the entire backside of her trousers comes away from her skin, torn to shreds by his irritation with her. "I'll fuck it out of you if you refuse to yield."

"Pascal, no," she shouts again as she tries yet again to get away from him. His hand clamps her neck as his feet kick her legs wide, perfect precision in his movements as he aligns every part of his body to cause damage. I can see it coming a mile off, hear it in her screams, and taste it in the air around us. This is the master at work. This is probably the man who found Alex, helped him and channelled him into the man he is now. There is not one bit of forgiveness or pleasantness about him. He's as comfortable with what he's doing as he is with breathing. No, maybe more so. One final forcing of his thigh into the back of her knee to hold her in place and her plunges his fingers into her so hard she screams and shoots across the table, and at the very moment I hear the noise, Alex's fingers push into me forcefully. I can't breathe, it's so intense, so very intense. Stars are almost on top of me before I even realise what's happening. I hear more screams and swearing as she tries to get away from his hand, which is ramming in and out with such power I find myself mesmerised by it. My core begins pushing into Alex's hands as I almost feel her body writhing about, her thighs slamming forward with every thrust of his arm, her neck being held down precisely as he turns her to face us and snarls more foreign words at her. The look in her eyes is sheer anger, ferocious even. There is nothing she's enjoying here, and yet there's nothing she can do to stop it other than beg and presumably safeword. Unfortunately for me, I can't help but feel even more excited by that, whether it's because of what she's done or because she's actually in pain I don't know, but there's no denying my reaction to it. It's potent, very nearly spellbinding.

Alex slowly draws his fingers out of me and brings them up to my mouth for her to witness.

"Suck them," he says to me. I'm one part infuriated by the command and two parts horny as hell. My legs are trembling, my stomach is warming, my brain is firing with all sorts of visions, and my core is crying out for more of his hands. Or maybe Pascal's hands, which are now leaving her body and, with one loud crack, spanking her so hard she screams again and tries to kick out at him. Fingers still hover in front of me as I try to make my mind up what the hell is happening to me. "Now, Elizabeth, before I make you." His slow tone is so scathing and threatening, I move my mouth straight to his fingers and pull them inside. The first taste of myself is almost enough for me to explode, and I sense my core trying to find some sort of purchase on anything – anything to make this ache go away. My vision swims as Pascal's hand hits her again, and again, and again. So hard, so very hard, and it's all I can do to keep myself upright instead of leaning toward them to feel her pain even more.

"Pascal, please..." she tries to say as he backs away slightly and wrenches at his belt with one hand.

"Do you not remember my name? Let me remind you, my dear," he says calmly to her as he unbuttons his jacket. There's not even a hint of anger anymore. He's utterly in control. Every move, every thought, every clearly sadistic process is measured and prepared like it's his very nature, like he was born just as he is now.

"Are you ready for him, Elizabeth?" Alex asks behind me as I continue to lick my way around his fingers, my groin still whimpering for his touch. "Are you ready for him to show you? Get you ready for me?"

I have no fucking idea, but if someone doesn't do something to me soon, I might just explode.

Pascal doubles over his belt and delivers the most frightening sound I think I've ever heard. She screams in pain and I watch as her eyes well with tears. Then I hear more gasps, screams and whimpers of pain as he does it again.

"Name, my dear?" he asks again as he releases her neck and waits for an answer. He shrugs from his jacket and places it over the back of a chair with precision, as if it's far more important than her.

"I won't do it," she chokes out between sobs. He flips her over, so quickly I hardly see it happen, and tears at the front of her trousers until all covering has gone. She clamps her legs closed and somehow manages to find a glare to throw at him. She's rewarded with what can only be described as evil, pure sin, rolling off a smile that I once considered amusement, and one I'll never look at in the same way again.

"Open your legs, my dear," he says smoothly. She shakes her head and scrabbles her hands around for something on the table, presumably to defend herself with. "No? Hmm. The hard way, then? Your defiance is intolerable. What happens to ill-mannered little girls, Lucinda? Do you not remember?"

She's physically shaking now, her whole body trembling in fear as her eyes start to search the room for a way out, and I can't help but begin to feel nervous for her. Pascal is eerily calm, just like Alex is sometimes, and I know I haven't even begun to see what he's capable of yet. My mouth opens to stop it but hands are instantly at me again, soft hands, almost caring, caressing and gently folding fingers into me. My core ignites again as he quickly takes my mind off the threat in front of me.

"Do you understand why you're enjoying this?" he says. "Should I fuck you while you watch? Would that make this easier for you to comprehend?" No. Yes. Christ knows. His other hand wraps around my throat, intensifying every illicit thought that's threatening to overtake me, and as it squeezes tighter, my body grinds into him to try and increase the pressure again, and his hand backs away. "You want it like that? Want it as viciously, as sadistically? Watch him, Elizabeth. Learn him. Let yourself want him."

"Last chance, my dear," Pascal says quietly with a step towards her and a lick of his lips. Fuck, so horny, so fucking horny, and I can't relieve my ache with Alex because he won't let me. He just keeps teasing me with quiet strokes and holding me against him so I can't gain leverage. I'd get up and ask Pascal for it if I could damn well move, but no matter how I struggle, his hold is vice-like.

"Slow, Elizabeth. You're mine, and you'll wait till you're told," he breathes in my ear, goading and teasing with his fingers as he draws them through me, over and over again.

Pascal's on her the moment she begins to shake her head again – head pinned, legs ripped open and forced to obey with no ability to fight him at all. His hands are instantly on every point on her body before she can think about moving to a new position to avoid his grasp. The belt is raised high and slammed down in between her legs so hard I wince in response to it as she screams in agony and bucks off the table. My involuntary response is to try and close my legs, but Alex's hand stays put as I watch the smile Pascal gives her in response. It's just as sadistic as the last, but now with a twist of that amusement creeping back in.

"Again, my dear?" He raises his arm. "What fun we're having, hmm? A pink little cunt on display for your hoards to see. Should we give them a real performance? It has been some time since my wrist has felt your innards." I can't even speak at the thought. Wrist? Is that possible? She shakes her head slightly and he whips the belt down again, harder this time, which causes her to cry out and begin begging for him to stop

"Please, no more. Please... Please. I can't. You know I can't." Again, he lands the belt on her, and again, and again. Tears pour from her eyes, her body reeling and wailing and groaning under the strain he's putting on her. "SIR!" she screams as he raises his arm again. He stops and inclines his head sideways.

"I did not catch that, my dear. Blame it on the excitement. I am quite fired up. Do say it again, and somewhat louder this time so your underlings might hear, too. I'd hate for them to be unsure and cause more disruption to my reputation." My eyes fly to the window. I'd almost forgotten about them. They're all standing there, watching, panting, and waiting for his next explosion. My legs try to close again at the thought that they're watching me, seeing me. Alex's hand squeezes my throat in response and tips my head back to the action in front of me.

"Sir. Your name is Sir." She pants as her legs come together and she rolls onto her side.

"I'm not entirely convinced of your acceptance. Open your legs. We shall try again, I think."

"How much do you want him, Elizabeth? Is it him you need, or this?" Alex asks as he slaps between my legs so hard I squeal and shoot back into him to get away. Stars erupt and lights flash as he does it again, and there's nowhere for me to go, no way of stopping the sensation or halting its progress. Another blow and I'm struggling to brace my knees against the impact of it. Wet slapping noises assault the air, and I watch Pascal turn to look down at us as butchering hands twist at my clit and pinch brutally. He's got a wicked smile firmly plastered on his face and green eyes sparkling with mischief and debauchery as I pant in reply to the vicious tugs. He's home, and I suddenly realise that Alex is home, too. This connection they have together is where he's most at peace, where he can be anything he needs to be without condemnation or repercussions. There's no need to explain or think about his actions; he can just be, and Pascal just knows, allows it, accepts it and pushes him to be more.

Sparkling green eyes fix into mine, and I'm lost in him. I can feel his thoughts swimming around in all of me, and Alex's, too, guiding us, guiding me, like some kind of ethereal whisper in my ear. His hold relaxes slightly behind me just before Pascal's hand extends towards me, and I know I've been asked to go to him. I don't know how I know, but I do. It's a request he's unsure of. I can feel that in the miniscule seconds between their differing movements and the continued hold on my waist. *"I love you. Do you want this? Leave if not."* He loves me; I know he does, because I simply wouldn't be a part of this if he didn't. He would have considered this rude to Pascal if he didn't love me. He wouldn't have brought me in here and let me witness any of this unless I was part of it with him – part of what he wanted us to be. His unasked question hangs in my mind. I heard him say it even though he didn't, and whether it's part of this show or just the inevitable, I know the answer because the very heart of me is somehow yearning for Pascal's grasp on me, and Alex's approval of that.

"I want to," comes out of my mouth, answering his concern that kept me held to him, and as I feel warm lips on my neck and his fingers leave my throat, my body leans forward to crawl across the floor.

"Be good," Alex growls from behind. Good? Nothing about this is good. It's all bad, wrong somehow, and yet so very right. There's no one else here anymore – just them, and me, together, and I'm struggling to remember there's another woman in here until I hear her panting in pain again. Pascal sneers at the noise and delivers another blow to her backside, almost as if she was vulgar to interrupt out little internal dialogue. She wails again and damn near falls off the table to cower in the corner of the room. Bitch. I couldn't care less. The only important things in this room own blue eyes and green. "Only her," Alex says sternly from behind me, so I turn my head to see him now standing behind me, all six foot four of him now towering above me and smirking a little at my arse in the air. I don't even know what he means but I halt my progress to look at him from down here. It's so comfortable, so normal, so fucking irresistible to be down here for him. If I could wipe the smile off his arrogant bloody face, I would, because I'm still so fucking angry about everything, but in this moment, right here, right now, I can do nothing else but just be. Just be what this moment is, the three of us.

There's a whistle to my left, which breaks my moment of completely irrational lust and adoration for the man in front of me. My head slowly turns to find yet another smirking arsehole who is removing his shirt as if tempting me to him. He really doesn't need to bother. My inner slut is crawling me all the way to that bank as fast as she can.

"Come, my rose," he says. "We have a cane to acquaint you with." I so wish my knees would stop at the thought but they don't. They just keep crawling me forward until I'm beneath his feet. "Up. That is no place for you. Only sluts and whores belong on the floor. Unless you'd rather it, that is? I can do either way."

"Table," that velvety voice says quietly. Pascal raises a brow and looks up.

"But, she-"

"Pascal."

"Hmm, it appears you have no choice, my rose. Up you get. We wouldn't want you to dry out down there," he says as I get up as gracefully as I can manage and stare back at him. "On the table with you then, legs spread. Let us see what you feel like, shall we?" Not with that attitude.

I raise my hands to touch his chest and feel him shudder from the contact. He instantly takes a step away and nods to the table again. I take a step closer to him again because he isn't in control of me, and I've got as much right in this as any of us. I won't be broken, or told, or cajoled into anything by him. We are equal. The only person in this room that has any power over me is Alex, and when he asks, I will probably do, but I will hold my own with Pascal. I will demand and not be frightened or pushed by him anymore. I will command the same respect he has for Alex and he will honour that, regardless of the fact that I'd let him do just about anything at the moment because I can feel myself dripping down my thigh.

"Say please." The words are out of my mouth before I think any more about it. Alex chuckles a little behind me, and for once, I understand his amusement. Pascal clearly doesn't.

"I have never asked pleasantly for anything, my rose. You should know this. You reminded me of it yourself." Okay, now we're going to have our own little battle, it seems. Fine.

"You will for me." He stares as I hold my hand on his chest again and gaze back, willing my conversation to enter his thoughts so that he gets it. So that he accepts it and we can all find a way through this. He flicks his eyes over my shoulder and frowns. I can only assume he's not being helped by Alex. I can see his mind working through the possibilities. What does Alex want? That's all that concerns him at the moment, how not to offend his new master. Eventually, he smiles and nods at the table again.

"Please."

My eyes narrow. He so doesn't mean that, and his utterly tempting smile does nothing to conceal his amusement at my trying to be in control, only confirms it. My hand is grabbed, and I'm spinned around so sharply my body has no choice but to follow the twirls until I land arse first on the table. Damn heels. Then, before I'm aware of my balance again, he's shoved the cane into my mouth lengthways and pushed me down onto my back so hard the air rushes out of me. His body hovers over me, those green eyes glinting and warning of all sorts of trouble that I should be saying no to. "Bite down, my dear. It will help with the screams."

Alex suddenly appears again from the gloom and gazes at me as he crosses to the window, one slight curl upwards of his lip as he raises his hand and lowers the blind. Apparently the viewing isn't welcome anymore.

Chapter 11

Alexander

He stood still and fought the demons inside as he watched her being turned and moved, every instinct conflicting with the others as he fought to feel comfortable with what was about to happen. Pascal was now in malevolent mode, primed, ready, and very willing to obey.

This was new to them all, nothing like the times before, no sense of normal or easy. Every touch on her skin was like a lightening bolt being delivered to his heart, every crass word used like a dig at perfection. *Cunt* – the word shouldn't be used within two miles of the woman he loved, and yet that beast raging inside loved the sound of it, wanted to hear her scream and beg and howl in the same pain he'd heard from Roxanne.

Roxanne. She was still here, wasn't she? How fucking dare she intrude on this? She shouldn't be here to see such utter perfection in action, shouldn't be able to hear Elizabeth mewl and pant with desire, or watch Pascal at his finest. It wasn't hers to see anymore. They were supposed to be alone for this. He was supposed to have organised it, got ready for it, made her aware it was going to happen, but watching Pascal bring himself out and deliver his punishment to Roxanne had been all any of them had needed to start this. His cock was burning, her pussy was on fire, and Pascal was more vicious than he'd seen him for a long time. The very air around them was crackling with arousal, and the smell, sounds and heat was damn near indescribable. Roxanne needed to leave. It wasn't fucking happening with her in here.

"Wait," he said to Pascal as he crossed to the whore on the floor, who was still cowering in fear. She fucking deserved it. Never before had he seen someone be so rude to Pascal. She would never do it again, not while he had the man's obedience anyway.

"Where is his collar?" he asked, as nicely as possible given the circumstances. Frankly, his cock just wanted this out of the way as soon as possible so he could throw her from the room. She scowled up at him and clamped her little mouth shut. It wasn't a wise move. He had far more important matters to attend to. "I will choke you on my cock if you don't speak up." Her eyes widened. "Did he do that to you? Choke you till you couldn't breathe? Choke you until you gagged on your own vomit?" She shook her head a little and scuttled backwards. "No? Well it would be one way to show you who's in control now, I suppose, although you could just give me the FUCKING COLLAR," he roared.

She jumped in response and scrambled away again, so he grabbed her boot and yanked her back to him, unzipping himself as she snarled and kicked. Fucking irritating dominants and their utter lack of respect for the rules. Who the hell did she think she was? She knew the rules, must have. Pascal was her Dom, for fuck's sake. She kicked again, so he grabbed the whip from the floor and threw it around her neck. Two turns later and she was beneath him as he sat astride her and pulled out his cock. He had no intention of putting Elizabeth through that again, but Roxanne didn't know that.

"Rapunzel," she shouted as he angled himself at her mouth. What? He stared for a few seconds and then waited for Pascal to answer, who was far too close to the love of his fucking life for his liking, regardless of the fact that he wanted what was happening, had asked for it, to be fair.

"Safe word," Pascal said in a bored tone, waving his hand idly as he dragged his fucking teeth across Elizabeth's collarbone slowly. This might not end well. He could already feel his instincts kicking in to drag them apart again. Safe word, not a surprising one given the princess beneath him. Was he supposed to honour that? It wasn't their safe word. He didn't even really know the woman, for fuck's sake. He waited again for some sign of sympathy from Pascal; it wasn't forthcoming.

"Alexander, please stop," Roxanne said, pleadingly. Hmm. He looked at his love's eyes and watched her watching him, her mouth parted around the cane, her breath almost reaching him from here, her throat pulsing and begging for touch, Pascal's hands wandering, closer, lower. Her expression morphed into that lust-filled gaze he adored. She was ready, willing, waiting for him to show her, love her. Her every thought seemed to be screaming, *"Leave her. Come here."*

She didn't need to see violence at the moment. She needed support, guidance and help to deal with what was happening.

She needed him.

He needed that damn collar, though, fucking rules of obligation. He flicked his eyes at Pascal and growled. The man instantly stopped and looked across at him from her chest, eyes almost lost but for his command. A piercing stare was all it took for Pascal to take a step away and lift his hands in surrender. He looked back down at Roxanne and tucked his cock away.

"Shall I let him back at you? I may have some respect for your safe word, but you know he doesn't." She shook her head again. "I stopped it before, thinking you were ready. Now, I'm not so sure."

"He doesn't deserve to have it back," she spat. The woman had some guile; he had to give her that, and that may have been true but he still fucking wanted it, if only to prove the point to Pascal.

"You have unfinished business down here. Finish it. I want that fucking collar," he said as he stood, walked straight in front of Pascal and wedged himself between Elizabeth's thighs, his thighs, his throat. She looked up at him through the thick air in the room, their eyes connecting again as she dismissed Pascal's and joined him again. He lifted her silken leg and wrapped it around his back, suddenly desperate to get closer to her and show her how he'd missed her, how much he wanted her, needed her. She pushed the cane from her mouth and let it roll down her chest towards him.

"I believe that belongs to you, Mr White," she said, that sexy little smile gracing her mouth and sending all kinds of thoughts to his cock. Choking was one of them. She had no idea.

"That is does, Miss Scott," he replied. "You can keep it if you like." The mere thought of Pascal's face was enough to curl both of their lips into a smile.

"I hate you," she said out of nowhere. He raised a brow and tightened his hold on her leg. "That's what you wanted, wasn't it? You wanted me to hate you. Well, I do, sort of."

He smirked a little in reply and lowered his head to her dress, which was in the damn way. Three tugs in the right direction and her astounding breasts popped out of the top, nipples tight and desperate for biting. He clamped his teeth down so hard she wailed and arched her back up into him, searching for more. His finger drew up those milky white thighs to find her dripping and mewling and panting as he dragged more harshly and let her feel his need.

"Do you want me to fuck you, or him?" he breathed out around her nipples, clamping again and releasing, creating the rhythm, the verse she needed. Why he was asking was a mystery. She'd done as she was asked so far. Maybe he should just tell her.

"Him," she said. He could have roared with jealousy, could have beaten Pascal to death at the mere thought that she wanted him more. Did she? His head came up to gaze at her, chocolate brown eyes completely owning his every thought. Love – the man was right. This shit did complicate everything. "If that's what you want, too." It was a slight reprieve, but it still damn well pissed him off.

He turned to watch the commotion that was now happening in the corner and tried to realign the internal commotion that was occurring. It was no use to anyone, especially not her. No matter how strong the temptation to just give in to the darkness was, he wouldn't allow her to be manhandled until he knew she was ready for it. This was the first time. She would be cared for.

Pascal suddenly dragged Roxanne across the room by her hair. She winced, and kicked and screamed but his body simply grew and ignored it, his long strides yanking her all the way to the cross on the wall and then hauling her up against it with perfect dexterity. His was an art form in himself, pure undiluted sadism, not one hint of regret or thought other than sheer dominance. Controlling him wasn't going to be easy. He watched Roxanne's eyes widen in fear and wondered what she'd had over him for Pascal to allow it. If the situation weren't quite so tetchy, he'd ask her.

"Is it Christmas yet?" his angel said beneath him. His eyes swivelled back to her.

"No, it can't be. I haven't got a bow to tie you up with." She smiled and licked her lips. Fuck, he wanted to kiss her. He wanted to do a lot of things but kissing her was on top of the list.

"I want a bow, and a tree, and decorations." She glanced over his shoulder. "Why is she still here?"

"Collar," he growled irritably as her thigh pulled him closer and she ground her pussy into him. He groaned and pushed back harder. With nothing but a scrap of material in the way, he wished Pascal would get the hell on with it. "New responsibilities."

She stared for a few more moments before reaching in between them for his cock, grasping and tugging and squeezing through his trousers until all that was left was her hand and that fucking mouth, lips shining and begging to be forced.

"Take me, Alex," she whispered. "Show me. I want you. I need you."

He savoured the thought as his hand pushed inside her as hard as he dared. She squirmed and ground back down onto it instantly, spreading those legs wider as she bucked and tried to find purchase for more. So wet, dripping and pulling him in further. Fuck, he wanted to beat her, hold her, rip every shred of decency from her and make her just for him, like him. Fuck morals, fuck obligations, fuck every other person in the world who knew nothing about this. Just them, the two of them, three of them even, bound, gagged, bleeding, screaming, coming, panting. Blind sweat and howls of desire, and tears, beautiful tears – fuck, he wanted her tears, her fear, wanted to watch the terror leak from her as she fell into him again and gave him everything.

"Pain," she mused, mid-drift, those eyes now beginning to cloud slightly as he rammed his hand in again. Her breathing evened out to a steadier rate, waiting for the more he was offering. She pulled herself up to get closer to him, her lips hovering around his as she locked her eyes with his and promised him the world with them. Grabbing at her, he twisted her breast until those eyes screwed shut and she shrieked in pain. Pain... That he could offer, and he could give it with no need for consideration, no worry as to how much she could take anymore. She'd let him know if she needed to stop, wouldn't she? She wouldn't be agreeing to any of this if she didn't understand by now, would she?

"I'll listen this time," he mused quietly, gazing at her panting mouth. It was a promise, because after all he'd put her through, she was still here, yielding, begging, wanting him. "Let me push you."

He unzipped again and grabbed at his cock. He had to get inside her again, had to feel her clenching around him and giving him everything. She mewled and begged in his ear while she fidgeted and yanked at his clothing to get him closer, deeper, just like she always did. One heated shove and he was exactly where he wanted to be, balls deep and watching her gasp for air. Her moan of desire filled the air with only her as her fingers tightened on his collar and pulled him towards her lips, his fucking lips. He bit down onto them and felt her breath panting into his mouth, felt her legs tighten around his waist, felt the constriction of her pussy pulling him further in love with every grasp.

A hand suddenly arrived over his shoulder, dangling a thin strip of burgundy leather.

Fucking responsibilities. Why was he always in the fucking moment? Inconsiderate bastard.

"What would you like me to do with it, Sir?" Pascal asked, as sarcastically as he could. He could think of a few things at the moment, none of them particularly helpful to Elizabeth, or himself. She groaned beneath him and shot a death glare at Pascal.

"Really?" she snapped. "God, give me a fucking break." She rolled her eyes and lay down on the table again with a thud. "This is not going to sodding work until you pair get this crap sorted out. I will not share this moment, at all." What the fuck was that? Pascal smirked, and waggled the strap again. She shook her head and shuffled her body away from him until she was on the other side of the table, staring at them and reorganising her dress. "Do you know how long I've been thinking about this, trying to deal with it? For fucking ever, and it's your fault, and yours, too, I suppose, and that's fine, ish. But don't think I'm doing this half-arsed. It's all or nothing. And is there a possibility of a bloody bed being involved? I mean after the, you know, other stuff. Or during it, maybe, and possibly it would be better to not be in here with that watching." She pointed over their shoulders in disgust.

Alex stared back at her in shock. Where had this version come from? He turned to look at Roxanne, who was still strapped to the cross as she hung her head and sniffled pathetically. Pascal smiled serenely as if he hadn't caused any harm at all and continued leering at his angel.

"What did you do?" Alex asked, glancing over her scrawny body for other injuries and suddenly remembering now was probably a good time to put his cock away, again. He glanced back at Elizabeth. He could still fuck her and deal with this other shit later. She stared at Roxanne in horror so he turned back again.

"She is quite anxious around bodily fluids, other than come, and your knife was within arm's reach," the man replied, casually. Alex raised a brow in reply and looked back at his angel for her opinion. She shot another glare at Pascal.

"Knife? That's my sodding knife. What did you do with my knife?"

"Not a thing. I simply held it in front of her. She is squeamish of such things. A good incentive, yes?"

"So you actually went in my bag, how dare you? That's personal for God's sake."

"Your cunt is not personal, my rose? I've been inside there." It was a fair point. Alex waited for a reply and tucked his cock away with a groan as he looked back at her. Compliant fucking was off the menu for a while it appeared. She threw her hands in the air and scowled.

"Actually you haven't, yet. On it maybe, around it even, but in it? No. And a lady's bag is her secret, Pascal. You can't just go poking around in it whenever you like."

"I will poke around in whatever I feel like. Is this not what we are doing in here? Alexander, enlighten your woman," the man replied as he twirled his way around the table flamboyantly and halted a step in front of her. She snarled a little, grabbed at the cane on the table and mumbled something about having to deal with this situation. Then, with her own flurry of dramatics, she stepped around him and stormed across to the door.

"I'm leaving," she snapped. "With this, because it's mine now, because he gave it to me." She stopped and poked her tongue out at Pascal. "So would you deal with whatever this is and then meet me by the front door?" And with a click of the door handle she slammed the door closed behind her and left.

They both stared at the door for a good thirty seconds before Pascal spoke and interrupted Alex's thoughts of teaching her more obedience. It wasn't going to happen. He still liked that fired up version of sexy as hell anyway.

"Do you have no control over her at all?"

"Not much, no."

"Did you really give her my father's cane?"

"Yes, I thought she deserved it for even entertaining this."

"Hmm, I didn't get to taste her, again, and why have I not been inside her yet? You blocked my progress. It was unreasonable of you."

"Pascal." The man was pushing the boundaries of acceptable behaviour with his honesty.

"Oh, do stop growling at me. I am too tense to behave appropriately," he replied sharply as he wrapped the collar around his fist and looked at it. "If I knew what that was, and I need to fuck something interesting." He unwound the collar again and wandered over to the window to lift up the blind. Alex flicked his eyes to the scars on his ribcage and smiled – his scars, his markings, his property. "Now, what should I do with this?"

"Put it on."

"Excuse me?"

"Shall I do it for you?"

"No, I..." There were no words coming from the man, just a strange stare as his mind clearly ran through every reason why he should not put it on.

"I've just battled for that, Pascal. I may attach a leash to it quite soon. Put it on," he said as he made his way to the door to follow the woman he loved. "And deal with that-" he pointed at Roxanne, "-however you'd like. But have your collar on and be at the car in ten minutes."

He grabbed the handle and pushed against the wood until the room full of people came back into view. Various masks and subs hung their heads in apparent humility to a dominant in Pascal's life. Control of Mr. Van Der Braack wasn't something any of these people had ever seen, he was sure. They didn't even know about Roxanne until it had all started an hour ago. He'd seen all their damn questioning eyes as he'd stormed in and demanded that she release him and do the honourable thing. Fuck them. Pascal would never be looked at again in that manner, with their shaking heads and their surprised gasps as they'd sneered and laughed at him because he was owned. He'd been submissive, quiet, almost lost over how to behave, how to handle the jeers around him. It was not a version of Pascal he liked a lot, not one he felt comfortable with at all. Not in public anyway. A small red head came and sat by his feet, offering herself up for a beating. His mind raced to Elizabeth again. Her skin was going to be battered if Pascal didn't get rid of some energy, and these people needed to remember whom Mr. Van Der Braack was, regardless of what had transpired. He turned and looked back into the room to see Pascal still standing there with the collar in his hand, staring down at it in mystification.

"Pascal."

"Yes?" Alex raised an eyebrow. "Sir." It still didn't sound right. They'd have a conversation about that at some point, unless he could use it to his advantage anyway.

"Before you put it on, you should fuck her. It should be interesting enough and might get it out of your system. Show them. You can have an hour." The man nodded his head and put the collar on the table, then smiled and crossed the room, thankfully with green eyes full of interest again.

He left the door open for others' viewing pleasure and walked towards the exit to find Elizabeth, and whatever would be coming out of her mouth this time.

The walk through the club was full of memories, and he stopped as a blue door came into sight. He'd been in there when he was here last. That was the room Conner had dragged him from, stopped him from going too far by allowing him to vent his frustrations on his friend instead of random women. Why had he done that? He'd needed Pascal, that's why. He should have called him and accepted it at the time instead of believing he could handle the situation with Elizabeth himself. It was all so obvious now. He needed them both in very different ways to allow him to be who he needed to be. Elizabeth wouldn't have to take his rage because Pascal was there to do that now. He could just love her, play with her and push her. But when the time came, when those moments were too much for her to endure, then Pascal would be there for him. A new three-way bond of trust needed to be formed, one of unspoken conversations and liberation. They just needed to find the rules.

He hovered by the door for a moment before knocking. When there wasn't any answer, he pushed it wide open and stepped into the space, which was almost empty. There were only a few tie hooks on the wall and a small bench in the middle. It was just his sort of room, with no need for thousands of objects. He could do as much damage with his own body weight as he could with kink supplies. There was only rope that he needed, and teeth. Asphyxiation took no more than a firm grasp, and holes could be used for any purpose when the participant was pliable enough. He breathed in the smell and let it settle for a few minutes. Stone and metal, it reminded him of the mine he'd had that dead fucker in, the one who'd been stupid enough to try and rape Elizabeth. Idiot. Elizabeth, the only one to ever hold his heart, the only one to ever let it beat at its own pace without recrimination. Pascal might allow him to be himself and give him a certain sense of peace, but Alex didn't feel the same way for him as he did for her. There wasn't the warmth. There was care. He did care, greatly, but that underlying feeling of love just wasn't the same.

The door closed behind him, and within seconds, her perfume changed the scent of the room. He smiled to himself and kept looking around the room. This would be interesting. If she wanted the truth, she was about to get it.

"Why are you in here?" she asked quietly, all venom having left her voice. "And where's Pascal?"

"I'm remembering, and he's relieving himself."

"Oh," she said in response. He turned and held his hand out to her. She walked straight to him and clasped onto it so he guided her to the bench and then walked off around the room.

"I want to tell you something, be honest with you."

"Okay," she said as she crossed those mile long legs and looked at him with interest. His cock needed to get a damn grip for a few minutes. Its time would come. He shook his head and fiddled with a ring on the wall for something to occupy his hands with.

"What do you want for Christmas?"

"What?"

"Christmas, what would be your ideal gift?"

"Umm. Well, London would be a good start. A healthy mum." She furrowed her brow and glanced at the floor. "And some peace, I suppose. I'd really like some peace."

"Do you think I can give you that?"

"I think you can if you're honest." He chuckled at her and walked back across to sit. There wasn't anywhere so he crossed his legs and sat on the floor beneath her. It was an unusual place to be so he stared up at her for a few minutes.

"Do you still want this, us, all of us? That collar is still yours if you want it, but with Pascal now, the circumstances have changed," he said as he stared at the diamonds around her neck. "What happened in there could have just been the air around us. I want to be sure." She

158

pondered the question for a few moments, not a hint of nerves as she continued to gaze straight into his eyes. If he didn't know better, he'd have sworn she was a Domme. That face was almost eclipsing in the hold it had over him, transfixing him almost to the point of forcing him to look away. It wasn't the same stare she'd had when they met. She was so much stronger now, so much more in control of herself. He hardly ever saw her looking downward or acting edgy now. She was just pure, true to her core. The term 'switch' really wasn't far off base at all, and Christ, he loved her for it. She eventually opened her mouth, still not removing her eyes from his.

"If I forgive you for the plane, will you promise to never do that again?" she asked. "I do hate you for it, and I don't know how to believe you won't do it again." He couldn't blame her. He'd been a fucking bastard. "And I want Pascal, not as much as you, but I do want him, whether you like it or not, but I won't be beneath him. Do you understand that? We will fight about it between ourselves, and you will let us find our balance. And I want to understand what this is between you two. Why were you fighting with Roxanne? For what?"

She put the cane on the floor between them and rested her chin on it, her hand around the shaft, looking strangely comfortable, almost relaxed, as she grazed her fingers across it. "I'll probably allow you anything you need, Alex, including him, as long as you ask me if it's okay first. You can't force this, or me. It just needs to find a way, find its peace somehow and settle, in all of us."

He could force anything he damn well wanted, both of them included, but he loved her all the more for accepting him, *them*. He grabbed her hand, kissed it lightly and stood up again. It was time she really understood. No games, no manipulating, just the facts.

"The last time I was in here, there were about six women, I think. They screamed, Elizabeth, all of them. I can still hear their cries ringing in my ears. It's quite beautiful in some ways. I had them in so much pain that Roxanne had to pay one of them off to keep quiet about it. I fucked them, hurt them, beat them, used them and degraded them. All of them. Do you understand? I once told you I wasn't a good man. Do you get that now? Did you feel it when I sliced that dress off you? I need that, want that, will never not need or want that. How I behaved on the plane was an extension of that man." She kept staring upwards at him, still with an unreadable face, nothing to give away any sense of fear or disgust. "It happened when we were apart, when I left you after the ball." That did make her eyes widen a bit. She clearly had no idea. "Conner made me attack him so that I would stop. He knows me well, because I wouldn't have stopped, Elizabeth, and he knew it. And the real problem is that Pascal is right. You did that to me. The loss of your love did that to me, made me lose control, again. For the first time in a long stretch, I lost my control."

She just continued staring at him, as if she was waiting for more and accepting his statement as normal. It really wasn't normal. He turned his head and wandered around the space again, searching for the right words in his mind. Scared? Was he scared? Edgy, maybe. This whole scenario was untested, unproven. He didn't know if he could cope with Pascal and hold himself together when it came to her, let alone actually make it happen. Maybe that's why he'd held off for so long, not really accepted this was going to happen. He stared at the concrete and tried to organise his thoughts. Truth – she wanted the truth.

"I can try to justify my behaviour then to some degree, but I am more concerned with where we go now, if you still want this. The reality is I am sadistic by nature, and am now dealing with a jealousy I wasn't aware I owned. My behaviour will more than likely cause you pain, and anguish. Our rules have not yet been formed, and because we are both immoral, Pascal and I, you are about to become part of something you can't imagine, that even I can't quite imagine. He is waiting for me to say yes. He can smell it all over you, all over me, I should think, but he's so much stronger than you, Elizabeth, both physically and mentally, and I..." Words failed him at the thought of what might happen. He wouldn't let it happen, though, would he?

"And?" His head shot round to look at her again. What the fuck did that mean? Wasn't she scared or nervous in the slightest? She stood up and walked towards him, a slight smile gracing those full lips. She took long, elegant strides that glided her across the floor until she was a foot in front of him. The red of her dress swayed at odds with her hair. Christ, he loved that hair. He put his hands in his pockets to stop his cock taking over his thoughts, and waited to see if she had more to say. "You're scared, aren't you?" He chuckled a little and gazed down at her. Trust her to understand his confusion.

"I don't know if I can control him, or myself, or if I even want to, and I've never had to care before you," he replied honestly. It was all he had, and she wanted the reality, said she'd stay no matter what. She smiled again, a breath-taking smile that had him falling over himself to grab her, kiss her, love her, keep her all to himself and hide her away from prying eyes. He shoved his hands deeper in his pockets and frowned at his own ridiculous dilemma.

"You're thinking too much," she replied as she swung her body around again and began walking. He watched her arse with a smile, watched her tapping the cane across the floor just as Pascal would, perfectly in time with her legs as if she'd been made to hold it, perhaps made to use it. "He's as aware as you are that I'm breakable, and you haven't broken me yet, have you? He won't either. I know what I'm doing, Alex. You should trust me. I'm done with being broken."

With that, she winked at him, opened the door and left. He stared at the door and mused the statement.

"You haven't broken me yet, have you?" I haven't tried to.

"He won't either." He hasn't been given permission, yet.

"I know what I'm doing." No, you don't.

"You should trust me." I do. I also love you.

"I'm done with being broken." Sadist.

"Done with being broken."

Pain, tears, fear.

Chapter 12

Elizabeth

Holy shit. Did I just say that?
Did I just give him a way to not bother controlling Pascal?
What the fuck am I doing?
I have no idea. I don't even know how I walked out of that room looking vaguely composed. If it hadn't been for this bloody cane, I might well have fallen over. Jesus, he looks good, all broody and moody and dominant, fretting around with rings on walls and trying to get me wound up. He really doesn't need to bother. Again, my inner slut is walking me all the way to that bank as well, at speed. Why I feel the need to be compassionate, I don't know. Maybe it's just because I love him, all of him, even the bastard in him. I felt it the moment we all connected in that room, felt the passion ebbing backwards and forwards between the three of us. And I refuse to deny it any longer, or let him. Whatever will be, will be. He brought me here, introduced me to Pascal, showed me this life of his and told me he wanted me to be part of it. So what the hell is he worrying about? He's the one that's supposed to know what he's doing. This could all go very wrong, and I'm not allowing it.

The club is still in full swing around me, full of life and spirit and beautiful people all dressed in their odd outfits with their whips and cuffs and blacks, everything you'd imagine of a kink club. And yet, beyond that door in front of me, the one Gage is guarding, they'll all be normal people again, won't they? Just normal, average human beings, dressed normally, having a drink normally and chatting normally. Okay, not completely normally given the fact that they're going into the back rooms, but to everyone on the street outside, they just look normal. Aren't we all like that really? Maybe hiding a little something behind our normal exteriors? Maybe being something that the outside world doesn't allow, something different, unusual, fascinating even?

I'm one of them now, too, aren't I?

My hand reaches the door and I gaze at my bracelet, his ownership of me, my marriage of sorts, to him. My other hand skims the diamonds at my throat, his throat, my ownership of him. We're so well interwoven, and if we can just let it all go and make that connection richer together, we'll be fine. I want to hear him in my thoughts more. I need that so much. I don't ever want to have to question his behaviour again or fathom the whys. I just want more of whatever that was in the room earlier. That conversation with them, that flowed inside of me, was fascinating, exhilarating, enthralling maybe, and so natural, in an utterly deviant way. I don't even have words for what that was, but I'm having more of it, and soon.

I'm just about to push on the door when it opens and two couples fall through, giggling and laughing as they go. They're so comfortable in their togetherness; perhaps they're a foursome? Perhaps they do this all the time? I giggle a bit at them and turn my way through the door to find Gage towering over me again. He nods at me, smiles, and then looks away again. It seems I've made a little progress in the doorman department.

Some nifty footwork later and I've managed to make my way back to Roxanne's apartment door. I look down at my dress, her dress. I should give this back really. However, having nothing else to wear, I ignore the thought and wander straight past it towards the exit. Alex will meet me there.

The foyer is empty, apart from a woman at the front desk, another immaculately dressed lady looking every inch the hostess with the mostest. She instantly reminds me of Belle with her perfectly done hair and her precision make-up so I dig around in my bag to find my phone and yelp out as my fingers find the knife at the bottom. Fuck. Pulling my hand out again, I inspect to see the damage my idiotic delving has caused. Nice, Beth. Well done. There's a small slice across my index finger, but apart from that, nothing too bad. I could almost laugh at myself really. I'm about to put myself in the hands of two sadists and I yelp like a dog at a small cut, one I've caused myself, for that matter.

Pathetic, Beth. Sort your shit out.

Carefully venturing into my bag again, I eventually find my phone and a tissue then go outside to the street to phone Belle. Christ knows what time it is but I need to tell her something because the barrage of texts from her don't sound best pleased with me. The cold air catches me by surprise and the shiver that rides straight across me sends a chill down my spine. Why don't I have a bloody coat? I need to toughen up, for God's sake. I don't know why I expected it to be warm near Christmas. Maybe it's because it was so hot inside. The burst of laughter that escapes my lips almost has me choking myself to death. Choking, choking on his cock – shit, he said that, didn't he? Even mentioned vomit. Wow, fuck me, that doesn't sound good.

"Hello? Hello? For fuck's sake, Beth, answer the fucking phone," my sister dearest interrupts my daydreaming, or squirming, as I try to wrap the tissue around my finger.

"Belle, yes, I'm here. Sorry, connection issues, I think."

"What utter bollocks. Daydreaming, are you? Where are you?"

"Still in New York. I've been with Alex and-"

"Oh my fucking God. What the hell is wrong with you? I thought you were coming home. Why aren't you home yet?"

"Calm down, Belle. You know I couldn't get home without a passport, and I needed to talk to him to get me home."

"So why are you still there. Honestly, Beth, go to the damn embassy. Or I'll send it to you. Give me an address."

"I don't need you to now. I'll get home with him."

"With him? How? Because if you mean *with him*, with him, then I swear to god I'm disowning you. I will not let you screw up your future with that bastard anymore. What a prick."

Oh god, how am I ever going to make her understand this? Even I don't understand this.

"How's Conner?"

"Gone, and don't change the fucking subject. What has he got over you, for fuck's sake?"

"What?"

"Shitface White."

"No not that. Did you say Conner has gone?"

"Yes, I got bored, and he was all 'have you heard from Beth? Is Alex okay?' Alex? Wanker. As if I give a shit about Alex. And you shouldn't either. So you-"

"Wait. What do you mean? Have you broken up with him?"

"What does that matter? I'm more concerned about you and getting your sorry backside home."

"Belle, you call him now and tell him you love him."

"Fuck off."

"Belle, I have no idea why you've let him go but you get him back. He loves you."

"Just like you think that dick loves you? Grow up, Beth. The man's an arsehole. They all are. He left you once and broke your heart, and now he's manhandled you out of your own country, kidnapped you for fuck's sake, leaving no ability for you to get home, and you still think he loves you? He's a fucking control freak. What the hell is going on in your head? You've been a disaster half the time you've been with him. He's an arrogant pig who needs chucking, immediately. I'm not watching you go through it again. Enough."

My hackles rose half way through that statement, not at her having a go at him – well, maybe a little – but more at the fact that she's right, isn't she? Every single word that's come out of her mouth is utterly correct. And yet I keep forgiving him, still keep wanting him to show me how much he loves me. Am I an idiot to feel like this? Should I just leave and be done with them?

I lean my back against the building wall and bang my head against it repeatedly in the hope that clarification might ensue. It doesn't. The fact is that when I'm with him, he makes it feel right, even when it's wrong. Yet the moment I speak to someone in the real world, I can see how bloody ridiculous I must seem, how bloody ridiculous this whole world must seem. There's no way anyone outside of this relationship could ever understand or comprehend what just happened in that room, or what we've been through so far, who he is, why he is, and there's no way I can explain it to them.

"Are you still there?" she says quietly.

"Yes." Just, my brain is still reeling with thoughts of how much he's hurt me before now. Visions fly through my mind of his hands on Tara, not listening when I screamed my safe word at him. I was so wounded, and so completely at his mercy. He did that to me, with ease. It doesn't even matter if I say I forgive him because it's still sitting inside me, nudging and reminding me what he's capable of, even if it might have been his random way of showing me something. I do hate him for that, no matter how much I love him. I hate him for making me carry this with me now, this underlying sense of nerves that he'll do it again.

"You need to let this go, Beth. He's no good for you. I know I said give it your all, but honestly, honey, the man's barking mad." No, he's not. He's different, yes, captivating, definitely, an overbearing idiot who needs a damn good slap, more than likely. But mad? Absolutely not.

"I can't, Belle. I don't expect you to understand why, but it's my choice. He's my choice. I'm a big girl now and I can handle him. And Conner is your choice. You said yes to him, and if you had the faintest clue what he's been through with Alex then you'd understand why he's protective of him, why he cares so much. Life is not so simple, Belle. It's not just black and white and fuck the rest, no matter how much you want to make it that way."

"What the hell is that supposed to mean?"

"I can't tell you. It's not my place to say anything, but Conner loves you, Belle. He adores you. Please don't throw that away because of me. Call him and tell him you love him, that you're sorry. If you have to ask him why Alex means so much, make him explain, and then perhaps you can fathom how I feel about him and why."

There's an awkward silence as I pinch at the cut on my finger and let the pain ease into me, just like I did at school, just like pushing on a bruise to strangely appreciate the sensation and revel in it. Squeezing it and then releasing, squeezing and releasing. I sigh as the pain dissipates.

"You're being stupid, Beth. Mark my words, he'll do it again. He'll break you until you're nothing but snot and tears and I won't pick you up again. Not this time. You should know better. Like you said, you're a big fucking girl. So this time you can damn well deal with it own your own."

The deadening of the line only mirrors her words. She's cut me off. She thinks I'm so ridiculous that she can't even be bothered to talk to me about it anymore.

I gaze down at the phone in my hand and keep squeezing my finger in some vague hope that she'll call back, but I know she won't. It's not her style. She's said her piece, and if I want her again, I'll have to crawl back to her for help. She'll be professional and work with her normal effective perfection, be civil even, but when it comes to emotions, she's just closed the door on me. Probably because she can't handle her own as well as mine, let alone deal with Conner's or Alex's.

I fucking hate him for making me do that to her and driving a wedge between us, because there's never been one there before. For all our differences, she's always been there to support me, look after me, help me, guide even. And now his actions have taken her from me, all because of his strange sense of normal.

Closing my eyes and sighing out another huge breath, I try to think of a way around all this. I just want everyone happy and settled. It's Christmas, for God's sake, and normal people are happy at Christmas. They giggle and drink and discuss fun times together while making new ones. They don't deal with all this crap and walk around with canes, pretending to be in control of something they're really not handling at all. Pascal's cane... Why have I got that? Why did he give it to me?

I scan the road in front of me and wonder what happens next. I need to get home. I need to get to Belle and try to explain so that she doesn't think I'm completely mental. My head is so not ready for them at the moment, not after that conversation.

Yellow cabs fly up and down the road, honking and blaring their horns as if it's perfectly acceptable to do that just to let someone know you're pulling out. It's nothing like London. There's no sense of reservation here. It's all loud and in your face. I hadn't noticed on the way over, but in these few quiet moments, I remember where I am. New York, New York. A city I've always wanted to visit, and now I'm here, and I can't help but wish I was happier about it. I wish I had come here on better terms and didn't feel the need to get away from it so quickly so I could make things right with Belle, see my mum maybe, do normal things.

It's all his fault.

Why didn't he just bloody talk to me, for fuck's sake?

"He didn't know how to get the point across effectively enough." My head lazily flops to the side to see him walking across to me and taking off his jacket. Strong, blue eyes search mine for the answers to questions he hasn't asked yet. "Your nose is blue," he says as he holds his jacket out to me.

"Did I say that out loud?" I must have, I suppose. I must look like a deranged idiot, chatting away to myself on the pavement. Or drunk

167

maybe. He nods and leans on the wall beside me as I shrug his warmth on. The cane gets in the way, so I tuck it between my legs and fidget about until I'm comfy again, crossing my arms to try and warm up.

"I wouldn't let him see that," he says as he grins down at my thighs clamped around the cane, the silver tip of it glinting in the moonlight. "Not until you're ready, anyway."

"Can I slap you?" The thought is so tempting.

"If you like."

"Several times?"

"If you like."

"Something more than 'if you like' would be good right now."

"What do you want me to say?"

"I don't know, Alex. I've just had an argument with Belle because of you, and I despise myself for that, and you. I don't know how to make everyone okay with this, any of it."

"I'll talk to her."

"You absolutely will not. Besides, she wouldn't speak to you anyway. I just need to get home and then I'll talk to her. Did you know she's broken up with Conner because of this?"

"No," he says as he hangs his head a little.

"Well, she has, and it's unforgiveable that we caused that. Have you even apologised for the last fuck up you made with him yet? That Caroline girl? And when you said he let you attack him, was that why he had bruising all over his face? Conner... Your *friend*, Conner? You know, right after you fucked all those other women?"

"Is this the telling off part?"

"Fuck off. You're such an arsehole sometimes."

"Yes, and I agree, but I still quite enjoy the telling off parts."

"This isn't funny. They're hurting, Alex, because of you. I'm hurting because of you. Are you going to hurt Pascal, too? Because for that to have happened in there, I can only assume he's told you he loves you, too. How did that happen? And are you really doing that collaring thing with him? Why?"

"We'll go home if that's what you want. You can talk to Belle and find a way to-"

"Why do you always do that? Deflect the conversation? Take some fucking responsibility for the pain you've caused, Alex, and just tell me the truth for God's sa-"

"If you gave me a fucking chance to finish, you would have heard the rest," he cuts in.

"What?"

"You can find a way to talk Belle into seeing me, and then I can explain my past. It might help her to understand." I'm gaping at him, and he's just standing there looking utterly beautiful as a slight shyness creeps across his eyes.

"You'd do that? You'd tell her about what happened to you?"

"For you, yes. If you think it's what she needs to hear."

"And Pascal? Conner?"

"Conner will be fine once he's got Belle back. And Pascal is for a better time than this, preferably somewhere warmer. It will be a long conversation, and I'll need a drink."

Talk of the devil.

A very relaxed looking Pascal wanders casually down the steps from the door in his pristine white suit, looking every bit the royalty he is, and immediately glances down at my thighs, which are still holding the cane between them.

"Elizabeth, my rose, really? That is entirely disrespectful of my superior status within this tryst of ours, and hazardously attractive. You should not be so brainless around me with it."

"What is your actual royal status?" It's out of my mouth before I know it. His brow arches as he drags his eyes back upwards and goes to light a cigarette.

"Not so brainless after all. And if you must know, I no longer have one, my rose. I declined it some years ago now."

"Declined? Why the hell would you decline it? Whatever it is?"

"For my brother. Fabrice was more worthy than I. It is something of a shame he no longer holds that accolade. However, I have no choice now, unless I kill him, which is still under consideration most of the time."

"But-" Alex cuts me off.

"Elizabeth, now is not the time," he says as he yanks the cane out from my legs and walks off down the road with it over his shoulder. "Pascal, are you relieved?"

"Mmm, quite thoroughly for now," he says quietly as he offers his hand to me and nods at Alex. I take it and wonder where the hell we're all going now.

"Pascal, are you coming home with us? What happens now, between the three of us, I mean?"

"Home? Hmm. I am unsure of his wants in this matter. We should define it after some nourishment. I find myself ravenous all of a sudden."

"Where's he going?"

"To the car, I assume."

"And then where?"

"You ask a lot of him, my rose. Why do you not just follow sometimes and let him lead you? It is his strength, is it not? You should question him only when the moment requires it, when he is being... difficult. Enjoy the peace he gives your mind in the meantime. It is quite rewarding." Peace? I stare over at him. Not much of that happening in there, if I'm honest.

"How are you at peace with him? He's so bloody confusing,"

"Not to me. He is perfection, and you bewilder yourself, my dear, with your morals and standards, and your infuriating decency. There is no room for anything but him. Do you not see? You must concentrate entirely on him, feel him, and absorb him into you. That is how I remain at peace with him."

"Bully for you."

"Che cosa ha detto?" The foreign words roll out of his mouth like they're second nature to him.

"What?"

"Italian for *what*? Do you not speak any other language? We shall correct that. Italian is a must, as is French. I am surprised he has not already taught you." Well, he wouldn't. It's the language he uses to hide things from me. I need to learn it in secret. "Dutch will come in time," he says, breaking my mini thought process.

"Is that the other language you speak? Dutch? You do that when you're irritated, don't you?"

"It is the mother tongue. We all revert to our roots when we are truly livid. Such anger requires no thought, only action. I rarely use it. There are only a few circumstances that condone such infuriation. You have been one of them." Oh...

We arrive at the car, which, of course, is a limo, to find the door open and a very relaxed looking Alex lounging inside with a paper. You know, just checking out the bloody broadsheets like you do after you've just been in that place, and done those things. I roll my eyes at him as I slide in and make myself comfortable. Pascal gets in behind me and sits across from us, so I fiddle with my finger and try to dab the still weeping blood off it.

"Put it inside yourself, my rose," he says. I lift my gaping mouth to see if I understood him correctly. He looks quite serious. "The blood, my dear. It will stop on contact with more palatable fluids. Is this not something everyone is aware of?" Alex chuckles and shuffles his paper about until he can grab hold of my finger as the car pulls away beneath us. I still have no idea where we're going.

"What did you do?"

"Sliced it on your knife."

"Hmm," is the only reply I get as he pulls my finger to his mouth and sucks on it. It's strangely erotic. Although if anyone in this car enjoyed the taste of blood, I would have assumed it would be the vampire sitting over there, not Alex.

"Were you a Count by any chance?" My own amusement at my Dracula reference has me giggling instantly as I stare over at him.

"I was, yes." Hysterics ensue. I can't believe the coincidence if I'm honest, and the perplexed look now plastered across his face only furthers my laughter. God, it feels good to laugh. When was the last time I did that, just laughed and relaxed?

"Why is this so amusing?" I'd reply if I could, but I can only sputter air in between my laughter. And Alex is now also looking at me with a bemused look on his face, having let go of my injured digit. I eventually find the wherewithal to collect myself and gaze over at him, still with a smile and occasional giggle.

"Well?"

"I thought maybe you were a vampire. When we first met, you were all Edwardian, with long hair, and the club was such an eye opener. You know, chivalrous and devilish, snappy teeth, weird abilities to read minds and make me do things I didn't want to do. I was only just beginning to get my head around him, and then you, well I couldn't fathom you at all. That morning in the kitchen, when you..." I instantly cut myself off at the thought of what happened next. That dance was highly erotic and absolutely not allowed, I'm sure.

"When he what, Elizabeth?" Alex asks from my side, his tone cool, but I can hear his question, and it has nothing to do with what

171

actually happened. It has more to do with whether I'm going to tell the truth, where my loyalty lies, so to speak. Pascal smirks, and I'm glad he finds it funny. I have no idea what to do.

"Umm..." It's all I've got. I no longer have any clue as to whom I should be honest with. If I tell the truth, will Pascal get in trouble? Will I? I should lie, shouldn't I? Make up some random other story. *Think quick, Beth.*

"I believe she is trying to protect me, Alexander. You had made it quite difficult for me to behave fittingly that morning with your antics the previous night. Her moaning and screaming had me quite dishevelled, and you allowed her to wander around half-naked in my company. It was unwise of you," Pascal says as he pours himself a drink and holds up the decanter to Alex. Well, at least he was honest.

"You touched her?"

"Yes, it was glorious, quite enlightening," he replies with no remorse whatsoever. This could get ugly. I shrink away into the seat and bite my finger. It's the only thing I can do to break my own tension. Fucking stupid, stupid, stupid. I should keep my mouth closed, permanently.

"Why? I told you not to."

"Alexander, look at her. You took her to my club in an almost transparent dress, with a cuff on, and those perfect collarbones on display for me. You chose that dress, didn't you? Hmm? You knew where you were taking her and chose it anyway. Did you not think I would try my luck at some point? You should have seen her ferreting around in your cupboards, quite exquisite in her natural state," he says as he fills a glass for Alex and passes it to me. "Hold that, my dear. He may beat me in a moment." I snatch it off him and recede back to the safety of the seat. "I wanted to know how loyal she was, whether she could be turned, and I wanted to know what speciality she offered without you being there to guide her out of my appraisal. One dance was enough. She neither fought me nor accepted me. It was refreshingly fascinating."

"You disobeyed me," Alex snarls as he folds his paper and leans forward a little, his size seemingly increasing as he does so. Oh god, what have I done?

"Yes, and I will continue to do so if it is for your own benefit," Pascal replies as he leans away and takes a sip of his drink. "Do not concern yourself with the outcome. I can assure you she wouldn't have gone through with it had I pushed her." Really? I'm not so sure. It was him who twirled me away if I remember rightly. I didn't stop anything.

"That's not the point, Pascal, and you know it. Had I wanted you to share her, she would have been offered at the time." My head snaps to his. How dare he assume I would have done that? Even if I might have, that's not the point at all. He doesn't even look at me, just continues staring at Pascal, who somehow still manages to look completely unaffected by Alex's harsh tone and size as he lounges on his chair and smirks again.

"You amuse me, Alexander, with your puzzlement. It makes you all the more appealing. If you didn't want to share her, why did you let me hear her scream? Hmm? Did you want me in there with you that night? Ice, wasn't it? Come here, my Rose. I'll show him now," he replies as he delves his hand into an ice bucket. Images fly through my brain of the time in his limo after I'd run from them – his hands on me, his distinctive grasp, unlike Alex's. Oh god, I'm drooling at the thought. The clinking of the ice bucket brings me back to reality as I watch Alex grab an ice cube and hold it out to Pascal.

"Open your mouth," he says quietly. What the hell is going on now? Pascal leans forward and does just that until Alex shoves the cube between his teeth. "Don't let it melt." What? Pascal just relaxes back again and still manages to smile while holding onto the ice cube.

"Umm... not sure that's possible," I interject, sarcastically.

"No, but it will shut him up for a while at least, stop more of that incessant intelligence pouring from his lips. Why didn't you tell me about what happened?" Shit.

"I... Well, I... It's difficult. He's difficult, and I didn't want you getting angry about what happened. He's right. Nothing happened, not really. Well, that's not entirely true, I suppose." *Honesty, Beth. Just be honest.* "You know what he's like, and he... We... Okay, I wanted him, even then. It stopped, but I don't know if I wanted it to. You can't put a girl in front of him. It's seriously not a safe thing to do." A chuckle emanates from the other side of the car. It's vampiric to say the least. I narrow my eyes at Pascal as Alex takes his drink from my hand.

"Hmm, so you're telling me that even at that early stage, before you really knew anything, you would have fucked him?" Christ, does he have to be so blunt?

"Yes, I... uh, yes, if you'd have asked, I suppose looking back on it now, I would have, maybe."

"Interesting," he replies. That's it, nothing else to give away how he's feeling about the fact that I just said I'd have screwed his friend when we started dating.

That's not normal, is it?

But the hand that's suddenly on my thigh and gripping tightly is very normal indeed. Pascal chuckles again and looks down at my legs while mumbling something through his teeth. I'm not sure what it is but it sounded very much like 'won't be owned by anyone' to me.

I have no idea what he's talking about.

Chapter 13

Elizabeth

We've been on the plane home for about six hours. We drove straight here from the club because it appears Alex was very serious about making this right with Belle and Conner. Apparently, it's important that I'm okay with her because, and I quote: *"You need to be ready to concentrate."*

I can only assume by that he's referring to that concentration thing I did at the auction, and then when he took me to Pascal's office. He's right, to be honest, because the only thing that keeps flying through my head is worry for whether Belle is okay. Well, that and him screwing other women – that little vision isn't leaving me any time soon, it seems. I know she may seem to the rest of the world like the biggest bitch alive but I know her better than that. She will be in pain about Conner. I've tried phoning her again but she won't pick up. She's clearly refusing to budge on the topic and I can't say I blame her, but I still wish she would. I just want her to understand. Even if I don't quite get it myself, I need to know that she accepts this, that it's part of me now. She wanted me to get out there a bit more, and that's what I've done. Okay, maybe this is a bit more than she thought I'd be delving into, but I am stronger now because of this. I am more aware of who I am and what I need. I have a good business, which should be moving into a new building very shortly, and a good man. Well, not a good man, but one I love nonetheless, and one who I know loves me, in his own way. I know he'd kill for me, I know he'll always protect me, and I know he'll be there with me as long as I want him. I know these things in my core somehow. They're like a part of me now, swirling around inside and creating a bond I never knew was possible. There's no denying or running from this anymore because we're like a force of nature together, a storm and a silver lining that flit between light and darkness. So comfortable, and yet so on edge as we continue to lose ourselves in each other and drift in and out of differing realities, to find our balance together, so I can help him, and he can guide me, over and over again. No matter how much I may dislike who he's been or what he's done, he is mine. Mine. He means it when he says he won't leave me. His own set of standards wouldn't offer that lightly unless he meant every single word. It's like having my own personal Mafia guard, who happens to want me to screw other men, too, and be in love with him. I'm to show him those emotions he's never had before and accept everything that comes out of his mouth unless I disagree. Then I'm to fight him. Simple really.

I don't know why I've found it so confusing before now. I just need to shake off some of my own lingering thoughts regarding the mayhem that is his past and all will be perfect. I'm positive it will be.

I've been sitting here most of the journey, dozing in and out of sleep and watching them both together. Neither of them have slept, only proving my point that Pascal is indeed *Count Dracula*, and Alex is some sort of demigod, maybe because I couldn't keep my eyes open two minutes after entering the plane. They've been more relaxed than I've ever seen them, as if they've found some sort of peace together that they've never found before. I haven't even asked them to explain it because I can see it as plain as day. Pascal is home, like being here with Alex is everything he's ever wanted, and Alex clearly feels like he has nothing to prove anymore. There isn't one ounce of a barrier in between them now. In fact, the only thing that is confusing either of them, I think, is me. I must be a conundrum to be worked out between them, a mystery of how this should work, who does what, to whom, when? Giggling to myself at the thought, I ponder if I should make their decisions for them – if maybe I should be the one to initiate something and see how that flows. Pascal clearly isn't allowed to, and Alex seems hesitant to for some reason.

I'm just building up to the idea when I realise I need a shower before I even entertain it. I need to scrub away the rest of this weekend and just relax. I feel like I've been in the same clothes for a bloody lifetime, and the plane is bringing back too many memories of Tara, who thankfully isn't on the plane. There's a very shy thing called Amy here instead. I'm surprised she hasn't joined the mile high club by now, to be honest, because Mr. Van Der Braack has been incredibly suggestive as Alex has looked on and chuckled. Never once has he joined in, though. He just keeps walking past me and brushing his fingers over my choker, reminding me that he's here for me, only for me.

"We're about twenty minutes out, Sir," Amy says as she scoots past Pascal's fingers for the hundredth time, clearly trying to remain professional. I don't know why she's bothering. We're all obviously completely deviant and neither of us would mind in the slightest if he screwed her, but I suppose it is nice to remember that some people aren't. There's not a hint of jealousy either, not from Alex or I. It's like a conversation we've all somehow had without mentioning it, that Pascal will still be able to continue being exactly who he has been with no interference from us.

I know I won't have another woman in the room with us, but I wouldn't stop him doing whatever he wants elsewhere. And given that Alex is still not gay – well, I assume he's not – he certainly won't be stopping him getting out there and doing whatever the hell he wants with anyone, which suddenly has me questioning the one thing I hadn't thought of at all.

"Umm, Pascal?" He swings his head round from the sofa and smiles softly. It's so very lovely when he does that. I could almost swoon. Alex continues with his chess game and frowns at the board.

"Yes, my Rose? What do you need me for?" That was so loaded.

"Well, umm..." I can't believe I'm even partially nervous talking about this, given the circumstances between us all. "Umm... Condoms?" He pulls three out of the inside of his jacket instantly.

"Who are you doing first? And really, you could have asked earlier. We are somewhat pushed for time now."

"Tests," Alex says opposite him, still frowning, although why he doesn't counter with his bishop, I have no idea.

"Ah, never fear, my rose. God here has made it abundantly clear that I am to be thoroughly poked and invaded before I indulge in you. It should be amusing if nothing else. I'm quite partial to that small, brown haired youngster that hovers around me at the clinic."

"Is that why we haven't-"

"Yes," Alex cuts in. Oh, right. And on that note, did he have tests done after that expulsion of aggression with those women? Because I might need to have some done if he didn't.

"Did you have -"

"Yes, Elizabeth. Would you like to see the file?" Arrogant bastard.

"Would you like to move your fucking bishop?" I snap in reply. I can be a smart arse, too, and I'm still not entirely happy about him having sex with other women.

"My bishop is becoming confused about whose bishop we are currently discussing," Pascal says as he looks at me and smirks.

"Both of your bishops," I reply, irritated, as I cross my arms and stare at Alex. I'm having another conversation about that at some point. It might not mean a great deal to him but it bloody well does to me.

"My bishop is flawless, and so is his as far as I'm aware. Actually, perhaps you should let me inspect it for you, Alexander."

"Pascal, shut up."

"My rose, will you please explain to this man how thoroughly tempting I am. I was hoping this -" he waves his hands around in a circle, "-*thing* might involve me actually attaining him at some point, preferably with his bishop involved."

Alex doesn't move, aside from a slight eyebrow lift as he continues studying the board, so I stare at his mouth and wonder how he feels about that. Does he want that? He always said he didn't, but now, looking at the two of them, I'm really not so sure. And oddly, I'm strangely comfortable with the idea.

He lifts his hand to move something and then licks his lips and replaces it in his lap again, almost as if he's questioning his thoughts on the topic rather than the chessboard. He's confused, and my heart thaws a little at the thought. That little boy in the rain keeps coming back up again to haunt him, doesn't it? Showing him he's not God after all, not quite as in control as he thinks.

I smile to myself and realise that this is nowhere near as clean cut as he would like me to believe, and that maybe Mr White is out of his depth, that maybe he hasn't gotten his head around this as much as I have, even though I don't actually know what's going to happen. Maybe I'm just more relaxed about the whole thing now I've accepted it. Or maybe it's just that I don't know any better and therefore nothing is too alarming yet. Either way, my body and mind are comfortable with this, as if fighting it, or over thinking it before just made it more difficult to comprehend. Now it just seems, well, almost normal to me somehow. Just an extension of what was before, now that we're all playing ball instead of hedging around the topic.

"You're smiling, Elizabeth. Is something amusing?" Alex says as he eventually lifts his hand and moves that bishop. "Check mate."

"I just think Pascal is definitely tempting, Alex. And as you've asked, I'll voice my opinion on the matter, in case you're confused about anything." He smirks a little in reply and wanders over to his seat for landing, still looking unfairly attractive in that black suit, with that ruffled, tired look.

"Clever girl," he says quietly as he sits opposite me and reaches forward to tug harshly on my belt. I wince a little in response and sit up straighter. "Don't be too smart for your own good, though, will you? You could get into all sorts of precarious situations."

"What on earth do you mean?" I feign an innocent voice. Flirtation has nothing on me, it seems.

"I haven't kissed you yet," he says, dead pan, not a hint of humour as I smile back and let myself melt into those eyes again. They're cool at the moment, light and airy, like a weight has been lifted from his shoulders now that he has me next to him again. "I haven't kissed you since we took off for New York."

"I'm not sure you deserve a kiss. I am still a little on the pissed off side of happy."

"I'm quite sure I don't deserve anything at all, but I'll be taking it the moment we're alone nonetheless."

"Right, well, I'll consider that then."

"I can watch you fuck, fuck her myself, but not watch you kiss her?" Pascal cuts in as he makes his way to his chair, still looking just as bloody good as Alex in a different way, although he's in a white suit instead. Blue, green, black, white. They're both beautiful in very different ways, bodies different, skin tone different, hands, fingers, gait, voice. As I watch Pascal tapping his thigh, I raise my eyes up to meet his. They're devilish again, harsh even, utterly intoxicating and dirty as hell. I tilt my head to try and hear his voice inside my head like I did at the club. What does he want? What's he asking for with those eyes?

"No," Alex replies, breaking me from my lust-driven daze. My head snaps back to him in an instant. His tone is firm all of a sudden, angry even, and I'm not at all sure why because he's watched us before, hasn't he? It shouldn't be a problem in the slightest.

"Alexander, really, what are you going to do? Pop in and out of the room naked for a linger of romance behind closed doors before you bring her back to me for another beating. My dear boy, you have not thought this through at all, have you? Elizabeth, do you mind if I watch you?"

Alex is out of his seat and towering over Pascal before I know what's happened, eyes of steel locked on as he glares down at him in fury. I can see the tension radiating out of him, as if another word uttered from Pascal's mouth might well drive him to cause some serious damage. Within seconds, Pascal has dropped his gaze and his frame to the floor in front of him. It looks so odd, Pascal down there. It's strange, and my eyes widen as Alex stares at him until those eyes deaden. I've seen them that way before, and felt them in all their might, so I suck in a breath and hope to hell Pascal just stays put, even if I don't like it much.

"Lower," he says. It's clearly a command, because just like Tara, Pascal's forehead is pressed into the carpet immediately. Two more minutes like this and eventually I watch as Alex's frame softens very slightly, just an inch of relaxation as his shoulders drop a touch. This is clearly my chance to intervene. His lip curls at me. Maybe not. Oh, this is ridiculous. We're supposed to be happy in this, aren't we? We're supposed to be comfortable with each other, learning each other. I unclip my belt to stand, but the sudden glare that's directed at my face has my arse planted immediately back in place. "Stay still, Elizabeth."

"But..." I hear a grunt of pain that has me glancing down at Pascal to find Alex's shoe on the side of his face, now pushing it into the floor even more. It's so wrong, to see him down there, to see him in pain and taking it. My throat constricts at the vision, part annoyed, part terrified, and part confused again. Why? "Alex, let him up." He just continues to stare at me, eyes now lost again to his other place as I hear another wince beneath us and watch his mouth rise into that deadly smile.

"Why?" he eventually replies. My mouth gapes because I have no idea why, other than the fact that it's not very nice, and this isn't normal. "Endure, Elizabeth. Just stay down. His leash is being clipped."

He turns his head from me, effectively finishing my involvement in the conversation, and stares down at Pascal again.

"What have you learned from this?" he asks Pascal as he continues to glower and squashes his cheekbone again.

"Never to question you, Sir," is the instant reply. My eyes widen at his submission – no come back, no typical Pascal naughtiness, just an immediate answer. I'm not sure how I feel about it at all, but I stay still just as he's asked and assume there's some reason for it I'm absolutely not aware of.

"And?" Alex growls again, that voice of his now low and aggressive.

"To always call you Sir, Sir." Alex's foot lifts away gently as he takes a small step forward and reaches his hand towards me, wiggling his fingers. I have no idea what he wants, so I just stare at his hand.

"Cane, Elizabeth," he snaps. "Get up, Pascal." I'm not sure what he's about to do, but I'm a lot more comfortable with the vision of white getting to his feet again so I pass the cane to Alex and narrow my eyes at what's to come. Pascal keeps his eyes very firmly on the floor; whether it's out of fear or submission, I don't know, but my body is primed for throwing myself in between them if this kicks off. After what feels like an eternity of staring, Alex eventually smiles again as those lighter eyes come racing back. "Lift your chin." Pascal does, but there's not a hint of humour or amusement in his expression. He is humble and ready to do exactly what Alex says, take whatever he decides to deliver. They stare again until Alex lifts the cane to Pascal's throat. "Grip it until I tell you to let it go." Pascal drops his chin again to grasp it to his neck, and with that, Alex turns and straps himself back into his chair.

"What...?" Yes, it's out of my mouth before I know it. The raised brow stops me in my tracks. It's his don't piss me off, too, face. The one he uses just before he launches, and while my groin might be asking for it, my brain very definitely is not, given his strange mood all of a sudden. I keep my mouth closed as he points at the other chair, and Pascal turns to sit in it, still gripping his own cane under his chin, perfectly.

"Have a drink," Alex says to me quietly as he looks out of the window and frowns a little. I tighten my belt again and raise my drink to my lips as I gaze at him and wonder what the hell that was all about.

181

I suppose there will be odd goings on between us, but did he need to be so vicious about it? And what's with the holding the cane thing? Is this a time for me to be fighting him or accepting his will? God knows, and the fact that Pascal is unharmed is clearly a bonus, so I decide to just let it go while I keep watching him. "Why do you question me?"

"What? I haven't said a word. I was just thinking."

"Your silence is louder than an order, Elizabeth. You want me to go easy on him, don't you? Want me to let this evolve naturally?" he says as he turns those piercing eyes on me and asks me to drop my gaze. I can feel that, too, now, that small difference between challenging him and being told to do something that's necessary. But he's right, I do want this to happen naturally. I can't see how it'll work any other way, so I stare back in a semi challenge and hope it's the right thing to do. "I won't do that, not even for you. I have my reasons for what's happening. You'll understand why eventually."

"Okay," I reply, because halfway through that, he pinched his brow and sighed. It showed me just how confused he is, too, how he's trying to do the right thing in his own way, perhaps trying to guide us all down a path that we'll just have to trust him on. And as he's said before, he's the dominant in the room. There's certainly no room for three of us.

"Okay?" he repeats in surprise.

"Okay, Alex. Just do it honestly and I'll trust you," I reply as I close my eyes and rest my head back. Another vision of him fucking women assaults me. I'll clearly never sleep well again. "I still don't like that you screwed other women, though. I'm pretty pissed about that. And we are having a conversation about your past. There are things I need to understand."

"Hmm," he responds cryptically. I don't reply as I doubt I'll be getting another apology, and I know I'll get that conversation from him at some point when we're all a little more rested, but I just know it's going to be okay regardless. We'll make it this time, won't we? Now that we're being honest and there's no need to hide anything, we'll be fine.

We'll all be fine.

~

"Belle, we need to talk about this."

I'm shouting at her bedroom door, but it appears no amount of me lowering my tone, being nice or generally trying to work things out is making her any more likely to come out of her room.

I got back about an hour ago, and the moment I put my keys in the lock to the apartment, I heard her door slam. So, after staring at the door for a few minutes, I decided on a shower and some comfy clothes in the hope that it might give her time to settle down. Apparently it hasn't, and I'm just about ready to give up and go back to Alex's, or boot the bloody door in. My eye catches the vodka set up on the kitchen surface, and I stomp over to it in the hope that a quick shot of the revolting stuff might calm my irritation. No good will come of me being overly defensive, and if I've any hope of making this right, I've got to tread gently with her. Alex will be on the phone with Conner by now, or maybe even at his place. I don't know. He said he'd talk to him and see if there's anything he can do to help. Where Pascal went off to, I have no idea, but when his driver picked him up at the airport, he was last seen getting into his car, still with the cane at his throat. Alex had stared at the car until he couldn't see it anymore, and then chuckled to himself. Something was funny, it seemed, but what it was I don't know because he wouldn't tell me when I asked. He just waved his hand at the car and asked me if I wanted a ride home or not. And then there was the Andrews thing to deal with – he who smiled and called me ma'am. Arsehole. He so knows I'm angry with him. I snarled a little and didn't reply to him, because regardless of whatever this has all been about, I'm not happy with him at all. I'm sure it will pass, but I thought I could trust him to help me out of random 'Alex' situations, and now I don't think I can. I understand Alex is his boss, but I thought he was my friend of sorts, that he would back me up if I needed help. Maybe he still will. I don't know, but I do know that I won't be relying on him for a while. We didn't even go back to Alex's. He just asked Andrews to drive us straight here so that I could deal with Belle. How I'm going to deal with her, though, I haven't got a clue. I just need to try and tell her the truth, or at least a version of it that she'll be able to accept somehow.

I swipe the vodka and glass, pour a double shot and down it as fast as I can. It still tastes revolting, and as my face screws up in disgust, I feel the burn hitting my throat and cough out the feeling as I put the glass down again. Good god, why does she like it? And how the hell am I going to get her out of her room?

Sudden inspiration hits me as I consider having another drink. Lord knows I deserve one.

"Come out here and have a fucking drink, you coward," I shout as loudly as I can. That'll piss her off. If there's one thing she's not, it's a coward. I hear nothing in response, no sound or movement at all, so I decide to try again. "Belle, hiding in there like a fourteen-year-old is not going to solve anything. You're supposed to be the big sister here and you're acting like a fucking child. Get your backside out here, now!" Still nothing... I pour another drink.

Having drunk two more double shots, I find myself feeling particularly drunk and collapse into the sofa for some much needed comfort. The room spins a little as I try to focus on the green wall by her doorway. Memories of walking the dogs when we were younger enter my brain from somewhere, and I giggle to myself at the thought of us both getting wrapped up in the dog leads when they went hurtling off after a rabbit or something. Long, gangly legs and red hair flew in every direction as we tried to untangle ourselves from the mess we'd gotten ourselves into, and she shouted at me because it was my fault. It had been. She'd told me repeatedly to keep the leads from crossing over each other so if anything went wrong, we'd be able to control the dogs separately.

Separately.

Keeping them on their own leashes and separate from each other.

Untangled. Not getting yourself into a mess. Keeping them separate.

Alex. Pascal.

My mind whirls again as I begin to question what the hell I'm doing. More vodka, that's what I'm doing. I scramble my way back up, and rather than try to walk, I succumb to crawling because I'm quite good at that, aren't I? Ridiculous it may be, but it gets me to the vodka safely, where I manage another triple shot of the stuff and sit on the floor to sip at it. It's now got that 'not quite so bad' taste about it, and I'm pretty sure after this one, it'll have that 'can't taste a fucking thing' going on that I'm hoping for. My confusion over why I'm actually drinking it only fuels my confusion over why the hell I'm here and not in Alex's bed, because that's where I want to be, letting him touch me again and remind me about us, letting him put his hands in all those familiar places and show me that this is going to be alright, that we're going to be alright, that we can make this work regardless of his past. Killer he may, be but I love him. I need him. Fuck, I need this to work. I can't do it again, not like before. I can't deal with him having strange moods and kidnapping me, and not knowing who the hell he is. I just need to keep that connected feeling and be one with him. I need to feel him in my bones and understand what he needs before he does. We had it in that room, all three of us, that bond of total understanding and acceptance. I want that back. I want that comfort and safety back. Now. I don't want to be somewhere I'm not wanted, not accepted for being just who I need to be, who I want to be. And I'm certainly not going to be judged by someone who has no clue what real love is all about, who won't even give someone like Conner a chance at happiness because she's still too messed up over a man who has long since left her. Yes, he was a monster, but she needs to get over her fucking self-righteous attitude and grow up. Life goes on. Life is complicated. People are strange and unusual. We all have our problems and issues, but we find a path to happiness and we grab it with both hands to make sure it stays close, safe and happy.

What the hell am I doing here?

Taxi. Yes, a taxi is required, I think. I crawl my way over to my bag and dig out my phone. I could call Andrews, the twat, but he's probably driving his boss around being all subservient with his 'yes sirs' and 'no sirs'. What an arsehole. If I could hit him, I probably would.

"Shit, fuck!" I hear my own voice saying in my mindless fuddle as I feel the blade slice through my finger again. For fuck's sake, could I be any more ridiculous? Mafia wife material I am not. I need to give this bloody thing back. Why he ever thought I needed it is still a bloody mystery. I pull my finger out to find another cut about two inches below the last one. I stick it in my mouth to try and stop the bleeding, because according to Pascal, sticking it inside myself will achieve this. I'm still not sure which hole he meant if I'm honest. Three slightly blurred taps at my phone later and I think I'm calling a taxi when her door finally opens. All I can see is feet, with a very nice shade of blue nail varnish on, kind of like Alex's eyes really. I stare at them for a while in the hopes of getting some cognitive function back for the battle that's surely coming in the next few minutes.

"Calling the dick, are you?" she says as the feet wander off in the direction of the kitchen. If I had control of my eyeballs, I'd roll them.

"No, taxi. I'm leaving," She can sod off with her holier-than-thou attitude.

"Hello, hello, Ching tong Szechuan," a voice sings into my ear. Fuck it, wrong number. I hastily end the call and stare back at my phone again, hoping for some miracle to save me from my idiotic, fumbling attempts.

"Well, I'm ready for a fucking drink now," she says. Really? What utter joy this will be.

"Right," I respond as I try to get myself together and aim my face towards hers. It feels like the first time I've seen her in weeks, and all of the pain and anguish come racing back to me. The whole nightmare hits me in an instant: Tara, kidnapping, screwing other women, Conner's face covered in bruising, murdering people. My heart instantly screams at me with undiluted emotion, every piece of which I've been trying to hide, push to the back of my mind and pretend doesn't matter. It all reminds me how much he's hurt me, how much I'm not the in-control person I need to be. My stomach turns at the thought that I can't do this. I can't be what he needs. I'm not strong enough for him, let alone them. One look in her eyes and I can see the fire he needs, and I haven't got it. That look that she wears permanently is the type of woman he needs, the type of woman who can dismiss emotions and simply be, with no thought to the whys. She wears it so easily, like she's owned it since she was born, that natural ability to shine her way through any situation and hold her own against any enemy. I know it's because of Marcus. I know he made her this way, but it just sits so comfortably on her now. How does she keep that up? How does she continue to be so strong all the time?

"Why are you so good at that?" I mumble. She picks up her full glass of vodka and sits on a stool at the counter, still just staring, obviously thinking about how to respond.

"What?" she eventually replies. I sniff back my ridiculous impending tears and shake my head in the hope of sorting my shit out.

"Being all strong and stuff. Staying strong," I reply as I heave myself back toward the sofa.

"I don't put up with shit. I did that once, and he hit me for it. I won't do it again."

It's all she appears to want to say on the matter and I can't say I blame her. I saw the bruising, witnessed the after affects, and watched her turn into someone new overnight, someone who would never let that happen to her again. I wish I had just an ounce of that ability, to be able to turn into everything I need to be to be one hundred percent happy with what's happening in my life.

"Are you happy, though?" I ask as I put my drink down and hear her sigh. She walks over towards me and sits in a chair opposite me.

"Happy? Depends on what you consider happiness. My conscience is clear, my mind is at peace most of the time and I'm comfortable with who I am. Business is good, and I have a great family, even when my sister is being a stupid cow. Is that what you mean?" I chuckle a little at her and tuck my feet up under me. At least we're talking again. It's a good start, I suppose. She smiles a little but keeps her eyes fixed on mine. She's not finished by a long shot.

"Everything you said was right to some degree, but I love him, Belle. And no matter what you say in here, I will still love him tomorrow. I can't begin to explain to you the whys but I need you to accept him. I need you to accept *us*. This is it for me. He makes me happy. I'm not like you. I can't just breeze through life and pretend not to feel, not to need someone."

"You can, Beth. I chose to do it, so you can, too. You can choose to leave him, choose to find someone who will treat you like a princess and look after you for the rest of your life,"

"But he will, Belle. That's what he wants. It's what I want. Just because he had a rough start in life and is confused about some stuff, it doesn't mean I should abandon him, or us, does it? I get that you don't understand it, and if I could make you see the reasons why he makes me feel what he does, I would, but-"

"Beth, stop. Stop. Do you realise how much I loved Marcus? Do you know how he felt like a part of me? How every morning when I woke up, after his last attempt at control, I made myself sick because I couldn't bear not to feel his skin on mine, no matter how fiercely? I wanted that more than you can imagine, regardless of how bad he was for me. Don't think I don't know how you feel. I do. I'm trying to save you from feeling like I do now. How I felt then was nothing compared to how I feel now. I feel fucking empty most of the time. I just want you to truly be happy, be able to live your life with no fear of uncertainty or stupid dramatics. To be able to wake up every day and get the same man in your bed, one you trust with your life, with your children's lives. I will never have that because of what I've been through. I will never trust enough for that – never give it a chance, and we both know it. You can. You can go and find a good man, and you can let your feelings guide you, but you can't with him. He will rip you apart. He already is doing, isn't he? And while that will make you stronger, it will also turn you into me. Heartless and cold – that's what you'll need to be and you know it, don't you?" It's all true, and I think I already am in some ways.

"So you're not happy then, are you?"

"I'm content."

"That's not happy, Belle. What about Conner? He makes you happy, doesn't he? You said yes. You said you'd marry him." I quickly scan her finger, and there's no ring. "Why would you send him away?"

"Whatever may have been isn't important anymore. I've made my choice. I chose, so stop trying to make me better because there's nothing wrong with me."

Really? The somewhat drunken sigh that leaves my body at her abrupt tone and clear ending of the conversation is only furthered by my complete inability to stay upright anymore. I've drunk far too much vodka. I roll back down onto the sofa and stare at the ceiling, trying to find some way to make this all okay again. Her happy, me happy, Conner happy, Alex happy. There really isn't any way when she's in this mood. There's no way to make her understand or even forgive any sort of strange behaviour. Alex is my only hope this time. If he can make her listen then maybe we've all got a hope, but I really don't envy him the task. I turn my head towards her to find her fidgeting with her ring finger and looking blankly at the wall. She's so not done with Conner yet.

"He wants to talk to you," I say quietly.

"Who?"

"Alex." I say even quieter for fear of her biting my face off or something. Her head snaps up and anger flares across her face again.

"Does he now? And how do you think that's going to help? His poor little boy fucking blue story won't mean anything to me, Beth. I'm tired of picking you up when he fucks up. Can't you see how wrong he is for you? What on earth do you think he can say to make me trust him with your life again?"

That he'd kill for me, that I'm wearing his collar around my neck, not that she'll have a clue what that means. That he'll give me the world and his emotions for my acceptance of him and his past... Surely she'll understand that. That ability to be honest about your whole life, about all the hurt and pain that you took and know that someone actually loves you, really loves you and still does even after the bad things you've done. She might get it if he explains that. She didn't go through half as much as he did and look how it's made her. She's got to understand when he tells her. She'll have to see why he's the way he is.

"He has things to say, Belle. Just let him explain himself, please? You might have a clue about the whys then because I can't tell you. I won't. And if we can't make this work together, I'm going to have to make some choices I really don't want to make. Please don't make me do that."

She stares at me for a long time, long enough that I can see her realising what I'm saying, that if it's a choice between him and her, I might well take him. That's how much this means to me, and it does because I can still feel him in me, I can still feel him swirling around and pulling me towards him as if I have no choice.

She slips herself off the seat and wanders back towards her bedroom, so I watch her and hope she's going to make the right choice. *Please make the right choice.*

"Okay, Beth," I hear as she closes the door behind her.

Okay.

Chapter 14

Alexander

"**W**hat do you mean he's been having dinner with my sister? When? Where?"

He watched the back of Andrews' head on the drive and narrowed his eyes. What was the woman up to? First she was looking into his accounts and now she was having dinner with Aiden Phillips. Fuck. Didn't she get enough of a show at the charity ball?

"I have video surveillance of them entering Tudors together."

"Without Amira, or Cecily?"

"Yes, just the two of them. He met her at the door and walked her in. They spent two hours doing something and then she left, alone," Andrews replied efficiently, with no other emotion involved in the statement. "I followed her back to her apartment where she stayed for the rest of the evening."

He was so close to making the man turn the damn car in the other direction. Driving towards Conner's was the last thing he wanted to be doing anyway, let alone now that he had a situation with his new-found family member to deal with. At least he could talk to Conner about that, too, he supposed.

"Is there anything else to report?"

"Mary's left for Christmas. She left you a present. The security on the east wing has had an overhaul, as you asked. The safe room has been upgraded. I have got some more intel on Aiden, but nothing more than we already knew really. If he's after you, it's all in his head, and as for the other dick and the photos, no, nothing." Two more turns and they'd be pulling up to Conner's apartment. He sucked in a breath and reached for the cognac. He was going to need it. At least the fact that he had Elizabeth back made this worthwhile. "Jacobs has been playing well in his field as far as I'm aware, no other deals of any significance or related to you, and Henry Deville has been quiet. He's just been organising his party from what I can see. "

If he was honest, the only piece of information that had sunk in was the part about his sister, and the thought of a possible betrayal. His mind was consumed with family and what that meant to him now. Conner, Elizabeth, Evelyn, and now Pascal – his family. He had a family and responsibilities to fulfil.

"When you drop me off at Conner's, go and get Ms. Peters and take her back to mine. I'll deal with her later. Find Pascal and tell him to leave her alone." That was all he had to say on the matter. He had some thinking to do, but first he had a friend to apologize to and some emotions to make some fucking sense of.

"You think he'll listen to me?" Andrews replied, astounded. It was a fair point.

"Tell him I told you so. He'll listen now." He'd better, although a good beating might be exactly what he needed to do by the time he got home.

The car pulled up at Conner's, so he downed the last of his drink and stepped out into the afternoon sun. It was warmer here than it was in New York. It was drizzling with rain, obviously, but the air had that smoggy, muggy feeling about it. He yanked at his collar to try and get some air and then chuckled to himself at the feeling. It was nothing to do with the weather. He was nervous. She'd have told him if she was there.

Walking towards the entrance to Conner's home felt like the long walk on death row – the Green Mile, he thought they called it. Only this mile was blue, and waiting for him. Every footfall felt full of lead, full of that emotion rising up inside him and telling him to go backwards, to trace his steps back to the car and head toward his angel instead, or Pascal, but not Conner. This was going to be painful, possibly physically, definitely mentally. He turned his head and watched the *Bentley* pull away. Fuck. The phone call had been bad enough, but the meeting was going to be ten times harder.

The man on the door pulled it open and waved him through, not surprising given the amount of times he'd been there, so he nodded and wandered towards the lift, which opened on arrival. He stepped in, closed his eyes and saw her face looking back at him. He could almost feel her hand on his cheek, telling him it would be okay, that he just needed to be honest and she'd trust him.

"Penthouse," he said as the doors closed. Was that how Conner would feel when he was honest? Would Conner understand and forgive him? Fucked if he knew, and he didn't deserve it if he did, did he? First, he screwed Caroline, and then he potentially destroyed his new chance at love with a woman that was made for him, regardless of how difficult she could be.

The doors opened, and before he could register what was going on, something hard hit his face, then his stomach. He heaved out a breath and splayed his hands to stop his fall. Dazed, he regained his balance and swung his head round to find the threat. There was nothing to see other than a sneering Conner, shaking his hand and staring at him.

"You're gonna stand there and take another one, dude. So get ready for it if you like." Shit.

He cracked his neck out to the side and shook his jacket from his shoulders as he screwed his face up around the pain. More was definitely coming. At least the physical side of it he could take if he had to, and with any luck this would all be over after that and they could just have a drink. "The first one was for Belle, the second one was for Beth, and this one," Conner said as he got closer and once again rammed his fist into his chin, "is for the last fucking time we were in New York."

He felt his head recoil as he stepped back half a step to get his balance again and rubbed at his chin. But try as he might to hold it down, he could feel that venom now, surging and coursing through his veins, tensing those muscles ready for action, ready for detonation, ready to kill. His heels bounced beneath him so he planted them down and tried to contain the need to beat the fuck out of his friend. If anyone deserved it, maybe he did, but fuck, why was everyone hitting him lately? He raised his eyes to Conner and found that blue hair glaring at him, body coiled, probably ready for more.

"I'll give you those three, Conner, but don't try again. I'm in no mood for it."

"Fuck you," Conner growled. Alex lifted a brow. The man really was pissed off. He ran his thumb across his lip as he felt liquid dripping from it and was surprised to find blood. That hadn't happened in a while, a split lip. He couldn't remember the last time he'd let someone get close enough apart from Pascal. "Looks good on you. You should keep it. I could do the weekly delivery for you, you fucking twat."

Well, this was going well. Two more minutes of staring while he tried to stop his fists from clenching, and eventually, Conner turned and walked toward the kitchen in that tell-tale gait of irritation. He supposed that meant he was allowed to follow, so he wiped at his mouth again and looked at the elevator door. He could just leave...

"You want a beer?" Conner shouted from somewhere in front. Alex picked up his jacket with a sigh and followed the sound until he came to a stop in the lounge. Lounge was a bit of an understatement really. In typical Conner style, the huge space was dominated by over the top gadgetry and high spec furniture. There were contemporary clean lines everywhere with stark modern art, and a high-tech bar that miraculously opened into the room from behind a concealed wall – clever shit that. He chuckled as he watched two small metal robots sweep their way across the floor in front of him and stop him in his tracks.

"Housekeeping?"

"Less expensive than a fucking cleaner, and I don't have to talk to them," the man grumbled as he sat in the long, blue, L-shaped sofa. "What have you come here for, Alex?" Straight to it then.

"We need to talk," he replied as he made his way over and picked up the beer Conner had left on the bar for him.

"Yeah, what about? About you screwing up with Beth, or about Belle? Or about you being an utter dick, who I'm pretty close to hitting again?"

"All of the above," he replied. "You ready for that?"

"Why not? I've got no one else to be doing, thanks to you," Conner replied as he tapped something into his *iPad* and the sound of *Audioslave* filled the room around them, very loudly.

"Conner?" The shit just put his hand to his ear. "Conner, turn the fucking music down." Still nothing, just an annoyed gaze as he turned it up even louder. Alex narrowed his eyes and took a swig of the beer. It was just as revolting as the last time he'd tried to drink it. This was going to take some thought. "One more time, turn it down." Or he would. Conner's head was now nodding side to side in time with the tune so he wandered casually over towards him, picked up the *iPad* and launched it across the fucking room. The result was sudden silence, a broken plasma screen and a pile of scattered plastic. He cracked his neck again and took another drink as his hand found his pocket.

"What the fuck, man?" Conner said as he stared at the floor. The two metal robots scuttled over to start cleaning the mess up. They were a good buy. Perhaps he should get some. It would save Mary some time at the apartment. "Jesus, Alex, that's like a hundred grand you just trashed."

"I'll write a cheque."

"Wanker." Alex smirked and took a seat on one of the bar stools. Pissed off or not, the man was cooling down. "Mind you don't fall off and break your fucking neck or something."

Maybe it was going to take a little more.

"Conner, I'm sorry, alright? I'm sorry. I'm here to try and make this right again. Elizabeth is trying to talk Belle into seeing me. Hopefully I can make this alright for you again."

"You don't deserve her, and I don't want you alone with Belle. You'll probably try to fuck her, too." Okay, time for the Caroline conversation then. He stared over at the man and thought about how best to broach the subject. There wasn't any delicate way really, was there? He'd fucked the love of the man's life. Whatever way he said this, it wasn't going to be a pleasant outcome.

"Why did you let me off with Caroline?" Conner darted his eyes around as if trying to avoid the topic. That was funny, given he'd brought it up for the first time ever. He eventually laid his head back on the sofa with a sigh and frowned.

"It didn't matter, Alex. It wasn't worth the fight. If you fucked her, she wasn't worth it, was she? Let's just leave it at that."

"At the time I would have agreed, but now, after Elizabeth, I know what love feels like. I must have hurt you. I don't understand why you wouldn't have-"

"For fuck's sake, Caro was a slut. End of."

"Well, yes, but-"

"Jesus, will you give it a rest? I couldn't have cared less about her, alright? She wasn't my priority at the time."

"What? You mean I was?"

"Get over yourself. You may be like a brother to me now but you weren't then. I didn't trust you as far as I could throw you. And the women fell all over you. They still do. You think I would have introduced you to anything really important to me back then?"

"I don't understand what you mean," Alex replied in confusion as he stared over and considered yet another thing that was not expected. Conner sighed and closed his eyes as if he were trying to decide what to say. The fucking truth would be a good start.

"Katie and Jonah were my life," he said quietly. "I wouldn't have risked them being anywhere near you, or your so-called acquaintances. Murderers, druggies, gangsters. You were a fucking nightmare back then."

"Who?" What the hell was the man talking about?

"It doesn't matter now. It's all gone. And so is the only fucking chance I had of a new life, so can you just leave it the fuck alone."

"What the hell are you talking about?" What was gone? And who the hell were Katie and Jonah? He just stared and tried to work out what secrets the guy had that he buried so deeply, and why he'd felt the need to hide them in the first place. Conner chuckled a little and took another swig of his beer as he sat up a little straighter and gazed back.

"You ever wondered why I take so many pills?"

"I suppose I just thought you were a user. It doesn't matter to me. I'd never-"

"Wolff Parkinson White Syndrome. I was twenty-one when I met Katie, twenty-two when Jonah was born, and twenty-four when he died, because of me. I didn't know until he was dead that I'd given it to him. I killed him. His heart couldn't cope with the strain, so that's the story, alright? Satisfied now?"

"I..." There was nothing to say. How could the man have kept this from him for so long? Why? Okay, he hadn't been the best friend, but he'd always had Conner's back, would have always done anything he could to help the guy. He opened his mouth again and still found nothing to say in reply. Nothing could answer that and sound as emotion-filled as was required.

"Just leave it, Alex. I don't want to talk about it. I'd rather know what you think you're going to do to make this whole fucking mess better."

"Why didn't you say anything?"

"Why should I? Caro was the perfect cover, and you did exactly what I thought you'd do. I know you, Alex. You just wanted something you couldn't have, didn't you? Do you still? Are you after Belle, too? Do you have your little green-eyed goblin perched and ready?" He sneered a little in response. That was below the belt, and he wasn't even discussing it. Besides, he wanted to know about the other woman.

"What happened to Katie?"

"She left me and then topped herself a few years later."

"Conner, I'm sorry. I wish you'd have said something at the time. I could have helped, could have..."

"Alex, I love you, man, but apart from in a fight, your idea of support back then was just to get me trashed. It's only since Beth's come along that you have any idea what reality is about. When they died, I kicked Caro to the kerb and we moved on. That's all there is to say really."

"She's been blackmailing me for years. Did you know that?"

"Really? Good on her. Was she worth the money?"

"No," he replied with a snort as he fiddled with the label on his beer. Fucking fiddling. He put the bottle down on the counter and stood up to try and calm that strange sense of guilt that was riddling him, yet again.

"So, Belle? Any fucking ideas? She won't even answer my calls anymore. She just said she doesn't want to see me anymore. We're done, apparently."

"She left because of Elizabeth and me. If I can prove to her that I mean it then maybe she'll lighten up a bit," he said, hoping that it might be true. Belle wasn't an easy manipulation, but he'd find a way around her. He had to.

"You won't touch her? I'm damn serious, Alex. She's off limits."

"I don't want Belle, Conner. I have two of my own to deal with now. That's plenty," he snapped as he thought of Pascal and the difficulties he'd placed on himself. He still couldn't decide what the hell to do with the man, or quite come to terms with why he'd done it in the first place.

"What do you mean by that? If you're fucking someone behind Beth's back, man, I swear I'll-"

"Conner, she knows. Calm the fuck down. She's part of it, too, told me she wanted it. I just don't know how to achieve a happy balance." Conner gaped at him and wandered towards him with a smirk. At least he wasn't pissed any more.

"Only you could find the love of your fucking life and have her want another woman involved, too. Jeez, man. How the hell do you manage that shit? What is it about you and women? Christ, it's like you've got a sign on your head that says 'God'," the guy replied, very nearly laughing and grabbing himself another beer out of the bar as he sat on a stool. Alex looked at him and pondered telling a lie, just ignoring this until he could fathom the reality himself and have a better explanation for what was happening. Conner smiled and winked at him, a typical Conner move, full of decency, regardless of their current altercation. Enough lies.

"Man," he said quietly, very nearly looking at the floor.

"What?"

"It's Pascal."

"Did you finally turn bi overnight? Wondered when that might bite your ass. Whatever the man's got, it's something I can't deliver, isn't it?" Alex raised a brow in surprise and stared back. "Don't do that shit with me, Alex. It's obvious something's been going on between the two of you all this time. But Beth, though? Wow, kinky shit. I would never have thought that of her." Did everyone know about it? It had never occurred to him that Conner might understand.

"It's complicated, different, and I thought I was going to lose him. It forced the issue."

"Those emotions finally catching up with you, huh? You're going to be an all-round normal human being soon, man. Fucked up and confused as hell pretty much all the damn time."

He chuckled at the thought and tried to push the visions away. He had enough difficult emotions to play with lately. Confusion and dilemma's concerning Pascal were not welcome. With any luck, this would all just fall into place without the need for games. "Listen, there's no way on earth I'm going to let you down on this. I'll deal with Belle. You've given me a family I never had, and you're the closest thing to a brother I'll ever have. I'll fix it, okay? Besides, Beth will never forgive me if I don't."

"There is that."

"Listen, I've got to go. Is this done?"

"Sort of. You owe me a hundred grand though." Alex smirked and picked up his jacket. One relationship down, one to go.

"By the way… Evelyn? Did you ever find out what she was up to in my accounts?"

"From what I could tell, she was tracking money movement, seeing what you had and where you had it. She didn't do anything other than that, but she's good, man. I changed all your access passes and re-routed the server, but if she wants in again, she'll get in. I never said anything to her in the end. I thought I'd leave it to you. I assumed you'd move everything about, which you have, so no harm done really."

Hmm, he'd see what Ms. Peters had to say about it. If Pascal hadn't got her over the arm of a chair by the time he got home, anyway. He made his way to the elevator door and turned to look at his friend.

"You want me to say anything to Belle?"

"Yeah," Conner said as he got up and wandered across to him." Give her that, and tell her I still mean it."

He took the ruby ring from Conner's outstretched hand and nodded. He wouldn't be bringing it back. Belle would know how much of a man she was losing by the time he was finished with her. They walked back through the kitchen area towards the door and he felt Conner stop behind him, so he turned to see why. Blue hair was looking at the floor and sighing as if his life was almost over, as if one more day without her and he'd possibly die. He knew the feeling well.

"I'll deal with this, Conner. I owe you that much."

"You could try just being a decent fucker for once in your life, Alex. And don't try to screw with her either because she'll walk all over your ass, man, mine too for letting you try."

He chuckled a little and made for the elevator. The man was right. It seemed the Scott sisters were anything but gullible. There really wasn't anything else to say on the matter so he kept walking until the doors opened. He turned again to see Conner staring at him, a pensive look engrained in his eyes as he took a swig of his beer and nodded his head. The conversation was over, and if he didn't come back here with some results, he wondered if he'd ever be welcome here again. The doors closed as he remembered the last time he'd messed this up for them. Conner had told him in New York that he'd choose Belle over him the last time he fucked up. Thankfully, he'd been able to salvage that situation. Whether he could fix it this time around was uncertain to say the least.

He walked across the lobby and realised he'd sent Andrews home, so he asked the doorman to call a taxi. No matter how much money you had, flagging a taxi down in London wasn't as easy as it was in New York. He stopped at the doorway to stave off the rain that was now pelting down and gazed out into the gloom – changeable weather, another difference between the two cities. A bit like himself really – unstable. No wonder the London disposition settled so comfortably inside him. It gave him the ability to change his moods in time with the weather, letting that dark, predictable place just linger inside and keep him company. It allowed him to recede into himself and allow the wash of London air to settle even deeper. It was dark and familiar, once again threatening the normality of hatred and loathing he was so comfortable with.

Why did she want him?

Why did Pascal?

A horn blasted somewhere, bringing his head back into the now, so he scowled at the black cab and hurried through the rain to the car. He hated rain. It reminded him too much of bathrooms, or rather the lack of them. Opening the door, he slid in and told the driver where to take him. The moron started to yatter away about the weather. Taxi drivers did that a lot, talked about nothing just to keep the air less tense. If only they knew how comfortable he was with that tension, how it radiated through him and relaxed him to that point of no thought other than action. Did no one else feel that? It wasn't the sense of peace she gave him, but it was the peace Pascal gave him, and it was something he realised he couldn't be without anymore. That's why he'd offered the man what he wanted, because the thought of not having that kind of peace was terrifying. It was his version of normal, his version of home. And no matter what she could give him, or how absorbing that was to him, it wasn't what Pascal gave him.

"So anyway, she said to me it was my fault..." The cabbie was still blathering on about something his slut of a wife had gotten up to, something she'd done with another man at some point. She probably wasn't getting anything decent from the man in front of him. It was unlikely the guy could even get it up by the look of the stomach rolling over his belt. He eyed the corners in front of him and watched as his road came into view, those recognizable gates glinting in the distance and letting him know he was nearly there.

"When was the last time you fucked her properly?" he said. The guy stumbled over a few expletives and regained control of the car.

"Guv, that's not the sort of question you ask a bloke," the dick replied.

"I assumed, given your rant, that you wanted my opinion, which is that you should try fucking her more appropriately. Then she'd have no need to go elsewhere." His own words rang in his head as he thought of Pascal. Did he want him to go elsewhere? Then Conner's words hit him again: *"Have you finally turned bi overnight?"*

Had he?

"I've screwed her every way possible," the cabbie eventually said as they pulled into the drive. Unlikely, was the best word he could think of. Had he shackled her, hung her, tortured her, starved her? Had he watched three men with their cocks in every hole? Had he fucked her arse till she bled? Had he strung her up and watched another man beat her until she cried and screamed and begged? Ripped her open and made her give him every ounce of fear she had? She shouldn't have the fucking energy to stray, let alone want for it.

"I doubt it," he said quietly as he handed over a fifty and climbed out into the rain again. The front door opened and he expected to see Andrews, but it was Pascal who stood there, now dressed in some Edwardian get up, long boots and a purple coat to match, looking every inch the lord of the manor. He smirked like an egotistical villain, leaning against the frame as if he owned the place.

"What the fuck is that supposed to mean?" the cabbie shouted as he began to turn the car around. It wasn't a conversation he was likely to continue. Presumably his sister was in there waiting for an explanation of some sort. He continued to the door as Pascal held it wider and lowered his gaze a little – just enough to show that submission Alex craved from him. Much as he wanted to tap his chin back up again, he needed that compliance for the time being, and he needed the man to know who was in charge.

"Queer fucker," the cabbie shouted behind him as the car pulled off up the drive.

Queer? He stopped and mused the thought as Pascal chuckled beside him. Queer, gay, bi, straight – they were all indistinguishable in his world, all meaningless in certain circumstances, and yet at the moment, it meant more than he could fathom. He slowly turned his eyes towards the still smirking idiot, who licked his lips and took his wet coat from his shoulders.

"Not yet, I think. Hmm? Maybe with time, yes?" Alex raised a brow and brushed past the man.

"Is she here?" he said as he carried on down the hall and listened to the clock delivering its normal tick tock. There was no other sound to disrupt the welcoming dull thud of normality, apart from Pascal, whose presence was always troublesome to routine.

"If you mean Elizabeth, no. But should you mean the female version of yourself who is currently drinking your finest malt, then, yes, she is. Why did you not tell me you had a sister? I believe she may be somewhat deranged, by the way." Not surprising given her abduction.

"Hmm. Did you stay away from her?"

"Mostly."

"Pascal, I told Andrews to-"

"Yes, yes, yes. I realise this. However, she was too tempting, and she also attempted escape on several occasions. I assumed you did not want that." Alex rolled his eyes and imagined the amusement she'd caused Pascal, probably got his temperature very high indeed.

He wandered into the lounge to find an irate looking Evelyn glaring at him as she put a picture down on the sideboard gently.

"Chess?" she said, a statement really. "Surely you're not intelligent enough for chess."

"I'm not. He is," he replied as he nodded at the bar where Pascal was already pouring some cognac.

"He is revolting, not unlike yourself at the moment. Make that driver of yours take me home, unless you've got something interesting to say."

He watched her making herself comfortable with not even the slightest hint of insecurity as she sat in an unknown home and sipped at his Scotch. Her hair was neatly pinned, and she wore an immaculate beige dress, fit for the boardroom. She was perfection really, the complete epitome of himself in female form. It was interesting that she'd become that way, regardless of her family home. Pascal raised an indifferent brow as he passed him a drink and took a seat over on the sofa opposite her.

"Evelyn, why were you looking through my accounts?" he asked. There would be no beating around the bush with this woman. He wanted her off guard, caught out. His phone vibrated in his pocket and dulled the moment, so he took it out anyway and checked the message.

> **- She says she'll see you. I'm going to stay here tonight I think. X**

Not a hope. He wasn't having another night without her in his bed, and the fact that they were back in London, near Aiden again, wasn't a comforting thought. She would come back here, where he could keep her safe.

> **- No you won't. I'll send Andrews over for you now.**

He raised his eyes back to Evelyn as he hit the intercom for Andrews and told him to go and pick Elizabeth up.

"Have you had enough time to think up an excuse so you can lie to me? Or are you going to be truthful?" he asked. His phone vibrated again. He almost rolled his eyes at the thought of what she'd likely be saying to his order.

"I was trying to find out why you lose about two and a half thousand every week in small pockets. Haven't you noticed? It's filtered out, quite cleverly really, but nevertheless it's not going to anything that you own. Conner didn't put the leak in there, so I was trying to work out who had," she replied, bold as fucking brass. If it was a lie, it was a damn good one. Why the fuck was he losing ten grand a month, and where from? More importantly, where to? He supposed he should ask her how she'd even got into his accounts, but that seemed irrelevant to some degree. Pascal turned and looked at him. It was his version of a shocked face, more humorous irritation to the bystander.

"Why were you interested?" he asked. He wasn't prepared to let her know she'd just told him something he knew nothing about, something Conner hadn't detected. He'd be having fucking words with him. "Maybe you should have just asked me."

"I wouldn't have known had I not been snooping. It's what I do. Then it became interesting."

"You just hack people's accounts to find out what they're worth?"

"Not everyone, only relevant people. Nicholas Adlin's worth and past is reasonably relevant to me now, as is Pascal Van Der Braack's," she replied as that smile crept across her face, the same fucking one he used when he wanted to twist the knife and let the world know how in control he was. Clever girl. Pascal laughed, completely unfazed by her apparent snooping.

"She's very good, Alexander. My dear, he has kept you from me. What is my worth lately?"

"Not as much as his, nor will it ever be if you keep paying whoever LC is," she responded instantly. LC, Roxanne, Lucinda? Pascal didn't flinch in the slightest.

"Well, I am more interested in fucking than he is, ferociously so. Tell me, are those hands as useful on anything other than a computer?"

"Dexterously so." And now they were flirting.

"Hmm, maybe we should find out. Up you get. Off with those clothes." She glared a little and crossed her legs as she sipped her drink again. Alex wasn't surprised.

"Pascal, go and make me a coffee. You're not helping." There was no way in hell Pascal was fucking his sister. It wasn't happening. His phone vibrated again so he swiped it out and found two messages.

- **We've talked about this ordering me around shit.**
- **I've spoken to Andrews and told him to piss off. He's sitting on your drive.**

Elizabeth clearly wasn't a happy fucking bunny.

He looked back up to find Evelyn and Pascal staring at each other. Pascal was looking disinterested, which meant an impending explosion, and Evelyn possibly egging him on into something she knew nothing about whatsoever.

"Actually, Pascal, go and get Elizabeth. Take one of the cars," he said, pocketing his phone again. It would get Pascal out of the house and his angel back here where she belonged.

"Is that abhorrent man servant of yours not retrieving her?" the man replied, not one muscle moving as he kept those green eyes trained on Evelyn.

"It appears not."

"Hmm," Pascal said as he stood up from the sofa and straightened his suit. "Then I shall go and liberate her. This chasing of your angel has become less restrictive recently."

Privileges or not, union or not, the man was not putting his hands on her until they were all in a room, together. Pascal wandered past him in his normal fashion and tutted as he reached for the chessboard. He snatched the white knight, removing a pawn in the process, then replaced the knight and made his way to the door. He'd obviously been playing chess while evaluating his next conquest, that being sister dearest, it wasn't going to happen. Still, it was a good move. He considered the board himself for a second or two and calculated the next position. Whatever it was, it didn't negate the fact that he was not touching Elizabeth, regardless of the man's tactics in trying to make him forget the threat.

"Belligare," he said firmly over his shoulder. It was all he could say with Evelyn in the room to tell Pascal how he felt, and he assumed the slight halt in his step meant that the man understood. He'd never had to use it before. He'd taken that fucking beating all night without asking the man to stop. He'd taken it to understand, taken it to feel what they felt, taken it to be taught, and had never intended to have to use it. But in this moment, his own safe word was all he could use without letting Evelyn know what was happening between the three of them. Pascal chuckled as he rounded the corner and wandered off towards the kitchen, more than likely in the direction of his damn *Ferrari*. He looked back at Evelyn, who was now studying the chessboard, too.

"Do you play?" he asked as he took a seat on the chair next to her.

"No," she replied, leaning over the board a little and narrowing her eyes.

"Would you like to learn?" He reached forward and moved his rook to counter Pascal then took a drink again as he tried to gauge her reactions. She was so like him – so closed, a wall of mystery.

"Yes, I think it looks rather fun," she said. Why was she so comfortable? Surely she should be fuming about being brought here under duress. Was she really as good at lying and manipulating as he was? Was it possible that this was all a lie, or was she being honest?

"Why did you have dinner with Aiden Phillips?" She smiled and leaned back on the sofa, giving herself time to think, a soft chuckle coming from her mouth as she clicked her head to the side and rubbed the back of her neck. Liar.

"Because he's relevant, too, isn't he, brother? You have quite a past that I'm finding out about. You've not been very nice at all, have you?" She crossed her legs and angled herself towards him in flirtation, an attempt at misdirection, maybe. "And he's actually quite attractive." It didn't work.

"You need to learn to play chess, sister," he said as he beckoned her forward to the table again and began to roll up his sleeves."

"Do I?"

"Yes. Your manoeuvring is clumsy, childlike." She scowled at him so he grabbed the decanter and filled their drinks again with a smile. "Would you like to be better at it? It seems a shame to waste a near talent, especially if your fingers are useful, too." She raised a brow as they stared at each other, the small upward lift of the corner of her mouth mirroring his. It seemed they were both thinking the same, probably both calculating risk and strategy, possibly in the worst way.

"Are you friend or foe, brother?" she asked. All he could see was himself looking back at him, distrustful eyes and a mask of unemotional response as she questioned his reason for existing in her company.

"That depends on who I think you are, sister."

Only time would tell.

Chapter 15

Elizabeth

Bloody man.

Honestly, I could throttle him. Who the hell does he think he is? Whatever my little drunken wobble may have been about earlier, I am so over that shit. Belle is still in her bedroom. Why, I don't know because it's only six pm, but to be frank, all I want to do myself now is go to bed, too. I nearly picked up the phone and called him to ask him to pick me up and then decided, having sobered up somewhat, that the best thing was to try and get some decent sleep and go over in the morning. Fresh, alert, ready for action, that type of thing. Besides, it's Christmas Eve tomorrow, and I still haven't got a bloody present for him, and I suppose I've got to get one for Pascal now, too. What on earth do I get him? As if Alex wasn't bad enough. Oh god, its Christmas Eve tomorrow! The thought has suddenly struck me again. The whole family is supposed to be at Alex's for Christmas. What about Conner? Are mum and Dad still coming? Has Belle said anything? Shit.

Anyway, now I'm sitting here trying to work out if I should go over there and give him what for. After all he's put me through, he still thinks he can order me around? Idiot. The text I sent to Andrews got an instant response of '*He's not going to like that'*, to which I replied, '*Sod him. Stay there.*' The poor chap is probably sitting on the driveway, still trying to work out what the hell to do. Not my problem. If he wasn't such a Neanderthal arsehole, I might have been kinder. Not yet, though. My kind days seem to be fewer and further between lately. It appears that they need to in order to deal with all these men. What I wouldn't give for a quiet night in with Teresa and Belle, one where we're all happy and relaxed, and I can talk openly about what's going on and they'll help me understand myself if nothing else.

Kicking my feet about as I lie on the sofa and try to concentrate on the *BBC News*, which is utterly un-fascinating, I decide to go and get some more coffee. That marvellous machine might go somewhere close to levelling my head back out again and help me to formulate a plan. Alex needs to see Belle. If he can convince her that everything's okay then maybe she can get back together with Conner. If we can achieve that by close of play tomorrow, then Christmas day is on, which means we need all the food to cook. Balls! Has Mary done that? Alex must have had the forethought to tell her about it so hopefully it's all there waiting. Cooking stuff I can do. There's order to the chaos when I cook. God, I miss cooking. I'd almost forgotten it's my job, to be honest, my business. I've been so swept up in this crazy twilight world of his that I'm struggling to remember my own kitchen. Did James sign the paperwork for his new job? Belle will know. Oh Christ, the new building! What's been going on in there is anyone's guess. Signage... Did I send the new graphics off for the new signs? I need coffee, and where's my notepad?

Ten minutes later and I'm suddenly on a roll of organisation. It seems a few hours back in my own space, a slight, vodka-induced meltdown and some irritation at him, and I'm miraculously back on form again. I'm ready to be Elizabeth Scott, caterer, sister, daughter. I'm ready to deal with all the things that need putting back into order and mentally organise myself. The world does not revolve around Mr. White all of the time, and while the last few days feel like an eternity of learning to some degree, I do have my own issues to get a grip on, regardless of Christmas. Two sheets of notes later, as I sit at the desk in my blue jeans, black t-shirt and *Converse,* I'm raring to go at the world. My brain is firing on at least twenty cylinders, possibly espresso induced this time, and my list seems to be getting longer. Unfortunately, I also seem to feel the need to bake something. Can I actually make a decent Christmas cake a day or so before Christmas? I know they should be made months before, but I just didn't get round to it this year. Oh sod it. My feet have me at the cupboard, looking for ingredients before I know it, and then sighing at the fact that we have nothing in the cupboards to make a cake with.

Grabbing at my bag, coat and umbrella, I swipe my keys up and head off out the door to go to the shops. Frankly, it'll be nice to get some air, and the shops are only a fifteen-minute walk from the apartment. A new guy greets me in the lobby and holds the door open with a smile so I nod back at him and notice as he scuttles out of the way and looks down a little. Clearly feisty Beth is making herself noticed as I storm onwards toward my target – the shops. Nothing is getting in the way of me making my cake. I am in control of that if nothing else. My cake is my piece of freedom, and I am on a mission to do just as I please with it. No interruptions, nobody getting in my head and telling me what to do, nobody manipulating a situation to suit themselves. No, this is me and my cake.

A car horn beeps at the side of me as I come to the crossing on the next street, breaking me from my silent, in-control moment. My eyes swing upwards to find a very flash looking car idling at the side of the road. Alex has one of those I think. Oh, it better not be him, and he better not have sent Pascal for me again. I'll bloody kill someone if he did, and I've still got this damn knife in my bag to prove it. I need to get rid of that. I think that's pretty bad here in England. I take a look around, MI5 style, to make sure nobody's following me, as if the bloody Mafia would be after me. My hand automatically clutches at my bag as the tinted window rolls down on the car. The first thing I see is a hand beckoning me – a hand I know far too well. I breathe out a small sigh of relief, because thank God it's him. Although, if I had his sodding cane with me, I'd hit him with it. Arsehole. How dare he send Pascal out for me again?

My head snaps back in the direction I'm heading, because nothing is distracting from my purpose, which, to clarify to myself mainly, is to bake a bloody Christmas cake.

"My rose, do not make me crawl suburban kerbs. It is beneath my status and quite ordinary." His voice comes from the depths of the car. I'd say it's shouted, but something about his voice makes shouting an impossibility. I just hear it because it seems to sing to me now more than ever.

"I'm going to the shops, Pascal. Please feel free to come with me."

That'll make him disappear. There's no way he'd ever be seen in a supermarket. I'm surprised to even see him driving a car, to be fair. Said car abruptly pulls to the side of the road, is abandoned very inelegantly in a bus stop and out he gets, utterly beautiful as he is. "You can't leave that there," I say as I continue on my way, completely ignoring his intoxicating eyes and listening to his brown boots coming up behind me.

"Why not?" he replies, as if the thought hadn't crossed his mind in the slightest.

"It's a bus stop. It'll get towed, which I'm sure he won't be happy about, unless that's yours?"

"Then we shall get wet together. It is a fetish of mine," he says as he takes the umbrella from my hand and holds it above us. "I shall have my driver take us back instead. I despise driving in this country of yours, and that thing is becoming sticky. He does not rev it frequently enough."

"I think I sense a metaphor in there," I reply as I fold my arms and carry on forward. "What exactly are you trying to say about the English?"

"Only that it is dulled by these English roads, my dear. *Ferraris* are not designed for leisurely pursuits. They should be thrashed with an academic finesse."

"Oh, really? Thrashed, huh?"

"Hmm. Why must you shop?"

"I want to bake a Christmas cake."

"It is somewhat late for Christmas cake baking. This should have been created last year, should it not?" Oh, so he's a cookery expert, too now? Fabulous. Is there nothing the man doesn't know how to do?

"How would you know what the hell to do with a cake?"

"We had servants, cooks, staff and such. On occasion I would, how do you say, lick the wooden spoon? Twirl it around my tongue."

"I bet you did," I mumble in response as I fix my eyes on the shop and halt my wandering thoughts. Nothing, and no one, is distracting me from my chosen pursuit this evening. Cake it will be. I so wish this fucking trembling thing would stop.

We continue on towards my goal for a while, my rampaging strides becoming tamed to a more leisurely pace as Pascal's presence seems to cool my irritated temper without him even trying. It's odd really, walking along a street with him. It's bizarre, as all the women around me stare and gawp at the utterly beautiful man who may look a bit strange in his get up. But to me, he's perfectly normal, perfectly natural. I couldn't imagine him any other way. He nods at a small gathering of ladies on a bench and graces them with his award-winning smile. They instantly blush and turn into each other, giggling and smiling as they bat their fuck-me eyes at him and stare back unapologetically, probably wondering why he's with such a mess of a girl. If only they knew.

"Pascal, stop encouraging them. They wouldn't last ten minutes with you. Do you have to be quite so blatant?" I could slap myself the moment the words leave my lips. The man's not even trying and I can feel my envy creeping over me.

"I smell jealousy, my rose," he replies on a chuckle as he points at the shop and dismisses the women. "I may have pledged my allegiance to him, but have sworn nothing to you, and it is good to keep one's options open, no?"

"I'm not jealous. I'm tired of men thinking they have all the power. I'm tired of them telling women what to do. Before you two came along, I was perfectly content, happily pottering along, and-" I am abruptly cut off as he swats my backside so harshly it sends me reeling into the shop doorway.

I couldn't be more surprised if I tried as my feet land me in front of the woman serving. Warmth pools immediately as my thighs clench around the moment. His face is full of untold promises as I turn my head back to watch that wicked smirk stare back at me.

"Oooh," the woman serving says from behind me, probably picking up her tongue from the floor as she does. "Found a handsome one there." I continue to stare at him, my skin now trembling a little more as he picks up an apple and bites into it maliciously. Visions fly through me at the very thought. Heat swims across my skin, only highlighting my need for what he's offering, what they're offering. I'd like to be irritated with him, but it's the truth, isn't it? And my inner slut is definitely confirming that. I may have thought I was happy before, but I very clearly wasn't.

"Cake, my rose," he says, as if nothing just happened. He doesn't acknowledge in the slightest that he knows damn well I will never be content with normal again, not now Alex has shown me, not now that I've felt the other side of this sexually intense world.

I turn away from him in a huff and walk towards my ingredients, snatching them off the shelf one by one as I pass by each thing and end up back at the counter.

Handing my card over to her, I can sense her still flirting with him over my shoulder. I can't even be bothered to watch. It's as bad as Alex, for God's sake.

"You can't just do that sort of thing in public, Pascal. I'm not your bloody property," I say sharply as we head back out onto the road and he takes the shopping bag off me.

"Only because he found you first, my dear. However, should you feel the need to spank me in public, I shall be more than willing to receive it."

It's a disturbing thought, although the memory of that whip landing at his side while he was on his knees has very clear connotations. I did that, and did it without thinking. I would never have contemplated the idea of throwing it in the direction of Alex, but something made me crack it at Pascal. Something inside of me wanted him to shudder in fear of me. Thank God I didn't actually hit him with it. Christ knows what I would have done. I huff out a small breath and head back towards my apartment again. Whatever this is between the three of us, however comfortable it may feel, I just wish I understood the complexities of it a bit more.

"Do you understand what's happening between us all here? The boundaries? Are there any? I don't know what I'm supposed to feel about any of this. I am comfortable with it, I think. I just never expected this thing between the two of you to happen, never thought it would be something I'd have to deal with, and I don't quite understand what that was with the..." I can't even finish my rambled thoughts, can't quite get the words out of my mouth in this ordinary suburban street. Maybe if we were in a candlelit room, the wine flowing and a more relaxed atmosphere, I could, but not here. He wanders along beside me some more in silence, heading for the car in the distance that luckily enough doesn't appear to have a ticket on it yet. He's clearly thinking, musing what I might want to hear, maybe what I need to hear. We eventually get there and he holds the door open for me. I screw my nose up at it and glare back at him. As if I'm going over to Alex's house. I've already told Andrews to piss off. I'll happily give Pascal a piece of my mind, too.

"There are many rules we will be learning, my dear, the first of which is that *he* is in control of *us*. You may try your hand at battling with me. However, I would suggest, at this tantalizing time, you do not tempt me onto his side any more than I currently am." Typical, and I can only assume that means I'm about to be thrown into the car if I don't comply.

"I'm hardly dressed for him," I reply as I slide in and give up hope of evading capture. "And I'm still baking my cake."

"You're hardly dressed. This denim thing you are so fond of is quite unappealing. Did he tell you of my ball?" Ball? What ball? He slams the door in my face and casually walks around the other side to get in.

"No, what ball?" I say, the moment his arse hits the seat. He revs the car far too much and pulls straight out into traffic without a care in the world. Having seen Rome's traffic, this is clearly how every other European nation drives. I grab a hold of the handle and sling on my seatbelt.

"It is in Berlin this year. You shall have to be dressed appropriately, although I'm not quite sure what that will be anymore. You're correct. This situation is a little confusing."

"When?" His mouth turns up into a smile.

"Five days from now." I could choke on something. Five days?

"What? I haven't got anything to wear, and what do you mean appropriately? It's Christmas, Pascal. I haven't sorted Belle and Conner yet, you know, got them back together, and Mum and Dad are coming over." The thought of my mother and Pascal together suddenly strikes me. It could be worrying to say the least. Her reaction to Alex is going to be bad enough, let alone two of them, possibly three if Conner's there, too. Mind you, it'll make her smile, I suppose. "Actually, are you staying for Christmas?" The car swerves to the left to avoid an oncoming motorbike and a potential near death experience. He does nothing more than smoothly spin his hand on the wheel and dig into his pocket for a cigarette.

"No, I shall fly home tomorrow. Alexander knows this. Christmas is apparently for relations, and regardless of my irritation in the matter, I have been summoned." Surprisingly, my body feels almost lost at the thought of him leaving.

"What family do you have?" I ask as I watch Buckingham Palace come into view and think of royal connections. "I know nothing of European royalty, I'm afraid." He snorts out a mild sense of disgust and carries on driving.

"If you force me to use the term *family*, I have two sisters and their respective moronic husbands; one brother and his slut of a wife who I will have to face, and a father who I shall try my hardest not to

212

face at all. It will be best completed in an inebriated state, I think. I shall begin the moment the flight takes off, and with any of your British luck, I won't remember a thing about it."

"No mother?"

"No," he says as a frown descends and he speeds up along The Mall. The conversation's closed, it seems. Yet another mysterious family past I'll have to deal with. "Why did you not tell me about Alexander's sister?"

"It never came up, and I think he wanted to keep it quiet. I keep secrets well," I reply as I smile at my own ability to hold information Pascal knows nothing about. It's a turn up for the books. The man normally knows everything. I'm shocked he didn't know about her.

"She is quite similar, no? I find her intriguing."

"Intriguing is one word for her, I suppose. I can't quite make up my mind if I like her or not," I say as I think about her. The long line of roofs comes into view as we round the corner and hit a mass of traffic trying to get past Hyde Park. "She's guarded, Pascal, seems to want to cause trouble. I'm not sure whose side she's on." He rolls the window down and blows smoke out of it as he gazes at a passing car full of women.

"She is young, and has had nothing to fight against yet. She is simply trying her hand at a game, trying to prove herself to him. There is nothing to concern yourself with, my rose."

"But with all this going on with Henry, I don't know..." Shit. Should I have said that? Surely Pascal knows. The sudden raising of his brow has me questioning that thought instantly. Balls.

"Henry De Ville?" he asks.

"Yes, but Pascal... Oh, shit. I shouldn't have said anything, and it doesn't matter anyway because Alex has it all under control, I think." I hope. Stupid, stupid, stupid.

"He has been keeping secrets from me, and you, my dear, are clearly hopeless at keeping them. This is something you will need get much more accomplished at. Our world is full of little clandestine adventures you will become part of."

That's it. I'm not saying another fucking word to get myself into trouble. Lord knows what will happen if I open my mouth again. Folding my arms in my lap, I stare out of the window as we start moving again, and I inwardly chastise my own ridiculousness. He stays silent, not questioning me more like I thought he would, just sitting there driving the car and softly breathing next to me. I can smell his aftershave washing over me, almost feel his pulse radiating through the car, but I don't have one clue what he's thinking. The bloody silence is damn near deafening.

"Pascal?"

"Hmm?" he replies, distracted.

"You won't say anything, will you? I didn't mean to tell you, and I don't want to get in trouble. If Alex wanted you to know, he would have told you, I'm sure."

"Don't you?" he replies as he turns the car into Alex's road, a twinkle of amusement in his voice again. "I would if I were you. He's at his most delicious when you have done something incorrectly, my dear. This is all the more reason for me to keep quiet about your faux pas, I think." Of course he would come up with something like that, wouldn't he? There's still nothing to let me know what he's thinking about, other than the ruse he's just given me. We continue along the road until I see the gates of home up in front of me, occasionally stopping for some other *Bentley*, *Rolls Royce*, or some other sporty looking number to turn in front of us into another enormously large house. Home. This will be my home if Alex still wants that. I stare around me at the wealth and think of where I'll be in the next few months, years. I've given him permission to be who he needs to be, told him I'll accept him and Pascal, shown him that he can't frighten me off with his games and murderous past. I am a potential gangster's moll, a woman of dubious connections, and one of three now. I am part of the high class underground that is London, possibly New York, definitely Europe. I swing my eyes to Pascal again, as he pulls through the gates, and watch him wet his lips in anticipation while looking at the house.

"What do you want from him, Pascal?"

There's a pause long enough to eclipse the sun as he pulls up in front of the portico and stares at the steering wheel, those green eyes of his almost dull for some reason. Time keeps ticking by as he just breathes and taps his fingers along the rounded leather. Eventually, he leans back and tips his head in my direction.

"I never contemplated this, Elizabeth. I was ready to leave the two of you and was as surprised by this revelation as you. I am not sure what I expect *from* him, nor what it is that I require *of* him. However, you should know this: whatever he requires of me will be given, whether you wish to see it or not. He has my collar now, and therefore my obedience. You, my dear, have neither to argue with." Not happy about that little line at all, my eyes narrow at him. He just gets out of the car and keeps his exquisitely serious face firmly in place. "Now, are you ready to go in?"

Stepping out of the car, I find myself staring at those red doors, wondering what will become of us in this strange harmony of three. Will we live together, with each other? Or just Alex, and I? Will we open our hearts to each other? What will children mean to us? How do we all make this normal, comfortable even? I haven't even had sex with the man but I know it's coming. I know this will be part of our relationship now. Fingers lace with mine as I stare and wonder, but something about all this still feels so right, so easy, in a very random way.

"Where is that fucking servant man he insists upon?" He sneers beside me. I swing around to see a grumpy looking frown glaring at the door as if he might have to do the extraordinary and actually open it himself. One step forward with my keys and I'm opening the door to my home, the one I'll be moving into at some point.

"You have his key?" he says.

"I have his soul, why would I not have his key?" Twin smirks smile at each other for a second or two as we both remember his apartment when he came for me.

"Do you wish I had taken you that night, my rose? Hmm? Wish I'd have forced myself on you and moved this along a little quicker?"

"Why would I want that? I wouldn't have had the pleasure of the tease, would I?" I respond as my foot hits the floor and I smell the house for the first time in a while. Evocative, heady visions and thoughts course across me as I hear the ticking of the clock and smell the familiar wood furniture. Lilies adorn the tables and the Christmas tree hits me square in the face as I look up at it and feel a little teary at its magnificence. Every colour under the sun is reflected in baubles twinkling in the low light of the hallway, lamps dimly illuminating the corners and highlighting all the architraves and pictures. The deep burgundy reminds me of his warmth as it stretches along towards the kitchen, past the study – his touch, his love. Home. Christmas at home. Where is he?

Dropping my keys on the hall table, I move towards the lounge before I know it. Regardless of my earlier irritation, I seem to have no ability to stop myself wanting to be in his arms again. All of a sudden, I need to be with him again, need to spend the night with him, need to have him inside me to remind myself of his touch, his hands made for butchery, for my butchery. Shivers course through me at the thought so I quicken my pace to find him.

I'm met with an incredibly amused Alex, sitting there chuckling about something as he stares at the front of a wingback chair. I can see nothing but a pair of unfairly beautiful legs and high heels. His head lifts at my rushed entrance and I'm greeted with him standing and holding out a hand for me. The cool blue of his shirt flawlessly matches the colour of his eyes, and his forearms stretch out to me as if commanding me to him with no other option than to go. One look at his mouth and I know I'm home, because that beautifully wicked smile has me thinking all sorts of things about his lips. But more than that is the heat that travels straight to my heart at the look in his eyes. It almost burns as it moves through my skin and pulls me to him, guiding me towards the love that keeps me with him, or stops me from running from him, and I know it all now, don't I? There's nothing left to fear.

"Did he behave?" he murmurs into my ear as he twirls me in closely and kisses my throat. His throat.

"He did," I reply, revelling in his touch, wanting more almost instantly. Those hands grip slightly and knead flesh in all the right places. So much so that I almost forget the other woman sitting in the room until she coughs a little. I'd know her voice anywhere. Evelyn? Interesting. I turn around in his hold to find her holding a pawn in her fingers and smiling quietly, still looking every bit the modern business woman with her perfectly made-up hair and her perfectly pressed dress. I so want to straighten my clothes, but I hold it together and keep my eyes fixed in defiance. I am strong. I am in control.

"Evelyn's learning to play chess, or learning to manipulate her life as your father would say." He chuckles behind me as he lets me go and wanders off. Ooh, something I might be able to beat her at. I'm definitely in control. "Would you like a drink?"

"Coffee, please," I reply as I sit in his chair and gaze across at her. Pascal walks off after Alex and I'm left here looking at her.

"Elizabeth," she says.

"Evelyn, how are you?"

"Well, thank you. I assume you're okay now after your rapid exit from the charity ball?"

"Yes, fine, thank you." I can feel the questions in her stare. Does she think I'm going to talk about it? I hope not. I've already dropped myself in it once with Pascal. I'm not about to do it again.

"So, you don't play?" I ask as I scan the board. It's very simply laid out, as if it's been completely restarted so I pick up a white pawn and move forward two.

"No, Alex was just showing me the rules of engagement. It seems quite simple." There is nothing simple about any *rules of engagement* where Alex is concerned – chess, underground sex auctions, or real life included.

"It gets more complicated the further into it you get. You need to learn to play at least six moves in front of yourself, and be ready to be knocked off course at any given moment." I could be talking about my own bloody life to be honest, certainly Alex's. I stare at the board and listen to my own words ringing in my head – six moves in front, more complicated the further you get, knocked off course at any given moment. It is my bloody life, well, now anyway, full of twist and turns, full of new problems to deal with, full of struggles and complications, but hopefully not anymore. Hopefully, this will all just slot in together and be fine now. If nothing else, it all proves how flexible I've become at dealing with him, how he's made me feel his world and understand how confused he's been in it, how he's taught me to play the game when necessary and learn those rules so that I can see him for what he is. He must close down emotion simply to make life easier for himself so that his brain has a chance to relax and be normal – his blissful idea of normal anyway. Is that where he wants to go with Pascal and I? Is that where he normally goes with Pascal alone, to that dark place inside where he can simply close the door and just be? Find his peace?

"Elizabeth?" Something's making a noise. "Elizabeth, are you okay?" What? Oh, Evelyn, yes. I look back up at her to find that brow raised, just as Alex's would be. I snort out a giggle and lean back into the chair.

"Sorry, I was just thinking about something and I got a little distracted. It's your move."

"It is not," Pascal says as he strides back into the room with a long grey coat over his arm. "It is time for the sister to go home. It appears I have become the fucking driver. Come, up you get," he snaps at her. She glares in response and gently sips at her drink. She really would be quite good for him. She's got Roxanne written all over her with her perfection, although I'm pretty sure she's not bat shit crazy, thankfully.

"Evelyn, you should go home now." Alex's voice comes drifting across my shoulder firmly. I'm swooning instantly. It's that tone of voice that makes my thighs clench, velvety, with just a pinch of that sadistic preference I can hear now. I'm here, and he wants her gone, Pascal, too by the sound of it. His hand suddenly lands on my collarbone as he stands behind me and I shudder at the small amount of pressure he uses to let me know what he wants – me, and a house free of distractions.

Pascal holds the coat up with a sneer. He probably thinks the material isn't good enough for him to hold or something. Evelyn just stares at all of us as if she has no clue what is happening. Thank fuck I do for once in my life. For once, I understand perfectly, and I'm suddenly very ready for it.

I rise up from my chair in the hope that it will get her backside moving. Thankfully, she gets up, too, and places her drink down.

"It's been amusing, brother," she says as Pascal puts her coat on her, ever the gentleman regardless of his clear infuriation.

"We shall do it again soon, Evelyn," he replies as we head out of the lounge and cross towards the door. He stops by a chest in the hall and opens it, then draws out a large wooden box and passes it to her. "Chess needs to be practised often. Use it daily with the app I showed you. You'll have some sort of chance the next time we meet." Sweet. Let's teach the sister how to be better at manipulating the world, too. Oh, aren't we a family full of deviants.

Pascal opens the door and marches through it to the car, barely containing the foreign language that's now pouring from his lips. Irritated grumblings carry on as the car revs beyond comprehension and Evelyn looks across at it.

"Is he safe in that?" she asks.

"He will be with you," Alex replies while holding the door for her. "He's been warned." Oh, I bet he has, and I dare say not just about the driving.

"Okay," she says as she steps out into the night and makes her way down the stairs. "Apart from the kidnapping, it's been quite lovely. Thank you." I narrow my eyes at the words. Has he been abducting her, too? Try as I might, I still can't work out how sincere that voice is. Something just doesn't sound right about it.

"Goodnight, Evelyn," I say as I watch her slide into the car. She turns and waves a little, that side of her mouth lifting, yes, just like Alex's.

"Good night," she replies.

The car door shuts and we both stand there watching the car race off up the drive.

"You don't trust her, do you?" he asks.

"I don't know," I reply honestly. "I want to, but something's not quite right." He chuckles and I hear him retreating back into the house behind me. I keep staring at the taillights until they eventually go out of view. I have no clue who that woman really is, and I don't like her anywhere near Alex or Pascal. I don't suppose I should be overly concerned, but I just can't put my finger on what's irritating me about her. Maybe it's just past experience and nothing to worry about at all. I mean, who would want to piss Alex off? Especially someone who's a relative newbie in London who works for Conner? No, it'll be fine. I'm sure of it. No problem whatsoever.

Chapter 16

Elizabeth

Oh, shit, my ingredients! They're in the bloody car, and no amount of me waving my arms around is going to make Pascal turn the around, so I don't even bother. I just stand here, staring at the dust kicking up off the gravel as the red lights dim into the distance. I just wanted to bake a damn cake, for God's sake.

I turn and walk back into the house to find him standing at the bottom of the stairs, looking at me as if he's about to pounce, and even if I wasn't interested, I wouldn't have a chance of running. Whatever it is that's going through his mind, I'm about to find out.

"Take your clothes off," he says, those cool blues now darkening a little. It's a quiet demand. He doesn't need to say it harshly or aggressively anymore because I want to, and he knows it. Toeing my shoes off, I pull my t-shirt up over my head and begin to unbutton my jeans. My fumbling fingers can't seem to get them down my thighs quick enough as I yank at them in irritation. Elegant undressing this is not, and I couldn't give a shit in this moment because I need him to remind me, to find me again. Finally, after much shuffling, I'm standing in the middle of the hall in nothing but my underwear. He raises a brow at me, and stares for a moment. "All of them." Oh, okay. Another bout of shuffling and I'm absolutely naked, and not in the least bit nervous about it as I stand, watching him watching me.

"Down," he says, so I do immediately. Knees slightly apart, just wide enough for his shoes, head gently dipped, just low enough to submit, just low enough that he'll be happy. Whatever I'm entering into with Pascal and him, it seems there are rules that need to be followed. What the hell they are, I have no idea. His feet walk over to me and then around the back of me. One finger draws up the length of my spine and has me moaning in pleasure at the feel of it. There's just the right amount of pressure to cause me to flinch away from him, and just the exact amount of tension needed for my core to begin that ache. "Seems you've missed me."

Much as I might hate to admit it, I have, desperately. I've missed this connection. All the drama, of his making I might add, has stretched us apart, caused a line between us that I don't want there anymore. I want to feel him on my skin again, in me, all over me.

"You caused the missing you," I say quietly, still keeping my eyes on the floor.

"Mmm," he muses as he comes around in front of me again. "But you understand now, don't you? You're here with all your information, so there's no reason to have anything between us anymore, is there?" I smile at the thought that he can read my mind so well. It's testament to how much he can feel me, too, how well he comprehends what goes on in my mind.

"We do still need to talk, though." We do, after this maybe, but we definitely still do.

He's silent for a while, and I just stay here beneath him, trying to stop some strange sense of need wanting to shuffle me closer to him and close the gap. His shirt falls to the floor by my knees, and I just halt myself from looking up at him. I haven't seen him naked for days, haven't felt the heat of him on me, or the weight of him. Tense minutes fumbling in that room while Pascal dealt with Roxanne were nowhere near enough to satisfy the craving I have for him now. I'm almost giddy with excitement at the thought of his fingers handling me again, almost lost in a closing mist of readiness waiting for him.

"Get up off the floor," he says as a hand comes down in front of me. I look up, slightly confused, and find him smiling at me, a twinkle of amusement in those deep blue eyes. "You'll take what you're given, baby, but you don't have to be down there for it, not now." I'm really not sure what that means, but I'm happy to oblige, I think.

I slip my hand into his, and lightening-quick, he's lifted me up and is walking us backwards to the hall wall. The shock of the impact against my back has me wheezing out a breath and groaning at the thought as his mouth assaults mine. Our tongues tangle in an insistent onslaught of moaning and growling as teeth nip into flesh and cause my legs to tighten in anticipation of what's coming. His hand roughly kneads at my backside as he grinds into me and pushes me harder against the cold of the plaster. Fingers grasp and I wrench my mouth away to pant out a breath as his mouth finds my throat, his throat, and he can take it, he can take it all.

"Fuck, I missed you," he grates out as his weight increases into me, grabbing and grasping onto my leg and picking me up off the wall again. Within seconds, I'm on the bottom step of the stairs and he's all over me. I'm desperately tugging at his clothes as I try to scrape his jeans down his legs so that he can get at me, in me, but I can't get enough purchase to do anything at all. His muscles grind against me roughly, and hot breath pushes any form of rationality out of my mind as he rubs into me with that expert pressure. His hand is suddenly around my throat, so I suck in air before he squeezes it tighter and let him push my head down onto the step behind me. He rises up slowly and towers over me with a smile, such a wicked smile, and as his other hand tugs at his belt and fly, his knees push my thighs wider. I'd look at what his hands are doing, but those eyes of his are nearly black now, so consuming, so dark in their intense stare. Is he still here with me?

His fingers tighten around my throat as he sneers a little and lowers his head to my stomach. There's no fun in this. This isn't a happy reunion. No, this is him reaffirming us, perhaps reaffirming him, to me. I gasp out in pain as his teeth find my inner thigh, then moan almost deliriously around the feel of it as he hooks my knee over his shoulder and growls. My core coils tighter as he moves his mouth to the other side and does it again, fiercer this time and with no restraint at all. My body relaxes into it as if this is normal. It is normal, perfectly normal for us, and the immediate release of tension as his mouth lowers again is almost euphoric. I still for seconds, waiting to feel his mouth on me, waiting to feel his tongue swirling inside and sucking on that place I need him to be. He hovers. He knows exactly what I'm craving and he just hovers there, prolonging the ache and causing more of it. I can feel him breathing on me, blowing air across me and teasing me. My back arches into him in the hope of spurring him on. He just pushes down on my groin to hold me still and pulls his head away slightly.

"Greedy," he mumbles. He's fucking right. I am, for him. One soft swipe of his tongue and I feel like I'm coming apart, writhing and bucking like a porn star hoping to stretch the moment out somehow. He touches me, just one finger poised at my entrance, and I try desperately to grind down onto it, anything to get him inside of me because this ache is becoming unbearable. My back grates on the stairs as he just holds my throat still and gently circles. Small, soft licks of pressure tease my walls until he dips his head again and sucks. Oh, god, I'm not going to last ten seconds. My legs try to clamp onto something, anything, but he won't give me anything apart from his shoulder, so I end up lifting my whole body from the ground until I'm pinned by my throat and arched across him. He sucks harder, and holds my backside up to his mouth so I can't get away from him, and then increases his sucking and lapping as he hooks my other leg over his shoulder, too. His tongue swirls and teeth bite into me as I continue to moan around every movement and flick, and I can't breathe. I can't get any air. I pant like a dog in the hope that I'll get some, all the time trying to stave off the inevitable explosion that's coming so I can revel in this build up more. My skin is on fire, every muscle taut with energy, ready to detonate and bring me those fucking stars I'm halting. His mouth suddenly stops and that powerful hand moves its grip on my throat around to the back of my neck. What's he doing? With one lift, he's got me against the wall again, this time with me sitting on his shoulders with nowhere to go at all. His hands pin my arms back to hold me in place, literally pinned by his mouth and his butchering fingers. He uses such force as his tongue swipes at me again, and again, and again, teeth biting, tongue dipping quickly. I try to grab onto the wall for balance, but as my orgasm begins to take hold, I can do nothing more than let it take me and hope he can hold me up. Stars flicker, then light behind my eyelids as his name comes screaming from my mouth. I'm panting, swearing and grinding myself into him in a blatant display of adoration for his mouth – a deviant mouth, *my* fucking mouth. Coiling and tensing as he continues to suck me dry and draws his nose along me. I can't move anymore. There's nothing left in me. If he let go, I'd fall flat on my arse, but he won't let go, will he? I just hang there on him, almost suspended by him somehow and realise that I am his property. I simply am his, completely.

And he'll never let go of me again.

I'm not sure how long I've been here but he's not moved me. He's still just got his face in my crotch, flicking occasionally and swiping that tongue up and down to prolong my euphoria. Small sparks of electricity are still riding all over me with every touch, and I know I'll be ready again the moment he starts intensifying himself. But he's just being quiet with me, almost loving – well, as loving as it can be with me pinned to the wall in the middle of the hall. My arms flex against his weight on them and he instantly releases the pressure slightly, acknowledging the truly wonderful pain that's coursing across them and giving me a small chance to regain some blood flow. I push again until I can move my hands to his hair, then coil myself around him as he manoeuvres my body back down on him so that I come to rest on the floor again.

"You still taste perfect," he says quietly, thoughtfully. I haven't got much to say to that so just gaze up at him, lips trembling with that emotion that always consumes me when he's near. "I hope you're ready, hope I've given you enough now."

My fingers gently move to his mouth as he licks his lips and stares at mine. They're soft and warm, full of love and undiluted care, and his eyes, softer than they were ten minutes ago, are far less intense. He wants me to understand, needs me to accept everything and to stop questioning. I don't know how I know that, but I do. I can hear it in his words, register it in my mind, and feel it in his actions somehow. I know that he's sent Pascal away to give us this time together, time so that we can become one again. And that's all I want, to bond with him again and find our way back, or maybe forward.

"I love you, Alex, all of you," I whisper in reply. There's nothing else to say in this moment, no worries or thoughts other than those of love and connection. He smiles and kisses the end of my fingers as he takes my hand in his and begins to walk us up the stairs, to a bed, thank God.

He waves a hand at the bedroom door and watches me like a hawk as I slowly wander past him towards the bed. Why I'm attempting nonchalance is beyond me because I'm so ready for this. My core is dripping with need, desperate for him to take what's his and own me again. My thighs clench with every step as I come to a stop by the footboard and remember holding on to the bedpost in Rome, being bound to it. Has he even got rope here? I need it. I haven't got a clue why I just thought that. Everything we've done together, every small kink he's shown me, and all I can think about is rope.

"Tie me up." The words are out of my mouth before I can stop them. Clearly this is a new thing for me, just blurting it all out there.

"I intend to," he replies smoothly as he opens the bedside drawer, and removes something small. He walks across to me, smirk now firmly in place, and after kissing me briefly, he keeps going with a wink. Where's he going? I swing around to watch him heading toward the locked door at the back of the room.

"What's in the cupboard?" I ask as he unlocks it and pulls the door wide open.

"Come and see," he replies. Why my nerves have suddenly kicked in, I don't know. My arms fold across my chest as if they might protect me from something, and I wander over to look into the cupboard. Oh, it's not a cupboard at all, more a small room, half the size of the huge en suite, I'd say. I stand just in front of him and gaze around the space, which is pretty much empty apart from a few mirrors on the wall. "In you go," he says as he shoves my arse and follows me in.

"Why do you have another walk in wardrobe?" I ask. He chuckles, but it's not a funny one.

He pushes on the wall over by the corner of the room and a large drawer appears from the wall. I peek over to see what's in it. Rope, it seems, and lots of it. My eyes shoot up to the ceiling and then around the sides of the space. There are ringlets everywhere. How I didn't see them before, I don't know.

"So this is your own private kink room then?" I say, trying for nonchalance, but not achieving it in the slightest. "You said you'd never had another woman in here?"

"It was designed for that, yes, but I've never used it." Oh. Well, damn good job too. "We're going to try something, and it's as much about trust for me as it is for you, okay?" he says. I slowly nod my head, having no idea why he would need to trust me in a sexual situation.

"Speak, Elizabeth," he says sharply, that velvety voice suddenly tense and a frown etched on his face.

"Yes, yes. I understand."

"Good," he replies, quietly again now as he draws out several lengths of red rope and drops them on the floor by my feet. Three strides and he closes the door to the room, locks it and walks back to me with the key in his hand. "Hold onto that. Don't drop it." Taking the key from him, I wonder why he's given it to me, or even locked the door, frankly. He could have just closed the door and left it unlocked, couldn't he?

"What am I supposed to do with this?" I ask as I scan my body, which is very clearly naked, and still bloody throbbing.

"Hold it." He bends and picks up the rope. "Stand in the middle."

I move myself to the middle spot and watch as he starts threading the rope through the ringlets, intricately lacing them backwards and forwards so that they start to form a web of sorts inside the room. I'm so mesmerised that I don't notice him pick up my foot until rope bites into my ankle, and that ache suddenly comes racing back again. He moves to my wrist and then my waist, wrapping and twisting the rope again until I'm becoming encased in it as well, a part of the web somehow.

Cuffs are formed around my arms in two locations, one close to my wrist, one on my upper arm, and then both ankles are cuffed, too. Another wrap and two plaits of sorts have somehow appeared over my shoulders leading down to my thighs, which are then also wrapped up. It's so pretty, if you can say pretty about a sadist in action. But it is, dexterous, clever, ingenious really.

"Are you comfortable?" he asks, slowly but directly. I'm entirely sure he's never asked if someone's comfortable before when he's done this. But yes, I suppose I am. I look down at all the rope work again and notice how symmetrical it all is, exactly the same on both sides of my body, as if there's a definite reason for the symmetry.

"Yes, I'm comfortable, and I trust you. I'm okay." He nods and wraps the two ends of the rope around his palms.

"Up you go then," he says, and with a very practised pull of his arms, my feet lift off the floor and my arms stretch out wide. I'm completely spread-eagled, and as I watch him tie off one of the ropes on the wall, I suddenly remember whose hands I'm in. Nerves race back again as I picture the plane, the arsehole behaviour, the slight sense of fear he's capable of making me feel. My body moves involuntarily as if desperately clawing for freedom, and in my struggle, the key falls from my hands to the floor.

"Alex, I-" What? What do I want? For him to let me down again? No, it's just...

"I'm claustrophobic," he cuts in. What? How can someone like him be anything phobic? It's not possible. He must be joking. I stare at him as he yanks the end of the rope tight against the ringlet and walks back over in front of me. "I'm claustrophobic, and I'm going to turn out the lights in a minute so that you can help me deal with that." Oh. I'm sure my mouth is gaping, positive in fact. He picks up the key from the floor, places it in my hand again and curls my fingers around it. "I'm giving you the key so that you can tell me when to use it. Do you understand? So that you can have the power over me in here, I'm negotiating." My mouth opens to say something, but I can't think of a bloody thing.

"Okay," is all I can find. It's not a lot, but all fear has rapidly dissipated so I just gaze at him and wonder what it's like to be in the dark if you're claustrophobic. He nods again and pulls on the other rope in his hand. I'm instantly lifted higher, and wider. I close my eyes and gasp out as the rope constricts tightly, causing that pressure to radiate within me. The rope burns into a more comfortable position and writhes me around until I settle still and eventually open my eyes to look at him again.

"I love you, Elizabeth," he says, his body absolutely still as his eyes pierce mine and remind me of his need for me, his need to find his peace in me. I gaze back into them and see the blue darkening. Whether that's his sadistic side or his own sense of fear, I don't know, but I will make this as easy for him as I can. I want him to love me, want him to show me the more we're both after, and if I can help him in the process then I'll give him everything I can. His shoulders sigh out a tense breath as I wait and watch him crack his neck to the side. His mouth parts. "Lights." And the room is suddenly black.

I mean pitch black. There isn't a shard of light anywhere. I blink my eyes about in the hope of bringing my night vision into play, but there's nothing, only the rustling of his clothes and the feeling of the ropes biting into my skin. A few minutes pass as I listen to my own breathing and still try to look around. Eventually, I realise there really is no point so I just close my eyes and take in a deep breath. Fingers suddenly brush my throat, and after the initial jolt of surprise, I smile at the tenderness in them. There's nothing harsh about them at all.

Although, the next feeling of rope travelling around my neck, albeit loosely, is not quite as reassuring. Something wet touches my arm. It's warm, and I quickly realise it's his tongue as his lips travel across my skin. Never has sensation felt so strange. Not even a blindfold creates this sense of darkness. It's as if there is nothing but the impression of heated air circulating. I can almost feel it on my skin, heavy, binding even, and the spikes of trepidation waiting for a touch, a reaction of some sort to ignite the temperature around us, are potent.

Skin rubs against my thigh and I try to work out which bit of him it is – hard, solid and muscular. It's only when his forearm wraps around my waist to draw me to him that I get some sense of positioning. It was his thigh. His hard cock jabs into my knee – that bit I do know – and I feel my legs start to lift a little as the rope becomes taut against them again. The weight on my arms relaxes, and I start to understand that I'm being lowered to a lying position as I hear the scuffing sound of the rope as it travels through the ringlets around me. I'm just about comfortable with the idea when the rope around my neck tightens, too. My heart rate spikes instantly. His hands are one thing; a hangman's noose is quite another.

"Stop, Alex," I shout out. Everything stops instantly. It's good to know that works even if it isn't my safe word. I suck in a breath and shake my head until the rope loosens a little. "I just... My neck, I can't..."

He chuckles. "Yes, you can. Stop being a pussy, Elizabeth." Oh, how fucking dare he? "Perhaps this will help." His hand clamps around my groin and he presses what feels like three fingers straight into me. The moan that leaves my mouth has even me surprised as my head tips back and sends me straight into that noose again. It immediately begins to tighten, but I don't care. All I can feel is his fingers working me, slow, tantalizing fingers pushing deep inside and stretching me, and oh god, that ache is raging again for him to go faster, harder, further inside, to reach the end of me and spark the magic so I can breathe through this. His thumb lands on my clit and starts circling, small forceful movements pushing me closer to my goal, his goal. I have no idea whose goal it is but I want it. And then my body is swaying back and forth. It's not his hand moving anymore; it's me. The web has created a swing and I'm being pumped onto his hand, harder with every rock into him.

"Yes," I hiss out, a siren's voice, the one reserved only for him. "More, please," I beg. I'm chanting it in my head, over and over again as he increases the speed and lets me bang onto his fingers, a perfect rhythm being created by a man who very clearly knows what he's doing. The ropes tighten again, painfully this time, and my body tries to coil away from it but there's nowhere to go so I just concentrate on his hands and let that mist of my happy place call. All noise disappears apart from my panting. All thoughts of anything other than my orgasm building evaporate into space. It's him that I want, just him, and to come as soon as I can. A sudden sharp pain in my hand reminds me of the key digging into my palm, and then another sting of pain across my arse from his hand, which burns deliciously, and has me screaming from the ferocity of it. Oh Christ, that was good, so good. I want another. God, I want another. Please hit me again.

"Again," I stutter out on a shaky breath. I immediately get one, this time on the other side, which equals out the blaze sending all sorts of shock waves to my groin. My panting increases to fever pitch. I'm so ready to come, so ready to explode all over him, and... He suddenly stops the swinging and removes his hand from me.

"Not yet. I want to be fucking you when you come. I've waited long enough for it." Bastard.

I blow out a breath in anticipation and wait again. The ropes on my arms loosen a little and I feel myself being dropped backwards, at the same time, the neck rope tightens again and forces me to tip my head backwards and down. I have no idea what this position is for until I feel his hands on either side of my head and his distinct scent under my nose. "Let's see how deep can you take me, Elizabeth." Oh god, I suddenly realise what's happening, and much as the thought worries me, I want him in my mouth, down my throat. In fact, I can feel the saliva pooling in my mouth at the very idea of it. But there's no room for manoeuvre here. I can't get away from him if I try, and I won't even be able to speak to tell him to stop, will I? He pushes his fingers into my mouth roughly and I instantly taste myself on them, sweet, salty. I suck for dear life in the hope of allaying my nerves. He pulls them out and I feel the tip of him brush against my lips. A stronger, salty taste assaults my airways as I swipe my tongue over him and revel in his taste. My lips reach out to draw him into me, hungry for more and very willing to comply with any form of deep throating he needs. He pushes, slowly at first, allowing me to find a comfortable access for him, and then when he reaches my gag reflex, he just holds still. I can't breathe, and a sudden panic sweeps over me as I try and swallow my gag down. My body tries to move away, but there's nothing to push against and he won't let me move. I can't speak. I can feel the shaking all over my body as I wrench my head about to try and get him out but he just increases the pressure on my head to hold me still again, with those fingers digging into my chin a little to keep my airway open and available to him.

"So fucking perfect. Fight me," he growls from above me as he enjoys my struggle, and then slowly shoves forward again, painfully slow. I feel him break through, and I'm left feeling completely choked on him as he holds my lips against his body. I can feel the hair on his groin tickling me as I try to get used to the fullness and find a way to breathe. After a few seconds, he slowly pulls back so I snatch air as quickly as I can and then suck down as he pushes back in again, deeper if that's possible. My throat relaxes a little as I get used to the forceful intrusion, and I find myself wanting him deeper, wanting him to ram back in again until he's fucking my face and drowning me in his come. If I could get my hands to his backside, I'd pull him in now and push him harder. The ache is only heightening every need I have to please him, because he's going to take that away from me, isn't he? He's going to make it better and fill me until it doesn't hurt anymore. His hands pull me back onto him so that I'm swinging again, backwards and forwards onto his cock as it somehow goes deeper still and begins to become fluid, a true rhythm of lust being created around slick sounds and groans of desire. This is why he's holding me so tightly, so that he doesn't hurt me, so that I stay at the right angle for him. It's strange, given his sadistic tendencies, but I can feel the love in those hands. No one else would see that, but I do. He could easily make this hell for me, but he's doing everything he can to make me enjoy this, and I am. His hoarse voice begins growling and groaning above me, as he gets closer. I can hear it in him, feel it in his cock, that slight jumping sensation as he rams in again and almost shudders from the intensity of it. "You feel so fucking good. I could come in you now. Do you want me down your throat?"

Yes, no, I don't know. Actually, no, I want him inside me, but I have no way of telling him that. No sound comes from my throat when

I try to say no, so I shake my head slightly in the hope that he understands, and somehow I sense the smile on his face. I can see it clearly in my mind as he slows his rhythm down and eventually withdraws completely. Spittle stretches across to him as I instantly gulp in a lungful of air and try to get some form of bearing again in the blackness. There's still nothing, no light, no flicker of anything to show me where he is. I feel like I'm back in the safe room downstairs, although this time I'm tied up, and hopefully we're not about to fight.

I just hang there, still lying flat with my head hanging backwards. It's actually quite freeing in a strange way, quite liberating to not have to take your own weight and be supported. The ropes seem to be touching all sorts of pressure points I wasn't aware I had. Like the pieces rubbing across my ribs, slowly grating on every inhalation of breath, teasing and causing a warming friction against me. I hear him move around me, and although I'm inquisitive, I'm so relaxed that my muscles stay loose. I have no ability to move anyway, and he won't do me any harm. Well, no more than he presumes I'm ready for. My ears hone in on the soft padding of his feet around the space, a slight anxiety now building again as his finger travels the length of my leg. No, it's not anxiety, more excited anticipation.

The ropes start to move again, lifting various parts of me, tilting and turning until I'm somehow facing the floor. It reminds me of the picture I saw on the internet when I was researching. My body's perfectly flat. All weight is being taken by my body. There's no excessive pressure on my arms, just my torso and thighs, but there's nothing supporting my head, and the ability to hold it up is taking its toll so I just let it hang down.

"Hold it up," he says from behind me, his hand gently encasing my ankle. I can't even fathom how he knows I've dropped it. It's pitch black, for God's sake. I strain it back up again and try to find a comfortable position, but it's no use. It's just hell to keep it taut. "Try harder. I can feel it in your legs. I can feel everything you do." *Oh.* "If you want to be fucked, you'll keep it up."

Suddenly, I'm using every available technique to keep it up. My neck screams at me as I try with everything I've got to keep it aloft. Pain begins to course across my back, my knees. Everywhere starts to hurt, my body trembling as I continue straining.

"I can't." Before I can finish, something's forced against my lips, coarse and rough.

"Open up," he says sharply. I try to recoil a little but again, there's nowhere to go, so I do as I'm told and the taste of rope scratches against my mouth. "Bite down." I clamp my teeth around it and find I can rest my head's weight into it. What's taking the weight I don't know, but it immediately relieves the rest of my body of its tension. And then he's gone again. I pant through the rope and blink my eyes about again, searching for something to show me where he is. All my senses are now on high alert as to what's coming next, but there's nothing, only the dark, soundless room.

Fingers grasp my hips as the ropes lower my legs. They must be almost on the floor, I think. Actually, I can't quite gauge where I am anymore, and although my balance has been changed, I still need this rope in my mouth to help keep me straight.

His hand is suddenly on me, and I moan out in relief of something to take the ache away. Fingers delve in as I hear the slick sound of myself. I'm pulled back towards him and then released, pulled then released. His hands are tightening painfully, reminding me of those preferences. One pull and his fingers come out, and the next shunt backwards and his cock rams into me as his holds me still against him. Oh god, the feeling of being filled is glorious, so tight. My muscles clamp onto him straight away, sending shudders of ecstasy into my stomach. That ache is almost obliterated by just his presence within me. I clamp down again, hoping to move him somehow, but I'm all in his hands. He's the one who'll dictate everything here. He teases me with tiny movements, just enough to cause more waves of delight to flicker across me, just enough to encourage the feeling of want.

His arm moves around my waist, trapping the wind in me with a quick yank backwards to him and another hard drive in. Yes. It's all I need, and as his size assaults me, I picture his face, that gritting of teeth as he takes what's his. My own teeth clench at the thought. Another ram in, brutally, deep enough that it hurts, and I humph out a noise that resembles speech. Oh god, it's good, so good, so deep and delicious. His pace increases and I can feel every ripple of him inside me as he pulls me backwards to him, harder every time. I can't breathe with this fucking thing in my mouth so I spit it out and moan out as he delivers another punishing stroke. I wish I could get his hands to my throat, wish his fingers were there, claiming me, owning me more with every thrust of his hips. I'm all his. This is all for him, me, *us*. Grunts come from behind me, and I'm swearing and cursing as I try to focus on not coming, on trying to prolong this until he tells me I can come. I don't even know how I know that because he hasn't told me I can't, but it's yet another thing I just know now. It's all under his command. It's all about what Alex wants, what he needs. He'll tell me when I can let this go, tell me if it's allowed.

My core screams at me for release. My throat is begging for his hands. Mewling and panting, drooling even, I just take the pain of his touch and revel in it, trying to keep myself from disappearing completely to the point where I can't hear him anymore, can't control what's happening to me. But that fog is closing in, and I can feel those lights haunting me, readying me for my climax. My body's humming and tensing, toes curling and a scream is building up inside me, desperate to escape.

"You'll fucking wait." He growls at me as he slams in again and again. The strain reaches fever pitch as he somehow changes my angle about again and my feet touch the floor. My knees buckle the moment they make contact. Completely unable to hold myself up, I'm saved only by his strength holding me, and his hand grasping at my throat to bring me back to him. Vicious fingers squeeze around my throat and I know there will be bruising, but this is us now. This is the sadist in him, and I don't want to control him anymore, don't want to question the whys or reasoning behind it. I just want him to give me it all, to show me how he wants it, to let me love him for all he needs to be.

I have no muscle control at all. It's all trembling and collapsing around me. The only thing I can focus on is the impending orgasm that is barely controllable as he keeps driving into me. Then my arms are suddenly loose. I don't know how, but the pressure from behind me to get down to the floor is immediate. It's not me who makes the decision to go to the floor. I'm just pushed there like a rag doll. My hips are yanked up high, my arse in the air so he can finish me off, or himself. I don't care. I just need to come.

"Oh god, please," I mumble as his hand shoves my head down to the ground and he keeps ramming into me, delving further into me with each violent slam of his body. Pain builds to excruciating levels and my mind takes over, that subspace not threatening anymore. I'm just there now, lost in my own world and not trying to stop anything as my energy dissolves into a calming void of patience. My cheek rubs on the carpet, causing a friction that intensifies yet another painful sensation. There's more pain, more aching, and more panting as his fingers ferociously tighten, grasping and yanking my throat back towards him as he drives in with force, again and again.

"Now," he shouts as he wraps his arm around my chest and pulls me up to him. I explode in relief, those fucking stars alighting with colours so bright I screw my eyes shut and just feel them pouring over me. I feel him as he powers into me one final time and hot warmth floods the inside of me. Everything clamps, every muscle contracts and coils so tight I can't even scream, can't make any fucking noise at all. His fingers keep squeezing, and I can't breathe again. I can feel him seeping out of me, overflowing and dripping along my thighs. He slowly pulls back a little and a wince leaves my mouth. He smiles in my ear. I can feel the corners of his mouth turning up as he bites at my neck and moves his hand in between us. I freeze at the thought.

"No, Alex, I can't..." I can't take anymore, and I don't want this moment tarnished or changed from the rush of emotion and adrenalin I'm feeling. He just tilts me away from him with firm hands and begins to press his fingers into my arse, his cock still buried inside me. I pant for some air and try to wriggle away, but his teeth bite in again, reminding me to stay still, and then he's in. I don't know how many fingers are there but I'm stretched wide.

"Put your head on the floor," he says quietly as he lets go of my chest and pushes me away from him. I doubt I've got the strength to keep myself up, but I roll forward and place my hands down until my head has come to rest against the carpet again. I go to open my hand but remember the key is still there, so get down on my elbows instead.

"You're incredible. I don't need to see you and yet I can imagine you. Arse high with my hand buried in you, cock seated deep and filling you with my come," he groans out as he pushes those fingers in and out slowly, rocking his hips into me at the same time. This isn't for my pleasure. He's not going to make me come again. This is him owning me, just putting his hands wherever the hell wants to because he feels that way inclined. It's almost degrading. Almost. "Fuck, I want to hurt you. Tell me I can. Tell me I can take it all from you now."

Yes, he can hurt me. Yes, he can take it all from me. I'm here in this dark space, with a locked door and a man who's just starting to show me what he needs, and I'm revelling in it. Power, force, anger, control, this isn't any dominant I've ever read about, tried to learn about. This isn't a man trying to be the good man he told me he'd be. This is a sadist, a dirty, disturbed sadist with only one thing on his mind, and I think I'm only just finding out how far he's going to take me.

"I love you," I say clearly into the carpet, feeling that friction on my face again and imagining the bruises that will be covering me by the morning. I don't care. They'll be his marks on me, his way of knowing I can handle him, that I love him, that he can't frighten me off. His fingers twist around inside me, causing me to arch away a little at the intensity of it, but the smooth, wet driving of his cock eases the discomfort, reminding me about the pleasure of his hands and what they can do for me. He bites down on my back, and nearly tears flesh from bone. My insides scream at the thought. Who could ever say no to him? "I'm all yours, Alex. All yours. You can do what you want."

Chapter 17

Alexander

All he had to do was keep feeling her, keep finding his way around her body and let her rhythm guide him. For once he didn't need to think about the darkness, or the fact that she was holding the key to escaping it. He wasn't focusing on the locked door or the fact that this was the tightest space he'd put himself in since he was a child. He kept pushing away the visions of his bastard father and just smothered her exquisite form with tension and release, tension and release. He let her relish in it and find out how much she could take from him, how much she was going to have to take from him, just giving her a taste of what was to come. Only once had a painful memory entered his mind as he'd listened to her skin moving beneath his hand, felt it quivering and riding around as she'd struggled for comfort, and her mouth around his cock had sent that fear away. The scared little boy had been banished by just one touch of her lips gracing him with her caress. Just like the ties, just like her hands at his throat, he could feel all her love and warmth driving away the negatives and telling him he was worthwhile, loved even.

She was panting now in front of him, trying to get away, or maybe change her sensation, but every time she did, he just held her firm, threatened more of that pain and felt her feeding off of that threat. She was more of a masochist than he thought. Her body continuously writhed under the pressure of hurt and torment, somehow finding another level of beauty he hadn't seen before now. He'd brought them in here for some time to be together again, but in reality, none of this was for her. It had all been for him, so that he could see if she could keep him from panicking, from losing it, and she had. He could have easily continued this out in the open, shown her all his love out there in the bedroom, where he could breathe, but he'd needed to trust her completely and know she could keep him together should the time come. So, he'd given her that key in faith, and thankfully, not once had he felt the need to ask her to open the door.

He'd been far too absorbed in her reaction to suspension to care about the threatening confines around him. Dark corners or not, she had held all his attention the entire time. He'd felt safe, needed, wanted and completely in control. Never had she been more pliable, more relaxed or more open to his hands. Her graceful limbs held muscle tension so well, as if she'd been doing this forever. She'd simply found her space and languidly relaxed within it. Fucking incredible really. Perfect.

So here they sat, his fingers still plundering her arse and her face pressed firmly into the floor as he slowly rocked her onto his spent, yet still aching cock. Forwards and backwards, away and towards, peace and hope. He could fuck her all night in here, fuck her raw and keep making her beg for more of it. The small boundaries of the room smelt of sin and sex, intoxicating, and his mind was firing all barrels at him. *Make her scream, make her beg, make her choke.* She'd taken it all so far, let him shove his cock deep into that perfect throat, let him still force his hand into her even now, even though she was exhausted. He could feel her body giving in to him, just letting him do whatever he wanted. She knew none of this was about her anymore. She was doing this simply to please him.

More fucking perfection.

He withdrew his hand and sat back on his haunches to see what she'd do. She pushed back towards him, offering herself up again. He smiled and gently nudged her away. It was enough for now. She needed to rest. He pulled out of her slowly and heard the wince of pain as his cock came out, which caused another smile of appreciation. He moved around her to feel his way to the cuffs and ties. All of them were removed within minutes until her body just lay there on the floor in front of him. He closed his eyes and ran his tongue along the curves of her hip towards her breasts, then gently lapped at the firm peaked nipple, still ready for biting, teasing. Her hand softly landed in his hair so he moved his neck around to feel her brushing that peace through his skull, every stroke like a divine right being given to the very nature of himself, to allow it free and let her tell him if she needed to stop.

"I love you," he mumbled into her nipple as his teeth nipped against it. She laughed quietly. He fucking loved that sound.

"Me, or my tits?" Well, fuck. That's not what he meant, although they were very good tits.

"You," he replied as he crawled up her skin and brought his mouth down on hers. She didn't move, just lay there and let her tongue dance with his, just let him manoeuvre his way around her frame and relaxed into it. Kissing was so personal now, so glorious in its privacy of two people in love. He decided in that moment that kissing should only ever be performed by lovers, because almost nothing came close to the intensity and emotion of her lips. She tasted of all things good in the world, of freedom, of peace and optimism. Every brush of her mouth was like a taste of happily ever afters, maybe following a fucking yellow brick road to some kind of sanctuary he shouldn't be invited to. He'd follow her anywhere. She wasn't ever leaving him again. She pushed her other hand into his hair and deepened the kiss – deepened it until he could feel her energy kicking back in and her body coming back to life. He pulled away and stood up. They'd never get out of here if he let her start this up again.

"Up you get," he said, as he pulled her weight up, not that there was much of it to pull anywhere. She stood and wobbled a bit as she clung onto his arms, those long fingers grasping on and refusing to let go.

"But-"

He cut her off, because in that moment it really wouldn't have taken much persuasion for him to push aside his love for her and treat her like a whore instead. "Baby, you need some sleep, and I need to go and see your sister."

"Oh," she replied. There really wasn't much else to say, and the fucking thought was disturbing enough. "But she doesn't know you're going."

That was probably for the best. He doubted she'd let him through the door.

"Open the door so we can get clean." The last thing he wanted was to go over there smelling of sex, although it might make for an interesting topic of conversation.

"Oh, right, yes," she said. "Umm, which way is it?" Her fingers let go as she walked away in the direction of a wall. He chuckled. Not all people spent so much time trying to get comfortable in the dark, he supposed, not like he did anyway.

"Lights," he said. The room lit up and he just stared at her, blinking and trying to shield her eyes. He scanned her body, noticing all

238

the damage he'd caused. Bite marks, red welts on her arse and thighs, a raw area on her cheek, and reddened patches all over her from the ropes. The twining of crisscross marks was embedded into her flesh beautifully. And her throat was covered in what was going to be some impressive bruising.

"Alex?" she said. He shook his head a little at the noise. "Alex, are you okay?" Was he? What was going on in his head? Why wasn't he happy about this, horny even? That odd sense of guilt seemed to be nagging him again, telling him he'd done something wrong. He hadn't. They hadn't.

"Yes, fine. Open the door," he replied without looking at her as he held out his hand to her. She unlocked it, all the time looking at him quizzically as if asking a question. He avoided answering and went for a shower instead. He needed to think about what the fuck had just happened, and why he wasn't comfortable with it. He had been before he'd seen the results, results that would normally have pleased him. So why was he suddenly feeling uncomfortable?

He came out from the shower and found her sitting on the edge of the bed, now with his shirt draped around her.

"I need to get going," he said as he pulled some fresh clothes from the wardrobes. "Have you eaten? Get some food and then some rest. I'll be back as soon as I can." He shoved and tugged until he was standing in jeans and a jumper and grabbed his keys from the side.

"Alex, what's the matter?" she asked quietly, her eyes searching his as she gazed and scrunched the covers up in her hands. She looked nervous, intimidated even, so he walked across to her and squatted in between her legs with a smile. Regardless of his own confusion, he wasn't having her a mess, too. Not anymore. She needed him strong and in control. She already had enough to deal with now Pascal had arrived with them, so that's what she was going to get.

"Nothing, Miss Scott. Nothing at all. It's Christmas Eve tomorrow and I assume you want your family here, yes? That means I have to deal with your sister. If I don't go now, I can't let Conner know it's okay, and I'll have let down not only you, but him, too. I love you. I'm fine. Everything is fine. Have a cold shower and get some rest, okay?" With that, he kissed her forehead and made for the door. He'd apply the balm later tonight, when she was asleep.

"Cold?" she said.

"Cold. It will help with the…" Bruising? Pain? He couldn't even bring himself to saying the fucking words out loud. "Marks on your body," he finished quietly, suddenly disgusted with the thought.

"Okay," she said behind him. It wasn't a convincing okay but he hadn't got time to dwell on it, and he needed some fucking air.

He was at the garage and in the *Aston* before he gave himself another chance to think about it. What the fuck was wrong with him? She'd just done everything he wanted of her, offered it, delivered it, and now he wasn't comfortable with it? Jesus fucking Christ, what a screwed up son of a bitch he was. Where was Pascal? He needed to talk to Pascal about this, although why that man would have a fucking clue he didn't know. Or maybe he would? He seemed to know everything about him most of the time.

He floored the car up the drive and stopped at the top to think about his direction. Pascal had gone to Eden after dropping Evelyn off. He could go now and have a drink. What time was it? He looked at his watch. 9.30pm. No, he needed to go and see Belle, needed to put that right first, so he turned towards their apartment and blew out a breath in anticipation of the oncoming fight.

He was there before he knew it. The car idled over the road in a back alley as he scanned the area for troublemakers. There didn't appear to be any in this neighbourhood but he gave the car a pat on the bonnet as he got out, just in case. It wasn't that he loved it that much – more that she did. And Christ did she look good in it. He walked over the road, avoiding the dick on a motorbike who very nearly ran him over, and wandered into the lobby. Cool, calm, he needed to keep it together because Belle would no doubt be launching into a tirade about how terrible he was for her sister, how he didn't deserve her, and what a useless piece of shit he was. He got it. She was right. She'd still be sitting at his dining table having Christmas dinner, though, right next to Conner. One way or another, that's exactly where she'd be. He pressed the elevator button and waited as it rose up beneath him to their floor. Deep breaths, calm, intelligence was going to win this fight, not brute strength. He walked along the hallway and rapped his knuckles on the door then waited for her.

"Who is it?" she called through the door a few seconds later.

"Alex," he replied, keeping it as informal as possible. Perhaps she'd be more relaxed if he was pleasant.

"Fuck off."

Maybe not.

"Belle, I'll break it down if you want?" Just a bit of brute strength might be necessary, useful even.

He heard the stomp of feet coming towards the door and moved sideways a touch. If she was anything like her sister, she'd definitely try to throw something at him, or scratch his eyes out. Sure enough, the door opened and what appeared to be a large, glass ashtray went hurtling into the wall behind him. He looked down at the remnants and smirked as he turned back towards her. These Scott girls were going to be the death of him, he was sure. She wasn't smiling in response. Shame. Ferociously dressed in a red dress, she glared at him and folded her arms, once again blocking his entry, just as she had last time.

"Fuck off," she reiterated. Eloquent as that was, and as much as he got it, he hadn't got the time. And Elizabeth was in his bed, waiting for him to tell her everything was going to be okay.

He pushed forwards and watched her eyes widen in surprise as he grabbed her forearms and forced her back inside. Her heels tripped a little as she tried to fight back so he lifted her and dumped her on the kitchen counter.

"Get it all out, Belle," he said as he took off his jacket and reached for a bottle of Vodka. Didn't they have any decent alcohol in here? Christ. He took two glasses from the cupboard and filled both to the top.

"What the fuck was that? You think manhandling me is okay?" she asked, still clearly bemused by his actions as he offered her a glass and moved away to the couch.

"I'm feeling determined, so say your piece and then I'll have my go."

"Say my piece? I said I'd listen to you. That's all. I have nothing to say to you," she said, that shorter hair of hers being pushed behind her ears and a look of loathing firmly embedded on her face.

"Really? You don't want to tell me what you think of me?"

"One thing you're not, Alex, is stupid. I'm pretty damn certain you know exactly what I think of you. And it appears it doesn't matter what I think, anyway. She'll still choose you. The really irritating thing is, in a roundabout way, I sodding told her to."

He took a step back in amazement; she'd been nice about him at some point? Well, that was a fucking turn up for the books.

"What do you mean?"

"You want me to answer that, tell you how fucking good I thought you'd be for her? Tell you how I told her to give you everything because it wouldn't work if she didn't? You egotistical bastard, you are so unworthy of her love. You live in a damn fairytale world where everything is bright and shiny and new, and there's nothing else than what Alexander White orders, what gets delivered to him because he so desires it. What a wanker you are. You have no idea of how love hurts, the pain that is caused by actions that happen without thought."

"Belle..."

"No, you asked. Now you can damn well listen," she said as she hit the floor and stormed toward him. "Did she tell you about Marcus? How he abused me, how he beat me and emotionally battered me until I had nothing left to give? Do you have any idea what bruises look like when they're littered across your body? Can you imagine the fear that is caused by the person you love most in the world treating you like shit, manipulating you, treading all over you like you don't exist other than to be a physical sounding board for paranoia and hatred?"

"Yes, I-"

"No, shut the fuck up. Listen to what I'm saying. You treat her just like that. You walk all over her with your whims and fancies. Kidnapping her? What fucking planet do you come from? Why would you think you have the right to do that? Is she not allowed an opinion, a chance to say no?"

"Of course she is, and I would never-"

"What? Hit her? Really? BDSM, the ability to relish pain from the deliverer, sound familiar? I read it in a kink forum. Quite insightful it was. How do you deliver her pain, Alex? Whips? Shackles? Or do you prefer to just order her around and treat her like a fucking slave? Do you think anyone really enjoys that bollocks? Fuck you, you're a piece of shit, and I hate you. You're ugly in here," she snarled, tapping her fist over her heart. "You must know that. You must know you'll never give her what she deserves. There is nothing you can say to make me believe you're worth her love. Nothing. Do you understand? Is that enough of me saying my piece for you, you dick?"

He pulled in a breath and waited to see if anything else was coming. She just stood there staring at him without a hint of fear or apprehension. Belle Scott meant every word she'd just said, and it wouldn't surprise him if she'd be happy to die for it, die for her sister. At least they agreed on that. It suddenly all made sense – her attitude, her hardened edges, her ability to manipulate and control everyone around her. Her abuser was still her keeper, the person in her mind that kept nudging information around to prolong the agony, just as his bastard of a father had been to him, until his angel came along.

"Have you finished?" She didn't answer, just continued staring and then downed the vodka in her hand without so much as a slight change of facial features. Still stern, still obviously very angry. "Would it help you if I told you about my past?"

"I couldn't give a fuck about you. There is no excuse for-" It was his turn to cut in. She was going to see that he knew exactly how she felt. He yanked his jumper over his head and watched her face change instantly to surprise as she started to back away.

"I don't know what you think you're doing, but..." He moved towards her.

"I had at least eight broken ribs by the time I was five," he said as he offered his hand to his ribs to point out the small lumps. "My arm is still slightly bent because of an unset fracture. My shoulder still dislocates due to being dragged about so much. I'm claustrophobic, scared of the dark and up until recently could barely breathe if I had a tie on for fear that it might choke me. You can't see a mark on here, can you? It's all clear now, isn't it? Perfect, some would say, but I can assure you those bruises are still there, Belle. I know very well what it feels like to be abused by the one person you love most in the world – actually, the only person you know in the world. And I'm very aware what a piece of shit I am. That statement was rammed home enough for me to never forget it." He snarled out a breath at the memory and watched her mouth soften a touch, just the faintest hint of care. She looked like his angel in that moment, which made him smile as he imagined her. She still didn't trust him, though. That was fine. That would come with time. "My father was, is still, a monster, who took great delight in reminding me of how worthless I was as often as possible. But she takes those memories away for me, Belle. She makes me feel like I have a point, a purpose. She is giving me another chance at decency, and a life. She is the only one who has ever given me any sense of peace, and I'm afraid I refuse to lose that. I'm not letting her go, regardless of how you feel about me, so we need to get past this."

She was quiet, her hands still folded as she stared at him some more and sneered a little, possibly in revulsion.

"Right," she said quietly. He wasn't entirely sure if she gave a shit about his past, but at least the venom had left her voice. They might have a chance at a normal conversation now.

"Belle, sit back down for God's sake. Whatever this animosity is, I need to talk it through with you, help you understand," he said as he went to fill their glasses. She suddenly moved and stopped him with her hand as she reached into the cupboard. What the hell was she doing now? Did she have another glass ashtray in there? He narrowed his eyes at her and got ready to duck. She pulled out a bottle of brown liquid and put it in front of him. Whiskey. He nodded at her and opened it as she poured herself another vodka.

"That must have hurt," she said, sipping it as she slid onto the stool beside him.

"Yes, it did." If he thought about it, he could still feel the impact of that bastard's hands every day.

"I didn't mean the bruises. I meant having to tell me. Did she make you do it?"

"No, she would never do that and you know it. I thought it might help. I knew nothing about your past. She didn't tell me. I'm sorry."

"Mmm..." She sipped again and he heard the sound of her heels hitting the floor beneath them as she gazed at the counter top. "You can put your jumper back on now. It's hardly appropriate to have you parading around here half naked."

He chuckled and walked over to his discarded jumper to pull it back on. Funnily enough, she was right. Something about being undressed in front of Belle didn't feel appropriate at all. He pondered the thought while shoving his head through the jumper. It had never happened before. Being naked in front of women had always been very easy, thoughtless even. Perhaps it was that he'd just explained his past, or maybe it was just that sense of moral decency kicking in. He ruffled his hair and looked back at her.

"How do you feel?" It was strange to use Elizabeth's words. He wasn't sure he'd ever used them before, but fundamentally, he was interested in Belle's response.

"Irritated," she replied. It wasn't what he was hoping for, but at least it was better than furious. "Is this supposed to make me think you're okay now? That you're not going to be a dickhead anymore? Because, while I, too, am sorry for your past, I still don't think you're good enough for her."

He stared for a few minutes. She had a point. How he was going to make her believe he would look after, love and protect her sister for the rest of his life, he didn't know. He found himself rubbing the back of his neck and chuckled at the very thought of trying to manipulate the sister, and what was the point anyway? He needed her to actually believe the truth, to believe that he would die to make sure Elizabeth was content and her future secure.

"I'm not good enough for her, but I intend to make her happy, and for that I need you to be pleased about us and satisfied in your own life, preferably with Conner." She scowled over her shoulder at him and then pointed to the back of her dress. What the hell did that mean?

"The zip, Alex. Undo it." He stared at her back in shock for a moment and tried to fathom what the fuck she was doing. "Just undo the bloody zip, will you?" He walked over and unhooked the catch then peeled the zip downwards a little.

"All the way, please," she said as she straightened up, her voice suddenly softer. Surely she wasn't coming on to him? He pulled it down a bit further and then backed away to his whiskey again. It was safe over there. "Well, I never thought you'd turn this down," she continued as she began pulling the dress from her shoulders and turned towards him with a seductive smile. Interesting game she was playing.

"What are you doing, Belle?" he asked as she wandered towards him, her dress pooling as she stepped out of it and continued forward, leaving her in nothing but a red bra and thong.

"We're the same, you and I," she whispered, shaking out her hair and smiling at him. "I never thought I'd meet someone who understood it. The pain, I mean. We could help each other out, you know." Her fingers landed on his chest, then she walked her way around his body, dragging those talons on the way and reminding him of his angel. His cock hardened instantly at the thought as he briefly closed his eyes and imaged her at home, in his bed, waiting for aftercare.

"Belle, you need to stop." She had no idea of his pain, and this was most definitely not going to happen. Her hand lowered and grasped at his cock through his jeans.

"Someone doesn't think I should." He raised a brow at the thought.

"My cock will fuck most things," he said quietly as he grabbed at her fingers and moved them away. "I won't, not anymore. You should be careful of the game you're playing, Belle. You're making yourself look as bad as me."

"Maybe I am," she said, her lips brushing his ear and gentle kisses raining down his cheek towards his mouth. His mind briefly tracked the possibility that this could be useful to him – that he could blackmail her with this moment if he let it go just a bit further. Then he saw his angel's eyes gazing back at him, the vision of them in tears if she ever found out. It wasn't something he ever wanted to witness again. That was enough. He grabbed Belle's hand harder and pushed her away. She instantly smirked at him and wandered off to her drink again, all elements of seduction apparently gone as she knocked it back and threw a blanket from the sofa around her, chuckling. Clever bitch.

"A test, I presume. Did I pass it?" he asked. He hadn't fucked her, so presumably he must have.

"I don't know. Did you? Do you want to fuck me? How's that cock doing?"

"It's thinking of Elizabeth." She chuckled again and sat down on the sofa.

"Good. Everything else she's had has wanted to fuck me, so I guess you've at least got some morals in that brain of yours. Let's talk a little, see what else you've got to persuade me with," she said as she pointed towards the chair and tucked her feet up in the blanket.

They talked for what felt like hours. He hadn't really got a clue what they talked about, but she was actually easy to talk to, easy to discuss matters with now that she was calmer. She was also very different to her sister, scarred maybe from her past. He didn't know, but every word that left her mouth was prepared, thought out. She had the ability to measure her words succinctly and to not beat about the bush where her opinions were concerned. She'd get on well with Evelyn. Either that or they'd hate each other instantly. He watched her direct the conversation away from Conner every time he tried to get to his next point: getting them back together. If he could figure out exactly what had driven them apart it might help. She got up and disappeared off into her bedroom, so he dug around in his coat pocket to retrieve her engagement ring. Placing it on the coffee table, he mused the ring and wondered what he'd need to say to make this right again. She emerged a few minutes later in cut off shorts and a t-shirt, her hair flowing around her shoulders and a relaxed smile on her face. He didn't think he'd ever seen her look quite so much like Elizabeth. The family resemblance was striking to say the least. Then she saw the ring. Her face screwed up as she stood there and frowned at it.

"Why is that here?"

"He asked me to give it back to you, to tell you that he still means it."

"He doesn't love me enough. Take it back to him," she spat as she reached for the bottle of vodka again.

"He adores you, Belle. How can you say that? Whatever's happened, it needs resolving. He's miserable without you." She simply stared at it for a few more minutes and then looked back at him in distaste as she snatched up her vodka.

"I'm sure you'll make it all better for him," she replied, sarcasm dripping from her as she sat as far away from the ring as she could.

"What happened?"

"You did. You always do. You're always right there in between us to cause a rift, to make him choose. I took his choice from him this time. You're not someone I'm prepared to compete with or play second fiddle to. It's difficult enough to deal with you having control of my sister, you think I want you involved in my own love life, too?"

"He would have chosen you. He told me that last time."

"He shouldn't have to choose anyone. He should love me enough to not question his loyalty. I don't know what you have over him but it's not going to work if-"

"Loyalty? Grow up. He's not a dog. He's the closest thing to a brother I'll ever have, and the most decent human being I have ever met, except for maybe your sister. You have no right to make him choose anything. Do you honestly believe the way to keep someone like Conner is to force him to make him choose who he cares for more? You talk about me being a control freak? Jesus, Belle, he loves you. Even with your tempestuous behaviour, maybe even because of it. You'd be a fool to let him go."

"It's nothing to do with you. Just take it away."

He noted the resolution in her face and knocked back a shot of whiskey. In most circumstances like this he'd just find a way to force the correct response, make someone do what he wanted without them even knowing he'd achieved it. But the woman was potentially family, his angel's sister, and his best friend's fiancé. Truth was the only way forward.

"Belle, I need you," he said, his throat constricting at the very thought as he stared at the floor. Christ, he hated this feeling – disadvantaged, desperate, dependant on someone else's response to a situation to make everything morally fucking acceptable. His irrational, overbearing and irritating emotions were now drenched in distress and inward conflict. It was the very reason he'd never allowed anyone inside, so that no one had the ability to make him need them, physically or emotionally. So that he would never need anyone in return. But he did need Elizabeth, and therefore Belle. Fuck.

"What was that?" she said. He lifted his head and tried to stay calm. "Did you just say you needed me?" She looked a little shocked, was even frowning at him in confusion. He blew out a breath and looked back into his now empty whiskey glass.

"For whatever reason, you are right. She will choose me over you, but she'll never forgive me for it, not truly, and I can't have that in between us. We will all suffer if that's the case, you included, and none of this will work out pleasantly. I love her, Belle, and I want her to want me entirely despite my flaws, but you're preventing that. Your attitude towards me makes her uneasy, flighty, anxious even, and I refuse to allow that in her life, regardless of whether you're right in your beliefs or not. She should be worshipped, adored, left to fly free with her dreams and aspirations. You shouldn't tarnish her with your own past, just as I'm trying not to over-paint her with mine. She's inspirational to me, a light to shine through the dark memories and help me find a future to be proud of, worthy of even."

"Well, that's all very sweet, but-"

"No, I haven't finished. You need to be bloody honest with yourself because Conner is that for you, too, isn't he? He gives you that solidity you need, that feeling that, no matter what you throw at him, he will always be there, ready to take more punishment just to show you that he loves you, will always love you, that he'll stay and protect you. So you push him away, don't you? You squash him down into a box and you put the lid back on, because that feeling of needing someone is so overpowering that you could kill it for even daring to enter your mind, couldn't you? You destroy it before it gets a chance because it's not worth the risk to your heart, is it? Not again? We are alike, Belle, and we may have had some similar experiences, but I'm not hiding from my chance of happiness. I'm going to fight for it and bow down to her, and no one's going to stop me, Belle. You included. Take that how you like because I couldn't give a shit what you think of me, but you should perhaps try the same, before it's too late."

He picked up the ring and looked at it. It really was stunning. Conner's choice had been perfect. He considered what colour Elizabeth would need. This red suited Belle, suited her anger, her venom. His angel would need something less intense, more dreamlike, virginal even in a strange way, less corrupted. Marriage. He chuckled at the thought. He'd already given her his throat. She'd never need anything else to know he belonged to her, unless she wanted it of course.

"Quite a speech," Belle said as she plucked the ring from his fingers and sank back into the sofa. "You're very good at that, turning a conversation to suit yourself. Do you do that to her, too?" He smirked and shrugged his jacket on. She was one of the few people who refused to let him do it, unless it suited her purpose.

"She doesn't let me anymore. She sees through it. So I'm honest, probably for the first time in my life, with the exception of Conner."

"He does that to me too," she mused softly, now playing with the ring and twiddling it around in her hand. He stood up. There was nothing more he could say. She was holding the ring and thinking about her future; that's all he'd hoped for, and he wanted to get back to the woman who loved him.

"He's had a lot of experience looking through bullshit," he replied as he thought of their years together. He walked towards the door and placed his glass on the counter as he went by. "He loves you, Belle. You shouldn't let anyone take that away from you, least of all someone in your past. And certainly not me."

"Hmm." He heard her mumbling as he opened the door. "Ask Beth to call me, will you?"

Beth... It still didn't sound right to him. He mouthed the name and closed the door behind him. Bethy. Her mother called her that – Bethy. It was quaint, loving. How was she? He assumed they were still coming for Christmas, that Belle hadn't put them off. He turned back to the door and knocked again. She answered it a few seconds later.

"Did you tell your parents Christmas was off?"

"Not yet. I was debating it when you arrived."

"Then you'll all be there?"

"Just ask Beth to call me. I'll talk to her about it tomorrow. Maybe we can avoid a catastrophe somehow," she replied as she closed the door again, with her left hand. The ring was on it.

Chapter 18

Elizabeth

I wish I knew the number entry code for the garage. If I did, I'd be able to get in one of the cars and slip out of here to see Belle before anyone got up. Alex is still sleeping. I have no idea what time he got in, but I know it must have been late because I was awake till 2.30 and he wasn't home then. My other choices involve taxis or Andrews, and he can still stick a foot up his own backside as far as I'm concerned. I suppose I'm going to have to speak pleasantly to him at some point, but I'll string the irritated behaviour along for as long as I can, just so he gets the point. I may have forgiven Alex for the strange kidnapping thing, but with Michael it just seems harder somehow. I wonder where he is. I haven't seen him since we got back from New York. He just drove us home from the airport and then disappeared. Maybe he's already left for Christmas.

I could just phone Belle, but it doesn't seem enough. Having a chat about whatever occurred between she and Alex last night on a phone just seems inadequate, as if I should give it the same respect it would deserve if he'd been talking to me about his past. His past. We still need to talk about that. There's no denying that what happened upstairs last night was illuminating and pulled us back together in a way we needed desperately, but I still need to understand why he's a murderer and what happened to make him that way.

I'm fiddling with an ornate bowl of glass baubles that's sitting in the middle of the kitchen table, reds, gold's and greens, all the colours of Christmas daring me to have a good time, to enjoy myself and play with the ones I love. As if that's going to happen now. He might have spoken to her, she may well have understood, but even if she does come over, everything is going to be awkward, isn't it? We're all going to be tense and uncomfortable. I might as well just cancel it and stop this pretence that we can make it alright. It's not alright. None of it is all fucking right apart from Alex and I, just. Pascal is still going to be a conundrum until we get whatever this is moving forward; Conner and

Belle are still not together as far as I'm aware; my mum still has cancer; Evelyn is still a complete unknown, and there's also Henry and now Aiden Phillips to contend with. I should just be happy about life given my breakthrough in understanding Alex, but I just want to crawl into a hole until I can at least sort one of these issues out. I need to feel useful, need to feel like I'm putting things right and making some positive decisions about my life again.

I need to bake my cake.

I'm up and clattering around the kitchen looking for utensils before I'm aware I'm doing it. Cooking will make everything better, won't it? It will almost definitely make sure Belle and Conner get back together, and there's the highest probability I can make Alex's past just piss right off by whipping up some icing, isn't there? Maybe a quick bashing of alcohol soaked fruit can show cancer what a pain in the arse it really is? For fuck's sake, what am I doing? I need to get a sodding grip. Mixing bowl. I couldn't care less how much of a prat I look. This is my way of bringing it all together again, of making everything happy in the world. Cook it, bake it, potentially thrash it, that one might actually work in some circumstances. My hand reaches for the butter just as a waft of a familiar scent comes into the kitchen. He's really not what I need at the moment.

"Butter this time, my rose? I believe it was honey last time we were here. Hmm, slippery, we could use this for many delightful activities." I'm actually waving a wooden spoon at him as I scowl at his amused indifference to my chaotic thoughts. Not that he knows what they are, but that's not the point. Why is he always so relaxed? And why does he always look so damn perfect, with his pristine lines and effortless sophistication? He's wearing an olive green suit this morning, beautifully fitted of course. Is it possible for him to be a mess?

"Sod off," I eventually respond as I snap my face back to my cake. I will bake my cake. I can actually hear his brow rising behind me as his arms encircle my waist and pull me back towards him.

"Did he not fuck it out of you? I had assumed you would be more tranquil this morning, less troubled in your thoughts," he says as his hand splays over my crotch. It's a damn good job I've got skintight jeans on because I'm sure his hand would be inside them if they were looser. His other hand brushes my hair over my shoulder as his lips descend on my neck. They're soft. In fact, he's being soft. Why? My eyes narrow. "These bruises suit you, my dear, but why does this tension still consume you if he gave you all you need, hmm?"

Bruises? What does he mean by that? Oh shit, last night. Damn it. I knew it at the time. My eyes flick to the stainless steel splash back to see the damage but it's not enough to get a clear sight of them so I try to move away from him. He just increases his hold until it's more like his normal grip, heavenly frankly. That inner slut of mine wakes up instantly and begins the pathetic panting thing that's only meant for Alex. I really need to just accept this as normal for both of them now.

"I want to see them," I reply. It's not that I'm scared of the thought. I can always cover them. It's more that I actually want to see his collar on me, the real imprinted version. Not the diamonds that are still on the bedside table at my apartment, I mean the imprints of his hands around me, his hold over me and mine over him.

"Why?" he asks softly, still nuzzling around my neck and making all sorts of reactions collide within me. Are we allowed to do this now? Is this okay? What if Alex walks in? Oh god, I'm horny. What about my cake? Oh, and the bruises. I stiffen up and push back against him as hard as I can to try and move again. He just laughs, dirtily.

"Pascal, please, I need to see them, and this is not happening. I'm not even sure if this is allowed to happen. Are you?"

"What is not happening? We are not doing anything. I am simply showing you I care, like a lion would his pride," he says as he gently releases me. Really? And what is all this gentle stuff about? I wander away from him and towards the hall mirror, tugging at my white shirt collar as I go. I have no idea why I didn't notice this earlier.

"Why are you being so gentlemanly all of a sudden? It's not normal. Stop it."

"Because I told him to behave more appropriately around you." Alex's voice comes drifting down from above me as I finally reach the mirror. Behave? Well that's a highly inappropriate word for either of them given the shades of purple that are dotted around my neck. It's like a necklace really. In fact, as I gaze at the marks, I can't help but wonder why I've never had any before. Was his grip that much firmer last night than it has been before? It didn't feel it, but it must have been, or maybe I'm hardening up to his hands. He comes around behind me without touching me, and stares into the mirror. It's his concerned face, the one he had last night when we left that small room. Not the one he had when he lied and told me everything was alright. I mean the one before that, when everything definitely wasn't alright. He licks his lips as his calm blue eyes watch me watching him. He's trying to gauge my reaction to these marks, in his own way trying to ask me if they're okay, if I'm okay.

"I don't think either of you should ever behave at all around me." I don't know where that came from. I'm positive I just wanted to think it but it just came out, fell from my lips as if destined to drop me in the shit. He smirks at me, those crippling eyes of his crinkling in amusement as he softly sweeps his hand over my throat and covers his own fingerprints. I can't stop the reaction that erupts within me. The want is instant, and I could so easily fall into these hands so he can use me again. I cover his fingers with mine to let him know it's alright, that I wanted it at the time, and that I'm happy with the result as his frown descends a little. This is him, and I asked for it, begged him for it, and he's finally revealing it all to me. He stares for a moment more and then pulls his hand away and walks toward the study. I watch him leave and glide my eyes over the dark blue pinstripe suit that encases his form. It's cut to perfection, just like the body it holds, and it's clinging to all the right areas. Very appealing indeed. I so want him right now, so want to grab hold of that hair and prove to him that these marks are completely okay and that I need more of them, as soon as possible. Pascal follows him, which leaves me feeling a bit left out so I pop my head around the door to find them sitting opposite each other, very seriously. "Umm, last night?" I ask. He looks me over, and smiles, one of those dazzling ones that completely steals my breath away. I cling to the door for support as I watch those eyes sparkling to life again, not one bit of remorse there now. He's so not thinking of Belle. Well, I hope he's not.

"Do you need more?" Yes, clearly, but I'd also like to know about the current festive dining arrangements.

"Actually, I meant the thing with Belle." Pascal turns to look at me with an astonished looked.

"Is your sister joining in also, my rose?"

"No," Alex and I both say in unison as I gawp at Pascal. The thought is slightly worrying. I'm not even sure I'm comfortable introducing them to each other. That's a point. I need to organise

Pascal's behaviour around that situation. She isn't going to understand this set up at all, not that I really do either. At least he won't be here for Christmas.

"She asked that you call her," Alex says, stealing my gaze from Pascal. I turn back towards him and find him leaning on the desk, his fingers steepled on his lips as he watches me carefully.

"What did you say?" I ask, somewhat hesitantly. If she knows he's killed people for a living in his past, it is not going to go down well at all.

"What was needed," he replies. That's it apparently. A very serious frown is all I get to help me out with that statement. Helpful. Right, well I better get going then, and see my sister.

Within ten minutes, I've managed to organise myself, done some covering of my throat and applied an acceptable amount of make-up to make me look semi presentable. Although the ridiculously expensive beige silk scarf and fedora hat combination that I've got going on probably lets the whole world know where I shop, or rather where Alex shops. I find my way back into the kitchen and realise I still haven't baked my cake. I must do that later, but first I need to talk to Belle and get Alex a present of some sort.

"What's the garage code?" I call as I throw my leather jacket on and grab the *Aston* keys off the table.

"Why?" he replies. "You're not going anywhere. I have plans for you today," he says as he rounds the corner and comes down the hallway towards me. I bet he does, and I'm more than willing. That point is clearly made by my buckling knees, as he owns me with every damn step. But I have no fucking present for Christmas Day, and good as that suit and the man in it are, I have to get out to find something for him. Actually, why is he in a suit? Where's he going?

"I have Christmas shopping to do, and I want some privacy to talk to Belle. Why are you in a suit?"

"I have some business to attend to. You're still not going out." Really? Both my hands have found my hips because he's got that look going on that I'm not at all fond of. And what business anyway? It's Christmas Eve for God's sake?

"I thought you had plans for me."

"I do. I plan to tie you to the dining room table, half fuck you, use one of your choices of butt plug, and then gag you until I get back.

255

I was considering leaving Pascal in charge of you while I'm gone, but I'm not sure he'll understand your signals, yet." Well, that was honest. Very honest. And I'm pretty sure my gaping mouth proves my utter surprise at the statement.

"Oh…" Not surprisingly, that's all that comes out as I watch the upward curl of his lips. There's no other movement. He's completely still. It's absolutely possible he might just pounce any minute and give me no choice in the matter.

"I thought it might make for interesting Christmas lunch conversation." He's sodding right there. I try to hide my smile and keep up the pretence that I'm being firm, but frankly, what's the point? Those dazzling blues and sinful smirk have me thinking all sorts of interesting things. I take a step backwards in the hope of evading capture – ridiculous, I know. His smile broadens.

"Well, yes, interesting indeed, but I still need to go out so I'm afraid it's-"

I don't know why I bothered. Three strides is all it takes for me to start screaming as I'm hoisted over his shoulder, giggling like a child. Teeth sink into my thigh as his fingers tighten and I catch an amused smile coming at me from the study in the form of Pascal as we go by. "Alex, please." I squeal as I try to stem my laughter and catch my hat, which has tumbled to the floor. A very healthy swat lands on my arse, making me yelp out again. God, I love him when he's like this – fun, happy and relaxed. "Put me down. I really have to go shopping."

"No." We're now in the dining room. It really does look very Christmassy, and I'd happily spread myself out for him, but I have to go.

"Alex, don't make me safe word you." He stops and leans down to swipe at the things on the table, pushing them out of the way so he can make room for the Christmas Eve lunch he intends to eat. "I really mean it." It's my last-ditch attempt to stop him before the *Chess* word comes out. Pascal arrives at the door and looks at us, that look of amusement now embedded in his stare as he scoops up my hat and crosses his arms to lean on the frame. I'm in so much trouble. I throw my hands out to him for support of some sort. I've no idea why, as if he knows why I need to go out.

"Alexander, it is imperative you desist," he says, quite forthrightly. It's very much his dominant tone and I freeze a little in anticipation of what's coming next. My arse is suddenly swung around towards Pascal as Alex turns and probably glares at the command. "It is a very appealing thought. However, I believe it may be in your best interests to put her down for the time being. I can drop her off on my way to the airport."

After a few minutes, Alex's tense grip is softened and I'm slowly lowered to the floor. Wow, okay, Pascal's on board. I like him more today, as if I ever really like him less.

"I want you back by three." It's all I get as he lets me go and walks out the room in a huff. It's a definite huff. I move to walk after him as he knocks his way past Pascal, but I'm halted by a hand and a slow shake of his head.

"Let him think about himself for a while. His present will be worth his infuriation, I assume? Hmm? What do you have in mind?"

"No idea at all," I reply as he drops the hat back on my head and offers me his arm. He chuckles and picks my bag up from the stairs as we wander along the hallway and into the kitchen again. Lord knows where Alex has disappeared to. Three turns later and the garage door opens to reveal the beautiful array of vehicles, one of which has Alex climbing into it and slamming the door behind him as the main entrance opens up.

"I love you," I mutter quietly as Pascal fetches the keys for the *Aston*. The bleep of the alarm makes me jump a little as I watch the man I adore leave without so much as a backwards glance. What have I done now, for God's sake? I had hoped this emotional rollercoaster would disperse now that we're on the right track, now that I've told him I'll take everything from him, and now that he's being honest.

"Do not concern yourself with his frustration. It is self-imposed and therefore of no importance to you," Pascal says, looking around aimlessly. I think it is of importance actually, huge importance. I've just been shunned because I said no to something, again, all for his benefit, I might add. Pascal's still fidgeting. It's bloody awkward and very distracting.

"What are you doing? You look ridiculous, and very un you," I snap in irritation.

"I miss my cane. I feel quite bereft without it." Well, that's his present sorted then, not that I'll ever find one as good as his. Maybe I should just give it back to him, or share it with him. I'll have a talk with

Alex about it later, if he's fucking talking to me by then. "Come, let us go. I have a plane to board."

We both slide into the car and I gaze at the dust still kicking off the drive as the door closes behind us, and wonder what I'm going to have to deal with later. Yet another unknown response to a perfectly normal situation – will he ever be less confusing? Hot then cold, black then white, happy then angry. Fucking twilight worlds and bizarre Alexander White oddities. A hand lands on my thigh as we head out onto the main road. It's comforting to some degree so I blow out a breath and look across at him with a small smile. Sometimes I think I understand him better than I do Alex. He's far more honest about who he is. It's written all over his every move.

"Why are you so much easier to read than he is?" He chortles to himself and straightens his perfect green tie. I have no idea why he bothered. He still looks overly handsome.

"I am not easy. I am a performance, my rose, a show that must go on. You read only what I allow you to. Do not presume to understand that which has no reality or depth. Your reality is with him alone. I am simply an added extra as one might say." What the hell does that mean? I roll my eyes at the wing mirror and stare out into oncoming traffic instead. It's less confusing. As if Alex isn't conundrum enough. I need to talk to him about all this, need some confirmation in my own mind as to what the hell is going on, regardless of how comfortable I may be with it.

Twenty minutes later and we pull up outside of *Harrods* and he walks around the car to open my door. Very gentlemanly I'm sure. If only the gawping females that have suddenly appeared knew a thing or two about what he'd like to do to them. My crotch unfortunately twitches at the thought. He smirks. It's no longer funny. Does he know my inner slut's thoughts, too? Jesus. Present shopping, then Belle, and then baking the cake while getting Christmas lunch prepared for maybe only two people.

"Let me taste those lips. It may douse the tedium that is to come," he says out of nowhere as he slams my door behind me. Really? Here?

"I don't think..." Apparently, that wasn't the correct response because I'm dipped into an exaggerated dance hold and lavished with an exquisite set of lips in the middle of the high street. I'd like to say I

258

fight him off, but I really don't as he pulls me back upwards and releases me with a sinfully wicked smile.

"I shall see you in Berlin in three days, my rose," he calls as he rounds the car and opens the door. Nothing else, no goodbye – he just leaves me there, panting like a sodding dog as I hear the giggles of women around me and watch him drive off. Wow, well that was interesting. Am I supposed to have done that, openly? I need a serious conversation with Alex about this sort of shit.

Flicking my eyes around, I scan for anyone I might know and hurry my arse into *Harrods* to see what I can find for Christmas presents. At the same time, I delve into my bag to dig out my phone to call Belle. The moment I do, I catch the handle of the blade again. I have to get rid of that. My eyes flick around nervously, just in case the knife police are around, but unfortunately they land on Teresa, standing about ten feet away from me. Oh shit. I smile in reply to her cross-armed stance, trying for casual. She saunters over with her *I know better* face on. Shit, shit, shit.

"Hi," she says. "Great to see you. You look fantastic. You want to tell me why you were just kissing Pascal Van Der Braack out there?"

Shit. Bollocks. Of all the people to bump into... At least it's not Belle, I suppose.

Oh, this is going to get messy.

~

Three hours and a very stern telling off from my best friend later and I'm sitting at a small coffee shop on my own, trying to figure out how the hell I'm supposed to tell Belle the truth. She's meeting me here in ten minutes, along with Teresa, and I have no idea how to even begin to explain what's going on. Teresa made complete sense at the time with her *"You can't lie about this stuff,"* speech. I'm sure she's right, and I'm positive Belle deserves the truth, but how do you tell someone about this sort of lifestyle choice? The royal bitch fest from Teresa was bad enough, because of course she'd worked it all out in the three minutes she had to look at me flustering around outside with Pascal. She'd just glared as I opened my mouth and attempted a lie of sorts, just held her hand up and then pointed towards the restaurant. At no point did she give me a chance to deny anything, and to be honest, I hadn't got the will to try anyway. I need to talk to someone about all this stuff. I need an outsider's opinion on things. I can't spend my time with both of them and just take their word as law, can I? It felt good to nod my head when she asked and know that someone else understood, even if it did take a bit of explaining on my part. And although she was shocked at first, probably a little angry, too if I'm honest, she was typically Teresa, my friend first and my adjudicator second. She hugged me as I tried to explain with tears running down my face. I don't know why they were there. Maybe it was just the relief of actually admitting it all to someone. Clearly she knew what we were into but she certainly didn't know Pascal was involved, and much as she may have been pissed off with me, she just sat and listened for a while, let me get it all out if you will. I stared at her as she bitched at me about being honest with the people that loved me, to stop pushing people away and at least give them a chance to comprehend the basics so they could help. 'They', being her and Belle, obviously.

So now I'm sat here, outside because the shop is crammed full of people, drinking a disgusting coffee, scanning the street for them to both turn up and waiting for Belle to berate me some more. If she knows about Alex's past, the murdering bit, I'll have no hope of convincing either of them that this is okay. Murderer, abused child and part of a threesome... This is not going to go down well at all. That I love him and that it's none of their business what we get up to will not be good enough. I could walk away from this lunch with no sister and no best friend because of the man I'm in love with. Merry Christmas to me. At least I found a present for him, kind of. It wasn't from Harrods, either.

I watch the street until I see her height above the crowd, her red hair standing out over her thick, white winter coat as she strides along and shuffles between the crowd. I've got to find a way to just tell her and hope she gets it, hope she understands and just says, okay, snotbag, it's okay. Then suddenly, I see blue hair behind her. Oh my god, she's with Conner. His frame comes into view as I stand up and wave my hand at them. Every worry disappears as I watch her smile in response and wave back at me. Just the fact that she's back with him makes this somewhere near worthwhile. He wraps his arm around her shoulder and barges his way past a gang of youths that are in the way. All of them look up at him and nod their heads, as if they respect the rocker who just pushed past them. I'm not surprised by their appraisal. Little would anyone know that he's possibly the richest computer geek out there. Belle giggles at something and my heart melts at the sight of them together again. Whatever happens in the next half an hour, I know she'll be fine now. Whatever Alex did, or whatever he said, it worked as much as I really wanted it to. Regardless of whether she accepts me and Alex, or the Pascal situation, she's got her man back, and that's all I need to know. I beam as I see him rest his forehead on hers. She closes her eyes and leans into him as they blindly push through towards me. Pure love is so uncomplicated when you get down to the core of it. Just take all the irritating other things out of the equation and let yourself love completely. Feel it in your soul and smile in the face of adversity as if it hasn't got a chance of beating you down or driving you apart. Be strong, love with your whole heart, accept all past mistakes and move on to something even more spectacular.

Alex.

"Hey, Snotbag," she says as she leans in and kisses me on the cheek.

"Hi," I reply, as I move the chairs around so there's enough space for us all. Conner leans in and kisses my cheek then winks at me.

"You're looking hot, Beth. I'm not surprised given your new arrangement. Two, eh? Kinky bitch," he says as he holds out a chair for Belle and then hovers behind her with his hands on the back of it. What the fuck? My eyes fly to his as I inwardly pray that nothing else falls from his mouth. God knows what he knows about Alex.

"Umm, I'm not sure what you're talking about to be honest, but nice to see you too, Conner." More shuffling of chairs ensues. I have no idea where to look. "Anyone want a coffee?" I may be able to make a run for it, if I'm lucky.

"I told her," he says. Told her what? Shit, what the hell is he talking about? I close my gaping mouth and turn back to Belle, who has a very good impression of Alex's eyebrow going on.

"Yeah, he told me. Interesting choice." What the fuck does that mean? I should leave. The fact that my feet are frozen to the floor and I can't speak really isn't helping me at all. Eventually, their combined stare prompts me to find actual language again.

"You told her what exactly?"

261

"About Alex's decision to finally turn bi." Oh my god! Language rapidly disappears again.

"I... I'm..." I flick my eyes around in the hope of some kind of miracle. Namely Alex or Pascal arriving to save me from my public mortification. Not that I care about the bisexual bit, obviously, although how the hell does he know that's a possibility? I shake the thought away because this is my sister, who knew nothing about any of this, or so I thought. "Going to get some coffees," I eventually say. Coffee, yes. Queuing for coffee will give me ten minutes to think, to find a way of making this sound normal, to some degree anyway.

"Beth, sit down. Conner will get them. He's going to meet *one* of your men anyway so we can talk properly, openly maybe, honestly." Honestly, okay. My arse slowly slides its way back onto the metal chair to do the honesty thing.

"You and Conner are good again then?" I'm just trying to avoid the topic to be fair. Perhaps she'll forget.

"Shut up, you idiot. When were you going to tell me you're part of a threesome? What possessed you to keep this from me, for fuck's sake?" Clearly not.

"I didn't really know, not officially anyway," I reply as nonchalantly as I can, trying for utter control over the situation. "And why did Conner feel he needed to tell you my personal business anyway?"

"He promised me he wouldn't hide anything from me anymore, not it if it might cause problems between us," she says. I can't argue with that, so I nod my head and try to look anywhere but at her. "And didn't know, my arse. How long has it been going on?" Okay, here we go.

"Well, it sort of hasn't. Not yet," I reply quietly. "Well, it hadn't until New York, but then I got out of the car earlier and Teresa was there and she saw me and Pascal together and I didn't know what to say. She told me I had to tell you, so I called you to see if you'd calmed down about the Alex thing and to find out if you were still coming for Christmas, and then I see you with Conner, which is great by the way." Oh, it's all tumbling out now. I can't control my mouth in the slightest all of a sudden. "I suppose I was going to tell you now. Not that I've got my head around it completely, and I'm more bothered about you being okay with Alex because I love him, Belle. I can't not be with him.

I just can't, and I don't want to have to choose. Please don't make me choose. This is me now. I don't know where it's come from but it's just me. This is all me. He hasn't made me do anything. Well, apart from the New York thing, but that was different. He was trying to show me something. And yes, he's got a past, but he doesn't force anything on me." That's not quite true. He sort of does in reality, but he has my consent. My smirk at the thought doesn't go unnoticed as she smiles back at me and puts her hand on top of mine. "I'm just me, Belle. I'm-"

"Doing absolutely fine, honey. A bit of a mess, yes, but I'm not surprised anymore. You should have just told me. I could have helped."

"How on earth could you have helped?"

"That's a very good point, but I could have tried. Us big sisters do know a thing or two, you know."

"About this? I don't think so." She's so not pulling the big sister thing on this one.

"No, okay, but I do know a little about what he's been through. I could have offered insight into that fucked up brain of his, helped you see past the shit. Although, it appears you're doing alright all by yourself," she says as Conner arrives back at the table with three large coffees. One takeaway.

"Right, babe, I'm going. See you back at home later, okay? This is way too deep for me to get into. Beth, just do them both and keep being awesome, will you?" he says as he leans in and kisses her. "I'm going to get him drunk now. I have a big thank you to say. Not sure what he said, but it worked."

"Bye," she says as he waves his hand and wanders off into the crowd.

"Home?" I ask.

"Yes, home. Given that you're moving out, I thought I might too, at some point." Giggling happens, lots of giggling as we sit there looking at each other.

"You're really doing it?"

"I still don't trust him, Beth. Alex, I mean, but he talks some sense when he's not being a dickhead. Let's hope you can keep that honesty up. You're a big girl like you said, and I can't make your decisions for you anymore. If you think he's worth the risk then he must be, for you. I've got my own life to live. Besides, I came onto him and he turned me down. He's the first one who ever has."

"You what?"

"Took my clothes off in front of him. He didn't budge an inch, said his cock was thinking of you. I thought that was a fucking good response to be honest."

"I can't believe you-"

"Oh, stop it. It's boring. Tell me about Pascal. Have you done him, too? What was it like? Both together?"

"Oh my god, Belle, please! We're in public, for Gods sake."

"Whatever. Let's go to a bar then. We can get pissed. Where's Teresa? Actually, how was she about the Pascal thing? Was it a little close to the bone? Think she might have been a bit hung up on him," she says, sipping at her coffee and waiting for all the gossip.

"I don't know. She said she'd be here by now. She seemed okay really, a bit floored, but, you know Teresa, chilled I suppose once she'd got used to the idea." She's ringing her phone before I finish the sentence, putting the coffee back down and starting to get her bags together again. A short conversation with the woman in question later and she's staring at me and flicking her head at the road.

"Come on. She's at a pub over there. She thought we needed space. As if? We need a fucking drink. I think we could all do with quite a few actually."

Oh, okay then. That's possibly the finest idea I've heard for a fair few days.

Chapter 19

Elizabeth

It's 8 o'clock ish, I think. I can't even see my watch. I'm in a taxi, though, heading towards Alex's home, my home even. Pretty sure I should have been home by three. That's what he said, wasn't it? *"I want you home by three!"* Well, sod him, the arrogant bastard. Light of my life. I've been having far too good a time getting tipsy with my girls at some random bar that I can't even remember the name of. Belle's re-engagement was something to be celebrated, laughed about and enjoyed, as was my fucking two men debacle, and it was pretty there, had pretty people in it. It was full of London's high society, all of whom I couldn't have given a shit about anymore.

I'm suddenly flung to the left as the taxi turns into a street of some sort, then I realise the crunching of the gravel beneath the car probably means I'm home. I smile into the fabric of the seat, where I've face planted, at the thought of being in love and then remember I'm going to have to deal with angry Alex. I've disobeyed a direct order, haven't I? Whoops. Whatever. He can go jump off a bridge or something, murderer or not. I can go out whenever the hell I like. I am strong, I am independent, and I am in complete control of all things Alex. I really need to talk to him about the killing people thing.

"Fifty-two, sixty," the cabbie says. My eyebrows rise into the fabric. Where the hell have I been? Up north or somewhere? Christ. The place was in Mayfair, wasn't it? Jesus. I haul my body back upright and search the interior of the cab for my bag, which is nowhere to be seen. Or rather I can't actually see it. It's not surprising. There are at least three of everything swimming around in my line of sight. Perhaps if I get out I'll have a clearer view. I lean against the door in the hope that it will opens. It doesn't. It just stays in my way, propping me up quite nicely. In fact it's quite lovely in here in general. It's quiet, and the hum of the engine has a serene quality that's making me feel all drifty and relaxed. Sleep. Sleep would be nice. I could just curl up and chill in here until the morning. That would be comfy, wouldn't it? Nice and quiet, comfy, snuggly.

I'm not sure what happens in the next thirty seconds, but the rapid tumbling feeling that suddenly assaults me has me spitting out gravel and staring up at the stars above. Oh, they're nice, too, twinkly. Look at them all up there, flickering and sparkling. They must be angels saying hello. My hands rise above me to pluck one out of the sky, or wave. I'm not really sure which, but I find myself tracing across the shapes with my fingertips, dot to dot. A cock appears in the shapes so I grab out at it and giggle to myself as I find another one and try to pull them together, knocking the heads of them together. No bloody angels up there anymore, it seems, just horny devils and naughty thoughts. There they are, my men, both of them, with their dicks out dancing around the sky. Oh, the possibilities. I grab the second one and stare at it. I don't know what Pascal's cock looks like. Does it look like that one? Maybe it's bent the other way? Who knows. I'll find out soon enough, I'm sure.

Something darkens the sky above me. Oh yes, it's the darkness coming to take me away and lead me into another kinky world of depravity. And yes, I'll go, no problems there. If I can just get my body to move, I'll be right there. Just need to make my legs work, just lift them up, and... Nope, I think I'll just stay here for a bit longer and enjoy the view. Snow angels... I could do those instead. I love the snow, love it when it's all over the place and covering the ground. It's Christmassy, pretty. It's all so very pretty. Ooh, snowmen. I want to build a snowman. I need some coal and a carrot.

"What the fuck are you doing?" Oh, lovely. It's my version of an angel's voice. Where is he? I can hear him – so pretty, so velvety. He can help me build a snowman. I bet he's never built a snowman. Poor little thing. He needs to build a snowman. Alexander White builds a snowman. It would be the biggest damn snowman the world has ever seen, with an enormous cock. "Elizabeth." That was rather loud. Why would someone be so sodding loud? Jesus. Too loud. Calm down. Enjoy the view, for God's sake. Look, it's so pretty, and...

My body is suddenly floating. How fabulous. I'm floating across the ground, and all the world is spinning around me. Hundreds of millions of stars just whirl around in the sky and map out different routes, strange new worlds and civilisations. I shall boldly go where no woman has gone before. James T. Kirk. Is he alive still? I don't know. Perhaps he's up there in the stars with my cocks, star trekking his way across the universe, and... Fuck, that's bright. What is that? Oh my god. Aliens are coming to get me. I need to run or something, but I can't move my legs. Why can't I move my legs? I'm going to die. I'm going to die at the hands of horny devils and James T. Kirk and aliens. Fuck, I have to do something. Have to keep everyone safe. My arms and legs flail around, searching for a weapon of some sort, something to beat off the threat, to reduce it to ashes and challenge the menacing evil that may prevail, but the light keeps blinding me and I can't see anything.

"Stop struggling," his voice says. "Trust me. You're safe." Ah yes, Alex. There he is. Trust him, yes, I'll trust him with anything. He can have it all – my body, my heart, my life. He'll protect me from the aliens, won't he? He'll look after me for the rest of my life with his butchering hands, because he won't let me go, will he? Can't. Belle told me he said that. And I won't let him go either, because he needs me to keep him safe and show him what love is, doesn't he? James T. Kirk will have to deal with the aliens because I'm needed here, to protect my man, to keep him happy and relaxed. Yes, relaxed. Let's all just relax and calm down, shall we? Just enjoy this darkness again, lovely darkness. Where have my stars gone? The sky is black again. The monsters have taken my stars. Why have they taken my stars? I had cocks in my stars, two of them. They were lovely, and mine. Fucking cock-stealing monsters, no one's taking my cocks from me. They're mine, just for me. I refuse to share them with anyone. Yum. Oh, now I'm floating on a lilo in the sea. That's nice. It's all soft and squidgy. I can relax here in the sea. I'm not sure how it's suddenly the middle of the summer but I'll just snuggle down and enjoy the rays of the sun as they bake me. I hope I put sunscreen on. I wouldn't want to burn. Mustn't tan these bruises away either, no. I need those. Maybe I should pull this towel over me, shield my collar marks from the evil rays. Yes, good idea. I'll just wrap this over me and then I can doze quietly and let the sea drift me off to Alex land, where all is rosy and comfy. Lovely.

Nice and quiet and dark.

Just lovely.

"Up you get." What the hell is that noise? Good lord that's loud. Leave me the hell alone. "Come on. Up, up, up. It's Christmas and we've got your family coming over in three hours." What is he talking about? Oh, fuck. Christmas! My eyes fly open to find him smiling down at me in a blue shirt with a glass of orange juice in one hand and what appears to be tablets in the other. Shit.

"What time is it?"

"Ten." Oh. Oh god, Christmas lunch. I haven't done a thing. How the hell am I supposed to cook Christmas lunch in a couple of hours?

"Why didn't you wake me, for fuck's sake?" I snap out as I throw the sheets back and hold onto my head. If I don't hold it, I swear it might fall off with the amount of banging that's going on inside it. Who gets drunk on Christmas Eve, and how the hell did I get back here, anyway? Where did I actually go?

"I thought you might like the rest after your battle with the universe last night. Did you win?" he replies with a chuckle. What is he talking about? I haven't even got the time to question him about it. I scrabble over the bed in the direction of the shower in the hope of salvation. I can't help noticing his fantastic backside on the way. He should come in there with me. That might liven me up somewhat.

"Come and wake me up, will you?" I call as I round the bathroom door and turn on the shower. I go back to the cabinet to brush my teeth and notice that I do look like I've been in some kind of battle. It makes me giggle a little as I remember the first time I looked in this mirror. My hair and face looked rather like they do now – a right bloody state. "What time did I get in?"

"Couldn't give a fuck," he says as he saunters in, fully dressed, and starts backing me towards the shower, my toothbrush still in my mouth. I throw it nonchalantly in the direction of the sink and hope it doesn't land in the toilet.

"You couldn't give a fuck? Looks like you could give several fucks," I reply as sexily as I can, given my exploding head and disastrous hair. He smiles a little and steps us into the shower, still fully dressed. "Alex, what are you-" I'm cut off by his mouth over mine, fiercely delving in and promising that strength I'm after to wake me up. My hands grab at his shirt as it begins to stick to his skin, fumbling fingers trying to grip the buttons as he glides those dastardly fingers along my spine and eventually lands them on the back of my neck.

"Turn around," he says into my mouth as he pulls away and watches me. I slowly turn and put my hands on the tiles in front of me. He taps my hipbone from behind, telling me to step under the shower a little more so I do, and then I feel his hand wrapping around my hair. He reaches around and drags one of my hands towards him, which lands on his extremely hard cock. "Stroke it," he says, so I do as he leans my cheek into the wall. I grip onto his shaft to create the pressure he needs and listen to the groan of appreciation that leaves his mouth. I love that sound, and I love the feel of his thin skin over the hard muscle in my hand. God, I want him inside me – no foreplay, just a damn good fuck. I just need this to remind me, and to wake me up, get me ready for the day, stretch me and make me less tense. I don't think I've ever asked this of him, just told him what I need.

"Just fuck me," I mumble out as I reach my other hand back and push my arse back to him. "Just do it, Alex. Make me come. I need it." He keeps still, no movement other than the rocking of his cock in my hand. "Please, Alex," I continue. Maybe the begging will work. He likes that.

"Take what you want," he says. "Show me." I smile to myself and widen my legs a little to accommodate him as I move closer and angle myself forward. I just want him inside me. I'm desperate actually. I try to pull him in but he continues to stand stock still so I back onto him and moan out as I feel him slowly inching inside, so much so that I clench around him harder and push myself even slower. Oh god that's good, so full, so complete. Pulling away a little, I gently rock back onto him until the friction starts to create that delicious burn I'm after. My core contracts around him again as I feel the build starting and increase my pace. His hand tightens in my hair as his fingers splay and tip my head back upwards, throwing me off balance. I'm suddenly reliant on his hand to keep me upright as I keep backing onto him, again and again. Deeper, faster, quicker, and my throat is screaming at me for his hand. My own fingers move to my clit to bring me on quicker because this is all me. He's not doing a thing, just letting me fuck him, use him. For the first time, I'm in complete control of this. He's letting me have the control, letting me get what I need for a change, and god, I love him for it. He's not punishing me for disobeying, not having a shit fit and acting like I expected. He's just letting me ride him harder and deeper until I release myself.

269

"Faster," he growls. My thighs burn with the pressure I'm putting them under and my fingers keep swirling and turning, trying to reach that orgasm, but there's no pain. I need some pain. I slam myself back into him. His cock hits hard but not hard enough and my nails scratch at the wall for something, anything. "Not enough, is it?" he says into my ear, his teeth nipping gently, and his breath teasing those thoughts into me. No, it's not enough. Why isn't he giving me anything?

"Alex, please. I need to come," I stutter out as his fingers tighten a little more. There, that's what I need. He tips my head up further so that the water begins running into my eyes and face, trickling into my mouth a bit as I try to pant for the air around it.

"You don't deserve to come," he says smoothly, grabbing my hand away from my clit and yanking it up behind my back. Yes, pressure, pain. My core clenches again as the onslaught of a rush begins.

"Please," I gasp out again, still punishing myself on his cock. He backs away from me so that I've got no friction to pound myself on and pulls my hair further down until the water is pouring into my mouth and nose. I can't breathe at all. Gasping and spluttering, I try to move my head away from his hold, but his grip is vicelike. I haven't got a chance, and as he increases my arch even further, I'm only just perched on the end of him.

"I said be back by three," he says firmly, a hint of that cold indifference back in his voice as he runs his tongue across my shoulder and I cough against the water, trying to breathe through my nose instead. "Three, Elizabeth. What part of that did you not understand?"

"I... Alex, please. I can't... breathe," I stutter out around my gasps. He just holds me there and removes his cock from me altogether until there's nothing but his hand in my hair and his fingers around my wrist. He just lets me nearly drown in the torrent of water that's gushing into my nose and mouth as I try to desperately grab for air. My head feels dizzy as the water just keeps running across my eyes and lips, torrentially pouring down and stopping me from getting the precious air I need. Suddenly, I'm pushed down onto my knees and spun around to face him. I splutter out some bile and heave in a breath as his soaking, jean-clad legs come into view. I chance a glance up to see what I'm dealing with. He's staring down at me, now stroking his cock around his jeans and daring me to open my mouth to speak. He's pissed off. I get it, so much so that he's not going to let me come. This is a punishment. I'm being punished for misbehaving, and it only increases my need to please him again. I hate that he's angry with me, hate that he's not going to let me come, and at the moment, regardless of my confusion, I couldn't love him anymore for it.

"Fuck my mouth then," I say. I have no idea why. I just know that I need to make this better. If he rams himself down my throat then maybe he'll let me come, or make me. I don't know. I just need him inside me, somewhere. He blinks once, and it's enough of a softening for me to shuffle my knees forward and offer my mouth up for him. Tentatively, I reach my hands forward to touch his jean-clad legs. "I love you. I'm sorry." He reaches for my chin and holds it there securely as he increases the pumping of his hand and keeps gazing into my eyes. The water still gushes over me as I watch his face relax a little. But he's not even going to allow me his come, and I quickly get the fact that he's going to just come on me, mark me. He's not even going to allow me the pleasure of knowing I made him come. He just keeps himself about a foot away from me and doesn't utter a sound other than a grunt as he shoots his come onto my face and then catches his breath. I lap at my lips to try for a taste as it drips down my cheek, but the water washes it away before I get a chance. I just stare up at him and wonder how the day is going to pan out if this is his mood – dominant, angry and irritated with me.

"How do you feel, Elizabeth?" he eventually says, still holding onto my chin and not letting me pull my eyes away from his.

"Disappointed," is the first thing that comes out of my mouth. "Frustrated, maybe." He continues to stare with no emotion whatsoever, those blue eyes of his boring into me until I find some more words. "Told off." Pathetic really, but there it is. That's exactly how I feel, and it's all my own fault. I don't think I even called him to let him know I wouldn't be home till later.

He eventually chuckles and pulls on my chin until I get the message that I'm supposed to get up. Both hands hold my cheeks gently as he tilts my face up to him.

"There is a reason I need you to do as I ask, Elizabeth, several actually, and none of them because of what you might think. I need to know I can trust you to do exactly what is asked of you. Do you understand?"

No, not really. Not at all, in fact. I just wanted to get drunk with my friends, and he's just had a snot fit about me disregarding his command and going for a bloody drink. After all he's put me through.

"No," I reply, because we're doing honesty now, and I want to know the real reasons behind this.

He pulls me from the shower and wraps a towel around me, then plonks me unceremoniously down on the toilet, lid down, thank God.

"I love you, and I don't want to hurt you. You said you wanted everything from me, but everything is difficult enough without me having to worry that you'll make your own judgments. I just want to keep you safe, baby." Oh, for fuck's sake. I only went into town.

"I just wanted a damn drink, Alex. Whatever this has been, and after everything you've done recently, it's just wrong to make me feel bad about going out, and-"

"I couldn't care less about you drinking. I'm glad you had a good time with your sister. What I do care about is the fact that when I let Pascal at you, when this begins, I'm not sure I'll be there with you. Do you understand that?" Oh. That's what this is about?

He kneels down between my legs and scoops me towards him, those blue eyes relaxing as he lowers his head and gently kisses my thigh. I rest my hand on his hair and wonder what's coming next. I hadn't even contemplated him being worried about any of this. He's supposed to be the one in control, isn't he? Pascal thinks so anyway. "He has a way of tempting me past caring, and I understand now that it's why I care for him, too, because he gives me that freedom. I have to trust you both. Don't you see that?"

"What do you mean you might not be there? You said you'd stay with me. You said that you'd keep me safe." He sighs and pulls away again then points back to the shower.

"Get cleaned up. I'll meet you downstairs."

"No, you will answer this, right now. I do trust you, but I have to know what you mean." Apparently I couldn't give a damn that it's Christmas anymore. I just want this endless backwards and forwards to end, and my fucking headache to go. I need to get on with it so that we're all comfortable, together or separately. The games end, now. He starts to leave the room, so I follow him out, towel wrapped around me. "Don't you fucking dare walk away from me." Happy sodding Christmas. Let's do this full-on, shall we? Who the fuck does he think he is? He swings his eyes back to mine, and they're scowling. It seems he's suddenly as pissed as me.

"Watch your tone, Elizabeth," he sneers.

"Why? Fuck you... You put me through the shit you have done, and then you dismiss my questions when I try to deal with you? Seriously, screw you. I am tired of not understanding your brain. When were you thinking of discussing this with me? Ten minutes before you disappeared into your oblivion and left me in the hands of another sadist who more than likely couldn't care less about my welfare? I deserve more than that." I can see the fury building in him, see his fists clenching and his eyes hardening as he tries to hold it back. Fuck him. If I'm the only one who'll question his orders, then so be it. That's what love is, and he's going to have to deal with me.

"Stop this. It isn't the time for it. I'll answer when I'm ready to."

"You'll damn well answer me now. I will not be-" One hand immediately grabs at my throat and yanks me towards the bed. It happens so quickly I don't even realise it until I'm pinned and turned onto my front. Without warning, his hand comes down on my arse with such force that I squeal out a yelp and try to move away. Not a hope. He keeps me still and delivers another, then another. Heat and pain radiate across my thighs and backside until I'm panting and trying to distract myself from the fact that it feels incredible, delicious, and yet frighteningly hard. Another comes down and I hear the grunt of satisfaction behind me as he pinches roughly at the exact spot he's just hit and then drives home another slap. "Stop, please," I cry out almost automatically, as the pain intensifies. My eyes start to water with tears but there's no denying the ache that's once again building inside. I need that, more of it. He flips me over with ease and wrenches one of my legs back to my shoulder, knee bent and pinned to the mattress by his weight. Those piercing, angry eyes have been replaced by the monster inside him, sending all those confused signals flying around within me. There's no point in struggling, no point trying to get away from him so I just stare with wide eyes into black holes of lust and gulp in thin breaths as his thumb pushes down on my throat, *his* throat. I'm not worried or nervous. I'm strangely relaxed in his grip, given the beating he's just given me. I feel safe somehow, regardless of the scratching of his jeans against my now heated and sore skin. He tilts his head a little and watches me with interest, as if surveying something he's never seen before.

"I won't be there with you, Elizabeth. I won't care, and he knows that. I will do this, and far worse. I will use anything I can to hurt you, or him. I will feel every second of your pain and push you for more of it. Without him, when it's just us, I can control it. With him, I won't want to. Do you understand that?" he says, squeezing his fingers tighter and moving his other hand across my stomach. "Your brittle little neck could crumble, you could be ripped open, you will be filled with pain, and unless you do what you're fucking told, you're not going to love me much at the end of it." I'm sure he feels the gulp of nerves in my throat at his words. He is, after all, holding it in his hand.

"I..." I manage to squeeze out of my mouth, but there are no words to follow. For the first time, I finally get what he's trying to tell me. He won't be there to look after me, and presumably doubts Pascal will either. What feels like two fingers slowly insert themselves inside me, and the moan that leaves my lips is consuming. I'm so ready. How the hell does he make me feel like this when he's being so malicious? Is it that that I don't understand more than him? Is it my need for it that I can't fathom?

"I'm a sadist," he growls out proudly, for the first time as his fingers begin stroking in and out. It's yet another moment of me falling hopelessly in love, another moment of pure honesty from him. He's not hiding anything from me; he's just being what he is and hoping I'll cope with him. "I want your pain. I want to have you begging me to stop, and I love you. Can you possibly imagine how scared I am of destroying you?" If I could smile without the need to pant for air, I probably would. What a lovely thing to say in the midst of manhandling me. I am so fucked up. I think I may be as bad as he is. And all I can feel is his butchering hand slowly drawing me to orgasm while my inner slut reminds me how much I want this, need it. There's nothing frantic about his movements, nothing aggressive really. It's almost loving as he holds me there with deadened eyes and clearly depraved thoughts. I twitch my head around to get some air.

"I'm not scared of you," I pledge. I'm not. He will stay with me even if he can't see that yet. He could leave me now. I can see it in his eyes, but he's still looking after me, isn't he? Still giving me what I need from him. He wouldn't have fought so hard to keep me if he wanted to destroy me, would he? "Let me up." He doesn't, just keeps those fingers driving forward, deeper, bliss, torture. Oh God, I could come so easily. Just a few more twists of his hand and I could explode around them, but I have a point to prove in this moment. "Alex, let me up, now." His hand stills a little but his grip on my throat is still relentless. "I love you. Let me up."

"Why?" he replies as he pushes another finger in and drags his thumb across my clit. In, out, round and round, rubbing, more pressure. Yes. My back arches into his hand as the moan leaves my mouth and gives him all the power again. I so want him to do it, just take me and let me forget this need to understand him, make my mind go quiet like Pascal's must. Somewhere in my muddled brain, I grab hold of the need to show him again and back away from his fingers. I will show him he loves me, that he can stay in control of himself when the time comes.

"No, let me up," I pant out as I push on his stomach muscles through his soaking wet shirt. He slowly pulls his fingers out and smirks a little as I rapidly scoot away, for some reason absolutely bereft at the loss of his fingers. Get a grip.

"Where do you think you're going?" he says as I reach the other side of the bed and get to my feet. Christ, my arse hurts.

"I have a point to prove," I reply. He just stands there, looking at me with amused eyes. Where the hell have they come from? I'm still very confused.

"Which is?"

"That you will listen when I need to be heard." He chuckles and snatches the towel off the floor to throw it at me.

"Hmm," he says as he walks out of the bedroom. What the hell? I'm pretty sure we were just in the middle of a reasonably important conversation. Am I going to have to talk to Pascal about this instead? Jesus. God, my head hurts, too. I rub at my arse and wince at the tender area around it. That'll bruise. He's suddenly at the door again with a smile on his face and his hands behind his back. I grab the towel because God knows what he's about to do. He gets to about three foot in front of me and flicks his eyes at the floor. He wants me down there. I stare back at him in defiance. "Did we not just have a talk about you doing as you're told?" Bastard. "Down you go." I narrow my eyes in response and continue my glare of superiority. "I could make you..." He doesn't bother with the ending. What's the point? I huff out a breath and sink down onto the carpet, noticing all the wet patches from his sodden clothes all over the floor. He takes a step forward and puts a small white box in front of me. "Merry Christmas."

Oh my god, he suddenly wants to do Christmas?

"Could you be any more bloody confusing? We were just fighting." He smirks at me, those blue eyes now sparkling again with amusement, and then crouches down.

"The supreme art of war is to subdue the enemy without fighting, Sun Tzu, which you just tried, and won in a roundabout way, I suppose. Well done. Very clever. Open your present."

"I..." I don't even understand what that means. Did I? Great, yes, well done, me. Although I thought I was just proving that he loved me enough. "I'm not your enemy, Alex."

"Far from it, Miss Scott. Now, present. Come on. We have work to do." Okay. There's no way we're making lunch for my family. Are Chinese takeaways open on Christmas Day? I hope so. I slowly unwrap the box and lift the lid only to find another smaller box. My eyes shoot back to his because that looks suspiciously like a ring box. "If I was going to ask you that, do you really think I'd do it here, or spank your misbehaving arse before doing so?" Christ knows, to be honest, and what's wrong with here anyway? But at least he's clarified the point.

My hand shakily lifts the lid and my hand flies to my mouth. I thought I'd seen the most exquisite diamonds in my life before now, thought there would never be anything more beautiful than my necklace and bracelet. I was wrong, because the utterly breath-taking ring that's twinkling back at me has me gaping in response. That's all I've got, a gaping mouth and no words. It's a replica of my bracelet. The banding is exactly the same, and its clearly part of the matching set, but the main baguette stones are huge. I don't know what I expected for Christmas, but this wasn't it. I just continue to stare at it as if it may morph into something less stunning if I remove my eyes from it. "Are you going to put it on at some point?"

"I can hardly stuff my hand up a turkey's arse with that on," I reply. Frankly, just the thought of wearing it terrifies me. He laughs out loud and falls back onto his backside while still shaking in hilarity.

"Only you would say something like that. What have I done to deserve you?" He chuckles as he pulls it from the box and raises a brow, almost as if he's asking me which hand I want to hold out to him. Given that he just said he wasn't asking, I go to lift my right hand. "Are you sure?" he cuts in. What? Is he asking me now? He will not fuck around with asking me to marry him. He's right. He'll do it properly, if he ever does, that is. I raise my right hand further up and hold it out to him. He nods knowingly with a smile and gently pushes the diamonds along my finger. Of course it slides on perfectly. It doesn't surprise me in the slightest that he knows my ring size. Andrews probably dusted my finger for size specifications, too. Arsehole.

"I don't know what to say."

"Don't then. Get ready. You can show me how appreciative you are later, after I've done battle with your father." That's a fair point, given the fact we haven't made Christmas lunch. What time is it anyway? It seems I still don't care because I can't stop admiring my ring and sitting on the floor. Beautiful just doesn't cover it at all. "Up you get," he says as he offers me a hand – very gentlemanly I'm sure. I stare at it for a moment, remembering what that same hand did to my backside just a few minutes ago, and then back at my ring.

"We have a lot of things to talk about still. I'm not letting any of this go. I want to know everything," I say as I take his hand and he yanks me to him.

"And you will, as much as you want, just not today. Today we do Christmas, your way."

"Okay." Yes, Christmas.

Having showered ourselves again, I watch him leave and set to with donning some clothes. I choose a rich green, long sleeved silk dress and throw my hair up into a messy bun, which, quite ironically, has the exact opposite effect and looks like I've just stepped out of the salon. I'm getting good at this looking elegant thing. It appears the rich life is rubbing off on me, as did Mr. White himself less than an hour ago. I laugh to myself at the thought as I touch up the foundation around my bruised neck and run my final layer of brown lipstick on. I wouldn't want Daddy seeing those in a hurry. As I hit the bottom step, I hear Alex singing in the kitchen. Singing? And Christmas carols, no less. Bing Crosby doesn't have a thing on Alex, it seems. I can't stop the images of family Christmases running through my mind as I walk along the hall and envisage two small children laughing and chasing each other about. I run my thumb over my shiny new ring and sniff back a small tear that's threatening at the very thought. Marriage, children, a real life with a man who's no longer hiding from me, just being himself and letting me find my way through his layers, bit by bit. I still haven't asked him if he wants children. Well, there's no time like the present, I suppose.

"Alex, we've never talked about..." Oh, holy shitballs. Everything is done, and I mean everything. I just freeze in the doorway and gaze around the kitchen at the array of chopped and prepared food that's engulfing the pristine white surfaces. When the hell did he do this? He's bloody well smirking at me. I don't even have to look at him to know he's doing that. I can see the tea towel over his shoulder as I watch him moving towards me out of the corner of my eye. I'd love to be unimpressed, but I can't. How? When? Why?

"No need for hands up arses, I've done that bit," he says. I'd quite like a hand up my arse if I'm honest. I can't believe I thought that.

"When did you do all this?" I mumble out as I sweep my fingers over the endless jars of sauces and packaging.

"You needed to sleep, and I needed something to do to take my mind off things. The spanking also helped with that," he replies as he grabs two bottles of red wine and walks straight past me into the hall.

"Where are you going now?"

"Dining Room. Bake something."

"What?" I call after him.

"I don't do cakes or deserts. Make a cake." Oh right, yes. My cake. Have I got time to make a cake? The doorbell rings. Obviously not. Shit. I spin on my heels and launch myself at the cupboards to see if I can at least knock something up in time. Scanning quickly, I find everything I need for a take on Christmas pudding, maybe, ish. It'll have to do. Just as I throw the flour into the mixing bowl, I hear Conner's laughter sweeping along the hall and smile to myself at his family. Conner's the only one really. Evelyn may be related, but I'm still not comfortable with her.

"Sticky fingers, dude." He says as he whistles his way around the kitchen. "Jesus, you've been busy, Beth."

"Not me," I giggle out as I mix furiously and tip the sugar in. "I've been sleeping." And being spanked for being a naughty girl. "Pass the eggs, please." I nod at the top cupboard and watch him reach for them.

"I thought Mary went home for Christmas?" he questions as he passes them over. Alex comes in behind him, holding a bottle of Champagne and some glasses.

"She does," he says.

"Where's Belle?" I ask.

"Sorting her lips out. Who did all the cooking then?"

"Him, the love of my life." I smile over my shoulder at Alex and watch those blue eyes crinkle back at me as he pops the champagne elegantly and pours. I return to my furious mixing and giggle at the thought of those hands half an hour ago. Would I have it any other way? Absolutely not. I'll never deal with dull again, not in this household anyway.

Chapter 20

Alexander

Christmas, at home. She couldn't possibly imagine what this meant to him.

He watched as she gave Belle a tour of the house. She guided her around with boundless enthusiasm as if she'd decorated and prepared every room herself, as if it were made just for her. It was, even if he hadn't realised it at the time. She was his reason to live. She was the explanation for every breath he would take for the rest of his life.

Elizabeth White. He pondered the thought for the thousandth time as he moved across the room and waited for the doorbell to ring again. This time it would be her parents. She could have said yes upstairs. She could have accepted his offer, but he knew she wouldn't. She'd want it all, wouldn't she? She'd want the whole proposal, not a quick spanking and then a quiet *what do you think*? And she'd probably get it one day, when they were both ready. She'd get everything just the way she needed it to be. He chuckled at the thought of marriage again and wandered over to throw another log on the fire.

"You scared?" Conner asked from the chair, now on his fourth glass of Champagne. What the hell sort of question was that? His phone beeped in his pocket so he swiped it out and trawled through an email about the rising cost of shipping transference, then another about some delay in the legal department.

"That's a very unlikely thing for me in any circumstance," he replied shortly, trying to distract himself from the very thought.

"Yeah, but Christ, man, her parents for Christmas? At what point did you think that was a good call? I've never even met them."

"She loves her parents. I want them to like us." Fucking emotions, still addling him and telling him he wasn't good enough. He fucking was, should be, could be at the very least.

"Us? You talking me and you, or you and her?" Conner replied, laughing at his own joke.

"Everyone likes you." No one liked him, not the real him. Only three people even knew the real him existed, and their opinions couldn't be trusted because they loved him, for whatever reason. He watched Conner smile his typically arrogant 'of course they do' smile and reach for the bottle again. "Stop drinking so much. You'll make a dick of yourself," he said as he put his phone away and fiddled with his cufflinks. Fiddled? For fuck's sake, he was as nervous as a hormonal teenager, again. This shit had to stop. He'd met them before and it was fine. He took in a deep breath and pulled at the collar of his shirt to loosen the restriction, not that there was any there. Dad. Daddy. Bastard father. He'd been hearing the bastard's voice in the back of his mind all morning.

"*Worthless little boy, useless, tedious. You'll never amount to anything. Look at your puny little body. You're weak, Nicholas. You disgust me. Christmas? There's no Santa Claus for little shits like you. You don't deserve anything nice. Why would he come for you? Why would anybody come for you?*"

He could still feel the rats that his father had *given* him as a Christmas present biting and crawling over him. He'd dumped them into the cupboard with him on Christmas Eve and whistled carols as he'd screamed for help. Help never came, only laughter and jeering. He'd killed every one of those fucking rats in the end, broken their necks and shoved them into a hole in the corner while he shook and cried like a child. His first kills, but not the last by a long shot.

Why would anyone ever come for him?

"Alex?" He squeezed his fists closed and pushed the memory away again as her voice softened all the edges. She'd come for him, the real him, in more ways than one. He smiled and turned to find her questioning face staring up at him. She knew something was wrong, could read it a mile off now, and fuck he loved her for it. She placed a hand on the front of his chest and crawled it up towards his throat. "Mine now," she said quietly, softly rubbing her finger backwards and forwards. "You'll be fine." He smirked down at her and tilted her chin further upwards. If it was anyone else but her, he'd probably have to show them just how *fine* he could be. But she was too deep inside to fool anymore, and she deserved his honesty because of it.

"I love you," he said quietly as he ran a thumb along her cheek.

"I felt that this morning," she replied instantly, a very cheeky smile suddenly erupting. "Your hands were full of emotion." Trust her to break his mood. "They'll be here in a minute. Shall we meet them outside?" His phoned buzzed in his pocket again for the hundredth time. He went to grab it, but she snatched at his hand with pleading eyes. "Not today, Alex. Just put it away for today, please?" He hadn't got a hope of defying those eyes when she used them to full effect. Deep liquid pools of chocolate bored into him and reminded him of decency, of honesty, of integrity, and of love. He smiled at her and imagined them later, preferably drowned in lust instead. He reached for his phone and put it on the mantelpiece, then took her hand to lead her towards the front door, now trying to push away every other thought that was of no use to him while meeting her parents.

"Anything for you, Miss Scott," he said as he wrapped a scarf around her neck and opened the door. They were both immediately hit with a few flakes of snow. Nothing really, just a small flurry, but she began to jump up and down in excitement. He frowned at her heels and reached for her but she broke away from him.

"Oh, it's snowing," she said as she leaped off the porch area and twirled around, apparently trying to douse herself in as much snow as she possibly could. "We can build a snowman." He frowned at the thought. He couldn't remember if he'd actually ever built one or not. Perhaps he had at the home, or maybe with Conner. He certainly remembered having snow shoved down his shirt by the idiot at some point, and a hard shot to the groin by a snowball.

He watched her spin round and round, looking upwards at the sky as if it were the answer to all her prayers. She really did like snow it seemed. No wonder she could ski. He assumed that was why she was rambling on about carrots and coal last night, and big cocks. Although what James T. Kirk had to do with big carrots and cocks he didn't know.

He ambled down to her and then dived in to wrap her up and help her spin safely. She squealed and grasped hold of his neck as they spun around together in a private moment of joy, forgetting everything else around them and being in love. No past nightmares, no thoughts of hatred, just a man alive and the woman who had made him realise it. His angel, and his chance at a new life, to make new life, children, his children, their children. A little boy who'd always be loved, protected, cherished, and a little girl with her eyes and smile.

The crunch of the gravel brought his attention back to the present as he heard her parents' car coming down the drive and stopped the spinning. She giggled in his arms and wobbled a bit as he put her down. What the fuck was that thought about? Jesus, he wanted to rip her to shreds for making him think that he could ever be a father. How did she do that all the time, make him believe he was good enough? Murderers weren't fathers. They didn't deserve that right. What the hell had he got to offer a child other than money? He shook his head and linked his fingers through hers.

"Are you ready to play happy families?" she asked, with pink cheeks and a radiant smile as she brushed at the snow on his chest. Was he? For her he was. He'd play anything for her, and her parents did seem like nice people. As long as he kept the father away from his toys, that was.

The whirlwind of arms that was her mother exited the car and practically ran to her daughter for a hug, so he let her go and wandered across to her father to help him unload what appeared to be several hundred presents from the boot. They were all wrapped perfectly with intricate bows, just the thing normal people did at Christmas. They wouldn't have made a call to *Harrods* and had gifts picked and tied. No, they probably spent days searching for just the right things, each filled with love as they'd sat in that farmhouse kitchen and poured all their hearts into individualising the presents, probably drinking tea from that old teapot and reminiscing over Christmases past. Love, parental responsibility and guidance, honouring your children with the best you could possibly be for them.

"Alex," her father said as he extended a hand. He smiled back at the man and hoped to ignore their last awkward moment.

"I'm sorry about the last time we... Well, I shouldn't have tried to, you know..."

Alex nodded in reply and remembered that hug, that fatherly intent of kindness, of decency. He wasn't sure what to say in reply so simply smiled and started picking up bags instead.

"Quite a gaff you've got here."

"I like it. I bought it a few years ago. It was a bankruptcy sale so I got it quite cheap. It still needs work but it'll make a good..." *Family*

283

home one day... He shook his head again and chuckled to himself at the thought as he gazed at the mother daughter exuberance that was still going on.

"Well, Dianne's ready for a whole bunch of grandkids whenever you're ready, and you've sure got enough room to fill the house up with them." Alex stared in response. What the hell was he supposed to say to that? Thankfully, blue hair arrived to interrupt the conversation.

"Mr. Scott," Conner said as he stuck his hand out, looking uncharacteristically nervous. He smirked to himself at the vision and grasped hold of yet another bag. Christ, how long were they staying? This evening's entertainment would have to involve a gag at the very least, tape too, maybe. He shook his head again and chastised his own thoughts, given the father figure standing beside him.

"You're the computer genius then?" the man replied as he scanned Conner.

"Yes, Sir." Sir? What the fuck was that all about? Mind you, he remembered saying the very same thing to the man in question. He chuckled again and began to walk back to the house to avoid the rest of the interrogation, hopefully her mother's exuberance too. No such luck.

"Alexander White, put those bags down and give me a hug," she yelled as he mounted the first step. It was shouted as if she really were his mother, that type of voice that demanded he respected his elders and yielded to her order. He rolled his eyes and put the bags on the floor to turn back toward her. She stood there, flapping her hands towards herself. Christ, Elizabeth looked just like her. The resemblance was uncanny really. She was still a very beautiful woman in her own right. "Come on, I need squeezes," she called. He walked back and was instantly wrapped up into a tight hug, then she patted his backside a touch too energetically. He frowned a bit as Elizabeth dragged her away and sighed in disbelief.

"Mum, will you please stop groping him?"

"Can't help it, darling. He's just too delicious. And talking of delicious, Bethy tells me you've cooked it all yourself. Is there anything you're not good at? You must marry this man, Bethy. Have you asked her yet?"

Jesus Christ. Fuck. The woman was very slightly insane with her directness.

284

"No, not yet," he replied as he tried to think of a way to change the subject.

"Why didn't you just put this rather exquisite ring on the other bloody finger? Honestly, you men. Tick tock, tick tock. You wouldn't want anyone else to snatch her up, would you? She could be tied to someone else before you know it, and then-"

"Mum, please," Elizabeth cut in. He stared at her mouth. It was safe there, and she would be literally tied to someone else soon, wouldn't she? There wasn't a thing he could think of to rebuff the discussion. He wanted her tied to someone else, fucking someone else, screaming and begging and panting, sweat pouring off her as she arched, then crawled...

"How old are you anyway, Alex? Those swimmers don't keep swimming forever," her mother said. What? He looked at his cock at the same moment she directed her gaze in the same direction. His swimmers were perfectly acceptable in their swimming task, often, as far as he was aware anyway. Did he need to get that checked out? For fuck's sake, when was the woman leaving?

"Oh my god, Mum. Stop. Come inside so I can give you a tour." She jumped at the chance and began to head away from him. Thank God. Was this what he was going to get all day?

He carried the bags to the tree in the lounge and took each one out carefully. Blue, green, yellow with spots, some ridiculous children's Santa paper wrapped around what must be a jumper of some description, and white packaging wrapped in pink bows. He stared at the fluffy ribbons and bows for a few minutes and wondered if his mother would have done this for him? Would she have taken the time to show him how much she cared? Or would she have thought him useless, too?

A hand landed on his shoulder. He flinched at the contact and spun his head around.

"She got this for you to wear. We all have to, I'm afraid. Conner's being made to put his on now," her father said with a chuckle. He rose to his feet and looked at the man's hand. He was holding a tie. The sneer that crossed his face was so instant he couldn't remove it until it was too late.

"Problem?"

Yes, there was a fucking problem. No matter how Christmassy the tie was, with its snowman scene on it and flashy lights, there was no way it was going anywhere near his neck. She said he never had to wear one again, and he wasn't about to let that bastard in his house now.

"I don't wear ties," he said as he moved around the man and headed for a safer place, anywhere but here, probably the study. Maybe he could do some bloody work instead of all this happy crap.

"Stand still, son," the father said. Son? He kept walking until he reached the door then braced his hand on it to check his temper. "I don't know what you've got going on in that head of yours, and I don't care unless you want to make it my business. But I'll tell you this once: if you let any of my girls down, if you think their laughter isn't worth your pain, then you're not the type of man I want involved with my daughter. Do you understand me?" He raised a brow at the strength of tone and stared at the hall floor in annoyance. Worth his pain? Her laughter and joy and beauty were worth every second of his pain, but a fucking tie, all day?

"Put it on, Son. Let's see how much you can take. Make you stronger than the pathetic piece of dirt you are. That's it. Now tie it to the banister. Reach for me..."

He took another step out into the hall and walked toward the banister in front of him. The spindles echoed misery every damned day. He'd chosen this house because of the curved sweep of the stairs. There was nothing harsh about the lines. They were soft and forgiving. Not like the straight, rigid contours of the house he grew up in. His fingers traced them as he thought about the importance of that, the decisions he'd made almost unconsciously at the time to shield his thoughts and keep him calm, safe. He turned back to find Elizabeth's father hovering in the doorway, a firm, unyielding look on his face as he questioned the decency of the man standing in front of him, whether he was worth his daughter's time or not. He wasn't, in all reality, but whether he was or not was irrelevant. She wasn't going anywhere anyway. He snorted back a chuckle and held his hand out.

"Give me the tie, then," he said quietly. A small smile played around the man's face as he took a step forward, handed him the tie and slapped him on the back. He flinched again at the contact and barely contained a growl as the man's smile widened into a happy grin.

286

"Knew I liked you for a reason," her father replied as he wandered off towards the dining room where everyone was gathered. He held the bloody thing in his hand for a few minutes and cracked his neck, trying to quieten the voices reverberating around in there, then closed his eyes, trying to sort them back into their appropriate boxes.

Piece of shit.

Worthless.

Murderer.

Sadist.

You'll never be anything... Don't worry, I'll beat it out of you, make you more.

A sudden noise brought him back to the moment. Jingle bells? He opened his eyes to find her standing in front of him. There was just her, her and that halo she seemed to damn well wear. She smiled and ran her fingers over his. No words, nothing, just her eyes and lips as she curved them up into a smile and kept staring into him. Deep inside him. She could feel it all, couldn't she? She may not have been the one to take the pain, but she could see it etched into him, see it riddled in his soul, and feel it in his expressions, even when he tried to hide them.

"You don't have to," she said quietly as the jingle bells music started again. He suddenly realised it was coming from the tie. He raised a brow at it and kept staring at her mouth moving. "I'll explain and it'll be fine. Just put it down somewhere." How could she explain? And how would her father ever accept him afterwards with no explanation to clarify why?

"Put it on for me," he replied gruffly. "Just kept talking, or do something with your mouth, will you?" She giggled and took the fucking thing from his grasp, pressing the tune again. "I'm going to hate that song by the end of the day." She looped it around his collar and started her work, quietly, methodically, gently.

"You can whistle it while I suck your cock later. I might even let you fuck my arse if you're lucky," she said softly, flicking her eyes over his shoulder. Nice thought. In fact, could they do that now? *Not enough time, White.* "Got any rope handy? I've been thinking about dildos quite a lot recently, too. Perhaps you could double up on me. You know? Prepare me. And butt plugs, what sizes are available? And why haven't you used a whip for a while? I enjoyed that... " His brow went higher. It seemed she'd found her dirt-ridden vocabulary quite nicely. Pascal would relish that as he watched his come pouring from her lips. "I quite enjoyed that spanking I received, too, oddly enough. Perhaps we can discuss it when I give you your present later. This aggression's all well and good, and you know how I love it, but I'm pretty sure you've got more kinky shit than that going on in that brain of yours. Please don't go all dull on me just when I'm finally starting to understand." He stared at her in amazement, suddenly fighting the rising issue in his trousers. "There, perfect. How's it feel?" He couldn't give a damn about the tie. Not one thought was targeted on the restriction around his throat as she crossed her arms and winked at him. Winked? *Witch. Fucking angel in disguise.*

"You're not going to be able to walk tomorrow, so I'd start thinking of excuses to give your parents in the morning."

"Christmas first, Mr. White," she replied with a smirk as she jiggled her tits at him. "And I think your hand's required up an arse again. Let's go get on with it, shall we?"

He watched her stride along the hall towards the kitchen in awe. She was utter perfection. Her hair was twisted into some exquisite style, the picture of elegance with slut's thoughts slowly embedding themselves into her. "I love you," he whispered to himself as he continued to gaze at her legs and arse.

"I should fucking hope so," Belle's voice said beside him as she strode past him, too. He kept looking at Elizabeth and then followed them into the kitchen. Lunch was about to be served. He'd have to wait for his present.

~

"Check," Elizabeth's father said as he moved a rook and smiled triumphantly. He was quite a good player really, not that Alex had actually played to win. He assumed letting the potential father-in-law win was probably a good thing. The mother giggled and drank some more of her eggnog cocktail that Belle had been producing all day.

"Dad, you can't possibly call that a win," his angel replied from his lap, laughing gloriously as she did so and trying not to slur the words.

"Whether the man played to his full cipacity or not," Alan said as he tried to get up, failing and falling back into the chair again. "I shall claim my vactory and bid you all a very goodneet." He tried once again to get up, and failed miserably for a second time. "Dianne, where's our room? Don't you have a butler? Fuck, I can't move..."

He relaxed back into the chair to watch the family at its finest with a smile. He could sit here all day and watch this, this honest, morally good family. They curled around each other like a cocooning blanket of safety, held each other together and supported one another in everything. The mother and daughters seemed to understand one another so well it was unnatural, or maybe natural was a better description. They were just as a mother and her children should be really, he supposed. They'd played so many games today he couldn't even remember them. They'd eaten too much, drank too much, and now he was sitting here in a Christmas jumper, having thankfully been allowed to remove the fucking tie. He'd been subjected to too many rounds of jingle bells every time a Scott woman had been within ten feet of him. And Conner's version of The First Noel at every available opportunity had been truly horrendous, but the day had been wonderful, happy, and serene. For the first time in a long time he felt like he was a part of a family, a family other than the one he grew up in, or the one he pushed away in Rome when he was a boy.

"Alan? Alan Scott? Have you gone to sleep? I can't believe he's made such a fool of himself. Come on, you'll have to carry him upstairs, Alex. The blue haired one's useless – pretty, but useless nonetheless."

"Hey, that's my man." Belle snorted at her as she rested her feet on Conner's stomach.

"He can't even keep up with your drinking, and you're a lightweight, for God's sake."

"I am so not a lightweight."

"Are, too," his angel cut in. He smirked at the love floating around and stroked her knee as she sprawled herself in his lap. She'd been sitting there most of the evening, permanently tsking at his clearly inadequate chess moves and rubbing the back of his neck. It was almost as if she was trying to comfort him through the day, keep him safe from any feelings he might be having. He'd had none of any adverse consequence, only ones of happiness, of love. Maybe some of sadness but they'd been overruled by the Scott attack on Christmas.

"Come on, big boy. You'll have to help him," Elizabeth's mother said as she disappeared towards the stairs. He picked his angel up and dumped her back on the chair where she shuffled herself down to get more comfortable. He walked around to Alan, hoisted him up to his feet and propped his arm over his shoulder, then dragged his form through to the stairs.

"Be careful there. That could be considered a hug," the man said as they reached the stairs, sounding incredibly *not* drunk. He stared in response and loosened his hold of him. "Every time I see you, I'll do that, try to give you a hug, and every time I'll expect you to try a little harder to hug me back, okay, son?"

"I thought you were drunk?"

"We can all play games when we need to get a point across. Bethy loves you, and that means we do, too," he replied as they began to walk the stairs together.

"You don't have to love me," he replied, frowning at the sentiment attached. Regardless of the day they'd had together, he couldn't possibly mean it, and he wasn't worth the love anyway.

"Yes, we do. It's our way, and as long as you make her smile, we always will. Just keep making my baby girl happy and keep her safe and we'll love you as if you're our own." With that, he slapped him on the back and turned into the landing, effortlessly negotiating the furniture. He watched him walk along just in case and chuckled at being played into a hug, a meaningful touch from a man he hardly knew, which felt... What did it feel? Comfortable? "Which room is it, by the way?" the man called, looking at the corridor of doors

"The fifth on the left," he replied. As far away from his room as he could possibly manage given the noises the man's baby girl would be making within the next hour or so.

"Merry Christmas," was the reply as his feet moved and turned into the west landing.

Alex turned back to the stairs to see Belle and Conner making their way up towards him.

"We're going, too," Conner said as he rested his hand on the back of Belle's neck, possessive really for Conner. He couldn't remember ever seeing him show quite so strong a display of dominance around a woman. It was a clear message being sent; he could almost hear it with every touch. *"Don't you fucking dare, White."* He didn't need to worry. He wasn't going anywhere near Belle. He briefly pondered if she'd have fucked him the other night. Would she have actually done it? She smiled at him from Conner's grasp; possibly, there was a hint of mischief on her face as she stood there. Who knew? He didn't care anyway.

"Okay, sleep well," he replied as he stuck his hand in his pockets and headed back down towards his angel.

"Thank you. It's been really nice," Belle said quietly behind him. He smiled to himself at her pleasantries. She'd been reasonably nice all day to be fair. She even actually talked to him on several occasions. "I'm still not sure I like you, though."

He rolled his eyes and kept walking downwards. That was much more like it, and far more comforting. Dislike he could deal with.

He wandered into the lounge to find it empty. Where had she gone? He turned and headed for the kitchen. She wasn't there, either. He listened to the air around him in the hope that he could hear her somewhere. Nothing, and no music so she clearly wasn't in the music room either.

"Elizabeth?" he called, turning back towards the dining room. He looked into the study on the way but only saw the dim blue lighting. Where the hell had she gone?

He rounded the corner of the dining room door to see scurrying mile-long legs encased in a short, black, leather skirt trying to stand up on the table. She managed it milliseconds later and finally stood still, hands on hips and a slightly nervous smile on her face. Fuck. The hardening of his cock was instant. He could hardly think as he raked his eyes over her form.

"Christmas present," she said as she pointed at the table to a black box, and then waggled her finger up and down herself. Happy fucking Christmas. Jesus. The skirt was damn near a belt with long knotted plaits of leather hanging down, the bra leather, too, with zipped fronts, the highest heels he'd ever seen and a thick black choker around her throat. She looked more like a Domme than a sub – something about the way her face was changing as he gazed at her. Pascal was right. It was all there, just as it had been when they were in the room with Roxanne. Switchy. She wouldn't be if he had anything to do with it. He wandered around the dining table quietly and looked at her from every angle. She couldn't be more perfect if she tried.

"How strong do you think the chandeliers are?" he said as he finally got back in front of her. She looked upwards and frowned.

"I've never really thought about it. I was hoping that this," she replied, waggling her finger at herself again, "would be more interesting than the light fittings, to be honest."

"Hmm..." He turned towards the light switch, flicked it off, locked the door, and then mounted the chair and table. She smirked and looked at his Christmas jumper.

"Not very kinky," she said. He looked down at it with a smirk.

"I don't know. How often have you sucked Santa off?" She giggled and blushed a little. Christ, he loved that blush, that hint of innocence she wore so well regardless of her current state of dress. "And I believe you said you wanted fucking in the arse. I'm sure Santa doesn't normally do that."

"More than likely not," she replied with a smile as she bent over and picked up the small black box.

"Merry Christmas, Alex," she said, her voice full of love as she gazed at him and offered it to him. He looked at it and then back at her. There was nothing in that box more interesting or tempting than she was at the moment, so he took it from her and pushed it to the end of the table out of the way. She frowned at him and looked back to it.

"But, that's..." He brushed past her and grabbed hold of the chandelier to test its strength. It bore his weight well enough as he hung from it and gave it a few tugs. "You cannot be serious, Alex."

"Can you do a handstand?"

"Uh, yes. Why?"

"Come on then." She looked at the chandelier, then at him, then back up again, then turned to take a few steps away from him so he beckoned her up with a brow. She sucked in a breath and gracefully stepped into him and kicked her legs up into a handstand. A fucking gymnast couldn't have perfected the move any better, and given his apparent butchering hands, he was a little surprised at the absolute trust she put in him. He twisted her to face him, then bent to pick her waist up and hoisted her legs over the chandeliers arms until she was dangling like a present sent from the heavens above. Her red hair hung down to skim the table beneath her as he let go of her and took a step away again to stare at the vision.

"Now what?" she said as he continued looking at her, imprinting the vision into his memory under the new title of Christmas presents. There really wasn't anything else in that box at all.

"Widen your legs and hook your heels under the other arms," he replied – better access and a stronger hold. Unless she wanted to feel scared... Either way was fine by him.

She shuffled a little then relaxed her arms down to trail her fingertips backwards and forwards. He stripped his jumper and shirt off and moved towards her.

"What's the plan, Sir?" she said, sarcasm dripping off her beautiful lips, which were about to be put to use. He crouched down to look at her face as he swiped a larger than average candle from the candelabra in the middle of the table. "Ooh, are we doing the hot wax thing? I liked the hot wax thing. Have you got a teaspoon, too?"

"No, you said you wanted fucking," he said as he held the red candle in front of her upside down face." Her eyes widened as she stared at it and got the drift. "Prepare you, I think you said. And I want your mouth around me, which leaves my hands free. Is every hole preparation enough for you?"

"Fuck," she muttered, barely audible, but enough for him to smirk in reply and stand up to unzip. He reached for the olive oil on the table and tore at the scrap of underwear covering her backside until it was out of the way. He held it high and poured the entire contents of the bottle over her legs and arse until it was dripping down her. Quick hands delved into both holes, lubricating and pushing in as she moaned and squealed at the intrusion, wriggling and trying to find a more comfortable position. He couldn't give a fuck about her position, and this would be at his pace, his force. She had no choice and no opinion in the matter. Happy fucking Christmas to him. His cock flexed and pulsed as he felt her insides clenching and kept listening to the mewling and moaning beneath him. He rolled the candle into the oil and began to apply pressure on her pussy with one hand. Pushing it in inch by inch and watching as she expanded to take it inside of her, he grabbed hold of his cock and found her mouth to keep her quiet.

"Open up," he said, meaning both ends. Her mouth suddenly encompassed his aching cock and he savoured the feeling for a few seconds, warm, wet and with that fucking precision of hers as she wrapped her tongue around him and sucked him in hard. Her hands grasped onto his calves and he felt her nails digging through the material, heightening every need he had to go harder, deeper. More. Slowly, he drew the candle out and then moved it to her arse. She stilled beneath him and dug her nails in again, so he moved his lips to her clit and licked across the length of her. Sweet, juicy, ripe for tasting and full of her scent, it was a fucking aphrodisiac to his senses as he drove his tongue into her and felt her legs tighten around the chandelier. Slowly, her mouth began to move again so he began pushing against the muscle keeping the candle out, harder and harder until her lips loosened and she panted out around his cock. He kept licking and sucking, all the time listening to the rhythm of her breathing, the very cadence of her body as she began to let it take all he was pushing for. Every fucking hole was filled, screaming for it and begging for more as she accepted more of his depravity, accepted it and relished it with him.

"Alex, I..." She panted. She what? Wanted more? She could have it. He pushed down on the candle until it hit the end of her and then drew it back up. In and out, twisting it as he did so and continuously licking like a fucking dog in heat as he felt his own release building. Those expert lips of hers were licking and sucking to perfection as she began to drag her teeth along with them. His stomach coiled and tightened at the thought as he lifted his head away and moved his fingers into her. Her juices overflowed with the oil as the slick sounds filled the air around them and he bucked his hips into her mouth for more, quicker. He intended to just watch his hands working, but he couldn't resist the taste of her in his mouth, couldn't control the need to have his tongue on her when she came. "Oh, god!" Her voice was muffled by the sound of his cock, now driving into her throat. The fucking angle was indescribable, and as his fingers continued working her, he watched her legs still, felt her mouth still on him. Her whole body tensed as she sucked him deeper in, so deep. One more lick, one more swipe of his tongue, or even a bite and she'd come. She'd come for him. Her inner muscles clamped tight around his fingers as he turned the candle slowly and then ravished her clit with bites, hundreds of them. He couldn't fucking stop himself from drowning in her come as she exploded around his face.

She swallowed beneath him, swallowed him in and then drew her head back to get away for air. His fingers left her pussy and clamped around the back of her head as he rammed in, again and again and again, until he couldn't hold it back anymore. He shot more and more of his come deep into her. Spasm after spasm shook him to the core as he tried to keep his legs upright and continued to push his teeth onto her swollen, throbbing clit. Fucking bliss, unadulterated fucking torture. His damn sadistic mind was in the fucking clouds somewhere as he pumped more of himself into her throat, savouring the feeling and scent as he did so. Sweet, sticky come drenched his mouth and nose as his lips moved around her and made her part of him, all for him, his fucking angel. His to abuse, his to use, his to do with as he saw fit whenever he chose to. She'd given him that, offered it, and he was going to take it. Fuck morals and their restrictions. It would only get worse from here. She'd learn so much more about him as she let him take her further, deeper into his needs, his preferences.

His legs hurt. What the fuck was hurting his legs and dragging him from his fucking bliss? His arse cheeks clenched as he shoved in one last time and breathed out a sigh of pleasure. That was a good Christmas present, one he'd never forget. Elizabeth, the perfect present wrapped up in rope bows and covered in his come. Pain suddenly shot through his cock and made him howl out in surrender as he automatically pulled away from the threat. He looked down at her to find her gulping in lungfuls of air and swearing at him on the release of breath.

"Fucking arsehole," she blurted out. He raised a brow and inspected his damn painful cock. Blood dripped from the side of it – not that much but still, she'd bitten him? Only one other person had ever hurt his cock. He shook the image from his head and scowled at her.

"Now, that's not a very nice thing to say at Christmas," he grumbled, still examining his cock.

"I was near suffocating down there," she spat back at him beautifully.

"So you thought biting me was a good idea?"

"It was the only-" Another deep breath, then another. "-way I could get you to listen. Get me down from here, for God's sake. I can't breathe." He tilted his head at her and pondered the best response to make her understand that biting his cock wasn't allowed.

"Say sorry to Santa."

"What? Fuck off. I couldn't breathe, Alex," she panted out. He smirked at the thought, as he looked at the candle still in her very appealing arse. Maybe he should do some real damage with that.

"You rarely do with my cock down your throat. Now, say sorry and I'll think about letting you down. Maybe even taken that candle out of you, unless you want another go, that is?" She looked at him in shock, the pink blush of coming still blooming across her chest, and her face very nearly matching the colour of her hair as she still tried to regain her breath.

"Oh my god. You think I'd do anything after-" He cut across her and snatched hold of her stunning chin. She'd do anything he made her do, and she'd beg for more of it.

"Don't ever bite my fucking cock again."

"Alex, I couldn't-"

"You ever bite it again and I'll make you wish you hadn't. Do you understand?" She nodded and looked down, which was actually up. He couldn't blame her for that one. At least she'd removed her gaze from him.

"I'm sorry. I just couldn't breathe," she said quietly. He stood up and yanked the candle from her at an angle. She winced in pain and mumbled another sorry beneath him. Good, his fucking cock hurt, too. Lifting her up, he unhooked her legs as he took her weight and she kicked herself down into a stand, which rapidly ended up in a sit as she tumbled to the tabletop, disorientated. He licked his lips and chuckled at the vision of defiance coming from her. Whatever happened between them, whatever journey they were about to take, he knew one thing with absolute clarity.

"I love you, Elizabeth Scott," he said firmly across the table. She smiled a little and stretched her legs out, suddenly looking like the cat that got the cream. She used her feet and legs to kick the black box towards him with a grin. It landed by his feet.

"I love you, too, Mr. White. Merry Christmas."

Chapter 21

Elizabeth

'm sitting by the kitchen window, staring out at the snowy ground. Okay, it's not overly snowy, but there is snow, and it looks so pretty. I've been watching Mum and Dad wandering around the garden outside with Alex as he points out different things to them. They really do like him. Dad's a little in awe, I think, since Alex showed him the garage, but Mum genuinely seems completely in love with him. It's not hard to understand why, but the fact is the man is a murderer. My murderer, my sadist and my slice of heaven. They are wandering around with a man who's killed people, aren't they? And they think he's wonderful. I'm not entirely sure how I feel about that. It's one thing knowing it myself, accepting it and finding a way to live with it, but that's my family out there, the people who've protected me from everything and just want me to be happy. They're good people. Why should they be involved with someone like him? They'll never know it, of course, especially given his absolutely perfect Alex behaviour, but I know it. I can feel it in every move he makes now, and I felt it in the way he swiped that candle out of me, purposely hurting me because I'd hurt him.

Bastard.

I sigh at the window and go back over to the sink to start loading the dishwasher. We've all had a very late lunch, having been up until God knows what time last night, and my parents are going back home in an hour. Conner and Belle have already left to go and spend Boxing Day night at some swanky hotel, an official function of some sort that Conner has to be at. So we all hugged and said we'd see each other at Henry's New Year ball. That's going to be fun, isn't it? I can't wait for that Happy New Year to kick in with a smile. I mean, what on earth are we all going to do there? Play nice and pretend no one's trying to destroy each other. It's like *The Count of Monte Cristo* or something. I've also been trying to get my head around whatever it is that's going to happen in Berlin, with Pascal and his idea of a ball. I'm a little concerned what his idea of a ball might involve, and the fact that Alex smirks very devilishly every time I mention it is also very worrisome.

His phone beeps on the table behind me, bringing me back to my dishwasher loading. I giggle at my wandering thoughts and switch the machine on to dispose of the Brie and chutney with bubble and squeak creation that I somehow dreamt up for lunch. Several more vibrations and beeps come rattling at me from the power house that is Alex's phone, so I go over and grab it up in case it's important and he needs it. I have every intention of taking it out to him, but it's been so nice without him having it permanently attached to his hand and ear. Maybe I should just take a look and see how important it is. I mean, if it's not life threatening then it won't hurt for him to keep wandering around with Mum and Dad, will it? Just being a normal human for a change and spending time with other normal, caring humans. That's pretty important to him, right?

My fingers swipe across the screen before I've thought about it too much. I immediately see what appears to be several hundred emails, nearly as many missed calls and a few messages. I haven't got a clue what's important and what's not, but I'm betting life threatening stuff doesn't come via email so I switch to the messages to see what's afoot, if anything. PVDB is the first one. It doesn't take a genius to work that one out, and for some reason, I feel completely comfortable opening it and reading it.

- **Do I now need your permission to kill my brother? It may liven Christmas up, no**?

That's it? I don't know why but I expected more from him, some sort of sentiment attached maybe, or a love heart. I run my fingers across the words and look back out to the garden to gaze at Alex while remembering the kiss Pascal gave me. He's Pascal's, too now. Will he give Pascal what he needs from him? Does he want to? I think I want him to. Well, I want him to do what he feels he needs to do. That's what this is all about, isn't it? Us all gaining some sort of bond together. It's still not clear, though, and I can't quite get my head around any of it, but I'm sure I will in time, as long as he's truthful with me about it.

He starts back towards the house with Mum hanging onto him, and I watch the vision of them together. Mum's beaming at something he's said, probably a joke of some sort. He's been doing that the whole time they've been here, trying to do anything to keep her smiling. I don't know whether that's because of the cancer or because he just wants them to like him for me, but either way, he looks genuinely happy doing it. As if he's found a family he can try to be normal with, honest with. I hit the next message and see some numbers, nothing else. It's not a phone number – more likely a code or something from MJ. I have no idea who that is but I can't see that a code is life threatening either so move on again. The last one has no name attached, and as I read the text, my hand slaps over my mouth, because that can't possibly be right.

- Happy Christmas, son.

It must be a joke, but who the fuck would joke about something like that? My flustered brain goes into meltdown mode. Do I show him this? I'm pretty sure I shouldn't even be checking his messages, given my *don't ever look at my phone* spiel when we first met. But I was doing it so that he could relax and just have a bit more time, wasn't I? Just like he said he was for me at the time. Whatever. I haven't got time to be concerned about whether I should have done this or not. I've done it, and now I need to work out what I should do about the message. My eyes flick over to see them coming up onto the terrace at the far end. I could delete it, couldn't I? Yes, then he would never know, and that bastard, if this is real, will never get to interfere with Alex's life again. Yes, good plan. My finger hovers over the delete button. Oh, but what if Alex wants to see him? What if he really needs to in order to be able to move on? Hiding this message from him would make that worse, wouldn't it? I flick my eyes up again. I've got about fifteen seconds before they're at the door. Delete, not delete. Hover, panic, fuck, fuck, fuck. Oh shitty balls, what should I do? I don't have any right to do anything. It's not my business, is it? Yes, it is though. He's mine, and I want him happy and able to forget all the shit in his past. Oh my god, I can hear their voices now, see his smile as he puts his arm around my mum and chats to Dad, completely oblivious to the fact that his girlfriend is scheming behind his back. *Stupid, Beth.*

I so shouldn't have done this. What the fuck was I thinking? Oh fuck. Think, think, think. Bollocks. I launch the phone at the table as if it's bitten me and watch the screen dull as he catches my eye and winks at me. He hasn't noticed. Good. I blow out a breath and spin back to the sink. Perhaps some sodding fairies can help me out of this when he does eventually read the message. Oh god, what's he going to do? All this lovely Christmas stuff is just going to disappear and be broken and ruined by Mr. Wanker Adlin. I briefly wonder if I need permission to kill someone, too. I could so kill that bastard. I could do that. I could take his heart and rip it out of his useless body then throw it to dogs so they could savage it and swallow it whole. Bury the fucking man in the dirt and watch his corpse rot in hell for the disgusting way he treated his child.

The door handle clicks behind me as their jovial voices come singing in. Mum's laughing again and Alex is talking about petunias. What the hell does he know about petunias? Other than he might need to take some to the funeral of his bastard shitface Father, as and when I get round to killing the fucker. What a knob. How dare he try to mess up my man's head again? Who the hell does he think he is with his nasty manoeuvres? Trying to break my man again... It's not fucking happening, not when I've just got him, just broken through and forged a path in. He'll close down on me. I know it, and it's not happening. I need that phone again. I need to delete that message and then none of this will ever have happened, will it? Plan. I need a plan to get the phone off of him and stop him touching it until I can. Sex. Sex is always good. It's a great distraction technique for Alex. Not with my mum and dad standing next to us, though. That could prove tricky to say the least.

"Coffee anyone?" he says, as he wraps his arms around my waist and kisses the back of my neck. "You smell of sin and my come," he whispers in my ear. I'm not sure I like smelling of come when my mother is ten feet from me, though. Sin is fine. Sin hasn't got a smell. Actually, it has. It smells like his suite in Rome, and his bedroom, and the study, and his hands – they definitely smell of sin – and anywhere that Pascal happens to be. Yes, sin has definitely got a smell. It's mostly called Alex. I smile at the thought and watch him fill the coffee machine up.

I need that phone.

"We're going to start packing up, Bethy," Mum says to me as she heads out of the room, followed by Dad. I flick my eyes to the phone. I could get it now. My feet start to move but I'm hauled backwards and lifted up onto the work surface.

"I've decided I don't like you in trousers," he says, spreading my legs apart and wedging himself in between them. It's a fair point. I'm not entirely sure I do anymore either. They do get in the way somewhat. "Let's make that a rule, shall we? No trousers."

"Ever?"

"Ever," he replies, trying to get his hand into the top of my suede trousers. Soft lips land on mine and he delivers one of his heart-warming kisses. The ones that remind me of the boy inside him, and the man I love. A warm, kind mouth lavishes me with a generous tongue and delicate promises of more, of cuddles and log fires maybe. My fingers run through his black hair and pull him closer to me, as close as I can get him, because these are the moments where I feel him most, where I can forget the man who hung me over a chandelier and fucked my throat till I couldn't breathe. I can just feel the Alex who needs me to love him, deeply, and let him know that anything he does won't stop me loving him tomorrow, that he can just be. He slowly draws back and smiles, an overwhelming smile that reminds me of all the happiness and fun in him. He's enjoying his Christmas. He's comfortable, relaxed. I so need that fucking phone.

"And where exactly is your very expensive Christmas present?" Maybe if he goes upstairs to get it, I can grab the phone.

"Upstairs. I took it off to shower. It's hardly my fault your mother stormed into our bedroom and dragged me out. Does she know nothing of privacy?" No, she's not known for it to be fair.

"Well, I didn't buy it so you could not wear it."

"Fair point, and I wouldn't want to piss you off, would I? My cock's painful enough this morning," he says as he lets go of me and wanders out of the room. Good, I'm glad it hurts. My arse isn't feeling so hot either, although it was possibly one of the hottest things I've ever done in my life.

My sore arse pushes off the table the moment I hear his footsteps disappear and I swipe the phone up. My finger hovers again. Should I really do this? What if's fly through my mind. What if he finds out? What if it's happened before and he's expecting it? What if it is a joke and he wants to find out who it is? Maybe they're threatening his company or something. This is so wrong of me. I shouldn't do it, or maybe I should. For fuck's sake. I wish I could make a bloody decision on this. I'm being ridiculous. I just need to do it and then I won't have to worry about it anymore. My feisty Beth should know how to deal with this, and she's not helping me in the slightest. What would Pascal do? He'd do what was best for Alex, wouldn't he? But what is that? Delete it. Yes, just sodding delete it. Decision made. Fuck it. What have I got to lose? Apart from Alex, that is.

"Why are you looking at my phone, Elizabeth?" Shit, shit, shit. My body freezes as confused Beth tries to find an excuse. There isn't one rapidly springing to mind so I keep looking away from him and wonder if I can sway my arse or something to distract him. "Do not fucking lie to me."

Perhaps not. Balls.

"I, umm..." Funnily enough, that's all that comes out of my mouth. I really need to learn to lie to him, or divert him better.

"Turn around, and be honest." I pull in a breath and turn slowly to find those piercing eyes in full irritated mode, a slight raise of his brow as he searches for some reason why I would be sneaking around behind his back.

"I just... I was trying to keep you safe." What a stupid thing to say. Why the hell did that come out of my mouth? His brow rises even higher. I'm not surprised, me trying to keep a murdering sadist safe must be mystifying to him.

"How, exactly?" Honesty, that's what I demand of him, isn't it? *Idiot, Beth.*

"You have some messages, but I just wanted to keep you to myself a bit longer, let you enjoy Christmas for a while more before you had to... And I didn't know if you should see this one or not. I just wanted to protect you from it. I didn't mean to be deceptive. I just wanted to keep you from hurting if it really is from..." My rambling knows no bounds, it seems, and I can't even bring myself to say the word Dad in front of him. My eyes find the floor in their normal fashion as I try to find the right words to show him that this is because I love him so much, because I want him calm and happy. His hands are in his pockets and I stare at the simple *Jaquet Droz* watch on his wrist that I bought for him, his present from me. Uncomplicated, simple, and elegant. It was my way of trying to show him how I want him to relax and not worry about all the complex stuff in life, just be as he needs to be.

"Head up." I draw my eyes up to him to see a now emotionless face staring back at me, features all hardening as his walls go up around him. "Better. Now say it more concisely."

"I think it's from your father." There's not a flicker of recognition. Not one hint of emotion or sensation changes his face. It's stone, like a mask of concealment. "One of the messages, I think, well, I think your father sent you a message," I say as I hold the phone out to him. He doesn't even look at it, just keeps staring into my eyes, very nearly killing me with the intensity of those blues. His frame remains stock still as I try to hold his gaze and show him I'm sorry for lying.

He suddenly turns without a word and walks away from me, and his phone. I have no idea what that means, so I watch his body turn into the study and slam the door behind him. What the hell do I do now? Is he in pain? Does he need me? No. He would have stayed if he wanted me. Actually, is he angry with me or his father? Oh god, what am I going to do?

"Bethy, darling?" Mum's voice calls from the hall. I swipe away the tears that have welled up and shake my face back into happy. They're leaving soon. I just need to make it through the next twenty minutes or so.

"In here, Mum," I shout back to her. She comes tripping into the kitchen as we both hear something come crashing down the stairs. I glance around her to see a suitcase roll onto the floor from the staircase, hotly pursued by Dad, thankfully not falling, too.

"When are you coming over to see us again?" she asks. I don't even know how today is going to pan out, let alone when we'll be going to see them again.

"As soon as we can, I promise," I reply as I help her on with her coat. She snatches my hand up in hers and stares at my ring. It really is utterly breath-taking. I've been staring at it in most of my spare time, too.

"You'll both make such wonderful parents," she says quietly. "He's so good for you, Bethy. Don't let him get away from you. Your father may be an intolerable fool sometimes, but a good man is worth every grain of sand on the beach. And he loves you so much, honey. I

303

can see it in the way he watches you. He comes to life around you." I smile weakly at her in reply and swallow the tears that are forming again. She has no idea at all how difficult my good man is.

"Okay, Di, are you ready?" Dad asks as he comes in behind us and wraps us both up in a hug. "Where's Alex?"

"Oh, sorry. He got a really important call and he's had to go and do some work. He told me to give you both a hug and that he'd see you soon." What utter bollocks, but what on earth else can I say? There's no way on earth he'll be out of that study for at least another hour. He'll be too busy brooding, breaking things or planning something despicable.

"Oh, never mind," Mum replies. "I suppose that's the life of the wealthy, though. Business never stops, does it?"

"No." Oh god, please just leave so I can deal with whatever's going on in the study. I urge them towards the hall as delicately as I can and keep talking all the way to the door in case Alex is actually destroying something in his office.

"Well, you both look after yourselves, won't you? You'll have to tell me all about this party you're going to in Berlin. Berlin, Alan? Our Bethy off to a posh do in Berlin, wonderful, isn't it?" If only they knew. I open the door for them and smile, nodding at the appropriate moments and throwing in a giggle at Mum's exuberance to show them how wonderful everything is. "And of course, say hello to Henry and Sarah for us, will you? It really would be lovely to see them again at some point." Oh yes, the really comfortable situation surrounding the other ball... Great. She wraps me up in another one of her mum hugs and then rubs both her hands along my arms. "Well done, Bethy. Look at you all grown up and happy. I'm so very proud of you. You know that, don't you? Good business, fantastic new man, marriage on the horizon."

"Thanks, Mum," I mumble. I have no idea how *well* I've done, and I certainly know nothing of marriages on the horizon at the moment. I'm not even sure if he's going to speak to me. Dad narrows his eyes at me over her shoulder so I throw him my brightest smile and walk them to the car. Perhaps that will speed up their disappearance.

Finally, after another ten minutes of hugging and telling me how grown up I am and how I've found such a wonderful man for myself, I watch their car go out of the top gates in a flurry of gravel. Dad appears to have been revved up by the garage. I watch the dust until it settles and then quietly turn back to face whatever's going on inside. "Merry Christmas," I mumble under my breath to myself as I reach the steps to the portico and glance back at the gates. I could have so easily gone with them instead of having to deal with yet another Alex problem.

I reach for the door handle, but it opens for me instead, and there he stands, the master of his castle. I fold my arms around myself to protect my heart from whatever might leave his mouth and gaze up at him.

"I didn't say goodbye," he says quietly with a frown as he watches me watching him. I keep my eyes fixed on his and wait for more. We might as well get it out of the way so I can make up my mind whether to just turn around and walk myself up the drive or not. "You look scared, Elizabeth."

I am – not physically, but emotionally I'm a fucking mess again, so I decide to be brutally honest.

"I am." He smiles a little and offers me his hand, so I gaze at that instead and wonder how he feels about things. "You're not mad?"

"Not at you, no." Oh, good. My beam of delight is slightly withheld as I look back up at him and take hold of his fingers. He chuckles and yanks me up to him. "Although, I need some help for a while, and you can certainly do that."

"Okay." I'll do anything to rid him of whatever he needs to get rid of. As long as we're back on solid ground again, I'll give him anything he needs. Anything. I know that now. He walks us backwards, closes the door, and then, quite surprisingly, lets go of me and heads back to the kitchen.

"Put some logs on the fire. I'll get us some coffee," he calls back to me. Coffee? What the hell is he going to do that involves coffee? Having said that, there's a teaspoon involved in coffee drinking, isn't there?

I chuck some wood into the fire and stare at the flames licking their way up the chimney. They're beautiful in their intensity as they climb and crawl around the stack, full of heat and passion, intertwining with each other and creating one flawed mass of energy. Is that what we are together? A flawed mass of energy, combustible, with me trying to endlessly rein him back into normality and morality?

Charlotte E Hart
ABSORBING WHITE

"Sit," he says as he rounds the corner with a tray perfectly balanced on one hand, waiter style. I wish I'd known him back then. Maybe I could have stopped his criminal life before it even happened. Maybe I could have helped him to accept that family in Rome and be a normal person. Normal? How bloody ridiculous. As if Alexander White even suits the word. I giggle at the thought and move over to the sofa, kicking my heels off on the way. Whatever's about to happen, I certainly don't need them. He places the tray on the table and turns to face me. His mouth opens and then closes again as if he's searching for the right words. I gaze up at him and try to appear open to anything, not that I know what the hell he's about to ask for.

"I want to talk about my father, about my life," he says. My mouth gapes stupidly, because that's the last thing I expected to leave his lips. 'Let me string you up and make you come until you can hardly breathe' would have been my best guess at what was going to happen. Or perhaps, 'I want to fuck you until this anger goes away'. Anything other than what he just said, to be honest.

"Okay," I slowly reply as he sits down next to me and makes a spinning motion with his finger. I assume that means I should turn, so I do and he pulls me back to his chest, then hands me a coffee.

"Comfortable?" he asks as he kisses the top of my head, and I feel a sigh leave his ribcage.

"Very." He squeezes me a little closer and rests his hand on my stomach. Okay, this is slightly weird now, although I suppose him talking about his father is very odd for him so I link my fingers over his and take a sip of my coffee. All I can do is wait and let him find whatever he needs to say.

Eventually, after what feels like hours, he starts to tell me things – vile things, things a child should never have to bear. There's hundreds of stories, days of beatings and cruelty. Every single word that's uttered from his beautiful lips sounds fragile, as if it's taking him immense amounts of strain to just keep the words flowing freely and remain calm. Words like broken, bruising, urine, pain, darkness, filthy, crying, torture, and hungry, thirsty even. Who does that to a child? Who? Why?

His hand tightens on my stomach every single time something really hurts him. I can feel it in every truly disturbing thing he says. It's the terms of sadness that do it to him, though, not the physical acts.

Words like *broken* and *bruising* don't cause the pain in his voice or the tension in his body. It's the ones like *crying* or *scared* that causes the panic in him every time he tells me about another day of nightmares. Every single day and night, every moment of his life was consumed by a man who made him into the hell that he became. He survived constant bullying, belittling and beating. I can see him shivering in the snow – the same snow that's outside now – snow that reminds him of being locked in a coal shed in the depths of winter, freezing, in nothing but his underwear as his father callously watched him and waited for him to try and escape just so he could beat him again. He didn't even have a bed to sleep in, just a urine soaked mattress on a hard wooden floor. I can see him there, too, that little boy.

I can feel him shaking and crying into the night to try and keep warm, to try and find reasons why his father, his daddy, the man who was supposed to love him, would do any of this to him. I can even smell that bedroom as he explains it to me and tells me why he's so scared of the dark, why he sits in his safe room and meditates in the hope of chasing away the memories, why he learnt to fight in the dark so that he could destroy anything that ever tried to hurt him again. I can feel my eyes welling up with tears, no matter how hard I try to stop them, as he tells me about killing for the first time, about how it made him feel like a God, and how it made him feel alive for the first time, gave him a new lease of life.

My body tries to move away from him as he describes, in detail, the first man he killed, but he tightens his hold and makes me listen to every single word until I have no power to try and break away from him. Hours seem to roll by as I listen to more stories of murders and of pain, interlinked somehow as if he finds a sense of solace in the acts, some way of ridding himself of the haunting of his past. In reality, they're just stories of a lost little boy managing to find his way through his nightmares. It's criminal, yes, but it's a way out nonetheless, his way out. A fighter's way out.

"They were all bad people," he says quietly over my shoulder as I sniff back another tear and try to stay focused on the positives. He's talking openly, letting me know all there is to know without me badgering him about it. He's just being honest so that I have everything I've asked of him. He promised, didn't he? Promised me he'd tell me the truth. Suddenly, I'm not so sure I wanted to know.

Because, bad people? He is the bad people, isn't he? He is the threat lurking in the darkness. He has been the menace your parents and friends warn you about. The man who sits behind me, Alexander White, the man I love, is a killer. It sinks in with acute clarity as I watch his hand twiddling with the ring on my finger, the very same ring that was offered with a proposition of sorts. "I never hurt anyone who didn't deserve it, Elizabeth."

"What's your definition of deserving it, Alex?" He smiles behind me. I can sense him doing it somehow, or maybe feel his amusement at my question.

"They had all acted as badly as I did."

That's it, his definition of what deserves killing.

"It doesn't make it alright. It's wrong to kill someone, for any reason." The moment the words are out of my mouth, I can't help but imagine what I'd do if his father was in front of me. The perverse type of anger that consumes my thoughts when I think about what that monster did very nearly tips me in favour of believing that it's fine to take the life of someone. "Do you think that message is from your father?"

"I don't know. I'll have someone trace the number. I could always go and ask him." What?

"I thought you had no contact with him," I reply as I spin around to look at him. He tucks a lock of my hair behind my ear and rubs his thumb across my cheek. It's a sweet moment really, considering what we've been talking about. I smile at him wearily and decide that I need a drink or six, preferably something strong. It is Boxing Day, after all. "Do you want a drink?" I ask as I make my way to the bar for something stiff. He nods, so I collect a couple of glasses and the cognac, and return to the other end of the sofa. He drags my feet up to his chest and begins to rub them, soothing me, showing me the other side to him again. The same one I first met, right here on this sofa. He takes a full glass from me and watches me with a smile.

"I know where he lives, although why he'd try to contact me I don't know."

"Maybe he wants to make amends." He laughs, full-on laughs.

"He is not the type of man to make amends, baby. You think the best of people far too easily."

"If I didn't, we wouldn't be sitting here now, would we?" I reply instantly.

"Touché," he says with another chuckle. I swirl the drink around the glass and wonder if there's any more to deal with.

"Is that it?" I ask, sipping at my cognac and trying to manage all the information into some sort of appropriate layer in my completely frazzled brain. "Nothing else I need to know?"

"I'm sure there's plenty more but that's most of it, the general gist anyway."

"Do I need to worry? Is anyone after you because of your past?" He continues with his foot rubbing but suddenly looks overly serious again, every trace of humour seemingly gone as he stares at my feet and then stills his hands on me.

"Someone is always after me, past or not. That's the position I've put myself in, and now you. It's why I like my games, why I've tried to teach them to you. It's why I need you to be able to fight, and why I don't want you to trust anyone. I love you, but you're part of this now. You asked for the truth, and so you need to understand what you're up against."

"I don't want to be like that, though. It's not me. You know it's not. I can't be a part of that type of world and be comfortable in it. Okay, I can play a game and have fun with it, but I'm not a killer, Alex. I don't manipulate, lie and cheat for fun or kicks on a Saturday night. It's just not me."

"All very true, but I'm afraid you're in it whether you like it or not, because if they want to hurt me, if they want to destroy everything precious to me, it won't be me they come for anymore. It will be you."

Oh, fuck.

Chapter 22

Elizabeth

We talked and talked and talked. All night we talked. I learnt more about him last night than in the entire time I've known him. It's like he opened the floodgates and finally let me all the way in, like he trusted me with every emotion he'd ever had, and gave them to me freely. Having scared the shit out of me with his little speech about me being the one they'd come for, I rattled him for every answer to every question I'd ever had. And he answered, just like he said he would, because he told me he'd tell me the truth. Okay, he threw some misdirection in there as often as he could, and he obviously tried to flirt his way out of the difficult questions. Of course I ended up being slammed, quite violently actually, and banged up against any object that got in his way. But that was just his way of finishing it off, of finishing me off, maybe. Every time I came, he pushed me for another one, asked me if there were any more questions, and then he'd shove me into a new position to make me come again. When I finally had a chance to answer by asking another question, he simply turned over and asked me to read out the dates on his back. He told me about every single date, the good ones and the bad ones, apart from our lunch date, and then he fucked me again. Apparently, his bitten cock wasn't that offended that I bit it, or maybe it was and that's why I got such a hammering. Who knows? Who cares, frankly? My inner slut certainly doesn't. Whatever it was, it was his way of showing me that he loved me, his own special brand of love just for me, his *only* brand of love, it seems. So now I sit here about thirty minutes out from Berlin, watching the ground fly by beneath us, hoping to god that nothing is going to happen with Pascal tonight because, frankly, I'm far too sore. I'm sure I'll still say that when his damned intoxicating eyes sparkle at me with some undisclosed innuendo directed at my crotch.

Alex is wandering about, looking highly fuckable, as he growls at whoever is on the end of the phone. The Christmas break has finished as far as his work is concerned, it seems. His long legs stride about in a tailored, three-piece grey suit, no tie obviously. I'm not sure he'll ever wear one again after Jingle Bells tainted the thought yet more. Not that I give a damn. I'd rather he never wore one again if it makes him feel anything close to the pain he talked about last night. Although, considering the issue, wearing it for my family was possibly one of the sweetest things anyone's ever done for me.

"That's not fucking good enough, Mark," he snarls into the phone as he pours a drink and tips the bottle at me with a smirk. Not a really angry Alex at all, well, maybe he is with the person on the other end of the phone, but certainly not with me. I beam at him in response with a nod and ponder the consequences of giving him a blowjob. That went quite well last time he was angry on the phone. He winks at me, licks his lips and waves his hand at the front of his trousers. How the hell does he do that reading me thing? I really need to work on that with him. I wouldn't want to become too readable, dull even. I giggle at him and look back out of the window again.

"Fifteen minutes out, Sir. Buckle in please," the pilot says over the speakers. We don't have a flight attendant today, and as Alex is still chatting, I push the button on the black console to acknowledge that someone's actually heard Phillip, and then start to buckle my belt up, although I can't really understand why anyone bothers. I mean, what is a seatbelt going to do at however high we are as we crash into a mountain or something? Sodding ridiculous design, really. He sits opposite me and continues with his unfriendly chat, now discussing a file and photos of some description. I have no idea what the hell he's talking about but it does remind me of that letter that Michael never let me see, which quickly leads me onto nearly being raped. What happened to that man after we left the club? Honesty, we might as well get that bit of information out there in the open, too.

He eventually finishes his call and looks at me expectantly. Apparently he knows something is coming.

"What was in the envelope that was in my shop? And when that bastard attacked me, and you beat him nearly to death, what happened next?"

"I would rather have the blowjob you were thinking about," he replies. Cute. My eyes flick to his cock again. I'm so in control. Not. My feisty Beth sits me up straighter and stares him down until the smirk disappears from his face. I'm getting quite good at that shit. He picks up his drink and hands me mine.

"I suppose it makes little difference now anyway. There was a picture in the envelope of me doing what I used to do, holding a knife. Quite incriminating, obviously. I'm having Andrews and a colleague look into it for me. Someone was obviously trying to warn you off me," he says with little emotion involved, completely businesslike, as if it's just another work problem to be organised and dealt with. "You look incredible today, by the way. That just fucked look suits you, especially when you're in pain. Keep squirming in that seat. Are you very sore? I have a balm?"

"And?" No way is he distracting me with sex, no matter how much I'm now thinking about his mouth and teeth. Yes, my inner slut is leaping out of her seat again but I grip onto the armrest to stop myself and gulp some alcohol down.

"What do you think happened to him, Elizabeth?"

"I don't know. I'm asking you."

"Yes, you do."

That's all he needs to say, isn't it? I do know. I've probably known since the moment he told me about his past. There's no way he would have let that man live, not after he attacked something so precious to him. Why, I'm still not sure. What makes me so special I'll never know. But to him, the very thought of someone hurting me, scaring me, let alone trying to get inside me, must have been like a ticking time bomb waiting to explode. Do I hate him for making me the reason he killed someone? Yes. I'm disgusted that another human has died because of me. In fact, I hate it and can feel it making me sick inside, churning my guts and screaming at my sense of justice. But am I bothered that he did it? That he took a piece of scum off this planet that may have raped other women? Absolutely not. People like that, and people that hurt children don't deserve another chance, do they? Why should they live? But what right do we have to make that judgment? What right does he have?

"I'm not comfortable with that thought," I reply quietly as I gaze out of the window in confusion. I'm really not sure what else I can say. Would thank you be appropriate? Well done? You shouldn't have? Not for me. Mafia queen of the world I am not. None of this sits comfortably with me, no matter how much I love him or accept his preferences.

"I know, and I'd still do it again tomorrow, regardless of your thoughts," he says with conviction etched into every word. My eyes find his again as he stares me down. There's a slight lift of his brow as he conveys his certainty. Nothing will ever change his opinion of being right on this. No amount of me telling him it's wrong to kill will make him believe that taking the life of this man was immoral. He may be right.

"You said you stopped a long time ago, said you hadn't done anything like that for years. You lied to me." He crosses his legs, smirks again and unbuttons his jacket as I feel the descent of the plane becoming more rapid. The brakes start to engage as the pitch of the engine changes around us, and I realise that I've only got until the end of this flight to gain whatever I need from him. He's about to see Pascal again, and I can feel his mood changing around that thought. His body is tensing slightly, his mind beginning to close down and change to that man that only wants his kind of fun, and me being part of it. He's excited, dominant, and full of ideas and manipulations as he keeps running his gaze over my body and seems to be losing the will to discuss this with me.

"I didn't lie. I just didn't see the need to drag that particular incident up again. He hurt you and tried to take something that wasn't his to take. The end result would have always been him in pain. It was reasonably therapeutic, quite liberating really." I've suddenly got all sorts of disturbing images flooding my brain – blood and bones, guns, knives, screaming and shouting. More of those gurgling noises he made the last time I saw him on the floor. Who was there? Where was it? Where is his body now?

"How? Where?"

"Elizabeth, don't ask questions you don't want the answers to. Your morals will confuse you, and subsequently us. And I quite like you liking my butchering hands, as you call them."

Very intelligent I'm sure, butchering arrogant arse. The wheels hit the runway beneath us and I feel my stomach lurch back to life at the thought.

"I still don't like that you did it."

"Of course you don't," he replies dismissively, nodding out of the window at something, which is apparently more interesting. I crane my head around to see what he's looking at and find two motorbikes and a car zooming towards the plane. I have no idea why the motorbikes are here so look back at him for some kind of clarification.

"There's been an accident. Take your clothes off." Umm... Okay. We unbuckle our belts and he speaks to Phillip through the console about something as I wonder why exactly I've got to take my clothes off. Funnily enough, it's not stopping me from doing it, though.

The plane eventually comes to a stop, and I watch as the door opens and the steps are lowered. I'd like to say I'm bothered about my state of undress, but given my hand on hip stance as I stare at the doorway, I've clearly become quite comfortable being clotheless around men. Shit, it's cold, though. A full set of black leathers walks through the door and hands a bag to Alex then removes his helmet. He's a youngish man, maybe twenty or so, and very pretty. There is nothing harsh about him. He's got a quiet aura about him, sweet.

"Sir," he says as he sweeps his eyes over me and then looks straight at the floor, possibly in fear.

"Is he waiting for us?"

"Yes, Sir," the young man replies with a strong Italian accent, still looking at the floor. The bag is tossed in my direction so I grab it and open it up to find a set of leathers for me. I assume I'm supposed to put them on, so quickly start trying to squeeze my arse into them. The boy watches me from the corner of his eye as Alex brushes past him and down the steps.

"What's your name?" I ask as I zip up the jacket and stuff my feet into the socks and boots also provided.

"Reubin, ma'am."

"Oh god, Reubin, please, no ma'ams. I really don't like it. Thanks for bringing these in for me." He looks almost shocked that I'm speaking to him, and still has that white glaze of fear imprinted on his face.

"That's okay. There's been a crash and the roads are busy. Sir thought it would be quicker this way." Sir? Alex, or Pascal? "I'll take your bags back in the car. I think you're going somewhere else."

"Oh, okay. Thanks again, though. Your English is very good. Where did you learn?" I ask as I shake my hair out of its grip and try to attempt a plait of some description. He gently folds my original clothes and places them in a small rucksack, then puts my shoes and handbag in, too.

"I schooled in Switzerland from the age of five. Papa thought it best," he replies with a sad face. My heart swells. He certainly didn't enjoy school, it seems. Bastard people, sending their children away to school. Why have any if you're going to do that? "You'll need to take this, ma'am, sorry, I mean, Miss Scott."

"Elizabeth or Beth, Reubin, whichever is easier," I say as I take the bag from him and shrug it on to turn for the exit. He gives me his helmet as we both walk down the steps, him three steps behind me as if it's only right to do so, his head down all the time. The relative normality of having Alex to myself has left, it seems. I'm in the realm of Dominants and submissives again.

Alex is standing near a bike with another man on it, fully kitted out in orange and black leathers with his helmet still on. I have no idea who it is. Maybe we've got a guide or something. Alex suddenly slaps the back of the guy's helmet and wanders over to the bike, pulling on some leather gloves and a wool coat as he does so.

"You ready?" he says as he climbs on, that excited schoolboy smile plastered on his face. I scowl at the uncomfortable looking seat and frosty winter ground, then attempt to elegantly stretch my leg over it. There is nothing remotely elegant about that manoeuvre, so I clamp on as tightly as possible to avoid the obvious possibility of death and roll my eyes at my ridiculousness. I'm pretty much clasping onto the grim reaper as I sit here, aren't I? Giving him my soul, so to speak?

He doesn't wait for me to get comfortable. He just revs the bike and skids us out into an arc. I coil myself around him even more as he begins to follow the other bike, quickly.

I've never been to Berlin. It's different, interesting, and as I gaze at all the buildings I've seen in brochures, I think about how much I love to travel. There are so many things to see in this world, so many cultures and religions and landscapes to visit. I want to go back to New York and do it properly. I think after we've got the business moved and settled in, I'll try and book some holiday and we can go back there. Maybe Conner and Belle could come, too. Whatever Alex said to Belle that night, it must have worked because they got on really well on Christmas Day. I actually saw them laughing together at one point. And he talked about skiing, and his yacht. I've never sailed either, and it's bound to have actual sails, isn't it? A proper yacht. There's no way would he have something he couldn't push to its limits.

He points at a large building on our left. It's almost like a palace with its intricate columns and ornate design features. Steps lead up to the entrance as it dominates the landscape around it and shows its majestic prowess. It's utterly beautiful. There's another building, too, and they both surround a huge park or garden area, a church or cathedral maybe. It's got that fairytale feel about it that all European castles have. Does Germany have a royal family? If it does, I'm sure Pascal knows them. Perhaps we could have high tea?

A sudden revving of the engine and zipping through traffic at rather excessive speeds has me hanging on for dear life again as he holds my thigh and drives one handed. He'd be getting such a fucking earful if we had those speaking devices in these helmets, but we don't, so I knock the back of his helmet with mine and feel his chuckle reverberating through his back. Fun Alex is back, happy, relaxed in his own way. Just for me, possibly Pascal, too.

Eventually, we pull up outside another quite extraordinary building. It's at least eight floors of old baroque detailing and a doorway that screams eighteenth century sophistication. We must look like a right bunch of idiots turning up on motorbikes. One should be in a horse drawn carriage or something, I'm sure. The man on the other bike gets off, pretty much abandoning his bike, and it's the moment I see him walk that I realise its Pascal. Even in leathers, he manages to look regal. He walks towards me and holds out a hand to help me as he pulls his helmet off.

"My love," he says with a sinful smile. I could practically faint. As if it isn't enough that I'm already wrapped around a bunch of deliciousness, I've now got the other one to contend with, too. I take his hand and remove my helmet, somehow managing a slightly more graceful departure from the bike this time.

"Fun," Alex says behind us. We both spin around to face him. He removes his gloves and throws them on the bike absentmindedly. "I like that one. Whose is it?"

"Lucinda's. I thought it might amuse you to ride it hard." My snort of amusement has left me before I know whether it should have or not. Given their battle for Pascal, I'm not entirely sure if it's funny or not. Thankfully, Alex chuckles and takes my hand.

"Where are we?" I ask as we wander toward the building.

"My apartment," Pascal replies as I scan the building again. "While you are quite divine in leather, I assumed you would feel the need to change."

"Lovely, although I was enjoying my tour of the city. It's very lovely."

"That building we passed is the Altes Museum, in the Lustgarten. It's where the ball is tomorrow, and we need to do some shopping before that," Alex says as we cross an exquisite marble floor and head toward a gilded cage of an elevator.

"Why? I have a dress?" In fact, I packed several. Why didn't he just tell me not to bring any if we were going to buy a new one? I shrug the rucksack off my back and Pascal takes it from me.

"Not the right kind, you don't." I frown in response and watch them both smile at each other. They've got that conversation going on again, the one I'm privy to on certain occasions. It appears now is not one of those times. Pascal holds a hand out to the lift and I walk in, hotly pursued by both of them. The gate closes behind them and I suddenly realise how small it is in here. I'm pretty much encased in a shit load of trouble. The floor leaves us and I look up at Alex with a smile. He's still the most arresting one of the two – bigger, stronger, his face infinitely more appealing – and those cold, calculating eyes still transfix me, regardless of the bastard behind them. He smirks and tilts his head at me, and in a split second, I see those eyes darken. Pascal's on me instantly. My feet are lifted from the floor as he pushes me back against the cage, harshly. I have no idea what's hit me until his mouth is on my neck, biting, grabbing, rough hands gripping me through the leather and squeezing with an uncaring grasp. I stare at Alex in shock and wonder where the hell this has come from, but I can see by his calm demeanour and cool face that he's given this to Pascal. He's giving me to him. He licks his lips and just watches me, and I can't help but love every second of it. Being watched as Pascal flicks the button on my leathers and delves his hand into them is mesmerising, mind-blowing even. I don't know how, but I know I've got to keep looking at Alex. This is for him. I pant out and try to move to aid his access because I want Pascal's hand inside me. I've been waiting for God knows how long to feel him inside me. He kicks my legs wider and rams his hand further in. The leather creaks around his efforts, and I swear he might tear them off with them force of his tugging. And then he's there, and two fingers shove inside me, brutally. Everything stills as my mouth parts and a puff of warm breath hits the air. I'm pinned to the cage and gazing at the man I love as the whole world stops spinning and Pascal's fingers begin to work me. Alex slowly pushes a button on the panel to stop the elevator, a flicker of amusement crossing his face as I squeal in response to the pain being delivered in sudden sharp bites along my neck. The next moan that leaves me is filled with near delirium as that hand drives in again like a wild animal, feral, foraging and claiming the prize he's been offered. He's overly aggressive. Not one part of him gives a damn if I'm enjoying this or not. He's clearly been let loose and he's going to take his opportunity. He delves in deeper, changing my angle again and sliding his other hand into the back of my trousers to keep me aloft. Time and time again, he's pinching and grabbing, forcing his weight into me, slamming me backwards against the metal rails because he knows it hurts, beautifully. So I close my eyes and let the build take me, let the fact that I'm being used be okay as his cock digs into my inner thigh. I can feel it straining to get at me. He hasn't got a hope because of the time we've got, and that's why Alex has done this, to tease him, and me, to get us ready. But I am going to come. It's taken nothing for him to get me to this point and I can feel it coming at me like a steam train, rushing across my body and forging a path through my surprise as he grunts into my neck and pushes his cock against me harder. I open my eyes to look at Alex again. I need to see him when this happens. I need him to know that it's because of him, for him. He presses the button on the panel again and looks at his watch with a smirk as the lift starts to move once more. My core begins to contract around brutal fingers and flashes of light blind me at the promise of bliss as his thumb pushes me higher into my orgasm.

"Fuck, yes, do it," I gasp out as I grab onto his shoulders and let him shove me back again and again. My fingers grip on, my nails digging in with no care, and pull him in toward me. His mouth... I want his mouth, his kiss, that one thing I need to make this more intimate somehow. Alex sneers. He can see I need it, and he clearly doesn't like the thought. Fuck him. It's my orgasm. I'll have it however I want it. I tug the back of Pascal's hair until his face comes up to mine, his fingers still ramming in and pushing me forward. Oh god, just a few more times and I'll come. My lips reach for his and he hesitates so I tug harder and instantly moan as they meet mine. Love, lust, I haven't got a clue what it is, but as his tongue swirls with mine, the feeling is explosive and everything goes white in front of me. My body stills against him as those deviant stars erupt and I feel him still groaning into my mouth, still rubbing his cock into me and sliding his fingers in and out. All I can feel is Alex for some reason, and all I can taste is Pascal, on me, and in me. Both of them, together.

My eyes slowly open again to see Alex over Pascal's shoulder. If I could remove my lips, I would but his mouth is divine, nothing like Alex's, far less intense, more romantic if that's possible in this moment. He's staring at me, his eyes now blackened and dirty. He's horny, extremely so, and we did that to him. Our performance has his abnormal brain conjuring up all sorts of depravity, I'm sure. I roll my lips around Pascal's and let my quaking slow down a little to relish it some more as I keep my eyes trained on Alex to show him how much I love him. It's strange, given my current positioning really, grinding on another man's hand, but there you go. This will definitely take some getting used to, but it has been for him, done with his permission.

"Take your hand out of her," he says, still staring at me. There's the briefest of hesitations before Pascal obeys and pulls away from me altogether, leaving me rather breathless against the cage to try and stand up on my own. He backs away to the corner and sucks at his fingers. I so want to do that. If I was any hornier, I'd probably be dangerous.

I'm not entirely sure what we're all supposed to do now – say thank you? That was very nice? I wish I could stop the giggle that's rising in my throat but I'm really struggling to be honest, and Pascal is not helping at all. His smirk is firmly in place as he continues sucking his finger in the corner.

"She does taste exceptional. You were right," he says as the lift stops, dings and the doors open. Alex growls at him and watches him carefully as he picks up my rucksack, exits and then wanders off down the hall. I look at him and try to hold back my giggle again because, seriously, what the hell is he growling about now?

"If it's not comfortable, why are you doing this?" He stares at me, an almost lost look on his face as he probably tries to work that out for himself. I button up my trousers again and lounge like a slut on the bars behind me. Christ, I feel nice.

"Just because I want to see him fuck you it doesn't mean I have to like it, or enjoy it quite as much as you just did." That's it. I can no longer hold my hysterics in. Really? Jesus. What the hell did he want me to do? Pretend I didn't? Oh my god. I'm almost crying at the hilarity of what he's just said, my stomach muscles clenching as he just continues with his stare and then yanks me towards him with yet another growl of annoyance. I walk my fingers up his suited chest and get up on tiptoes to kiss him, pouring all my love into his mouth in the hope that it relaxes him to some degree. It was his idea after all. He pulls away after a minute and stares at me again.

"I'll hate every minute of it next time, I promise." I giggle into his chest. I really haven't got anything else to say on the matter.

"Hmm. I can promise you'll hate every minute of it, too," he replies as he lets go of me and ushers me out with a small smile. I'm not entirely sure I'm happy with that response. What exactly does he mean by that? He walks us down two corridors and finally gives me a key and a rather dramatic slap on the backside as we reach a door.

"It's yours. Put it on your keyring. If you ever need a place to run to, this is it. Here or the safe room at home." He's very serious all of a sudden. "What was the code?" I gaze at him for a moment, trying to get my head around what he's just said, and then try to remember the code. Battle of Hastings.

"Ten sixty six, but I don't see why I-"

"Because you may need to one day, and if you do, I'll know where to find you. You go nowhere else but those two places."

I put the key in the lock and try to dismiss his strange words. I know we had that little chat yesterday but honestly, as if anyone's ever going to come after me. I may be his girlfriend, but this Mafia world he seems to be part of isn't anything to do with me. And why bring it up now? I was really enjoying my post-Pascal orgasmic bliss there, arsehole.

The door opens and I'm hit by the smell of sandalwood and flowers. It's a bright apartment, nothing like his apartment in Eden – London's Eden, that is. It still has heavy antique furniture but the drapery is cream and the wallpaper a relaxing blue colour with fleur de lis patterning on it. It's almost as if a woman lives here, too.

"Ah, there you both are. I had assumed he was fucking me out of you. It is not possible that I've exhausted you, surely?" Pascal says as he comes around the corner, now having taken his top and jacket off so I can see his upper body. It's completely unfair of him. I spin back to Alex to see if he's up for that. My crotch certainly is. He raises a brow and looks at a door in the corner of the room, then shakes his head at himself and takes off his coat instead.

"I've given Elizabeth a key."

"Of course you have. This way I can fuck her whenever I like. A truly marvellous plan, you are a genius, Sir."

"Pascal," he growls.

"You cannot possibly imagine I will be able to behave around her now?" he replies as he wanders back out of the room again, unzipping the front of his leathers as he does. I instantly chastise myself for trying to crane my head after him.

"Where's the coffee machine?" I ask Alex, because there has to be one, clearly.

"In the kitchen, down the hall on the left."

I walk down towards it and gaze at the pictures on the wall. They're all non-descript, just random paintings and prints. There's nothing to give anything away about Pascal until I reach a small silver photograph frame on a side table. I pick it up and study the two incredibly handsome men in it, both in full military livery of some sort with medals decorating their chests and swords at their sides.

"That's his brother, Fabrice, and his father." I turn around to find Alex looking at the picture over my shoulder, a slightly concerned look on his face as he takes the picture from me and gently puts it back on the table.

"You really do care about him, don't you?" I say as I gaze up at him. He turns past me and goes into the kitchen with a frown. "Alex, it's okay for you to be in love with him. I don't mind."

"I know you don't," he says as he turns to look straight at me with a smile. I look over his form, all six foot four of him, looking utterly beautiful in his small moment of confusion. His perfectly tailored suit is undone at the front, opening up his heart to me, just me. "And considering I've just let him touch you, it's a damn good job I am." I lean on the units and return his smile. He's finally admitted it, although he hasn't exactly said he's bi.

"Are you comfortable with that? You know, the bi part of the conversation." He sighs and turns back to the coffee machine so I walk over and put my arms around his stomach, then nudge my head under his arm. "You can be whatever you need to be with me, especially after last night, and certainly after the last half an hour. I'm hardly likely to judge, am I? And he is very attractive."

"His body doesn't interest me, not in the way he would like it to. Yours does."

"Have you ever tried?" He kisses the top of my head and chuckles.

"It's something I would know. I've been around enough situations to understand what I need."

"Well, I didn't think I'd enjoy kissing Tara the slut that much either but funnily enough, it was quite exciting. Have I told you how much I hate you for that, by the way? I do." He raises a brow and halts his coffee making routine.

"You didn't look like you enjoyed it."

"I didn't. I just said it was exciting. Under no circumstances will you make me do it again. Ever. Unless the woman is not Tara, then I might like it more. I'm not exactly thrilled that you fucked her mouth having tied me up to prove what a dick you were, still are sometimes. You do understand how much I hate you for that? I may need you to make that up to me. Perhaps I could tie you up and make you do something you're unsure of, too." The wink I deliver at the end of that has him tilting his head at me and hovering a teaspoon in my line of vision.

"Are you trying to manipulate me, because we could try some more negotiations?"

"Who would dare?" Although I am up for that type of negotiation any day of the week, "And I'm sure you'll do as you please anyway. I'll have lots of sugar in my coffee, and can I go take a quick shower?"

"The room in the corner is ours. Help yourself."

I swan off down the hall to let him think about his own reactions. I'll never be able to tell him how he thinks or feels. It's up to him to work that out on his own. I don't really even understand this collaring thing or the meaning of it, but I've accepted Pascal into our relationship. I know he's part of the equation now and I'm pretty sure he always will be. Whether anything actually happens between the two of them, I don't know, but I suppose we'll all find out in time. I cross the main lounge area to the door in the corner and am halted by a picture I didn't see when I came in. It's a picture of a woman in her late thirties maybe. She's smiling into the room but the gaze is stone cold, like there's no life in it at all. She's completely beautiful, with raven dark hair and bright green eyes, and I know without a shadow of a doubt that it's a family member. I wrap my arms around myself unconsciously and continue to look at her features. There's something decidedly creepy about them.

"You have met mother, I see." The sound makes me jump, and it's only when his fingers brush along my arms that I begin to relax a little again.

"That's your mum?"

"Indeed, quite the bitch. This is her house."

"Apartment."

"No, house. I had the building converted the moment she graced hell with her being. I do not envy it down there. Shall we go to heaven instead? We could cause a revolution."

"You're half German then?"

"Spanish. She was the bastard daughter of the reigning Prince of Spain at the time. My grandfather does not like to admit to our lineage. However, my father did do the honourable thing and married her when she fell pregnant with me. She never forgave me for that."

"That sounds sad."

"Excruciatingly so, but dull nonetheless, and quite irrelevant to my life," he replies with a soft smile, a warm one. I can't stop my hand reaching out to him but he moves away from me and picks up a tweed jacket as if he's going somewhere.

"Are you leaving?"

"I have been summoned to a very tedious encounter with a delinquent teenager who requires some manners beating into him." How very Pascal. I watch him flit around and wonder if we're supposed to talk about what happened in the cage or not. Is this how it goes? We just go back to being sort of friends again after every encounter? I don't want that. I have feelings for him that require a connection to be more permanent to some degree, more personal.

"Can I have a kiss before you go?" He stills and looks at me over his shoulder just as Alex walks into the room. His head slowly turns to look at Alex, as does mine. It's a moment of complete confusion between the three of us, all eyes flicking between each other as if hoping one of us will just make the decision and let us know what that is exactly. Should I? Or is it up to Alex? Pascal eventually speaks up.

"My dear, you may have a kiss whenever you like. As long as he tells me it is acceptable."

There is no verbal response from Alex, nothing, only him walking across the room to our bedroom and smirking the entire way until he's disappeared.

"Guess that was a no then, huh?" I giggle out quietly.

Pascal chuckles, picks up his keys and grabs my hand leaving the warm, imprint of his lips on them, before turning and leaving.

This is definitely going to take some getting used to.

Chapter 23

Alexander

Trawling through emails while he was getting ready was the last thing he wanted to do, but the sudden barrage of messages he was receiving regarding Tate had piqued his interest. He was being copied in on emails regarding the Shanghai deal that were usual in their content, however, unusual in their terminology. They didn't make any sense. Normal structure was applied, but the paraphrasing was in the wrong order. He'd been through enough of these documents to almost memorise the content and this wasn't right. Henry was copied in on most of them, and the wording just wasn't normal. They were complex legal documents relating to Tate's version of the sale process – a sale process that he wasn't actually managing anymore. They all went through the correct channels in Shanghai, to be completed in four days time – the channels he'd already shut down and moved over to a new legal counsel so that Tom Brindley could do all the negotiating and work without Tate knowing, which he'd done to an exemplary standard. The deal was set to close today. There was nothing getting in the way of it, nothing stopping the flow. He'd signed all the secondary paperwork required and transferred the money over to Louisa, who in turn was to send it to the designated account at 8pm CET. All he had to do was wait. In one hour, he would be three times richer than he was now and nobody knew a thing about it other than himself, Louisa, Tom, both lawyers and one member of the Chinese government. So why was Tate sending information through to Henry at such a rapid pace? And why was he being copied in on it? He looked over an email again and scanned it for some inbuilt code he hadn't noticed the first time he read it, then decided to open his laptop so he could see them side-by-side. They began dated 24th December and finished today. He chastised himself for putting his phone down for too long over Christmas and slammed his hand on the table in frustration.

"Alex, I can't do these buttons up. I mean, how the hell am I supposed to... Oh, sorry, you're working," she said as she stormed into the room, looking the epitome of sin. He looked up at her and tried to push the instant need to fuck her away. He needed to get this organised. Who the fuck decided today was a good day to merge this deal? Christ. It didn't matter how much he'd had his damned fingers inside her last night, he still couldn't wipe away the vision of Pascal's being there, too. He couldn't decide if that was a good thing or not, so he shook his head and looked back at the screen.

"I'll do it in a minute," he replied as he scanned the listed information again.

"Problem?" she asked as she walked over behind him and laid her angelic fingers on his shoulders. "Oh, good lord, look at all those lists and numbers. It's worse than my recipe sheets."

"There's something here I'm not seeing. Tate's being underhanded, and the fact that I can smell you isn't helping me find the issue." She slapped the back of his head. He wasn't sure what for.

"It's really impolite to say that. I do not smell." He spun around and stuck his head in her on display crotch and inhaled deeply. She did. The devil couldn't smell any better than she did. "Is it to do with Henry?" He couldn't give a fuck about Henry all of a sudden.

"Yes. This is a very good look for you. You should wear it all the time."

She snorted in response and braced her hands on her hips.

"Had I have known the dress scene was steam punk come Edwardian glamour with a hint of gothic masochism, I wouldn't have bothered packing all the other dresses. I'd have just dug around in Pascal's wardrobe instead. Oh, look, it spells a word."

What? He lifted his head to look up at her and saw that she was staring at the screen in front of him. She leaned forward and ran her fingers over a particular legal paragraph, then the next. "S H A N G H A I, break, S E T, break, T O, break, C L O S E..." He pushed her hand out of the way and began looking over the email himself.

"How did you see that?" She was right. Every letter beginning a sentence created a word, then the next paragraph started a new one.

"Henry and I used to play games. Whenever he took me home or something, we'd make up stupid games to keep ourselves occupied on the drive. He liked making up stupid languages and pretending he was CIA agent in the cold war to make me smile. It was something to do with his dad, I think. Anyway, it was quite funny when I was fourteen," she replied as she put some earrings in and leaned her highly intelligent arse on the desk next to him.

It wasn't funny now.

By the time he'd organised the emails into the correct order and scribbled the lettering down, he knew exactly what was going on. He picked up the phone to call Louisa and explained what to do. She seemed remarkably calm given the apparent shit storm that was happening, so he shouted at her some more and used as many threats to her job as possible. Within seconds of putting the phone down, more emails began bouncing through his account. Tom Brindley was on it seemed. How he knew what was happening was mystifying, but the man was on a mission because email after email began beeping at him.

To: Alexander White
From: Tom Brindley
CC: Louisa, Shen Guai, Max Libbington,

Sir,

Still all set. Tate's been running these slowly through the week. Found them the other day and began filing them into place. We assumed he might try something over the Christmas break.

We've countered the move and termed the deal stalled because of negotiation issues. Mr. DeVille deflected on all counts. The Chinese are backing us and have sent all pertinent or significant information back through Tate regarding the other deal.

All parties informed on 24/12. Both Lawyers have all legalities covered and are awaiting the closure of the transaction of monies. They are still ready for completion on the correct deal in 36 minutes with Catton Holdings Inc.

The new holding company, Catton Holdings, via Max Libbington, has been set up to conceal the sale, and is usable only by yourself upon completion. Louisa has security access only, and will inform you of the safe delivery of title deeds and all proprietary information.

Mr. DeVille is aware of your deception, but not that the deal is still in progress as far as we know.

Will send relevant notification of transaction closure upon completion.

Kind regards
Tom Brindley

Head of Land Purchasing,
Catton Holdings Inc.
Asia and Pacific.

Following that email was another, including all the subsequent emails from Tate, highlighting the correct code within the varying documentation, also, the other multitude of emails concealing the deal that was still in progress, the reciprocating replies from the Chinese, the counter offenses from the lawyers, and Louisa's hand scribbled notes. He smiled at the screen. She'd clearly been the one to find the buried deception.

Well, fuck. An organised team. He knew there was a reason he paid them so much. He fired off a quick reply acknowledging their brilliance in managing the situation, being careful not to be too commending about their sneakery. He also reminded them in no uncertain terms that he was, in fact, the boss, and it would have been fucking nice to be informed of what was going on. Louisa replied instantly.

- **We thought it would be nice for you to just enjoy Christmas with Miss Scott, and we had it covered. Merry Christmas, and you're welcome.**

He'd sack her for that. And then rehire her as something other than his PA. The woman deserved more. Maybe she could run this new Catton Holdings for him? She must have been the one to name it, after all. He leant back and smiled at the screen again as he watched the minutes tick by, then tried to formulate a plan as to how he was going to deal with Henry.

"Clearly no problem anymore, then?" she said beside him, still trying to do up buttons on the outfit he'd selected for her. Bright green organza material hung in swathes from a black silk corseted waist, which was the cause of her buttons issue, and cascaded to the floor behind her. The gathered front of the dress was pretty much at crotch level, giving the appearance of an elegant burlesque dancer's uniform. And she wore the most restricting garter belt and underwear he could find to make sure she was as uncomfortable as possible, because she fucking well deserved that for enjoying herself with Pascal. He chuckled at her scrambling fingers, and watched as she got more and more irritated with the tiny silk buttons.

"Come here," he said. She threw her hands in the air and turned towards him. "You look breath-taking," he continued as he began the laborious task of closing the front of her up. It would be a damn sight easier to get them undone later. "And you are a very clever young lady."

"Flattery will get you everywhere." He damn well hoped so. He expected to be everywhere on her as soon as possible. "What are you wearing around your neck? This does look very Pascal, by the way. How on earth did he manage to get you into it?" He skirted his eyes along the long leather boots and full black regency suit and smirked. Pascal got him to do just about anything once a year, just for the day of his ball.

"It's his day. He gets pretty much whatever he wants from me on his birthday. Apparently this year, it's this."

"It's his birthday?"

"Mmhmm. You were a present."

"Oh, right. Hmm, good job I bought his Christmas present with us then," she replied with a blush. He chuckled at her again and yanked the corset in tighter. She just sucked in more breath and let him. What present had she bought for him? "Well, they wore cravats with this sort of thing normally, and I've seen the black one hanging in our room. Are you going all Mr. Darcy? You know, the undone, dapper, save a damsel in distress look, or are you covering my throat up?"

Her throat. She was saying it as if she meant every word. It tumbled out of her mouth in ownership, and she was right. It was hers, to have and to hold, 'til death did they part.

"I've been trying to make up my mind whether to wear it or take you in blind."

"Oh," she said, now fidgeting with her hands and brushing down the front of her skirt as if it would cover her more somehow. "Do I need my choker? What do you think? Too much?" He glanced at her bracelet and ring then up at her chest and neck. The bruising was faded now, apart from the slight bite marks from Pascal's teeth yesterday.

"Do you want to cover that up or leave it on display?"

"That's up to you. They're not your marks, are they?" He thought about it for a moment and considered his response. He could put some more there, he supposed. They had half an hour before leaving, but then it was Pascal's birthday.

"Leave your neck bare. He'll enjoy seeing it," he said as he finished the last button and stood up. He checked his watch again and smiled at the beauty of it. Simple, stylish. Nothing too fancy or ornate like some of these other men wore. Why they needed a multitude of dials and different time zones all over them, he never could understand. Twenty minutes, that's all that was left. Pascal's car was coming to pick them up so he wandered into the bedroom to grab the silk cravat. "How would you like to feel this evening?" he asked as he came back into the room. She was sliding a hairpin into place to hold the small top hat into place as she slid her feet into her heels.

"Umm, how about not scared too much?" she replied. He frowned at her and draped the cravat around his shoulders.

"Scared?" he repeated, shoving his hands into his black breeches. His phone vibrated in his pocket so he reached in and grabbed it out.

"Yes, Alex. Scared, worried really, possibly just nervous, but scared was the first thing that sprang to mind. I try and do that with you, just say the first thing that blurts into my brain rather than try the 'let's play a game' stuff you're so fond of."

"What are you scared of?" She looked at the floor and kept her mouth shut as she fidgeted with her bracelet. If it was anyone other than her, he'd be excited, turned on, ready and very willing to take that fear and use it to full effect, but this love did strange things to his conscience. It wouldn't stop him in the right moment. He would revel in it when the time was right but this wasn't it. "Head up, baby. Tell me." She suddenly looked defeated, utterly lost in a moment of weakness as she wrapped her arms around herself and kept staring at the floor. He walked over and picked up her beautiful chin for her. "Elizabeth?"

"What if I do lose you? You tell me to do as I'm told, and then in the next breath tell me you're not going to stay with me. I'm confused. Who do I listen to? Who do I safe word if I need to? What if you don't hear me? I can do this 'we'll be okay' thing until I'm blue in the face, but I felt you in the Lake District. I felt you the other night. You disappear. You want to, and I don't know how I'm going to make..." She trailed off to nothing but moving lips and a sigh. He looked at her for a minute and then picked her up and put her incredible arse down on the desk behind her. Did she not understand this at all? He supposed he hadn't been that informative of the lifestyle, nor given her much explanation, but then he'd never really expected to have to live it with her.

"Why do you think I've been so hard on Pascal?"

"I don't know. I don't know anything about what's going on with you two. One minute you're making him kneel on the floor with your 'you will' voice, and the next you're all dreamy eyed over a picture of his family. And I have no idea about the whole collaring thing? Is that normal? Why have you even done it?" she replied, all spluttering lips and waving hands. He shook his head and said what he hoped would be true.

"I collared him because I refuse to let him leave me. I need him. Our relationship has always been about me beating him until he's had enough, which serves both our purposes. I couldn't give a damn if he kneels for me or not. He will always let me beat him and that's what I need." Her eyes widened as she leaned away from him a little and parted her extremely fuckable mouth, which was becoming ever more fuckable with every breath at the mention of beatings. "And I am hard on him because I need him to believe I mean it, that he will not survive if he disappoints me. And the only way Pascal could ever disappoint me, which I hope he knows, is to not look after you."

"Oh. I..." she started, still with wide eyes and a concerned look on her face. "You mean your plan is to let whatever happens happen and hope that Pascal is decent? Because, you know, he's not exactly known for that, is he?" He'd said all he could. He was as much in hope of a decent Pascal as she was. He'd seen the way the man touched her, kissed her. He was relying on this newfound love to get them all through this.

"No, he isn't." What time was it? He looked at his watch. 7.56pm. He fiddled with his cravat and considered putting it around her eyes again. She still looked a little nervous. Perhaps not. "Put this on for me?"

"That's it? The safety speech?"

"Yes, where's my drink?" he replied as he flicked open the laptop again and logged into the fund transfer page. She jumped off the table beside him, wobbled, and then slapped him so hard he didn't know what had hit him. He glared at her and then smirked at her hand on hip stance. Those legs really did go on forever.

"What exactly was that for?" Christ, he loved her.

"Just thought I'd get my shot in while I could," she replied with a giggle, now sipping her glass of champagne with the other hand. "Do your own sodding cravat, Mr. White." Hellcat. He rubbed his cheek and wiggled his fingers at her.

"Come here, and watch this screen." She was by his side in a second and resting her chin on his shoulder as they both stared at the monetary amount.

"Fuck me, that's a lot of money. Why are we...? Oh." The amount rolled down, and down, and down, until the closing balance was zero. "Where's it all gone?" Two minutes went by as he kept staring, and then his phone vibrated on the table at the same time as the email started pinging. Confirmation of fund transfer, confirmation of balance received, confirmation of terms, confirmation of land deed transfer, confirmation of sale. It was all there as she stood quietly behind him and held his hand. Finally, an email arrived from Louisa, confirming all of the above and attaching all the legal documents involved, with the note, 'Well done, Sir.' He immediately forwarded all the necessary information to Tyler Rathbone and waited for the answering email. That man was about to get a lot richer, too, but then he had funded the deal to some degree and helped him out of a bloody tricky situation when he needed a new investor. He shook his head at the thought of a smiling Tyler clapping his hands together in that American way.

"I just bought a big patch of Shanghai," he stated, suddenly overly anxious to get her reaction, which was odd. He'd never needed anyone's approval on anything before now.

"Good for you. Congratulations," she said. "Is that what you wanted? Have you avoided annihilation then? Decided on world domination instead? Is Henry off the hook? Is it over now?"

No, it wasn't at all. He smiled at her and clinked glasses as she stood there watching him. She really didn't care in the slightest about the purchase. Either that or she didn't know enough to understand how much money he'd just made.

"Are you ready to go?" he asked as he shut the laptop down and felt his smile grow wider. This was deception at its finest. Henry hadn't got a chance of beating him. He only needed to sort this other crap out and then everything would be fine again, quiet. He could just try for some of that peace she always wanted and just be happy. She wandered off into the bedroom, apparently in some sort of huff about something, and slammed the door behind her. He looked at it for a moment and considered fucking her back into a good mood, but he checked his watch and realised the car should be downstairs so scanned his phone for messages instead while she calmed down. He found yet another from the unknown person pretending to be his father. This was the third now, all similar in their tone – warnings. He'd dismissed the first two and just gotten on with Christmas and making her happy, but the third had been more intrusive.

> **- Son, do you remember how angry I got when you didn't get to me quick enough?**

Yes, he did, and the obvious warning in that message that the person was pissed he wasn't responding had cut too close to the bone to be just a simple hoax. No one other than Pascal and Elizabeth knew anything of his past, not in that detail anyway. His stomach churned again at the thought as he scowled at the new message and looked over the contents.

> **- We need to talk, son. I would hate for that life of yours to be a total waste, and the girl is pretty. I'm sure she'd be appalled by what you turned into.**

What the fuck did that mean? Who the hell was this person? Mark Jacobs knew nothing. Even the call to Andrews to get him back home hadn't proved useful, regardless of the fact that he should be home by now, dealing with it. Neither man seemed able to help him with who the person was. Son? Fuck off. Was the wanker threatening Elizabeth now? Threats to himself he could deal with, but not her – never her. He sent the message straight to the pair of them and threw in as many deliberate intimidation techniques as he could manage. He fucking paid them both to be better than the current shit they were producing. Whatever the threat was, it didn't matter too much because she knew anyway. He'd been honest and told her. There was nothing left to hide. She knew it and she was here with him anyway, loving him. He just wanted to kill the fucker that was daring to threaten her.

"I'm ready now," she said softly from behind him. He turned to look at her and was momentarily blinded by the vision as she held her cane up and tipped the front of her hat at him. Two people merged together in an instant: Elizabeth and Pascal, his aggression and need, her love and passion. He pulled in a breath and felt the warmth caress every part of him, coursing through the very soul of him and offering that peace he was in search of. It was coming. It was close.

It just needed a helping hand.

~

The car pulled up to the front of the Altes and he looked her over again. She was still a little nervous. Her fingers still fiddled occasionally with his cravat that she'd been holding the entire way.

"Are you going to put that on me or not?" he asked. She flinched and then picked up her drink again to down another glass of champagne. Those nerves of hers still looked overly attractive. They still churned his stomach and reminded his cock of exactly what he was after. He'd said all he could to allay her fears, and to be honest, he wanted that fear there a little, wanted it to circulate inside her and make her aware of the possibilities. Who wanted a dull life of boredom with disingenuous words whispered into the night? She wanted to see who he was, to feel him in his happy hour at the bar. Well this was it. This ball and all the people within it were where he could truly be himself, a version of himself that was accepted, warranted, fawned over even. Not that he gave a damn what they thought. It was just nice to allow his mind to quieten and be the animal rather than playing the gentleman.

He opened his door at her lack of response and picked up the long rectangular box she'd wrapped so carefully, then watched the driver open hers. She picked up her cane, looked at it for a moment, inspecting it as if searching for something, and then smiled to herself.

"Something amusing?" he asked as she tied his cravat around the hilt of it.

"Yes. Come on. Let's go," she said, and suddenly she was back. Her face was now the picture of fortitude as she exited the car and strode straight past him. All heads turned as she made her way up the red-carpeted stairs without him, the ruffled trail of her dress kissing each step as she did so. He watched her go and gazed at the sway of her hips until she made it to the top and then spun to face him. She held Pascal's cane – *her* cane – up and beckoned him with it, a radiant smile illuminating the space around her as the lights from inside the venue dimmed in comparison.

A few people spoke to him but he couldn't hear them. She shone too brightly at the top of those stairs, dulled the world into insignificance and reminded him how small he was. How utterly disappointing he must be as a human being when compared with the likes of her, because she owned her frame, she was all her. There wasn't a damn thing in this world that could ever corrupt the nature of her soul, let alone shackle it.

"Alex, come," she shouted. He chuckled at her command and waited for the next one, which might include one of those beautiful giggles if he was lucky. She shook her arse at him and then kicked her leg up a little in a faux cancan move while laughing at herself and tipping her head at the doorway. She was either quite drunk or suddenly very excited.

"Alexander," a voice said beside him. He started walking up the stairs and acknowledged the arrival of Draven Creed at his side with a nod. He didn't need to look. The shadow from the man was enough.

"You still have that one?" Mmm. It was probably an oddity in this world for him to be with one woman this long to be fair.

"Yes, she's interesting. Getting more so with time."

"I heard of the revelation in New York. Is it true?" Ah, yes. Pascal. This would need dealing with reasonably quickly or he'd be answering the same damn question all night. He briefly wondered what Pascal had told everyone before deciding that it was nobody's business but their own.

"I'll let him explain it, if he chooses to." He caught Elizabeth's hand in his and walked them in through the door to find the man in question.

"Oh my god," she said under her breath as they walked through the enormous foyer. He raised a brow at her as he considered that Pascal had indeed outdone himself this year. Money must have been poured into this party. Not that that was anything unusual where Pascal was concerned, but there wasn't a table in sight that didn't have crystal adornments and elegant fetish themed objects cascading over it. "Jesus, how rich are you two?"

"Exceedingly, it seems," he replied, as he caught sight of the man himself. He was in gold, a near perfect replica of the suit he was wearing himself, and stood in front of a gaggle of women. That small boy hovered at his side with a nervous smile on his face as the women fawned over the lord of the dance and fell to the floor for him. He smirked at the theatrics and wrapped her arm over his to make their way towards him. "I thought you didn't care for money. What did you buy him anyway?"

"We bought him. *We*," she snapped as she watched a woman sitting on some chap's lap, possibly fucking. He raised the other brow at her newfound temper and wondered what she'd been thinking in the car earlier. "Are they having sex? We've not even eaten yet. I hope we're not sitting at that table." She'd be seeing a lot more than that at some point. "Actually, it might just be me, I suppose. I'm not sure. I'm not even sure if it's a good present or not. Promise me you won't be mad? I mean it. Well, not until later anyway, then you can be a little bit mad." What was she rambling on about?

"What?"

"The present. Say you'll just accept that I want him to have it. I don't like him all bereft and lonesome." He still hadn't got a clue what

336

her lips were discussing, but he nodded in affirmation and led them towards the table. Pascal caught sight of them and smiled broadly as he took a seat at the top table and waved them both over. It was a genuine smile, a happy one. It seemed the man was completely comfortable with their new situation.

"It is not possible for you to look any more divine, my dear," he said as he took Elizabeth's hand and licked his way up her arm. Hackles that would have normally risen stayed quiet and relaxed at the sight as he watched them interact. She giggled and blushed slightly as he pulled out a chair for her and handed her more champagne. "Have you readied yourself?"

"Have you?" Alex cut across them as he put the box on the table in front of the man. Pascal turned and smirked at him, that far more normal devilish performance now coming back out to play with relish.

"I will always be ready for you," he replied. No 'Sir', just a slight bowing of the head as he turned back towards Elizabeth again. "Is this for me? I do adore a present."

"Yes. Oh, and happy birthday. Why didn't you tell me? Open it, please," she said as she picked it up and shoved it at him in enthusiasm. The man scowled at her then back at him as he glanced his head around.

"You told her? I could be cantankerous with you for that." Alex chuckled at the man and picked up a glass of champagne, trying not to stare at her tits jiggling about.

"Why?" she said as she started undoing the bow on the present and shuffled closer to him.

"I do not age, my dear. Somewhat like that vampire you consider me to be. Is it possible that I could open my present myself?"

"No, too slow," she said as she giggled and started ripping the paper away. "You do make a very good vampire, you know?"

"I do?"

"You do. It's very you. You look a bit like Gary Oldman tonight, only bigger and more attractive. You just need some little round glasses and- " Pascal grabbed her, yanked her towards him and bit at her neck so hard she screamed out loud. The entire room turned to the sound as the man continued to devour her in front of everyone and groped at her thigh like a wench in a pub. After a beat of squealing and squirming, she quietened in his arms and began to sprawl herself across him, those exceptional legs opening easily as he pulled his fingers higher and moved the dress out of the way.

"Don't push your luck," Alex said quietly beside them, still drinking and watching them in interest, his cock hardening beneath him at the connotations involved. "I'm still not entirely comfortable with the thought." Pascal stilled and then slowly removed his hand, gliding it over her skin as he kissed his way up her throat towards her mouth. She moaned again, possibly in irritation, and then sat herself upright, quickly dismissing the moment and aiming at the present again instead. She suddenly noticed all the guests still watching the show.

"What the fuck are they all looking at? It's just normal Pascal for God's sake," she snapped, all aggressive eyes and a sneer that had come out of nowhere. It appeared she was becoming possessive of her little moments. Alex chuckled at her performance and handed them the discarded box again.

"They're not watching Pascal, Elizabeth. They're watching you," he replied, licking his lips at the very thought and imagining her spread out on the table for him, for them. "You're an unknown quantity to them, a surprise of sorts."

"Well," she said as she took her seat again and knocked the lid on the box with her cane. "I'm not theirs to watch. I'm yours, and perhaps his every now and then," she continued with a nod at Pascal. "And now I'm all wet and excited again. Will you open your present, please?"

"By all means, my dear. I am extremely apologetic that I became distracted by your divinity," Pascal replied with a wave of his hand at the audience. They all turned away again and recommenced their inane chattering. He pushed at the clasps on the box and finally opened it to reveal some bagged objects of differing shapes. She began fidgeting excitedly in her seat and couldn't stop her hands diving in.

"Do I fuck with it? A new toy? I'm afraid I have never seen such a thing," Pascal asked with a look of utter confusion on his normally guarded expression.

"Nooo!" She giggled. "Well, actually you might, I suppose," she said with a very dirty grin. She pulled the first thing from the bag to reveal an ebony stick, or rather cane. She then pulled another and began screwing the two together. He chuckled beside her and rubbed her back. It was a thoughtful gift, given the fact that he'd taken Pascal's own from him and given it to her. Although she hadn't a clue what she'd just done. He shook his head to himself and watched as she reached in again and pulled out the silver top and began to screw that on, too, then handed it to the man. Could she make this anymore difficult for herself? Or him? "Its antique. I found it in a shop in London. Apparently it comes from Holland, late 1800's the chap said. I couldn't just leave it there. It reminded me of you. Look, it's got a bat on the top of it, too. Bat... Vampire... Get it?" Pascal just stared at her as if he were mesmerised. "Is it okay? Pascal? What's the matter with him? Have his batteries finally run out?" she said as she glanced at Alex, and then to Pascal again.

"I think he may be in shock."

"Really? Why? It's just a present."

"And a very thoughtful one, if not completely inappropriate. Well done."

"It was just there, and I... Pascal, speak for god's sake. What's the problem? I can take it back if you don't like-" The man snatched the thing off her so quickly she almost fell off her chair. He wasn't surprised at all. He'd probably do the same if the roles were reversed.

"Neither of you will ever take this off me again," he eventually said as he stroked his fingers over it reverently and smiled. "It's mine, as are you. Thank you. I am delighted by your offering."

"Well, yes. Good. I'm glad you like it, but I'm not sure what you mean by... It's... I... I just didn't like to see you so anxious. It's not very Pascal like, is it? And I-" He yanked her over to him for the second time and plonked her on his knee, this time having asked some kind of permission via a small unnoticed look.

"It is the most exquisite gift I have ever received and I may love you a little for it, Elizabeth. I can only assume he knew nothing of it, so thank you for your bravery in the matter."

"Bravery? It's only a cane. It's not like I've broken any underground rules, is it? Not that I have any idea what those rules might be. I just thought you'd like one back."

"Ah, but you have, my dear. You have just shown him that his power over me is of no significance to yourself, and have therefore given me free rein to abuse you with my new toy."

"Nope, not getting that," she said, looking back at the man for clarification. He just stared at her with a deviant grin and yet another snap of his teeth. The man was going to be the death of him. Either that or she was. Alex held out his hand until she climbed off Pascal's knee and sat on his instead. She felt so good there, all for him, his angel with her perfect body and perfect, if not innocent, mind. She frowned and glanced between the pair of them. "Alex? What's he... I don't understand what he's talking about."

"I gave you his cane to stop him misbehaving with it, Elizabeth, to protect you from it until I was ready for him to use it with you. You've just handed him another one of your own free will. Nothing to do with me at all. Do you see?"

She looked between the two of them again, that frown slowly receding and a look of astonishment replacing it.

"Oh," she said.

Quite. Oh.

Chapter 24

Elizabeth

"**O**h..."

Once again that's all I seem able to say. I've just realised what I've done. *Oh* is all I've got really, because I can't quite work out if I'm happy about it or not. I mean, the times I've been with Pascal on my own have been extraordinary, and he's always been gentlemanly in his own particular way. I'm damn sure there are plenty of people in this room that can testify that he's not quite as much the gentleman as he may appear, but with me he has been decent in a roundabout way.

"Should we just get on with it, my love? Hmm? How long should we let him control us?"

"As long as I damn well please," Alex says behind me. I can almost feel the growl reverberating in his chest at the threat.

"I think I'll wait, if that's okay with you," I respond as I watch his eyes dance in delight at the thought. I no longer have any sodding clue what is happening between us, not that I had much before.

The crowd suddenly erupts in cheers and wolf whistles so I turn to see what's going on. There's a man and a naked lady wandering towards a large clearing in the middle of the room. They reach it, and she immediately kneels down in front of him so he can circle her with what appears to be a large black sheet. He swings it around like a matador and eventually lands it over her completely until she's hidden beneath it.

"What is-"

"Shh, manners, my dear," Pascal says beside me. I continue watching until another man slowly emerges from the crowd and crosses the floor towards her. He's big. In fact, I'm pretty sure I know him from somewhere but I can't quite place him.

"You chose Draven?" Alex asks as he strokes my collarbone and pulls me back towards him a little more. Draven, yes, the chap from Rome. I remember him now, although I wouldn't have guessed because there isn't a hint of leather on display this evening. Pascal shrugs and hands me a glass of something that is clearly not champagne. I drink in anyway with a shrug of indifference.

"He offended you. It seemed the appropriate response given our innovative arrangement. And I've never seen his cock. He's overly shy about it, remarkably."

What the hell is about to happen?

Draven hovers near the woman, looking decidedly uncomfortable, and then the lights dim down until there's hardly any light at all, just a spotlight on them. I'm so engrossed in the pantomime that I don't even notice all the guests sitting down and servers bringing food to the tables until its put in front of me. We're supposed to eat and watch this? Wow.

Having tucked into my duck in port jus, and then memorised the entire dish because it was so fabulous, I glance back at the floor again to notice that nothing has happened yet. He's still just standing there and the woman is under the sheet.

"Come on," I say. "You have got to tell me what's going on here. Are they actually going to do anything?" I ask.

"Patience," Pascal says from beside me. He hasn't eaten anything, merely prodded it and then pushed the plate away, preferring his port in a glass. He has, on occasion, taunted poor Reubin with the occasional offering of a vegetable or two while he's been sat as his feet, but other than that, he's been non-committal on the food front. He really is a vampire.

"I am being patient, but this is ridiculous," I reply, now scanning the room for yet another intriguing piece of equipment and finding what looks like a swing of some sort. I tilt my head at the contraption and try to align my body with it's positioning. "And what's that for?"

"He means Draven's patience. We are not known for patience, none of us in here, and this is a show of our host's never ending power in this dominion of his," Alex drawls on the other side of me with sarcasm rolling off his tongue in waves. I swing my eyes to his and giggle at his relaxed smirk as he pulls my chin to his lips for a kiss.

"Why, thank you," Pascal says from behind us.

"You're very welcome," Alex says as his butchering hands climb a little higher along my inner thigh. I so could at the moment... It really wouldn't take much. He could spread me out on this table and help himself. "Are you going to end the man's misery at any point?"

"Perhaps Elizabeth should. It could be an initiation." Alex's hand instantly stops and he scowls over my shoulder at Pascal. "It is my birthday."

"She's not ready."

"I'm not ready for what?" I am. I'm very ready for anything with them. I turn to look at Pascal and find him standing up, and then quite harshly prodding my thigh with his new cane. I scoot away in response and frown at the thing. Present or not, it wasn't bought for that. Although...

"If it moves, it is ready. Is that not what you used to say? I'm positive I have-"

"No," Alex cuts in firmly. It's his 'don't piss me off' voice, and as he uses it to full effect, I watch Pascal raise a brow at him.

"You would deny her the pleasure of this?" he asks, knocking his port back and licking his lips. It immediately reminds me of his kiss yesterday, and I barely contain a moan at the thought.

"I said no."

"He is such a spoilsport, my dear. I am not sure how you have survived with him this long. Think of the fun you could have had with me. We could have fucked with abandon and desecrated the entire world with sin."

"Yeah, I'm guessing your idea of fun involves me being manhandled and used by varying other men at this point."

"Hmm... Can she at least begin proceedings?" Alex rolls his eyes and eventually waves a hand at the floor, offering me a chance to go with him. I'm entirely sure I should be saying no, but I can't stop myself from standing up and taking Pascal's very enticing hand.

Before I know it, we're walking across the floor through the party guests who have now gone deathly silent. It reminds me of the charity ball I went to with Alex, everyone looking and staring at me as if I'm some new object to play with. The main difference here is I'm sure most of them would be very happy to play with me in an entirely different way.

"What do you need me for?" I ask as we get closer, and I notice a few of the men removing their cravats.

"I want you to be yourself, my love. And when you have found yourself, the three of us will leave the rest of this gaggle to it, I think. I would normally choose someone I have little care for, but tonight you are here, and I quite like the fact that it annoys him."

"What annoys him?" I reply as he walks me in front of the sheeted woman and takes a few steps away with a wink. I could look a mess, I'm sure. I could crumble from all of these people staring at me, but I refuse to do it. I am Alexander White's girlfriend, and Pascal Van Der Braack's, well, whatever I am. I lift my chin, grab onto feisty Beth and stare him straight in the eye. That's rewarded with another delicious smirk.

"Take the end of the sheet, my dear," he says, tapping his cane on the floor. The sudden noise behind and all around me makes me jump a little and I realise everyone is banging their feet and canes on the floor. I gently pick up the end of the sheet and hear a moan coming from beneath it. Draven takes a step towards us but I see the flash of disgust grace Pascal's face and watch the man retreat again. "Now, ask me you to fuck you," he says, quite loudly. My mouth opens, but nothing comes out. I just stare in response as feisty Beth leaves at a rapid pace and sods off somewhere else. He can't be serious... In front of all these people? Does he mean here? Surely not. I glance across at Alex to find him studiously watching me, his gaze drifting up and down my body and a smirk creeping onto his lips. He so knew this was coming. "Find yourself, my dear. Ask for what you want," Pascal says again. Oh, for God's sake.

"I want you to fuck me," I say as quietly as possible. I flick my eyes around at everyone else and try to keep some composure. I will not look like an utter moron in front of these people.

"No, no, that will never do. Louder, my dear. Beg for it," he says, flamboyantly waving his hand around as if this is a theatre of some description, and looking like utter sin as he does so. What a bastard. If I could twat him with this cane, I probably would. How fucking dare he embarrass me like this?

"Fuck you," I spit out in fury.

"I think you may have missed some vocabulary. Try it again, with some begging." His eyes light up with that deviant animal that I know lives in him. He's waiting for me to give him a chance to show this room that's he's in control of me, regardless of that fact that I'm

Alex's. The room still chants and bangs the floor around us, and I consider the fact that it is, in fact, his birthday. My hands find my hips.

"I want to fuck you, please," I manage as sarcastically as I can, although I don't really feel the sarcasm because it's true, isn't it? I do, and I now can't stop imagining it because he's licking his lips while I stare at them.

"Then come for me," he eventually says. "And do it on your knees." There he is. That's his moment to humble me again. No matter how much I may want to fight with him about our ranking in this arrangement, he will always find a way to have me kneeling beneath him, whether by Alex's command or not. We stare at each other for a time as the banging and jeering goes on around us, and I listen to his words circulating in my head. I want to look at Alex for his thoughts but I know this is between the two of us, and I've got only two choices. Crawl, or stand my ground.

"Just fuck me," I growl out before I've thought too much about it. "Just get on with it, Pascal."

I have no idea why that popped out. I'm pretty sure it was just my brain wandering through my mouth with no actual thought involved. He raises a brow and continues with his infuriatingly beautiful stare. He couldn't look any better tonight if he tried, or maybe that's just because he's already had his hand in my pants. He eventually does the only thing he can do and looks over his shoulder toward Alex. The room goes quiet as he does so, and it becomes clear to me in an instant that this is new to the room, that nobody knows what this situation with Alex is. They're probably never been seen Pascal asking permission for something before. I'm also pretty sure that whatever should be happening between Draven and the woman at my feet is of no interest at all to anybody, so I swing my eyes over to Alex, too.

He sits there watching the show with no emotion on his face whatsoever. Nothing. I'm not even sure if he's still here or not in reality. If I was closer, I could see his eyes, but all I can see is his frame, draped in that black regency suit as he begins to pull himself upright at the table. There is no movement of his head, not a nod or a shake or anything other than a slight raise of that damn brow, and then he simply walks away towards a door in the corner of the room. My whole body tenses for the possible onslaught that is Pascal, because I have no clue if they've just had a conversation or not.

He just watches him leave and then turns back to me and bows. Bows? In the middle of the bloody room? What do I do with that? Am I supposed to curtsey or something? What does any of this mean? I look back at the doorway in the hope that Alex will appear to clarify what the hell is going on. He doesn't.

"After you, my dear, and do put the dear girl out of her misery," Pascal says. Oh, what? I turn back to him to find him holding a hand out in the direction of the very door Alex walked through. Oh, right. Umm... Does that mean what I think it means? Oh god, my ankles almost give way at the thought as I slowly move my frozen body forward and watch his disturbingly attractive one move backwards. The rapture of applause behind me has me swinging back around to see that I've pulled the sheet from the woman, and Draven has wasted no time in devouring her right there in front of everyone. I watch for a minute as he begins to undo his trousers while rutting at her backside like a starved animal in heat. My pulse quickens at the vision as I feel my core clenching around the sight. Fucking. Lots of fucking, and hair pulling, and pain. She's moaning and then screaming as Draven yanks her onto her back and then slaps her face. I pull in a breath and turn back towards Pascal, my chin as high as I can manage and my legs firmly striding onwards as I move past him. I refuse to acknowledge him or show any fear in this moment. I knew it was coming. I've waited for it for God knows how long, and yet every step towards that door is like torture. It's like all my dreams could be shattered if it's not right, or Alex disappears, or Pascal isn't decent. I reach the door eventually and hover my hand over the handle.

"Pascal?"

"Hmm?" He's so not thinking of anything other than getting his hands on me.

"Will you listen to me?" There's nothing but silence as a response. Nothing. No, "Yes, my dear," or "Why would I not?" just silence, and fingers wrapping around the back of my neck. So I just stand there and feel those fingers, try to listen to some hidden conversation in my mind that he might be trying to have with me, but again, there's nothing. Just silence.

Soft lips suddenly land on my shoulder, warm and caressing as they make their way across me and up to my throat.

"You think too much, Elizabeth." That's all I get to allay my nerves. Helpful it is not, and it sounds far too much like Alex for my liking, but those warm lips soothe me back to relaxing as he pushes the door open for me. "Would it help if I promised to kiss you the entire time? Hmm?" Yes, probably.

Oh god, what am I doing?

The corridor in front of me seems endless and Alex is nowhere in sight. I also have no clue as to where it is that I should be going, so I just stand there and wait for some instruction. He waves a hand in front of me toward the end of the blue corridor, so I hesitantly walk along it, wondering what's going to happen next. On turning a corner, I'm met with Alex leaning against a door looking at the floor, which halts my momentum. He slowly raises his eyes to me. Those light blues have disappeared, and he's consumed with darkness. I can see and feel it pouring out of every fibre of his being. He looks huge as he stands there, a slight sneer gracing an otherwise detached face.

"Is this what you want?" he asks. No pleasantries. He almost seems pissed off with me, although the thought that he's actually asked is comforting.

"If... If it's what you want," I mutter. I have no idea if what I said out there annoyed him or made him happy. He's so gone, completely and utterly in his twilight zone of need, and while that inner slut of mine is jumping all over the place, there's no denying my fear — fear of losing him and never getting him back. What if this destroys everything? What if this is enough to drive a wedge between us that there's just no coming back from?

He pushes backwards on the door and it swings open to reveal a room. He disappears into it so I lift my head again and follow him as Pascal chuckles behind me. Chuckles? Nothing is funny here, not one thing. I couldn't be more nervous, excited, or scared if I tried. This is my life I'm playing with, my love, my whole world. He might find it amusing to see me worried, but I certainly don't. I've spun on my heel and slapped him before I've even thought about doing it. He recoils from me and growls. *Growls.* I'm not sure I've ever heard him really angry, and he suddenly is, very, more so than that time at Eden. Within seconds, I've been lifted and thrown. I'm not sure where the fuck I'm going to land, but as something soft hits my back, I blow out a breath of thanks for at least some decency.

He's standing at the end of the bed I've landed on, yanking at his cravat and undoing his coat with the other hand. It's like a regency drama playing out in front of me, and I scoot my eyes around the dark room to find Alex. He's sitting in the corner of the room having removed his jacket and rolled his sleeves up. I gaze at him for a moment and wonder what's going through his mind. Is he happy? Comfortable? Relaxed?

"Take her clothes off," Alex says, an order directed at Pascal, I assume, because the moment he says it, Pascal grabs hold of my feet and drags me towards him. My instinct is to fight, but something inside me instantly relaxes at his touch. Something just clicks into place. I can't even describe the feeling to myself, but the peace that settles is immediate. In fact, I can't wait to get my clothes off all of a sudden. Could I be anymore sodding confused about all of this? There's nothing soft about him undressing me, nothing romantic or caressing in the slightest. He's ripping at cloth and handling me as if I'm something to be used, and every nerve in me is igniting at his aggression. He's precise in his movements, as if he's done this a thousand times before and knows exactly where to tear at clothes to remove them swiftly. I'm simply rolling around as he strips every inch of me away. Every piece of material like another barrier being stolen.

Eventually, I'm left naked and panting in front of him as he stands back up and steps away again. There's no movement from him at all as I squirm in turmoil on the sheets, occasionally trying to cover myself while waiting for something to happen. Why, I don't know, but it's just so raw, so clinical, and there's no love flowing here, which feels awkward. He just stands there as if awaiting another instruction, almost serene in his frame as he gazes at me and breathes.

"Her first," Alex's voice says smoothly from the corner. I suck in a breath and watch Pascal's green eyes sparkle back to life as he takes a step forward and rips at the cufflinks on his shirt. I immediately scramble backwards up the bed. I don't know why... Maybe fear, or nerves. "Stay still, Elizabeth. I don't want you chained." Chained? My body stops at Alex's command, and I watch as the bed dips with Pascal's weight. Oh god, it's really going to happen. I'm going to have sex with him. Oh Jesus, what am I doing?

"Alex, I..."

"Shut up," he says. "Beg or scream. Nothing else." I swing my eyes to him at the same moment as my legs are yanked apart and Pascal's fingers are rammed inside me. My body instantly opens to him, legs widening with every twist and turn of those fingers as he prods and fetters about, thumb flicking and swirling as if he knows exactly how to make me come. And Christ, he does. My back's arching, my legs trembling, my whole body screaming at him for more. I haven't got a hope of even trying to pretend I'm not enjoying this. I can barely keep from coming as he pins my arm to the bed harshly to stop me writhing around so much. Another drive of his hand and I'm begging. It's falling from my mouth like a chant of sorts. More, please, more, harder, faster. I can't keep my mouth shut. It's spilling out and driving me mad with the need to come. His mouth is suddenly on me, everywhere. My nipples are sucked and then bitten as his hand keeps working me, in and out, again and again as I feel his mouth moving downwards. My hand grasps at the sheet in frustration as I feel my wave of bliss coming at me, chasing its way across my skin and promising me those lights. I can't breathe. I can't even think, and the instant his warm mouth lands on my clit, I'm done. My whole body stills as I arch higher and shove myself into his hand, my sensitive nub into his mouth. Lights begin their flashing as shudders and trembling assault my body repeatedly, and he keeps pushing me for more. More. My leg is grabbed and yanked sideways again so I can't gain any purchase to get away from his mouth, and he keeps biting at me, keeps prolonging the orgasm until I can't stand it.

"Stop. I can't. Please..." He keeps going, not listening to me in the slightest as I moan in near delirium from his assault, his tongue flicking and dragging across me as if I'm a toy, just something to be played with and used until he's told to stop. I can't breathe. Please, stop. "Please, I'm-"

"Enough." Alex's voice comes sharply from the corner. Pascal immediately removes his hand and mouth and leaves me panting in front of him as he kneels back on his haunches and stares down at me. I gulp in breaths to regain some semblance of order and stare at him as he wrenches at his belt and unbuttons his fly. The creak of the chair in the corner makes me snap my head in its direction. The man I love stands up and crosses the floor towards us as I pant out breaths.

Everything about his movements tells me he's horny, the swing of his legs, the slight tension in his back, the small tilt of his head as if he's looking down on a scene he's not really a part of. My Alex is disappearing. The man coming at us is losing himself, and at the moment, I could love him more for it if I tried. My hand reaches out for him as he halts by the side of me and rakes his eyes over my naked body. He doesn't take it, just continues to peruse me inch by inch and eventually runs one finger across my breast. He takes my nipple in his fingers and pinches it roughly, causing me to arch into the pain and watch his mouth part in desire. He could so easily remove Pascal from this. He could push him away and take me himself, and I want him to do that. I want him to fuck me and use me. I want his hand around my throat, claiming me, owning me, reminding Pascal that I'm not to be toyed with. I want to feel him in his darkness, let him do his worst and prove to me that I'll still be able to reach him, that he'll still hear me when I cry out for him.

He tilts his head at my panting and lets go of my nipple, then draws his fingers through my core slowly. The need to come again is instant, so much so that I moan out again and try to force myself down on his hand. He doesn't let me, just moves his hand away and smirks a little, a disturbingly deviant look. He really is far too attractive for his own good in that dark place of his.

"I want to see her," he says as he walks away. I have no idea what that means but Pascal leaps at the chance. He's all over me, hands grasping and clawing as he flicks me over onto my stomach and I hear the scraping of chair legs coming across the room. My hips are hoisted high and my head is pushed down onto the sheets roughly as he manoeuvres me around. The scratch of his nails, every now and then, digs in and reminds me these aren't Alex's hands, that they belong to someone different. I gasp out in response to a sharp smack across my backside and then moan as he bites at the sting, heightening it ever more and increasing the level of pain. A chair arrives in front of me and I watch Alex sit down and cross his legs so he can see my face. He wants to see my eyes, and I know that because he taps my chin upwards as yet another hard slap echoes in the room and sends me reeling toward him. Everything in the room goes quiet, not literally, but all I can see is his eyes as he bores them into me, dark pools of lust as he just gazes at my reactions and watches me being shoved about. I can feel Pascal's fingers driving in and out of me again, aggressively, but I'm not with him. I'm with the man in front of me, the man I love.

"I love you," I pant out as he stares at me. He doesn't answer me, doesn't even flinch really as I feel the head of Pascal's cock begin to rub up and down my core. My need for it consumes me as I watch the lust in Alex wash over him. I push back into Pascal, push hard and widen my eyes as he forces his way in and grasps my hips. He's so hard inside me, and I'm trembling in seconds. He pulls back and then drives back in with a groan of appreciation. It's the most beautiful noise I've ever heard from him. I did that. We did that, together, and I moan in response to it and let him pull me back onto him again and again. He's so deep inside, and I can hear them both again, swirling around in my mind, talking to each other. Alex is telling him the speed, the pace, guiding his movements somehow and not allowing him a moment of his own choice behind me. I'm moaning and squealing in front of them both while Pascal increases his fervour, grating at the inside of me and filling me with a need to satisfy them both that I didn't know I possessed. Pascal suddenly grabs my hair and yanks it backwards towards him. I cry out at the force of it and let him drive in again as he pulls my whole body upright. He doesn't care how much it hurts. He probably wants it to hurt, and at the moment, I couldn't agree more because the feeling is exhilarating, consuming – nothing like Alex. He feels completely different as he grips me with more precise fingers and inflicts his version of pain on me. Less weighty, more biting with his hold as he slams into me, and forces me forward again. I can feel my orgasm coming at me now. It's clawing its way through me, and begging me to erupt.

"Fuck me harder," I call out as I continue to keep my eyes focused on Alex. "I need more than that, please..." I know I'm begging Alex for that, not the man behind me. I need his strength, his level of force, and this isn't it. The corner of his mouth twitches slightly as he lifts his eyes above my head and nods. The moment he does, all sorts of pain assault me from every angle – slapping, biting, nipples twisting and the deepest drive from him I've felt yet. He lets go of my hair and pushes me back down again until my head is on its side looking at Alex. My mouth parts as I feel the sting of tears pricking my eyes and try to pull them back, but the pain is so intense that I can't hold them in. I can't fight them. I don't even want to fight them, so I let them go and listen to the growling and groaning coming from Pascal.

His rhythm becomes erratic as he rams in and out, almost splitting me with his aggression, constantly driving and bucking and holding me in position as he gives me everything I'm asking for. Lights begin their flashing parade in my head, and I feel the drifty place calling at me, removing all the pain and just letting me float in that cloud. My muscles clamp, clench and grasp as I pant with every thrust and just let it all go. Heaven washes over me, pure bliss rolling over my whole body and tensing every muscle I've got as it releases in defeat. I moan my way through it and try to keep my eyes on Alex, but I can't. The moment I feel Pascal abruptly still inside me and call out something in another language, I need to close them. I need to allow myself a minute with him. Just with him. I just want a few minutes of connection with him to bind us closer as his come empties inside me. I can feel it filling me, hot and wet, as his fingers relax just a fraction and I get his version of a caress across my skin, a faint brush of his finger across my hip bone showing me a second of his care, of love maybe.

Minutes, or maybe hours, pass as I revel in the moment and feel him pulsing inside me. It's just him and me for a few minutes, together, for us. I sigh out a relaxing breath as I let his touch soothe me back down again and try to memorise the feel of it. He's so different to Alex, lighter with his caress now he's come, softer somehow as he lingers near my thighs and drifts his fingers over me again.

"Open them," Alex snarls in front of me. I slowly open them to find him gazing at me. "Was it all you hoped for, Elizabeth?" Oh god, what a question. How do I answer that? I can hardly breathe in my calm place, let alone think properly. Pascal's still moving quietly inside me, still pushing the last of himself into me and now licking his way around my back, and still mumbling in another language.

"I... I'm..." I have no idea what I'm supposed to say to make this okay. I've just been fucked in front of the man I love and I couldn't care less. It's not normal. None of this is normal.

"Hmm..." That's all I get as he slowly gets up and starts to undo his belt. I still my grinding and focus on him, because it's all about him. Whatever he wants, I'll do it. Whatever he needs from me in this moment, he can have it. If it makes him feel in control of what we've just done then he can take it and use it however he wants. Pain, binds, anything, he can have it all because he must be hurting from watching another man have sex with me, he must have felt that somehow. "Keep fucking her," he says neutrally, all emotion lost as he grabs the back of my head and pulls me up the bed towards him. The instant I feel his hands on me, I'm moaning for him. He's harder in his grip on me, bigger, stronger, and I'm melting into the remembrance of it. His hands, his grip, his weight are all so much more enticing than Pascal's for so many reasons. His love, his warmth, my man, my throat, and his lust for me, his need, it all comes pouring out of just that one hand.

He pulls out his cock and just holds it there in front of my mouth, and before I know it, I'm stretching away from Pascal for it. I'm desperate to show him I love him, desperate to have him inside me to counter Pascal and show him his importance to me. I lick my lips and moan again at the thought as he swipes it across my mouth and then pulls it away again, teasing me and letting the taste of his come assault my senses. Pascal rams in behind me, hard as steel again, and sends me forward to Alex. I open my mouth for the penetration. His cock is instantly shoved as deep as it can go down my throat, and I'm held there by that one hand, filled by both of them and struggling for any breath as Alex tightens his hold on my head and doesn't allow me to retreat. Again, Pascal drives in, and again, hitting the end of me and threatening my orgasm back to life. I can't stop the moan bubbling in my throat as my lips widen to accommodate Alex's cock, and I sense him thickening. He's so close. It's taking nothing but this show and me begging to get him ready to explode inside me. My hand taps his thigh gently in the hope that he'll hear me, that he'll remember I can't breathe, and the instant I do, he relaxes his hold and pulls back so I can take a breath. He's here. I've got him, and I'm quick to swallow him back down again in gratitude for him listening. He begins a pumping rhythm into my mouth and groans above me. It's ten times the sound of Pascal's voice and I can't stop my sucking and licking. I'm so desperate for him to come in me so I can show him that the man behind me is irrelevant to us, that it doesn't matter that he's fucking me. Love and lust begin merging together in some sort of communal tie that has me greedily nipping and salivating over the thought as his groans get louder. His pace begins to falter and I know he's ready so I let him take the weight of me by my hair and lift both hands up until they're on his arse, pulling him closer, deeper. Pascal's arm instantly wraps under me to support my weight as he starts grunting behind me, forcing his way in time and time again as his other hand now circles my clit rapidly and brings me close to another state of bliss. I just let them both use me, punishing me from both ends and filling me. It's the most erotic feeling of my whole life. Alex's cock keeps shoving in and Pascal's just drives me back to it, over and over again until I feel those lights beckoning and Alex tensing in my mouth. His hand claws into my hair and rips my head to the left a little to hold me in place for one final drive, and then he explodes down my throat. I can feel it rippling its way down his cock, nearly drowning me in his come as he growls and grunts above me. My whole body goes rigid and gives in to the feeling as Pascal pinches his fingers into my stomach and fills me again from behind. The second he does, I feel those lights flooding every sense and shrouding me in a blanket of sweet torture. Coming together, all of us, using each other as beautiful, sinful, delicious sparks of utter bliss roll over me in waves and remind me why I'm here.

For them, for him. For a different kind of love.

Chapter 25

Elizabeth

"I'll send Andrews for you at three," he says as I climb out of the car and blow him a kiss. I hover at the side and look at him as he smiles in reply and then points at the building. It seems I have to go in while he waits. He's been like that quite a lot lately, always watching me to make sure I get to wherever I'm going. In fact, most of the time he hasn't let me go anywhere without him, or that arsehole I used to call Michael, at my side. It's getting a bit silly to be honest.

I'm going to see Belle at home, although why I'm calling it home, I don't know. Alex has been busy sorting out removal men for all my stuff so that it can be moved over to his. It's all he's been talking about since we got back from Berlin. Well, that's not entirely true because he's also been back on his phone an awful lot, shutting himself in his office and being secretive about stuff I have no idea about. But he's been completely direct about me moving in with him, overly so, almost to the point of ridiculousness. I did try to say that we should wait until well into the new year, at least after we'd moved the business into the new building, but he wouldn't have a bar of it. He just picked up the phone and called a removal company while we were discussing it. He gave them my home address and told them to be there tomorrow morning, which happens to be New Year's Eve. What the sudden rush is, I don't know but he's adamant about it, and now I've got to tell Belle. I've also got to start organising what I'm going to take.

Pressing the button in the elevator instantly reminds me of the cage in Berlin, and thoughts of Pascal come flying back. I smile at the memory and watch the floors flash in front of me as I run my fingers over my lips. After it happened, we all just gazed at each other, each in our own state of bliss as I lay there butt arse naked in front of two of the most beautiful men I've ever seen. Nothing was really said, no words spoken of any really content, just small smiles and gentle caresses from Alex as he held me close to him and watched Pascal like a hawk. Eventually, the vampire put his coat back on with a simple nod of his head, brushed his fingers across my lips, and left us alone in that room. Whether Alex had asked him to leave or he went of his own free will, I don't know, but I felt the tension leave Alex the moment he did. Within ten minutes of him going, he told me he loved me and wrapped me up in his arms even tighter. Wandering his hands over my skin to check for bruising or breakages, he said he was sorry. I don't know what he was sorry for, and when I asked him, he wouldn't reply. So, we just lay there and mumbled sweet nothings at each other until he picked up a part of my dress and smiled. There wasn't much left of it, so after some faffing around with his jacket and belt, I eventually made myself look somewhere near decent and slipped my heels back on as we left. The crowd watched us walk through, regardless of their positions of utter debauchery. Some of them knelt for Alex mid-thrust as the floor parted for us. Others simply bowed their heads or curtseyed. The party was In full swing but we weren't staying to enjoy it apparently. He'd had enough and wanted nothing more than a bath with me to celebrate business, and fucking. I couldn't have loved him more in that moment if I'd tried. That he refused all that to spend time with me was overwhelming.

Pascal didn't come back to the apartment that night, and I haven't seen him since. I did ask about him yesterday and Alex just said, "He'll be back when he's back." I'm not sure what that means if I'm honest, but for once, I didn't question it. Whatever this thing is between us all, I'm sure Pascal will flit in and out of it as he sees fit, or as and when Alex sees fit, I suppose.

"Hey," I call as I walk in the door. I'm greeted with a very relaxed looking Conner sprawled out on the sofa, smiling at me.

"Beth," he says in reply and continues nodding his head. Oh, he's got earphones in, clearly listening to music.

"Belle, where are you?" I ask as I head to her bedroom and find her furiously throwing things in a suitcase. "Oh, are you going somewhere?"

"Yes, his place, under bloody duress," she snaps.

"Umm... problem?"

"Apparently, I'm his fiancée, and I should be living at his, immediately, and if I don't then he'll sell this building and we'll be homeless. I mean, what the fuck is that? Fucking arsehole... At what point did he buy the building we live in? Fucking stalker."

"Oh..." It's all I've got really. Besides, given that I'm about to tell her I'm moving into Alex's, none of it really matters, does it? And she is actually going to marry him, I think.

"Oh?" she shouts. "Fucking oh? What's that supposed to mean? Jesus, Beth, have some balls. Go out there and tell him he can't do this. It's just fucking rude," she shouts again, pointing at the door and flicking her finger at it.

"Do you want to move in with him?" I reply quietly as I pick up a discarded purple shoe and place it on the bed, reverently.

"Well, yes, but that's not the sodding point, is it? I would like to have made up my own mind about that fact, you know, kept an air of mystery about it somehow." I giggle at her in response and sit net to the shoe as she starts throwing things in the suitcase again.

"I'm moving in with Alex tomorrow."

"Oh," she says, her hand stilling as she looks up at me. "Are you sure? I mean, you know I'm okay with that if you are, sort of, but are you going to be okay with him? I'm... Well, he's... You know." I smile at her and think of the things he is: beautiful, difficult, hard work, and confusing, but mostly just mine, and I need him in a way I can't possibly explain to her.

"I'll be fine. It's what I want. *He's* what I want. Do you think Teresa would like the apartment?"

"Might do. I'm still considering burning the building down at the moment, though."

"Do you think you could wait till the removal men gets here in the morning then? I have no idea what to take, though. His house is fully kitted out already."

"Well, Teresa's stuff is shit. You know her mum made her buy it all from charity shops. Apparently it was good for her to understand how to earn the good stuff in life," she replies as she flings things from the wardrobe towards a different suitcase. "Maybe we should just leave it all here for her, apart from personal things, obviously." I nod at her and wander back out into the lounge to find Conner still in the same position. He pulls his headphones out of his ears and follows me over to the kitchen, looking decidedly hot in his casual rock god look, now sporting yellow tips on his hair.

"You okay?" he asks quietly, very un-Conner like. I push the buttons on the coffee machine and look back at him for clarification on his strange question. "With everything... Are you okay with everything that's going on?"

"Of course I'm okay that Belle's moving in with you. It's wonderful, and I'm very-"

"I didn't mean that, Beth. I meant you, Alex and the green-eyed goblin." My burst of laughter is out before I can stop it.

"Green-eyed goblin?" He has to mean Pascal.

"You know who I mean. I didn't think Alex would introduce you to that. I just wanted to make sure you're okay with it all, comfortable. I'm not being funny, Beth, but I never would have expected you to be so..."

"Up for it? Ready to fuck the world?" His head shoots back at my liberal outburst. "I'm a big girl, Conner. This is all my choice. I told him I'd accept it if he would, if it's that important to him. As and when he actually gets to grip with being in love with a man, too, I'm sure we'll be fine."

"My sister the slut." Belle's voice comes around the corner. "Always knew she had it in her."

"I am not a slut."

"You so are. I'm not the one fucking two men, am I?" she asks as she comes over and stands between us, grabbing another cup. Conner blinks at both of us.

"It's not possible that I'm hearing this conversation," he says.

"You started it," I say back to him.

"I was just trying to find out if-"

"What's two like anyway? I've never screwed two at the same time. And while we're at it, why have you never put handcuffs on me? I'm feeling left out," she says, turning back to Conner.

"Babe, if you want that then I'm all over it." She laughs. Conner frowns. "What the hell is that supposed to mean? You think I can't do handcuffs?"

"With blue hair?" she asks, still laughing. "I'm sorry, but while your fucking is tremendous, I'm just not feeling kink king of the world going on." He scowls at her and swipes some cups off the top of the counter in an instant rage of some sort, sending them flying across the room. "What the hell are you-"

"You want me to leave you with Alex for an hour or so instead? Call the fucking goblin for you, too?" The room is utterly silent as we both stare at him in surprise.

"Conner, I'm not sure what's going on, but we were only joking," I say quietly to try and ease the tension as they stare each other down. Belle now has her hands on her hips, and she's directing her most furious glare at him. He's returning it with equal vigour. Seems he has got a temper, just as she said.

"Fuck off," she eventually spits at him.

"Get your damn bags," he replies immediately. She just keeps staring, then eventually storms off into the bedroom and slams the door behind her, leaving me face to face with a very irritated Conner. The sudden memory of Alex sleeping with that woman of his pops into my head, and I wonder if that's what's got him so riled. I turn back to the coffee machine and carry on making it as I listen to him huff and puff behind me. Scraping sounds start and I peek back to see him picking up the broken cups and walking towards the bin with a slightly calmer looking face.

"Did he apologise for sleeping with Caroline?" I eventually ask, quietly. I never did find out, and if I can help him by talking it through then I will, no matter how pissed I might be at his little outburst. Conner stops and looks over at me in shock.

"Yes," he replies with a curl of his lip, turning back to the bin, clearly not happy to discuss any more than that.

"Is that what that was all about?"

"Yeah, sort of."

"You want to talk about it?"

"No," he replies, turning back towards me with a harder face. I narrow my eyes as feisty Beth works her way through me, ready to attack. Fucking men and their ridiculous mood swings, as if I don't have two to deal with already.

"Can you go and apologise to my sister then? Because seriously, blackmailing her out of her home and then having a fucking shit fit about nothing is not cool, and if you act like that to her again in front of me, I'll cut your fucking balls off with the knife in my bag," I spit out. He scowls and I watch the sneer of his lip as he takes a step towards me. Fuck him. Temper tantrums are not what I expect from him, and my feisty Beth kicks in with a vengeance. My hands find my hips as I glare at him in return and will him to try again. I can handle Alex in rage, and Pascal, and whip wielding maniac women. Conner's like a puppy dog sucking a lollipop to me.

"What the hell was that?"

"You heard. You think I'll put up with you doing that to her? You need to grow up and act like a man. She loves you, Conner. Stop being a dick or you'll lose her, and it will be all on you this time. Take a fucking look in the mirror and engage brain mode, will you?"

He just stands there and looks at me, all anger and resentment seemingly gone, as he suddenly turns and wanders across to the bedroom.

"You're going to be fine with him, aren't you?" he says, chuckling and shaking his head.

"What?" I have no idea what he means. I glare at his back, trying not to show any confusion and prove I'm in complete control of the moment.

"You just keep doing that and you'll be fine. I don't know why I was so worried," he says as he twists the door handle and walks in to Belle, closing the door behind him.

Several crashes take place in the next ten minutes, followed and encouraged by an enormous amount of screaming and shouting from the room, none of which comes from Conner, thankfully. I sip at my coffee and listen to it to make sure his temper doesn't include any sort of physicality. After a while, the noise dies down so I wander through to my bedroom to start the task of packing my things up.

The bedroom feels cold to me as I stand in the doorway and try to remember the last time I was here. It seems so long since I've spent any time in my own home, and the funny thing is, I don't care. I feel so close to Alex at the moment that I can't even begin to process the thought of not waking up with him, being with him, and spending the rest of my life with him. He's everything to me, and quite strangely, being with Pascal, too seems to have heightened that somehow, made the connection stronger, not weaker. I don't know why. Maybe it's because it's something so personal, a feeling just for the three of us. It suddenly strikes me that Alex purposely kept me away from having any real closeness with Pascal. He made me look at him, with Pascal behind me, and then held me to him and refused to let Pascal anywhere near me. Is he really jealous? How can a man be jealous of what he's asking for? Very random. I need to talk about that with him because I need that closeness with Pascal, too. If this is going to carry on, I need to know that it's okay for me to have cuddles, kiss him, hold him if that's what he wants. Does he? He is Pascal after all.

I shake my head at yet another confusing thing to deal with and cross the room to grab some suitcases. Having pottered about a bit, I realise that there really isn't that much here. Clothes and books, make-up and hair stuff, none of which I need because there's three times the amount at Alex's already. I sit on the bed and pull out the old photo albums from beneath it. There's years of memories carefully placed together to tell our family story. There are pictures of Mum and of Dad dancing, Belle growing up, me looking stupid in varying shots as I try to look like Belle and act all grown up. There's both of us with our lanky legs and stupid faces as we laughed or giggled, shots of holidays on the coast and one where Belle decided to give me candyfloss hair. I can remember Mum pulling it out and still feel pinch every time another sticky bit was stuck in too awkwardly. Then there's a shot of me on my first day at high school, wearing an astoundingly drab uniform at the school gates as Dad hovers off to the side. In comparison to Belle beside me, I look a mess, tired, dull, admitting defeat even back then. Her blazer and long socks of St. Peters, as she smiles brightly, seem to highlight every difference in us, as I look miserable next to her. Seems I was already feeling useless compared to her even back then. Not any more though. Whatever that was, it has gone.

I snap the book closed and look at the doorway to see if I can hear anything from her room. There's nothing but silence so I carry on chucking things into boxes until there's barely anything left. There's my life without Alex: two suitcases and six randomly packed boxes, pretty much nothing really. What the hell have I been doing for the last ten years? Hiding, clearly. Belle was so right when she told me to get out there more and sort my shit out. Whether I'll ever sort my shit out entirely is another thing, but look at who I am now. I'm stronger, wiser, fitter, more... More what? Just better than I was before is what I am, more who I should be. More who I need to be.

The click of the door has me spinning to see Belle coming down the corridor at me while Conner takes some bags the other way.

"You okay?" I ask as she comes in.

"Yeah, sorry about that. He just drives me mad sometimes." Not surprising given the twat behaviour. I turn back to my room and stare at the mess.

"That's me. That's all there is, or was," I say, pointing at the boxes and stuff stacked on the bed, now for some reason trying to hold back a sob that's threatening to erupt. She wraps her arm around my waist and hugs me into her.

"That's nothing but old memories and a different person, honey. You are so much stronger than you were then. You're going to be fine. You do know that, don't you? You've got this. You can be whoever you want to be now." I flick my eyes back to her and fold. I don't know why, but the tears that begin don't stop. They just keep coming at me from every direction. I try to stop them, but as she pulls me closer and starts to stroke my hair, they just get worse. I'm scared, worried and nervous. More thoughts of him with another woman plague my mind, him killing people, him being part of this underground world, all the fucking money and what that means. Drivers, planes, housekeepers, his family, childhood, father – it all comes together and I slowly realise it's everything attacking me, every fear, thought, worry, concern. Will it work? Will he be good for me? Can I trust him? It's all there, assaulting me and reminding me how hard it is to love him, to help him, and how damn easy it is to need him.

I eventually find the wherewithal to sniff back my ridiculous tears and straighten my body away from her. I will not let this consume me. I love him. I'm moving in with him because I love him. I need to get over this stupidness and sort myself out. Why this is hitting me all of a sudden I do not know.

"It's okay to be scared," she says. "I'm shitting bricks and you know how good I am at not giving a shit." I giggle at the thought as she smiles in return and straightens her dress out. "Into the valley of the shadow of death and all that, huh?"

"Rode the brave two? There's a few hundred missing there to protect us, don't you think?" She sighs a little then pulls a lipstick out from God knows where, and re-applies.

"I like this," she says, plucking out a picture of the two of us at some event we did. I'm covered in flour or some other foodstuff and she's got a hairnet on, looking decidedly messy for Belle. "It reminds me of being kids, the fun times. Can I have it?" I check my watch and realise Andrews will be here in ten minutes so pick up my bag and head out the doorway.

"I thought you hated that. You always said you looked stupid in it."

"I do," she says, catching up with me. "But that's the way I like to remember us, me being stupid. I'm not quite the bitch I appear to be all the time."

"I could question that," Conner says as he stands by the counter. She smirks at him and flings a coaster at his head, which he dodges efficiently with a grin.

"You two alright then?" I ask as I peer down at the street below. The Bentley is already there waiting for me, as per bloody usual. I roll my eyes at it and consider the fact that I might need to have it out with Michael, otherwise I'll be forever needing to smack him or something, and I did quite like him to begin with.

"Fine," they both reply in unison, smiling at each other. Could they be any more in love? "We're going. Are you okay to lock up?" Belle finishes.

"I'll come down with you. The dick is waiting for me."

"Dick?" Conner asks

"Michael. Andrews."

"The man's a legend, and one of the most efficient men I've ever known. Alex has a lot to thank him for, and if you ever need protecting, he's the man for the job. You might want to be a little nicer to him, Beth. You never know when you might need him."

We all make our way down to the foyer and I'm greeted with none other than the man himself holding the door open for me.

"I'll see you both tomorrow for New Year then, yes?" I ask as they walk toward another waiting car. Belle nods in reply as Conner hands a case over to a man I've never seen before, presumably his driver. "Take care, honey. Love you," I call out.

"You too," she replies, sliding into the car and waving. I watch until the car pulls out into traffic and then turn and look at Michael to find him smiling warmly. My finger is in his face quicker than my brain can keep up with.

"I hate what you did to me on that plane, and if you ever manhandle me again, I'll have you charged with assault. I have a fucking right to make up my own mind." He doesn't flinch, doesn't move, nothing.

"Yes, ma'am," he says, his warm smile disappearing from his face. I scramble into the back of the car in irritation and frown at the back of his bald head as he gets in the front. "And don't call me ma'am," I snap again. Arsehole. Although I do feel better for saying my piece.

The silence continues as we weave our way through the London traffic. I'd love to think he was uncomfortable with it, but he's probably not. Not nearly as much as I am, anyway. I may hate what he did, but I hate this discord even more. Why can't the world just get on? Love, live, enjoy and be happy, for God's sake. Why is there always so much in the background to cloud things and make them difficult? I just want some normality, some peace. I want to run my business and enjoy living, not worry about all the things that continue making life complicated.

"Has he told you everything?" Michael says as we turn into Mayfair.

"What?" I snap, although I can feel my heart warming to the man again.

"Has he explained it all? I can't protect you if you don't know the truth. He said he had, so I want to hear it from you."

"Do you mean about the hurting people thing?" I whisper in response. I'm not even sure if he knows. Was that reply scatty enough for him not to understand if he doesn't know? Christ, I'm confusing myself now. Would Michael know about that sort of thing?

"Yes, Elizabeth. I mean the murders." Clearly he does. I randomly look around just in case anybody's listening, because there are so many other people in this car. Stupid Beth.

"You could get sacked for saying that. Have you turned the bugging thing off?"

"No, it's on. I want him, and you, to understand the severity of your situations. I'm also happy to get sacked if he doesn't like it. My job is to protect you, and I can't do that if you fight me."

"I fought you on the plane because you were an arsehole."

"I did my job."

"You were an arsehole."

"And I'll do it again if he asks me to. It's what I get paid for."

"Michael, you can't just scoop me up and carry me where he tells you to. I have enough of that from him."

"Did he tell you about his past?"

"Yes." We've been over this, haven't we?

"Then he did exactly what I hoped he would, and therefore you now know who you're with. Now you can make a choice about whether you want that life or not. That is your choice. My job is to protect you, Elizabeth, at all costs. If you fight me again, I'll knock you out."

I have nothing to say to that, and my mouth is gaping at the thought. He wouldn't, would he? I mean, I know there's been some shady dealings happening in the background, but none of them worth knocking me out over, surely? I try again to find some sort of response but nothing is coming out so I just stare out of the window and hope the situation never arises. Whatever his reason for saying something like that, Conner's probably right. If I ever really need him in that respect, I'm sure he'll be there.

The gravel crunches beneath us as the car pulls into the drive, and I stare down at the house I'm now to call home. I'll only need to go back to the apartment once more to get my stuff loaded and then I'll never go there again. This mansion in front of me is home now. I look at the key in my hands and twirl it around my fingers as I imagine a real life here with him. Let's just hope that past doesn't catch up with him at any point soon. I've got quite enough to think about with Pascal and my new building; the last thing any of us needs is another twilight zone of Mafia shit coming to bite us on the arse.

"He told me to tell you he'll be back later," Michael says.

"Where's he gone?" I ask as we walk into the hall.

"I don't know. He took one of the bikes out at lunchtime and didn't say," he replies, walking towards the stairs and then taking them two at a time.

"How was he?" I call up to him as he rounds the corner and disappears.

"Irritated," he shouts back. Oh, wonderful. Let's hope he's got over that by the time he gets back then.

I dump my bag in the closet, having retrieved my phone, and head down towards the kitchen. Perhaps I could make some dinner or something because I'm not entirely sure what I'm supposed to do in this house all on my own. It's like a sodding mausoleum in some respects, wings that are never used, and rooms I'm sure have never even been looked at. We just spend our time in the same spaces, relaxing as if it was nothing more than a three-bedroom suburban house, with a swimming pool, and a view of the park. I snort to myself and continue onwards past the study. Dinner, yes. I could scavenge the cupboards for a lovely meal. That should be nice for him when he eventually gets here. And I suppose I'm going to have to get used to cooking a meal for two every night, unless Mary's here. What do we do about Mary? I want to cook every night. I don't want someone else doing that for us. Mind you, she can hang on to the cleaning if she wants. I've never been a fan of tidying my own home, kitchen maybe, but changing sheets has never been on the top of my to-do list. And this is a big house. Yes, Mary can stay.

"My dear," I hear from the doorway. My head shoots round to find Pascal sitting behind Alex's desk, shuffling papers and looking what can only be described as dodgy.

"Oh, you're here," I reply as I push the door open a little more and wonder why he's looking through Alex's things. He folds a piece of paper, puts it in his pocket and looks up at me with a smile.

"I am. I thought we might talk a little, some of your English tea, perhaps?"

"Well, Alex isn't here and I don't know when he'll be back, but..." He looks at me and then stands up, showcasing his absolute magnificence as he beckons me with his hand and licks his lips. I'm so not doing this without Alex being around, no matter how much I might want to.

"I am more than aware of this fact. We could occupy ourselves together while we wait, hmm? I am quite jealous that your lips have not been around me yet," he states, all green, sparkly eyes and dangerously tempting hands, tapping them on the table just like Alex does and reminding me where they've been, where his cock's been, and not been. My eyes are so quick to traitorously travel the length of him and his quite beautifully fitted suit that I bump into the wall while watching him.

"That's not talking," I say as I back my way out of the room and head for the safety of the kitchen again. I will not do this without Alex.

After his reaction in Berlin, I have no idea how he would feel about anything happening without him.

"You seem afraid of me, my dear," he says as he follows me in, actually sounding quite worried. "You look nervous, and while it is thoroughly intoxicating, I am uncomfortable with he thought."

"You are?" I reply, slightly stunned at the emotional reaction to my inner turmoil. He smiles. it's not entirely genuine; he's clearly not that emotional. I stare at him for a few seconds while trying to work out what to say. I'm not afraid of him in the slightest. I'm just not sure what the etiquette around us is. "I'm not afraid, Pascal. I'm bothered by the potential consequences. I don't understand what we can and can't do."

"Ah, yes. He is jealous, no? We should address this. Come here and kiss me." What? No. He flicks the button on his jacket and waits for me to launch myself at him. It's hard not to, to be fair.

"No. That's what I'm trying to say. He's-" He's across the floor and sweeping me up into his arms before I can blink, aggressively holding me and grasping the back of my neck to force my lips to his, and I can't stop melting into him. I wish I could, but his mouth is divine and I can feel my whole body trembling at just the thought of more. His frame moves us backwards until there's something hard behind me, stopping me from running from him. Not that I would, because all thoughts of Alex are disappearing, all thoughts of loyalty diminishing with every clash of teeth and grind of his thigh against me. He suddenly stops and pulls away, leaving me utterly breathless as he just stands there and reaches into his pocket. I stare wide-eyed in response, waiting for whatever he's about to deliver. He pulls out his cigarettes and smirks. Right.

"If I choose to, my love, I can have you wherever I like. Here, in the hall, perhaps in his bed? It is futile to concern yourself with the obligation you have to him. I have fucked most things he has offered with no moral implications in the matter at all. If he didn't want me to have you, he simply would not have collared me. He does not yet appreciate that," he says as he sits at the table and lights up. I continue with my stare and then shake my head at the statement. Could he make this any less emotional if he tried? My heart slumps slightly at the thought so I turn to the cupboards and try to focus on cooking some food instead. Maybe that's exactly what I should do –

just forget the feelings I have for him and use him as and when Alex asks for it. Just enjoy those moments and keep it businesslike maybe, a quick fuck or blowjob when Alex needs such an act. I can feel the sigh leave my chest at the very thought. That's not what I want with either of them. I need that connection to do this. I need to know Pascal has feelings, too, that he wants me not just because of Alex.

"Do you love me, my dear?" Interesting question. Do I? I keep opening the cupboards and retrieving ingredients as I ponder the thought. Alex asked me that once before and I said no, but now I'm not so sure. I would kill for Alex. I would lay my life on the line to prove my love for him, but Pascal? I suppose I did put myself in harm's way for him with maniac woman.

"I don't know you well enough to truly know." It's the only honest reply I have at the moment.

"Would you like to?" Oh my god, I'm so confused by this man. As if Alex wasn't enough. I slam the bottle in my hand down on the counter top and swing round to face him.

"What do you want from me? For God's sake, Pascal, what? Do you know how hard this is for me? I'm not one of you immoral sluts, Pascal. I'm me, and I'm in love with Alex, who is difficult enough without you adding to the mix. Can you even begin to imagine how hard it is for me to do all this and keep him happy? He's jealous of whatever this is," I snap out, flicking my hands between us. "And yet he wants it. And you. What the hell am I supposed to do with that? And why would you ask me that question and confuse what you just said about no moral implications. Morals? Really? As if you have any clue what morals are? I'm tired, Pascal. I'm tired of trying to work this out. I've just moved in with a man who wants me to fuck another man, too. Does that even compute as odd to you?" He just sits there, not a hint of a reaction to my tirade as he blows out another puff of smoke and watches me catching my breath. Fucking man. I could hate him sometimes.

"Hmm. A very fascinating speech, my dear. However, you have still not answered the question."

"What question?"

"Would you like to know me better?"

"Yes, probably." It's instant. I don't even think about it, and as one of his genuine smiles creeps across his lips, I turn my head back to the cupboards in infuriation. Lasagne. I'll make Lasagne. It's Italian, and he likes Italy, doesn't he? Alex, that is. I delve into the fridge to check for mince and try to forget the conversation that's going on. I'll just make food and pretend this is all innocent, that it's just another day in a normal household.

"Would you tell him that?" What? Christ. "Endure his wrath, for me?"

"I endured a whip for you, Pascal," I mumble in response as I grab an onion and start chopping, though at this moment, I can't for the life of me remember why. An arm wraps around the front of me and softly pulls me away from the chopping board. The hand holding the knife is pulled up to his mouth and kissed over my shoulder.

"Then we shall suffer his fury together, my love. If you wish for that clarity then I might force it from him for you." My whole body freezes at what that could mean.

"Pascal, I didn't mean you had to-"

"One must be ready to combat the inevitable, Elizabeth, at some point," he says as he lets me go and walks away towards the door. I turn to see his relaxed gait wandering away, and wonder what he's just inferred. Presumably it has something to do with beatings.

"Pascal, I really don't think... I mean, I don't want to see you..." *Get hurt.* He's gone, so I just stare at the door and try to get my head around what he means by any of that. He couldn't have meant that he considers me worth fighting for, could he? I suppose he did say that once, that if Alex fucked up again, he'd take his chance next time around. And he has, on occasion, offered me a choice between them, hasn't he? But he's collared now. I shake my head at the doorframe again and turn back to my chopping, still confused, and still tired of trying to work all of this out.

Chapter 26

Alexander

- If you're wondering where it is, brother, I have it.

He looked at the text again. Why did she have his fucking money? Why? And how the hell did she get it. He'd tried to call her but the phone line had been dead. It didn't surprise him, given the computer genius that she was, but why send the text and then not talk to him? He'd travelled to her apartment and picked the lock to find the space empty apart from furniture. Even a phone call to Mrs. Peters hadn't helped in tracking her down. It seemed the woman thought she was in Europe with friends for Christmas and the New Year.

Two days he'd been trying to find the money that had somehow disappeared from the Chinese lawyer's account. It had been there for a day in their holding account and then he received an email from Tom to say that the deal was off because the money was missing. He couldn't give a fuck what the Chinese were saying in all reality. He'd battle them and more than likely win because the sale was recorded and he had all the legal documentation to prove it. Whether it went missing while in their possession was neither here nor there in the eyes of the law, but some fucking moral obligation was now piquing his curiosity in the matter. Also, the fact that some other bastard was interfering in his dealings was intolerable. He would win, but this would take years to wrangle his way through – years he didn't have, given the peace he was trying to find for his angel. Several phone calls to Conner for his help had proved reasonably useful in that Conner scoured all his accounts again for any interference and found none.

He looked back up at the night sky and narrowed his eyes at the moon shining too brightly. It hindered his approach and made him feel like he was in the spotlight, never a place the real version of him liked much. So he stared at the old manor house on the other side of the

370

road and snarled at the thought. What the hell was he doing here? He had business he should be dealing with. Why he'd felt the need to ride all the way out here and drag up old ghosts was beyond him, but something was nudging him, that old sense of a lie travelling along his spine and telling him something was off.

"*I love you,*" whispered through his mind. Two voices now told him that, and both of them regardless of all his faults, one of them maybe because of them. He could face this and deal with the man, find out if he was the one sending the texts or if someone else was trying to scare him for some reason. He watched the dim lights in the house flickering and wondered what he was going to say to the bastard after all this time. He should have brought his angel with him. She would have known how to deal with the problem. He checked his watch again and wondered if the man ever slept. It was 1.30am now, and he'd been sat here for a little over an hour, waiting for the lights to go out so he could go in and look around, perhaps search the study for any relevant information. Son... The word kept droning on in his mind to counter the love. Son? Never once had the man used the word that he could remember. Little shit, prick, Nicholas on occasion, but never son. Why would he bother using the term now?

He wrenched his helmet off in frustration and climbed off the bike to push it further into the trees. Hopefully no one would steal it if he hid it a little. He snorted in derision at his thoughts given the quiet country lane in the middle of nowhere. It was highly unlikely any traffic would even come past while he was inside. He stared at the house a bit longer and eventually decided he was going in, regardless of whether the bastard was awake or not. Maybe he should just choke the information out of the man, demand he told him the truth and then just leave. Short and sweet, no discussing old fucking times or sneaking about while the man slept. Yes. Fuck it. He was going to find out what the hell the man thought he was playing at, if it was him. He'd got the element of surprise at least, and if he just went in there and asked direct questions then the man would have to answer him.

He sucked in a breath and pushed away the visions assaulting him with every step towards the house. He refused to feel intimidated by the air around him. Even it wasn't his family home, the connotation was the same. Just being within twenty feet of the brickwork was enough to bring those memories flying back. He could feel those broken ribs again, almost sense his fear returning with every crunch on the gravel beneath his feet to remind him of the crack of bone. His bones, the bones his father broke, repeatedly. He halted outside what appeared to be the lounge window and watched the back of a man wander across the room to a cabinet. The chills that crawled up his spine as that man turned and looked through the window very nearly had him turning back around again for his bike. Instead, he sunk back into the shadows to make sure the bastard couldn't see him. Those eyes were still the same, and his frame was still huge even though age had changed his features. Wrinkles lined his face and his black hair was now greying slightly, but other than that, the man was still exactly as he used to be. He was still evil in his appearance, or at least he was to Alex. He supposed to all his clients, Richard Adlin was the epitome of a decent old lawyer – good mannered and well respected in all his circles. They knew nothing of the man who killed his mother and beat him black and blue for years. Nor did they know of the man who locked all the doors and made him beg for a chance to go outside, just a chance to play with the other children in the street. His fists tightened as the bastard just stared back into the night and eventually made his way out of the room. He followed the frame with his eyes as it moved its way toward the front door and then sneered as it opened.

"Who's there?" the bastard's voice shouted, still abrupt enough in its tone to make him flinch a little in response. His body reacted in its normal pathetic state. Legs trembling, heart beating rapidly, throat constricting around words he couldn't get out. *"Fuck you, Dad."* He wanted to scream that out loud, shout it and show the man the monster he'd shaped, let all that rage descend upon the one man who truly deserved his anger so he could truly feel an emotion in the act, just for once. He listened to his own breathing and watched the air puff into the cold night sky, rapid bursts of energy filtering from his mouth as he tried to stave off the fear clawing at him. *"I love you. I will always love you."* Elizabeth's voice came at his mind again to counter the silhouette on the porch. His angel's voice breaking the moment and reminding him he was worthy, that he could do this, that he was strong enough to handle any threat, including his father. He cracked his neck about and flexed his hands out of their death grip on nothing. He just needed the information, just needed to know the ifs and whys, and then he could leave. "I've got a shotgun here." He smiled a little at the comment. It really wouldn't take much for that to be used for a damn good purpose.

"Then put it away, father," he said as he emerged from the shadows and walked slowly towards the man. For a split second the bastard looked shocked, but it was quickly replaced by arrogance and that same, never-ending smug smile.

"I wondered when you'd turn up, Nicholas."

"My name's not Nicholas," he replied quietly as he edged past the man and into the house.

It was yet another representation of decency – highly polished floors and quality antique furniture decorating the hallway as if he was being introduced to some kind of family home. All lies. The only aura this man had was one of lies and brutality. He could feel it with every breath the man took. The arsehole closed the door behind them and turned to look at him.

"You think because you made a new life for yourself that you are no longer my son? Your name is Nicholas Adlin. It will always be Nicholas Adlin," he said sharply as he walked past him and back into the lounge again. "Drink? Cognac, isn't it?" How the fuck did he know that? He followed him through carefully and stifled the need to take his leather jacket off at the sudden heat. He wouldn't be staying long enough for that.

"Did you send the texts?" he asked calmly, desperately trying to quash the terror holding him hostage, raking up old thoughts and terrorizing any element of control. Just looking at the man was enough to disable all rationality. Thoughts began to merge and blur into confusion as the clear game plan disappeared into the fire along with logical thinking. He shook his head to try and regain some calm as Daddy turned back and tilted his head with those same eyes bleeding hate at him from across the room. They were still the same eyes, still the same disgust and loathing pouring from them, damned liquid depths of black holes boring in and forcing him to look at the floor briefly. The fucker chuckled and snorted in contempt.

"Of course it was me, Nicholas."

"Why?"

"You're my son," the bastard replied with another snort of disdain, as if he were an idiot for asking the question. *Stupid little boy. Pathetic. Look at you.* He halted the need to break something. Looking at these walls adorned with pictures of happy families, none of which were real, was enough to send him crazy with fury and uncertainty. What sort of life was the man trying to portray, for Christ's sake? He turned away and stared at a picture of a woman he now knew to be his mother. He felt the venom leave his stomach almost immediately. It was a different one than the one he had. She was wearing a blue dress that sparkled the same colour as her eyes, but she was dull other than that, just sitting in a chair someone had presumably made her sit in and told her how to appear. A glass was placed in front of him on the table, so he stared down at it and wondered what the hell the man was trying to achieve.

"Did you kill her?" he asked quietly, nodding at the picture, not touching the glass in the slightest as he watched the man close the curtains.

"She fell. Your mother was a clumsy woman," he replied as he made his way to the desk and began signing documents. Did she fuck.

"What do you want? Why did you text me?"

"I want my son to behave appropriately. I'm your father and I deserve some respect," he replied, his back hunched over the desk as he shuffled papers about. "It's Christmas, son, time for families to be together." If it was possible for his eyes to pop out of his head they would have. What the hell was the bastard going on about? Happy families? Christ, he hadn't seen the man for years, and the last person he wanted to spend a minute with at Christmas was him. Christmas was for people like Elizabeth and her family, people who loved each other and wrapped intricate bows around presents.

"Respect for what?" he asked as the man scribbled on a folder and tucked it carefully into his desk drawer.

"You're alive, aren't you? And you've done well for yourself. Shouldn't I be rewarded for my efforts in teaching you?" He just stared at the bastard's back again, now wondering what teachings he was referring to. As far as he could remember, the only teachings he had received were those of fear and of turmoil. His throat tightened again as he watched the man's fingers working the pen in his hand. He could see the loose hold he had on it, the relaxed manner of the way he held it, the same way he'd held that fucking tie for all those years as he'd walked toward him with it. So familiar. He frowned at his own pathetic trembling again and tensed every muscle to combat it. "From what I can see, son, you are feared, respected, and privileged. Your business is thriving and you have a woman that is very appealing. Elizabeth, isn't it? I'm certain I must have had something to do with the creation of that." Anger rose up inside him with such force he barely tamed the thought of killing the man as he sat there. How dare he mention her name? Who would fucking miss him anyway? No one. Not one person on this planet deserved the pain of having to deal with such a man. He took a step towards the arsehole and inwardly smiled at the prospect. He could do it. He could just squeeze and overpower the old man. It would be quick, easy even.

"There isn't a reward for what you created. You should be jailed for what you did to me," he snarled out as his body reminded him of his job. The bastard turned his head from the desk and then lifted his frame out of the chair. He was still so big, and the instant feelings from his childhood came hurtling through his own bloodstream in sudden panic as he watched the man sneer in response.

"You wouldn't be the man you are today without it, son," he said, stepping toward him.

"Do you honestly think that's true? You're mad. Why?" he managed to reply as he took a step backward from the bastard and hit the table.

"Look at yourself, boy. You're not afraid of anything. You go after what you want and get it. You have everything you will ever need. You would be nothing without me and my guidance. You'd have ended up working in some mechanics shop fucking around with engines. That's all you ever wanted to do, mess around with that ludicrous little plane." His plane. His little red plane. He loved that plane, spent hours when he was alone dreaming of flying in it and being free in the air.

"It's the only toy I ever had," he mumbled, now taking another pathetic step away as the man seemed to grow in size again. "You never let me have anything else."

"Toys? What good would toys have done you? You needed hardening up. You were weak, just like your mother." *Weak. Weak and pathetic. Useless. Stand there 'til I tell you to move. Maybe you'll get a treat.* He was four when that happened, and he stood still for three hours, hoping to be rewarded with something nice as his father made phone calls. He just stood in the middle of the carpet, even pissed himself rather than move. *Must keep Daddy happy.* Instead, he was given a beating when he tried to sit quietly through exhaustion, just to keep Daddy happy. *Must keep Daddy happy.* Daddy. Daddy was never fucking happy. He frowned at the thought and felt the anger coming back, a rage building and quieting the noise in his head.

"I was four years old when you broke my fucking ribs. Why?"

"I did not break your ribs. You tripped on the stairs. You were as ham-fisted as your mother was." Both eyebrows shot up at the lie. Was he really going to pretend it didn't happen? Surely the bastard was man enough to admit what he'd done.

"You beat me until I couldn't breathe and then stamped on my ribs. You fucking did that. *You.* I fucking remember it," he said, his voice now finding a level of irritation and power again as that quiet kept swirling through him.

"I only hit you when you needed putting straight about something. And be careful with your tone around me. You're still my son."

He scowled at the man as he got within arm's reach and pushed the need to just kill him away. That fucking suit hid a monster inside. He shouldn't be here, shouldn't be alive even. He should rot in the ground with all those other repugnant wastes of life that he'd taken.

"You tied my fucking neck to the banister and taunted me. You left me out in the cold to freeze, burnt my face in the oven. I didn't even have a bed, for fuck's sake. I deserved better than that. I was a child, and..." The bastard held a finger up to stop him, and without thought, his mouth clamped shut. It always had done when that happened. It was warning enough for what would come next. Fucking ridiculous. He was a grown man now, for God's sake. He glowered at himself and inched forward to the man. He would do this. He wasn't afraid anymore, couldn't be.

"I think you better leave. You're clearly not thinking straight, son," the bastard said calmly.

"STOP CALLING ME YOUR SON, YOU FUCKING-"

The hit of something hard to his head caught him completely off guard and sent him reeling into the bookshelves behind him, then to the floor. Pain seared through him as he grasped onto the side of his head and winced like a pussy at the intense throb assaulting him.

"Stop whining, you little shit," the bastard said from above while swinging a large glass decanter in his hand. "Always whining. Whine, whine, whine. Where's my mummy? I want my mummy. You needed to grow up so that's what I did. I helped you. Don't you see? Do you still whine for her, still wet the bed like a disgusting little prick?" Alex cowered beneath the man and held onto his head as he heard the change in voice, the low tone of evil resonating like a death bell coming at him from all directions. "How does your new little thing like it when you cry like a baby?"

"Leave her out of this," he muttered quietly as he remained on the floor, suddenly not daring to get up and face whatever was coming next. *Stay down. Just stay down and be quiet. Be a good boy and he'll stop.*

"Why? She's a pretty thing. I'd hate you to ruin your chances with her, fuck that handsome face of yours up. Perhaps she needs a real man instead." He couldn't find any language to respond with. Nothing. But the mention of her was enough to force something from his throat, anything.

"Please, just-"

"How does she fuck, Nicholas?" the bastard asked as he kicked his thigh with the heel of his boot then ground it in deeper. "Look at you down there. You really are a disappointment. I thought you'd be stronger than this by now. It seems I was wrong. Do you need some more instruction?"

Panic reared its ugly head again so he just kept staring at the floor, shielding his head and wishing something would come and take him away. He could feel the thoughts of a young boy racing in as Alexander left him. All that was left in his place was a snivelling, terrified four-year-old, dreading what was about to happen. He tried to move a little to ease the discomfort on his leg but the bastard just ground his boot in harder and laughed. That laughter echoed in his head, louder and louder, until all he could hear was the sound of his bedroom at night. The sound of those shiny shoes clomping up the stairs towards him had him almost choking on tears but for the fear of actually doing it. His body tried to move again, tried to find a way out, but there never had been anywhere to run to, nowhere to hide either, and so he'd just waited there for his punishment. He'd just waited like a good little boy and tried not to cry as every blow rained down on him, just as he was doing now. *Mustn't cry. Just keep Daddy happy. Must keep Daddy happy. Be stronger.*

"*Get up, Alex. I love you. Be more than this.*" Her voice again, chanting in the background, swirling through him and dulling the pain a little. "*Show me more. I love you. I want it all.*" He tried to hang onto it, but the chiding laughter wouldn't go away, and he couldn't breathe all of a sudden. Why couldn't he breathe again? He pulled his hands to his throat at the onslaught of the attack to try and keep it at bay, but he couldn't stop it. All he could feel was the dull ache in his head, the piercing pain in his leg, and the fear of what was to come. Why was his daddy hurting him again? Why?

He pulled himself into a ball and let the inevitable come as another wave of punishment slammed down on his head. *Useless little shit. How many times have I got to show you this? You disgust me. You're not worthy of any of it.* He couldn't tell if the man was saying it or if it was just memories, but the voice was drowning out everything, killing any sense of reason and just destroying all she'd told him, all she'd promised. She was wrong. He wasn't worthy, and certainly not of her. She'd be fine with someone else. They'd protect her from this and give her the good life she deserved.

Another kick to the ribs had him howling in agony and grasping onto the shelf to avoid the next one. He didn't. It just rammed into another part of him as he lay there. *Keep Daddy happy.* He should fight. He knew that, could feel it somewhere deep inside, but he couldn't find the anger he needed. He was scared, terrified even, and all he could see was her eyes staring at him as he shook in fear. Her angelic face looked revolted as she sneered at him in disgust and laughed along with his dad. *Useless. Worthless.* "Elizabeth," he mumbled to himself as something wrapped around his throat, and he closed his eyes to the sensation. *Just keep Daddy happy. Stay down. Be quiet. Don't cry.* His body began to move across the floor, and he tried to kick his legs out for purchase but the fight wasn't there, and what was the point anyway? *My throat. Mine now.* Her voice came out of nowhere and sparked across his thoughts. Her throat. Hers. He'd given it to her. It wasn't this bastard's to have anymore. The vision of her face became stronger as his back dragged across the wood, a smile now spread across it as her hand floated in front of him. *I love you. Don't leave me, Alex.* He reached a hand forward for her but the pain in his throat was too much, too tight, and he gasped for air while trying to reach her.

"You got heavy, Nicholas." *Nicholas. Nicholas. Nicholas. No, Alex. Her Alex.* It was all for her, and she was disappearing. Why couldn't he see her anymore? Where was she? He wrenched his hand at the constraint around his neck and heaved to get back to her. Nothing happened, but his movement stopped and she was there again. That red hair of hers was flaming as her smile broadened once more and she beckoned him. He pulled again and watched her blow him a kiss and giggle, such a beautiful giggle, so free and wonderful. He wanted that giggle, needed it more than anything, and he wanted to hold her and kiss her and tell her he loved her, tell her that she completed him and made him whole, and that without her, his life was empty. *"Come for me,"* she whispered. *"Show me."* He needed to, with every strangled breath. He had to reach her, had to show her that she was his world. He had to show her that nothing would stop him from getting to her and keeping her safe. Only death would ever stop him. Death.

He hauled again on the rope and felt it giving enough that he could get the other hand in, too, so he wrenched at it again and scrambled his feet to the floor. The creak of his leathers caught his attention and cleared the air of the other confusing noise in his head. *"Up, Alexander. Be more."* Now Pascal's voice, clearing away all the others apart from hers. It was as if they were one and the same somehow. Guiding him, calling him, calling him home.

He snarled at himself and watched his own feet plant onto the floor in front of him as he rose, and with a final tug, he felt the rope loosen around his neck and then finally go slack in his hand.

"Got stronger, too," Daddy said behind him with a chuckle. He turned to find the fucker smiling at him, smiling with some expression he'd never seen before. Uncertainty. He looked down at whatever it was in his hands and found a tie there. A fucking tie? He threw it on the floor in disgust and raised his eyes back up to the man.

"Don't ever fucking touch me again," he growled out, barely containing the need to rip the bastard's head from his body. She wouldn't want that, would she? That would be wrong, immoral. The dick just stood there, still smiling, and reaching for the glass of cognac he'd poured earlier.

"Look at what you've become, son," he said as he took a swig and rolled up his sleeves. "It makes me proud to see you like this." Proud? He sucked in a breath and tried to walk past the man. He had to leave. He couldn't find any peace here. All he could think of was murder, death and revenge. Years of revenge, clawing its way around him and telling him to kill the threat in front of him. Sadistic, twisted thoughts now clouded over the love she'd created again to help him through all of this. The bastard put a hand on his chest to stop him. "Don't leave like this. We have matters to discuss." They had nothing to discuss, nothing. He was done here.

"I have nothing left to say. Stay away from me and my family, or I'll kill you," he replied quietly as he glared at the man's hand and watched it slowly pull away. His father's hands were the same as his own. In fact, everything about the man was too familiar, like looking in a mirror really. He frowned at the thought and clung onto the vision of her smiling at him as he stepped around the bastard and headed for the door.

"You'll regret walking away," his father called as he reached for the handle.

He might regret a lot more if he stayed.

The moment he hit the cool night air, he grabbed hold of his ribs and head to check for damage. At least one rib was broken. He could feel it moving, and his head was pounding as he limped up the drive. He swiped his fingers across the area and added more fresh red to the dried blood already coating his hand. There was a small gash, but he could feel the tenderness already filling with fluid as a lump started to form. After briefly considering going to a hospital, he made it to his bike and blew out a breath as he stared back at the house. The lights were still on, and he considered what his father meant by regretting walking away. What did that mean? He wasn't sure he gave enough of a fuck to think about it any longer so just climbed on his bike and gingerly pulled the helmet over his head. The bastard couldn't do anything to him now. He'd just proved his point. He may have needed Elizabeth to help him with it, but he'd finally done it, beaten the man at his own game and walked away with his head held higher. She would be pleased with him for that, proud of him. She'd think he was decent for his behaviour, given the scenario, and her opinion was the only one he cared about. She'd be proud of what he did.

He just needed to get home.

~

"Alex?" she mumbled, her voice full of the huskiness of sleep as she lay there in his bed. He climbed in beside her and pulled her close to him. He hadn't bothered with a shower. He couldn't face one more second without her wrapped around him, regardless of the taint of that man's fingers on him. The drive home had been torturous, as he'd remembered month after month of childhood memories. The beatings, the cruelty, the manipulation. "I was worried. Where have you been?"

"Out," he said in response as he pulled her tighter and let the warmth of her soothe him. He smelt the aftershave of Pascal mingled with her perfume and smiled at the thought as he kissed her neck. No jealousy coursed through his veins as it normally would. There was just some sort of peace as he breathed in the scent and let the hours of riding disappear. "When did he get back?"

"Around three, I think," she said as she grasped at his hands and laid one of them on her breast. She squirmed back into him, and he felt his cock hardening at her naked form as she moaned and sighed in front of him. He didn't need to worry that anything had happened between them. She'd never do that to him unless she was asked, no matter how hard Pascal might try. He caught the thought that he wanted the man in here with them now and tucked it back away for another time. This was for the two of them, just them. Her body writhed as he let his hand travel downwards across her flawless skin, and then she moaned again as he slid his fingers inside her. She was so ready for him, always ready for him to devour any time he wanted or needed it. She widened her legs as he probed deeper and felt her muscles clenching so he pushed her legs back together and brought her hand around to his cock. One touch was enough to rid him of everything other than her, and as she guided him towards her waiting pussy, he let her take the lead. His cock reacted in its normal way with her. It ached and pulsed for the second it drove inside. It constantly throbbed for her to take it and do as she wanted with it, to show him how much she wanted him inside her. Screaming for him, begging for him, and as he slowly delved inside her, she moaned aloud again, pushing back towards him.

He wrapped his arm underneath her and stroked at her throat as she ground back onto him, over and over again until she began to shudder a little. Fuck, he loved every tremble that left her body. It was a sign of their love, of something no one could ever take away from him no matter what happened. True love – unending, all forgiving love.

"I love you," he growled into her hair as her back arched away from him. He grabbed her and yanked her back to him. Close, he needed her close. Close enough that he could smell her and feel her body giving him everything.

"I... I love- Oh god, yes," she near screamed in reply as her pussy began contracting around him and he felt her coming on him. Glorious. He drove in harder, squeezing her throat a bit tighter as he did and watching her body try to get away from the intensity. She shifted and writhed until she was perched on the end of him, so he turned her until she was above him and pushed her astride him. He suddenly wanted to see her, to have her on top of him so he could watch her showing him she loved him. She sat up and smiled down at him, the same smile he'd seen earlier. She was breath-taking as she linked her fingers through his and lowered down onto his cock. Slow and steady, she began to ride him, grinding and building her own pace until he couldn't stand it anymore and forced her down onto him harder. She grunted and mewled like a starving kitten as she let him take her again, harder and fiercer until she folded her body so she could kiss him. All the time she needed that kiss, that closeness, and she could have it as she grasped the back of his neck to bring his mouth to hers. All the while, she let him slam in at his own pace and rid himself of any residual effect. Again and again, he rammed in to force them back together, bind them tighter, remind her that he loved her and would do anything to keep her safe.

"I love you," she breathed into his mouth as her tongue and teeth nipped lustfully and he felt his come rising through him. "I love you, more. I love you." She kept chanting it into his mouth, ear, and then throat as she folded her face into his neck and begged for harder, faster. Her fingers grabbed at his hair and he roared in pain as she ripped and scratched at the area around his wound. But she could have that, too. She could have his pain and use it as she saw fit because it was all hers, all for her. He grasped her hips tighter and closed his eyes as she moaned again and just let him take what he was suddenly desperate for. His cock swelled as he bit into her shoulder, the urgency to come inside her almost frantic as he fought to mark her again with himself and claim his prize for being a good boy, a good man. On and on he drove until his heartbeat was so frenzied he could hardly breathe, as she begged and told him she needed him. And then he was there, growling and groaning as he rammed in for the last time and felt his come explode deep inside her. It poured in as if it were the first time he'd ever fucked her, so he pushed again and let her feel his need for her.

"Mine," he grunted into her neck as he relaxed his hold of her a little and just lingered in his peaceful place. She pressed more kisses onto his throat and whimpered in response as he slowly pulled back and felt the wetness ooze out of her onto him. His come, her come, their love.

"Yours," she said without hesitation. "All yours."

He pushed back in again and bit her shoulder some more. She was right, and he was going to prove it again. He was going to prove it all fucking night, until she believed it in her soul.

Chapter 27

Elizabeth

I don't know what happened last night because he won't tell me. I could have a shit fit about it, but given that we've got about an hour before Michael will be waiting to take us to Henry's New Year ball, I'm really not sure this is the best time for a row. He did let me dress and clean the cut to his head, and he also let me help him put the strapping around his ribs, but other than that he's told me nothing. I'm not even sure if I really want to know if I'm honest.

"Are you nearly ready? I'll go and get some drinks," he calls from the bathroom as I slip my earrings in and look down at yet another ridiculously expensive dress. It's gold this time, with a halter neck. I turn to slip my heels on and find Pascal leaning on the doorframe, looking truly delicious in a black tux. He's coming, too?

"Exquisite, my dear," he says, clearly not daring to step a foot across the threshold. I could say the same frankly. I so wish he'd stop being so fucking tempting. It's quite disturbing.

"Are you coming with us?" I ask, slightly shocked by the revelation. I cannot cope with both of them in a normal gathering of people.

"No, I am at the mayor's ball. It seems I am my country's cultural representative for the coming of the New Year. Dull indeed," he replies as Alex walks back into the room. He stops suddenly and looks at Pascal with an odd look, not one I can ever remember seeing before, something like surprise.

"Why are you standing out there?" he asks, his voice terse, slightly angry.

"I was not aware I was allowed to enter the sanctuary, Sir," Pascal replies, smirking as he stands up and looks somewhat stunned. I giggle in reply and watch Alex wave a hand into the room as I switch the mirror light off.

"You have been invited," he says charmingly as he walks across and kisses me. I have no idea why but this quickly turns into a groping

384

session as his hands start wandering all over me. I begin to push him away to save my outfit and make-up, but there's really no point. I'll just do it again at some point. But as his hand suddenly tugs at the zip on my dress, I realise what's going on and pull my face away from him to clarify what's happening. We just stare at each other for a few seconds as I try to read his mind, or try to hear Pascal's. His brow rises to ask me a question. I'm not sure what it is but I'm pretty convinced it's to do with sex.

"We don't have time," I reply quietly. I want all night with them if this is going to happen again. I flick my eyes to Pascal and then back again. I want to revel in them and feel them both around me, in me. "If that's what you mean?"

"There is always time for fucking and debauchery," Pascal says from the side. I swing my eyes round to see Pascal untying his bow tie and flinging it on the bed. Those green eyes of his are suddenly full of interest as he scans the length of me again and removes his cummerbund. I turn back to see Alex smirking at me, the same devil may care smile he always has when he's thinking inappropriately.

"You want this?" I ask him. "Now?"

"Yes, right now. You wanted the truth from me."

He pulls the dress off without another moment's hesitation, and I feel myself being turned around like a rag doll until I'm standing in nothing but my thigh highs, thong and heels. "I want you sore all night. I want you to remember this," he says as he unzips and gets his already hard cock out. I stare at it in shock and glance back at Pascal who's now doing the same. "Touch yourself for me." I open my mouth in reply and wonder where this has come from. There's no warmth here. The room is suddenly ice cold and I feel like I'm just going to be used for no reason other than fulfilling a simple need. Nerves begin encroaching and I try to cover myself from their stare.

"Alex, I need more than that. You know I can't just-" Warm hands are suddenly on my back as I feel Pascal moving them around me and kissing my shoulder.

"Do as he says, my love," he says quietly while grabbing at my hand and guiding it around my body to the front of me. I can feel the length of him rubbing against my backside as he draws my hand downwards and places his fingers over mine to start me off. I can't stop the moan that leaves me as I begin circling my clit. Small, gentle rubs as I close my eyes and try to find a rhythm in the abrupt moment. "Are you ready for both of us, Elizabeth? Hmm?" he says over my shoulder, his voice now husky and low as if the other devil suddenly joined the room to play, too. "I have waited for this, waited to fuck your ass while he comes inside you. I want nothing more than to be close to you when he comes, to fuck you as he does." Oh god, that's working. I can feel the delicious sparks beginning to shoot across me at his words, and his teeth are grazing on me gently as I widen my stance a little to aid my own access. His hand works lower, pushing his fingers inside me along with my own and bending me slightly forward with the pressure of his weight. His other hand slowly trails along my backside, and as I sense where he's going, I look to Alex for help. He just smiles and licks his lips in encouragement. "You have a perfect ass for fucking. Do you need stretching? I think not. The tighter the better. Hmm?" he says as he pushes a finger slowly inside me. Oh god, I can't breathe all of a sudden, and those nerves come rushing back at me as I feel my whole body freeze. He just keeps pushing until he's all the way in both ends of me, working my own fingers against the one he has inside my arse. Alex strokes his cock in front of me and watches as I begin to moan into the rhythm being created for me and try to keep my legs from collapsing. I can't keep from widening my stance again as Pascal slips another finger in and moves it around, widening me, preparing me. I grab onto the footboard of the bed to steady myself, and grip tightly as I feel his feet kicking at mine to keep them open. I thought I'd have time to get ready for this, thought they'd give me a time or a date maybe, but I should have known that wouldn't happen. I should have realised it would be in the minute that Alex just let all his concerns go and took what he needed. He stares at me and then just steps into me and lifts me up off Pascal's hands.

"Hold on to me," he growls as he lines himself up and then drives in so forcefully I cry out in reply as he seats himself and just holds me there. "Remember who's fucking you," he says as he gazes at me and starts to slowly move back to the wall. "Who do you belong to?" I hardly have any words, but I know the answer to that one.

"You."

He plants his shoulders on the wall, leaving room for my legs, and lifts me up a little. I can feel fingers laving at my core and dragging the slickness back to coat me in my own juices, and as his fingers begin delving in and out to get me ready for what's coming, I moan into it again.

"Again," he says as he looks over my shoulder and nods. It's almost imperceptible, but I can see it, nearly feel it before he even does it.

"You, always. I love you."

I feel the intrusion so quickly I gasp in response and just stare into dark blue eyes as Pascal forces his way in with a slow shove until he's as far in as he can get. My mouth stays open as I get used to the feeling of both of them and wrap my legs around tighter to hang on. We're all completely still as I listen to the groan behind me and his fingers tighten on my hips. Why this has to happen so quickly I don't know, but as I watch those blue eyes looking at Pascal, I suddenly understand. This isn't about me, well maybe to some degree, but this is about them, being together. Alex's hold increases as he slowly lets me down on him again, filling me to the point of me gasping air in and clinging onto his neck for support. At the same moment, Pascal pulls away from me, sliding his cock out and making room for Alex's. Oh god, the feeling is indescribable, almost painful but somehow not. Like being toyed with, cat and mouse maybe. I don't know. I just need more of it. And more love... I want the warmth back in the room. My mouth trails along Alex's throat and eventually finds his lips to pull him closer as he lifts my thighs and gives Pascal his chance again. He takes it with relish as he pushes back in again, harder this time. I groan into his mouth as I feel the brush of material rub against my legs and back, so deep, so very deep, and then moan again as Alex lowers me. In and out, friction and tension. Constant pounding and grunting. Never empty. Over and over again as my body accepts the rhythm and revels in it.

"More," I breathe into his mouth as a hand leaves my thigh and is replaced by Pascal's. I'm just held here as they both use me and fuck me to the point where nothing is clear anymore. I can hardly tell the difference between them as fingers grasp and scratch at my skin. There's perfect synchronicity in their movements as panting and moaning echo around my thoughts, so I close my eyes to just feel the heat of them both. Overwhelming need drives me into Alex again as I hold him close and let him guide the pace, the cadence. It's all for him. He can have anything from me and take whatever he needs because I need to please him, love him. I'll do anything he wants to show him I love him, and that he deserves that love.

Pascal's tongue licks around my shoulder as I feel his body tensing in response to my cries for more. More speed, more power, more force. I can't stop the need for both of them to be less gentle with me. Rougher. I need the roughness. Alex wrenches his mouth away from me and looks at Pascal again. Just one a soft blink and Pascal drives in with such force that I scream out and tip my head back onto his shoulder. Yes, more. His mouth is on mine in seconds, his tongue swirling and panting as he increases his hold of my thigh and then takes the other to support me. He stills deep inside and we turn so that he's against the wall now, then he leans me away from Alex a little so that all I can see is the man I love looming down on me with darkness consuming him. Oh god, and I can't breathe again. As his hand reaches for my throat to hold me against Pascal, I can feel my core clenching around him, gripping and tightening as he drives in again, filling me so completely that I have nothing left to say. There are no words for the feeling as he plunges in again. So full, so inexplicably whole and needy, maybe complete.

"Are you going to come for him, my love? Show me," Pascal growls against my ear as Alex rams in again. Oh god, yes, more, yes.

"I can't..." And then the room is silent, and all I can see is Alex fucking me, fucking me and pinning me to the man he loves, the man I love. There's so much emotion in the moment as I watch Alex's face struggle to hold himself back. He's so close, and I can see the love in his eyes as he stares at me and then at Pascal. He's still here with me, with us. His shirted forearm is straining to stop choking me. I can see that in his eyes, too, as he shoves into me again and again. Teeth bite into my neck and I know I've moaned but there is no sound, only a blissful serenity as I just watch the motion of the man I love and let my body tremble for him.

"Come, now." His mouth forms the words. I know them so well, but I can't hear them out loud. They're just floating around my brain and dragging that feeling through my stomach as fingers dig into my skin. Sweating, panting, growling, moaning. It's all here in this room with us, but I'm drifting somewhere else, just watching those eyes and feeling every deep thrust inside me as he bores into me. My core clamps on to him to try and keep him close as he pulls away for another slam in. I need him deep when I come. I need them both deep inside to remind me what's happening, so I can remember the connection and love them. I reach my hand for his head and pull him closer, and he follows me and grunts into my neck as I clamp on again and again, and only then do those sparks start flying around me. Noise suddenly returns as I hear Pascal breathing heavily and swearing, and Alex grunting and groaning into my neck. Both of them are so close, both of them waiting for me, and so I let it all go, just let the tension explode within me and dig my fingers into Alex's neck. Those lights and stars engulf me as I sense Pascal coming in me first. His head tips away from my neck and he slows his movement to almost nothing and releases his own tension in me, his fingers furiously grabbing at me roughly to encourage my own orgasm. And then Alex stills, too, all of us suddenly lost in our own moments, or maybe sharing each other's as we moan out in pleasure and grasp at sweating skin with need.

Lips meet mine and I have no idea whose they are until I hear the words 'I love you' being breathed behind me. They're Alex's lips, Pascal's words. My eyes fly open at the thought as I wonder who he loves, but as Alex takes his mouth from mine and stares at Pascal, I just gaze at them in awe as their lips meet. Maybe it's for the first time. I don't know, but the moment is so private I feel almost humbled to be a part of it. Pascal is completely still as I feel his hands relaxing on me, and I slide to the floor between them. Their bodies crush into me as Alex presses himself onto me and wraps a hand around my back to bring me closer to him. I kiss at the shirt over his heart and allow him his moment with Pascal with a rush of love for him. I wish I understood the implications of what's happening, but I don't care. Whatever will be, will simply be. If the man I love can feel at ease enough to do this with me, then I can accept it and treasure it as yet another memory to cherish and adore. We are all one in a strange way, a twisted and odd way, and possibly something no one else will ever really understand, but it doesn't change the fact that we are together, all of us.

"I love you," I say repeatedly into his chest as I feel his heart hammering beneath the cloth of his shirt. He is home. This is it now, the three of us. I know this with every beat of my own heart. He's just being all that he needs to be, just showing me, and I couldn't love him any more for it. His honesty and the truth are all I have ever asked of him, and this is another part of it, finally. Truth.

He pulls away after a minute or two and just stares at Pascal. No words are spoken. He just continues gazing and softly rubbing his thumb across my back while his other hand plants on the wall by Pascal's head. He still hasn't moved. Not one inch of his body has changed position as I feel him gazing back and breathing quietly. I know he's doing that. He'll just be gazing with that softer Pascal smile and relishing his connection to the man he loves. I smile into Alex at the thought as I feel their come running down my legs for just a few more seconds, and then decide that they might need to say something to each other, maybe talk, or discuss something that can't be said in front of me. So I gently remove myself from between them, kick off my heels and head towards the shower again. One last glance back before I turn into the bathroom, and I find Alex staring at me with a small smile playing around his lips. It may be a confused one, but it's an honest one, and that's all I care about. I blow him a kiss and head in to clean myself up.

Whatever will be will be.

~

Two sodding hours it's taken us to get here. Two. I could have gotten ready in the car and had more time having sex with my two men. Go me. That would have been far more fun than the London traffic that has been an absolute nightmare, but at least it's given us a chance to talk, I suppose. Not that there's been any clarification on the Pascal thing really. Most of the time he's just sat there sipping his cognac with a smile, looking utterly delicious in his tux. Belle has texted me a few times to see where we are, but other than that, we've talked about business, the future and Christmas.

"Do you want that put on?" I ask as we turn into the drive at Henry's. I know we've got another five minutes because I know how long it takes to get to the Lord of the Manor's house. I've done this driveway a lot.

"Mmm," he says as he hands me his bow tie and turns to face me. "I love you, Miss Scott." Sweet.

He's said that about a thousand times since we got into the car, almost as if he's worried what happened with Pascal is going to scare me off. Not a chance. It may have complicated things in an odd way, but it doesn't make me want him any less.

"So what's the plan with Pascal then?" His brow rises with a chuckle, such a beautiful sound.

"And what does that mean, exactly?"

"Well, you know, he is married." His other brow shoots up. "He needs to do something about that, because whether you understand it or not, you did, in fact, just kiss the man. It was very erotic by the way, quite stimulating, but isn't that called having an affair?" I giggle out as I loop the tie over his neck and start my fingers working. "Did you know you were going to do it when you saw him in the doorway? I mean, he is rather appealing, obviously, but at what point did you decide you wanted that? I can't believe you didn't ask me first."

"He's collared. It's hardly an affair," he says with a smirk. "Last night, and you already gave me permission if I remember rightly."

"I did, did I?" The stupid girly giggle that leaves me has even me rolling my eyes.

"It's okay for you to be in love with another man, Alex. I'm certain you said that."

"I did say that, didn't I?" I reply as I gaze into his laughing blue eyes and feel my heart erupt with love. Truth: that's what I wanted, and that's what I've got.

"Yes, baby. You did. Thank you." I giggle and lean into him again to tie the rest of his bow up, and notice his breathing is restful, almost as if this means nothing to him anymore. His finger just caresses my arm as he relaxes and I pull it tighter then let go. I smile back at him and think of Pascal at his deathly dull duty for the night. He said he'd meet us later to talk. Talk? I'm not sensing there'll be much talking going on at any point really, certainly not with the slap he delivered to my arse on his way out. It still stings a bit to be honest.

"Are you very sore?" he says out of nowhere as I notice the lights of the house twinkling through the windscreen.

"Yes." There's no other answer to give. Being hammered in both ends by two quite big boys is playing havoc with my privates, in a rather delicious way. I'm such a slut. Belle was right. I snort to myself at the thought and watch his hand tighten around the glass he's holding.

"I'm glad," he says quietly. It's to the point, I suppose.

"I thought you said you wouldn't be able to stay with me when that happened, you know, that thing we just did."

"The fucking thing, you mean?" My eyes fly towards Michael in mortification, although why, I don't know. It's not like I'm the virgin bride, is it? But Christ, why is he always so abrupt?

"Alex, could you please try to be a little more discreet? Anyway, my point is, you seemed to be fine. See? Nothing to worry about at all."

"We had to go out. I didn't give myself a chance to play with either of you. We'll be elsewhere when that happens. Call it a moment of weakness if you like," he responds as he stares at the house distractedly and downs the rest of his drink.

The car pulls to a stop outside the rows of other cars, and I turn to see his face changing to an expression of irritation. I know that look now. I've seen it too many times to be able to dismiss it. He's angry, and if he thinks I'm going to be dragged into something distasteful after what's happened this evening, he's very much mistaken. I want to enjoy the happiness floating around, not have to deal with his ever-changing moods and get into a row about something. His hand goes to grab the door handle and I clasp onto his arm to stop him.

"What's wrong? I thought that thing with Henry was over. I assumed that's why we were here. Is something still wrong? Alex, I'm telling you now, I'm not going in there for a fight." Every ball we've been to has ended up in a fight. Well, apart from Berlin.

"I have some things I need to say and then we'll leave," he replies quietly.

"Why the hell don't you say them somewhere less public then?"

"Because *you* asked me to be moral, Elizabeth, and *you* asked me not to kill anyone else. I am trying to be decent about the fact that this fucker tried to ruin me," he says with a sneer. "I will happily do it my way if that's better for you? Is it? Shall we turn the car around?"

It seems we're going in for a fight one way or another then. My heart sinks with the realisation and the reminder of his past. No matter how much I try to dismiss it, he is a killer, isn't he? He's a murderer, who very clearly still has the same tendencies coursing through him, even as we speak. I couldn't feel any less like going to a party all of a sudden.

"Then I'll go home, I think. I can't just watch you destroy him, Alex. No matter what he's done, he's still a friend to me, and so is Sarah. I won't stand beside you while you ruin him. I'm sorry but I just can't." He turns back to me, and scowls, but I can see the real emotion there. It's a look of utter devastation, hidden behind a mask of fury.

"You will get out of the car and act properly," he eventually says, very slowly and methodically as he holds the handle and clicks it downwards. "And I will not ask you nicely again, so don't push this, Elizabeth. Your place is by my side, and I expect you to be there."

"No, not for this I won't," I say as I fold my arms over each other and glare back at him. "There are times when ordering me simply won't work, and this is one of them, I'm afraid. Welcome to the new fucking me. She's the one you created by the way, so shove it up your arse." I swear I hear Michael snort in the front. "Michael, take me home."

I have no clue how this is going to play out, so I stare straight at the front of the car and do my best to ignore the temperature that's suddenly risen at least ten degrees.

"Get out of the fucking car." His words are slow and very exact. I couldn't give a damn. What's he going to do? Carry me in there? I think not. I reach forward for my drink and swirl it around just to prove my utter contempt for his orders.

"No. Home please, Michael."

"Elizabeth, I'm going to ask you one-"

"Or what, Alex? Don't even bother finishing that sentence. There is nothing you can do or say to make me watch you humiliate or destroy him. If you make me choose you over integrity, you won't like the fucking answer. I've put up with everything you have thrown at me, given you everything, and do you know what? It's made me stronger, and far more capable of dealing with your bullshit than you give me credit for. You can go in there and do as you see fit, but I won't be going in with you. You told me I had the moral high ground in this, and you were right."

I'm pretty sure he's staring at me. I really wouldn't know because I'm still looking at the front of the car and hoping nothing untoward happens. With any luck, he'll realise my superiority in this and agree, then we can just go home and relax. I can almost feel his pulse racing next to me as he considers his options, but in reality, there is nothing he can do, is there? I lift my chin up higher and take a sip of my drink as I kick my heels off and lean back into the seat. Relaxed, calm, composed. He will not win or change my mind when it comes to decency.

"Fine, we'll talk about this later," he suddenly snarls out as he simply gets out of the car and slams the door behind him. I look at the door in shock and watch him put his hand in his pocket and walk across to the main entrance, ripping at his bow tie as he does.

"Home still?" Michael says from the front after several minutes of me staring at the door in the hope that he'll come back. I sigh out in resignation and nod my head. "Elizabeth?"

"Sorry, Michael, yes. Home please."

There's a very awkward silence as the car turns round and heads back up the drive. I can't believe that's just happened. After all we've been through, and after all he's said about his past, he still can't be decent about all this. I understand his need to get even, but here? In front of everyone? I dig my phone out to text Belle and tell her I won't be coming after all. Alex will probably tell her I'm ill so I go with that story and say I'm feeling a bit sick. She's so not going to believe it, but what can I do? I can hardly tell her the real reason, can I? I can just imagine her snarling at Alex as he lets rip at Henry in the middle of the floor. And what about Sarah? He told me she was the one to tell him in the first place. Will she be alright? Oh god, I should go back and stop him, shouldn't I? My mouth opens to tell Michael to go back again, but I can't get the words out through loyalty to Alex. Henry did try to ruin him, still might be doing. I don't know what to do. I turn round in my seat and stare at the house in the distance to see if I can see anything. What I'm hoping to see, I don't know. Alex running after us maybe? God, what a fuck up. Why is life with him never just smooth?

My mouth puffs out a long breath, and I slump back down into the seat again, shaking my head. Who do I talk to about this? I suppose I could call Pascal, but how would he have a clue about morals and decency? Maybe I could just talk it through with him, though, just get some perspective on whether I've done the right thing or not. He's the one always pushing me to stand up for myself, be more dominant. My finger has pressed the call button before I'm aware what's happening. It seems I value his opinion more than I thought I did.

"Are you alright?" Michael says from the front. Sweet. No, I'm not.

"Not really, but that doesn't change the fact that I'm not sorry about what I said," I reply quietly as I listen to the ringing in my ear.

"I may have to cut my own throat," Pascal says. My mouth curves into a smile immediately.

"It can't be that bad," I reply as I sip at my drink again and stare out at the dark country roads zipping by.

"It is. How does one endure such tedium? I should be fucking something, or strapping it over a bench. Instead, I am forced to behave appropriately and make your repulsive English chit chat." There's a brief quiet pause as I hear the scraping of chairs and the tapping of a glass. "And I am positive there is a fat man in a horrifying tuxedo about to make a speech. It is quite atrocious. Do you not have tailors in this country for gentry? How is your cunt?"

"Fine, thank you." It's not at all if I'm honest, but I'm damned if he's knowing that. "I think I just fucked up a little bit."

"Really? This sounds amusing. Enlighten me?"

"Well, I'm currently travelling back to the house having told Alex to shove it up his arse because he wants to destroy Henry DeVille. He happens to be one of my oldest friends, by the way. It's just not right, regardless of what he's done. So I told him that and then left."

"The plot thickens," he replies, sounding thoroughly bored again.

"Pascal, I'm serious. This can have not gone down well at all, and I don't know if I did the right thing."

"Did he fight with you?"

"A bit, but I just stood my ground and looked away from him."

"He does so hate to be ignored. Bravo, my dear. Let him poach in his own heat for a time and find his own path back to you. He will return. You should not concern yourself. Tell me to come home to you. We could cause some jealousy, no?" I roll my eyes and try for serious again.

"But what if he-" The car suddenly shoots off to the left and increases in speed, and I find myself being tossed across the seat. Fuck, seatbelt.

"Michael, what the hell are you playing at?" I grumble at him as I wrench at the strap and click it into place.

"Hold on," he says sharply as he swings the car into a right hand bend with the use of the handbrake. Jesus. I grasp the handle and pant into the phone as we zoom up a very dark, wooded lane, still at speed. MI5 arsehole is clearly back on form.

"Is something thrilling happening?" Pascal chuckles into my ear.

"No, yes, I don't know. Michael what are you doing?"

"We're being tailed. Duck down." What? Of course the first thing I do is look out of the back window. "DOWN, ELIZABETH!" he shouts at me.

I throw myself onto the seat and try to peek out of the windows as I snatch at my dress bag and remember the knife in it. He told me to keep it on me. I'm sodding glad I did now. Although what the hell ninja Beth's going to do with it, I'm really not sure.

"We're being followed, I think," I whisper into the phone as I scan the interior for threats. Apparently I can do covert operations now, too.

"Are you? How delicious. My balls are becoming more enthusiastic by the minute. Put me on loudspeaker." Why? I do as he says anyway and keep my face pushed into the leather, hoping for some of those pesky fairies to come help us out.

"Andrews, are you there?"

"Yes," he growls from the front.

"What is the registration?"

"Alpha, Delta, Six, Two, Quebec, Quebec, Alpha."

Several minutes go by as I listen to nothing more than Pascal breathing and Michael swearing as he throws the car around every available corner.

"It is registered to a company I have heard never of. I shall send you the information. Should I be concerned?" Pascal eventually clips, now sounding very businesslike and professional.

"Its professional, whoever it is." The brakes are suddenly slammed on and we skid sideways along the road, bumping and crashing into hedges as we go until we eventually come to a grinding stop. My head flies up again to see what the hell is going on, and I stare out into the foggy night and shudder a little at the image.

"Why are you stopping? For fuck's sake, Michael, shouldn't we keep going or something?"

"I can't. Elizabeth, whatever happens, you do as they tell you," he says, rustling about and undoing his seatbelt.

"What?"

"You do exactly what they say. You keep yourself alive," he snaps again, now digging into his boot and staring out of the window at lights in front of us.

"I... I don't understand, Michael. What are you sayi-" I cut myself off as I watch in terror as he pulls a gun from the middle console and places it quietly in his lap, hiding it with his own hand.

"Listen to me very carefully, Elizabeth," Pascal says quietly. "I want you to talk as much as you can if they take you." What? I can't believe what I'm hearing.

"What the fuck are you talking about? Take me? Why would anyone take me?"

"You are worth a lot of money, my dear. Do not be weak or unintelligent. You must remember everything you see and speak it, as shrewdly as possible given the circumstances, before they take your phone."

"Listen to him, Elizabeth," Michael says from the front. Oh my god, is this really going to happen?

"Michael, I cant..."

"You can, and you will, my dear." It's the most abrupt tone I've ever heard from Pascal. "I do not wish to lose you. You must be in control of yourself. Think, Elizabeth."

My brain scrabbles around for sanity as I sit myself upright and peer out of the window again. Nothing's happening, just a set of headlights shining at us. I swing my head around to the back window to see the same, and then watch in horror as a door opens.

"Oh Christ! Michael, someone's getting out. Do something," I snap out under my breath as I see two figures walking towards the car.

"Breathe, Elizabeth. Make them believe you knew this was coming. They will thrive on your fear if you let them," Pascal says quietly, soothingly. Okay, okay, breathe. Breathe. In and out. In and out. I blow out a shaky breath and grab onto Michaels arm.

"Tell me what to do, Michael. Oh god, I'll do it. I'll do it. What's happening?"

"Stay calm and do as they say," he says as he turns and looks at me, covering my hand with his. "Do as they say, okay?" I nod my head rapidly in reply and watch his eyes crinkle softly with a smile. He pats my hand again, then lets go and turns back to the front. "You'll be fine. Just stay calm."

A figure walks through the gloom in front of us, and Michael suddenly leaps out of the car and starts firing at people. My hands cover my ears, and the scream that leaves me sounds otherworldly. Real fucking bullets are flying around outside the car, and I can see him dodging and running. Where's he going? He's leaving me? I need to tell Pascal what's going on. Fuck.

"Pascal, fuck, there's lots of men. Shit, I can't see how many but Michael's out there and they're all firing guns at each other." I see Michael skirt along the side of the car as two men drop to the floor in front. He bangs his hand on the window by my head. I have no idea what that means, but I duck back down onto the seat in case that's what I'm supposed to do.

"What now?" Pascal says to me.

"I don't know. I'm cowering like a fucking baby on the seat because that's what Michael just told me to do."

"Good. Stay there."

"Pascal, I don't want them to take me. I can't... I don't know what to do." It's all I've got as I listen to yet another gun firing outside. I hear shouting, rapidly followed by another round of shots, so I curl up into a ball and try to stave off my tears. In control. Stay in control. Calm.

That's what he said, wasn't it? Calm.

Chapter 28

Elizabeth

"Elizabeth?" I think that was Pascal but I can't hear anything over my own breathing. I'm just trying to make the sound go away. If it goes away then it might not be really happening to me. "Elizabeth? Speak," he snaps loudly. It's so much like Alex that it drags me back from wherever I was, so I grab at the phone again.

"Yes, I'm here. I need Alex, Pascal. Where is he? I need him. I can't do this. Please...?"

Another shot and a gut-wrenching shout from outside have me swinging my head up in terror to see whose voice it was. Michael? I stare out in shock as I see a body collapse to the floor in the distance. The fog hinders my view, but I know it's him.

"I love you." What? I shake my head and keeping staring at the fog in hope of seeing movement.

"I... I think Michael's been shot, Pascal. I can see him. He's on the floor. Oh god, he's been shot. What am I going to do?" Tears begin pooling in my eyes as I watch the outline of three men gather around his body to kick at it like a piece of meat. He's dead. Michael's dead. No, he can't be dead. It's Michael, for God's sake. Michael's don't die. He has to be pretending so that he can do something else. I keep looking, waiting for him to get up, but he just lies there. He doesn't move. Even as I dig my fingers into the leather seats, he doesn't move or do something to tell me he's okay. He just lies there, looking dead. Dead.

"Elizabeth?" That's Pascal again. I can hear him talking at me quietly, trying to soothe me and make me feel okay, but I don't feel anywhere near okay. Tears are beginning to stream down my face as I keep looking for signs of life, anything. Move, Michael. Just move. It's going to be okay. You just have to move and then... "They're going to come for you now, my love. Listen to me."

"No, I can't. This isn't real. He's not dead, Pascal. He just... He can't be. I don't believe-"

"Elizabeth, I love you." *I love you, too.* My ears try to focus on his words as I watch the men start to make their way towards me, but I just keep staring at the lifeless body on the ground. I can't see or compute anything but Michael until they start to get closer and I can make out their figures coming at me.

"They're coming. I can see them, three of them. They're walking towards me, and Michael's just lying there, Pascal. He's just-"

"What do they look like?" I flick my eyes over to them and try to see, but it's misty and dark.

"I don't know. It's foggy and I can't see properly. One's much taller, though, with dark hair. They're all in suits." I try to make out some differences, something to give him a clue, but it's just too murky to see accurately. "The shorter one's got a crew cut, I think, and a slight limp maybe. I don't know. Michael's dead. He can't be-"

"Keep talking, Elizabeth. Keep holding your phone, and speak to me until they take it from you, do you understand?" he says firmly, now sounding slightly out of breath for some reason.

"Pascal, I'm scared. What if...? I don't understand what they want with me. I haven't done anything wrong. What if they hurt me? I can't do this."

"You are an expensive commodity, my dear. No one damages that which is of value. Just do as they say until I can find you. If they do try to harm you in any way, think of the man you love, remember how much pain you can take from him."

Pain? Fuck. I'm not sure if that's a comforting thought or not as they get closer. I can't stop the fear coursing through me as I pant into the phone and try to pull myself together. Michael's out there, and he's dead. He's been killed. I'm not ready for any of this. This wasn't supposed to be real. He told me and I knew, but I never thought it would affect us. Who would want me? I turn round to face the front and keep trying to regulate my breathing, stay in control, look indifferent. My feisty Beth tries to help me but I can't quite latch onto her. Michael's dead. This is real. I can hear their sodding voices now, too, chuckling and laughing to each other, and all I can see is another man hauling other possible dead bodies across the ground towards the car in front of me.

"They're here, Pascal," I whisper as I see the tall one's body at the window. A car door slams from his end of the line so I picture his face as the phone goes quiet in my hand, and I tuck it into my lap. My other hand is grabbing for my bag and wrenching it to my side. The car door opens and the man crouches down until I can see his face.

"Aiden?" I'm sure I couldn't look anymore in shock if I tried. "What are you doing here? What is this? Why are you...?" I can't even finish. I know he's part of this world, but I thought he and Alex were friends, sort of.

"Elizabeth Scott. You're quite hard to get hold of on your own," he says, chuckling and rubbing his thumbs around each other as he leans his elbows on his knees.

"I don't understand. Did you just... just shoot... I mean, kill Michael?" I stammer out as I try to hold eye contact.

"No, I think that was Mark." Laughter erupts outside as I nervously stare into the eyes of Aiden Phillips in utter confusion. The man touched my sister and manhandled me. He's the very reason all of this happened with Alex in the first place, isn't he? The reason he became a murderer. Arsehole. Some kind of anger begins in the pit of my stomach. It's like a lightning bolt of rage, grasping at my guts and telling me do something, anything. Hurt something maybe. Michaels dead, and this arsehole is bloody laughing about it? I swallow down the last choking sob that's weakening with my oncoming fury and turn my body to face the man. "Now, I need you to come with me and be a good little girl. Alex has something we want, and you're going to help me get it, one way or another." There's more laughter and jeering, as he holds a hand out to me, and chuckles to himself about something.

"Fuck off, you revolting piece of shit," I spit at him and scowl at his offered hand. I'm not sure that's doing as he says, but fuck him. He just killed my friend.

"Still wild, I see," he says as he backs away and nods at the car. Two men are on me the instant he does, and I feel the phone slip from my grasp in the struggle. I'm kicking and screaming at every available opportunity, clinging onto my bag for dear life and swiping it at heads as I do. I will not go fucking easily. *Do as they tell you.* The words come drifting through my head. *Be in control.* Shit. My body goes rigid as one of the arseholes grabs both of my arms and shakes me about to get my attention.

"Stop struggling, bitch," he snarls at me. I haul in a long breath and stamp on his foot with my heel. He howls in pain and pushes me away from him, so I stumble across the dirt and turn back to him with another snarl.

"Don't fucking touch me again," I snap out at the bald little shit. Feisty Beth is back, it seems. Thank God. "Just piss off."

"Knock her out if she's gonna be like this," the other twat says. I whirl round on him with my best 'fuck off' face and clutch tighter to my bag. If he takes one damn try at that, I'll stick this knife in his chest so quick he won't know what's hit him.

"He wouldn't be very happy about that," Aiden replies. Who wouldn't? Alex? You're fucking right he wouldn't. "Get the drugs." Drugs? What?

"No, Aiden," I near scream in response with my hands up at him. "I'll come quietly. No drugs."

"I bet you don't," he says with another chuckle. They all laugh again, and start leering at me. Nothing is fucking funny here, and as I watch one of them coming at me with a syringe, I realise that nothing is very funny at all. Not at all. I open my mouth to protest again, but Aiden's hand is covering it in seconds and I'm pulled across to the waiting needle. My feet try to halt the movement, but I haven't got a chance against him as he keeps dragging me towards it. He's too strong, and his grasp is just as firm as Alex's, in just the same places. Precise, practised.

Oh god, what am I going to do?

"No, Aiden, please..." I feel it pierce my neck and just stare into the eyes of the other man as he smiles at me while chewing on his gum. Eventually, Aiden's hold loosens a little, so I try to move, but I can't. Nothing works. Not even my speech seems to work anymore. Everything's so heavy. Every limb seems to be fighting against me as I start feeling lightheaded. Tired, I'm so tired. I can feel my mind trying to force my vision clear, but it's blurry. Everything's suddenly unfocused and fuzzy. Tired... Maybe sleep will be good. Maybe it'll all be over when I wake up. Michael won't be dead, will he? He'll be okay. And Alex will come for me, won't he? He won't ever leave me. He told me he wouldn't, that he'd protect from this sort of thing, that he'd always...

~

ABSORBING WHITE

I open my eyelids slowly to see a dark room. Shit, my head hurts. Why does my head hurt? And what is that smell? It smells like earth, or chalk or something. I stretch my face around with a shake to try and get my brain functioning again, but everything just seems hazy or dulled. My senses feel like they're not functioning properly at all, and why does my back hurt so much? I put my hand down to the bed but feel a cold bumpy surface instead. It feels like rock or granite against my palm, which instantly makes me turn towards it. Rock? Why am I on rock? Where the hell am I?

Trying to focus on my surroundings, I slowly, and quite painfully, pull myself upright to get my bearings. The whole earth seems to tilt a bit, but thankfully, as my night vision kicks in, I start to see the outline of the room, or maybe area would be a better description. There's a door at the far end, but above me seems more like a cave than a room. It's all grey, or very dark anyway, and I can hear dripping water or liquid of some sort, and Christ, its cold. Wrapping my arms around myself, I stand and instantly fall back down to my arse as my legs wobble beneath me. I try again and again until eventually, they begin to support my weight without concern. There's nothing here to notice as I edge my way around the blackness. There's no furniture that I can see, or light switch I can find as I travel my hands over the wall near the doorway. There is a lock on the door. I can feel it, but there's no key in it to help. I press my ear to the door in the hope of hearing something, but it's utterly silent. All I can hear is that dripping noise, and maybe the occasional tumble of stones or something, but certainly no voices. It's just me, in a large, very dark and cold space. So I go back to my piece of rock and sit back down again to try and think of a way out. *Just do as they say, my love.* Do as they say? They're not saying anything because no one is here. It's just little old Beth Scott in a fucking cave.

I can feel the tears coming, but I try to suck them back up because that's not going to help anyone, is it? And if I'm going to sodding die, I refuse to look like crap when I do. I suddenly remember my bag and search around for it, for my knife more importantly, but it doesn't seem to be here. There's nothing here. Only me, and a fucking cave. I tuck my legs up and sit cross legged so that I can wrap the material of my dress over me to cover as much as possible. If I can keep warm and hold myself together, someone will come. Eventually, someone has to come. It would be nice if it was Alex or Pascal, but even if it's Aiden, at least something will be happening.

I wish I knew how long I've been sat here. I have no idea of what time, or even what day it is. I've heard that drugs can knock people out for days on end. Have I been sleeping that long? Oh god, I'm cold. And I need a drink. Why isn't anyone coming for me? Pascal told me I was an expensive commodity; you'd think they'd treat me with a little more respect if I were. Some heat would be nice at the very least. Eventually, I can't stand my shivering anymore so get up again to see if moving around might help warm me up a bit. I could do some jumping jacks, I suppose, get my heart rate up and ready me for ninja Beth to take over at some point. I sneer over at the door and command myself into action. I need to be ready to kick some Mafia arse when it eventually comes, find that rage thing again and use it to full effect as and when I need to. The sodding drip of water keeps falling. Drip, drip, drip. Who am I trying to fool? As if Beth Scott has got any chance against these types of people. Drip, drip, drip. I so wish that fucking dripping noise would stop. I can't damn well think for that constant irritating sound. Drip, drip. Oh god, shut up. Drip, drip.

"Stop dripping," I tell it, quietly. I'll find it in a minute and block it up, or drink it. Drip, drip. Fucking noise. Where is it? My senses come into effect to help me find it as I remember his safe room. Quiet, dark. Think, block out everything else and focus on the sound. Use your body, scout out the threat, attack and defend. Be still. I stand perfectly still and close my eyes to find that peace that gives me the ability to feel the damp air around me, hone every sense on just that one thing so I can find it, and kill it. My feet walk me slowly across the rough ground until I eventually hit a craggy wall with my fingers, and I can feel the water running down it. Following it down, I find a small pool of liquid. How do I stop the sound, though? My hands swipe at the wall to try and knock the water off course, but the same sound just keeps dripping, never ending, drip, drip, fucking drip. I need to stop the fucking sound. I need to conquer the challenge, be the victor, and win the game. I can't stop the giggle that bursts through my throat as I think of Alex trying to solve his problems, or manipulate something to his advantage. He'd have a way of stopping the water. He'd have a way of stopping anything. Where is he?

I give up my fight with the wall and go back to my rock. At least I found the water. I solved the mystery, so to speak. Fucking water. Jesus, is anyone going to come and get me? What's the point of taking someone and then just leaving them in a room? Drip, drip, drip.

"SHUT THE FUCK UP!" I scream at it, hurling a stone along with my voice. "SHUT UP, SHUT UP, SHUT UP!" I'm suddenly across the room again and throwing any piece of gravel or dust or stone I can find at it. Then I'm down on my knees, scrabbling around in the dirt for anything to remove the pool so that it just stops dripping. The constant damn noise is irritating me. I can't think with that racket going on. I want some peace to think. Kill it, stop it, noise, noise, fucking incessant dripping. It's making me almost crazy. My fingers scratch and scrape until I'm filled with heat for my efforts. More and more gravel gets piled and tossed at the threat until I can hardly inhale anymore. "Shut up, shut up, shut, up," I keep mumbling to myself. I have to stop the sound, have to make it stop, just stop so I can breathe again.

A strange realisation hits me as I'm lobbing everything at it. Is this what Alex feels like? Is this what makes him do it, kill people? Is the noise too much? Is his childhood so constant that he can't breathe for the constant pain and disturbance of it? I launch more gravel at it before I abruptly sit back on my haunches and listen for the noise. Gone. No dripping. No noise. Peace at last. Fuck you.

I heave in a breath and stare into the darkness with a sneer firmly planted on my face. Round one to feisty Beth. Ninja Beth will be along shortly. Oh, god that is what he feels like, but with real human beings instead. My little wobble at the water might only be a snippet of what he feels, but it's the same, isn't it? Just an amplified sound nagging at him, telling him to find some peace, to stop the barrage of hurt coming at him all the time. That's why he does it.

A sudden clank behind me has me jumping to my feet and swinging round to face the door. The lock clicks, and then the room finally floods with some light. It's still dull, but at least I can see now to some degree. A man hovers in the doorway with a flashlight, so I cover my eyes as he points it up at me and laughs. I wish people would stop fucking laughing at me.

"Come on out, Elizabeth Scott," he says as he points the light back downwards again. The voice is familiar. I don't know it, but the tone resonates somehow. "It's time."

Time for what?

He turns his back and begins to walk away. Part of me is desperate to stay in my cave with my rock. Nothing happens here. It's safe. But I have to know what's going on. Does this that mean Alex is here somewhere? I'm walking towards him so fast I trip over a large boulder and crash to the floor before I get to him. He stops and turns back to me, his torch now trained on me so I can't see again. "Careful," he says as he reaches a hand down. My breathing accelerates three fold as I recognise that hand. All the lines are in the same place, the nail beds the same, the length of the fingers, width of the palm, even the tone of his voice now echoes around my head.

"Alex?" I mumble out.

"Close," he replies as he grabs my hand and lifts me up in front of him. I instantly stumble back from him as his face comes into view, snatching my hand from his as I go.

"You're, you're..." That's all I've got as dark blue eyes bore into me. So cold, just like his son's used to appear to me. There is no mistaking who this man is because I can see Alex in every feature. Every contour is etched with the same lines, cheekbones, brow bone, his mouth, nose. He may be older, but even his frame stands as Alex's does. Tall. Strong. Dominant. Evil.

"Richard Adlin, it's a pleasure to finally meet you."

I have nothing, absolutely nothing. The immediate urge to kill this man is coursing through me. My arms clamp around me to keep me away from him. He reeks of deceit and lies, and there is nothing warm in his voice. All I can see is a four-year-old boy standing by his feet and crying, bruises littered all over his body and broken bones aching as he waits quietly for the next beating to come.

"I hate you," I spit out.

"Yes, I thought you might," he replies slowly as he turns and begins walking again. "Still, if you want to see my son again, I would suggest you follow me."

Alex is here? I need to get to him and help him, or he needs to help me. I'm not sure which, but the arrival of his bastard father has me infuriated. Picking up the front of my dress, I stomp after him with my best in control face planted on and step out of my safe place. There are tunnels and corridors leading off everywhere, and it quickly dawns on me that I'm in a mine of some sort, or maybe an old nuclear shelter. The ground beneath us is still made of chalk dust as I clip along it with my heels and try to maintain my balance, but it's harder here, as if it's been trodden on for years and worn down. Dust flies around as I watch the bastard shining his torch towards the end of the tunnel and fight off the need to stab him in the head with something.

Eventually, a huge room comes into view. It's obviously an old meeting place of some sort. There are tables and chairs dotted around and a light source coming from the other side of it. I weave my way around things until we reach another doorway, where he turns and looks at me.

"I'll warn you now, it's not overly pretty in here, and if I didn't need you to make him see sense then I wouldn't make you part of it. Unfortunately, he's as stubborn as I am," he says with a smile and a nod at the door.

"What? I..." What the hell is happening? He opens the door and my hands fly to my mouth.

There's blood splattered everywhere. The dirty old walls are covered with red streaks of blood, and as I turn the corner, I can see why. Alex. He's handcuffed between his legs to a metal chair in the corner, still in the remnants of his tux, with blood across his face. One of the six men grabs me instantly and sits me opposite him on another chair, so I just gaze into his eyes and hope he's got some sort of plan. There is no pain on his face, no concern either. He just lifts the corner of his mouth at me and then looks back at the others again with a blank stare.

"Where is it, son?" the bastard asks behind me. Son? I could rip his head off for saying the word. He has absolutely no right whatsoever.

"I've told you. I don't know," Alex says quietly. "And no amount of beating me is going to help me find it for you."

"Come on, Alex. It was there and now it's gone. Stop being a dickhead. Don't make me hurt your little lady to make you see sense," Aiden says irritably as he comes into view from the corner.

"As if I give a fuck about her," he replies, drawing in a long breath and looking at the floor. Once upon a time I would have worried about that response. I would have been scared enough to believe what he said, but not anymore. I know how he works now. This is a distraction technique to make him appear not to care. Probably in the hope that they'll let me go, or at least not bother going too far on me. Well, I hope it's that anyway. I stare over at him and put my best shocked face on. Hands grab at the back of my dress and rip open the halter neck until it falls down in front of me, and I'm left with my breasts on display. I instantly go to cover them, but then notice the slight twitch of his mouth, that miniscule muscle that tells me he's pleased. No one else can see it, and no one else can hear him telling me to stay still, but I can. I can hear him talking to me, asking me to trust him, telling me to just do as he says and everything will be fine. I lower my hands nervously and watch him staring at me.

"Nice tits," one of the twats says. I stiffen a little as a hand reaches across my shoulder and grasps at my right boob, roughly.

"You're going to give me a floor show now?" Alex says with a chuckle. "I've watched other things fuck her. It's old. I'd frankly rather you just beat me." That's a little harsh. I scowl at him in reply and watch him sneer back at me. *Don't listen to me. Stay still.* I can hear it plain as day, swirling around my mind just as it did with the two of them – just as it always has, if I think about it. Every time I've been nervous of something, there's always been a voice telling me to just trust him, to just believe him and let him guide me. I never knew that was him, but now I do, and now I can finally hear it, crystal clear. *I love you. Stay still.* So I do, and I let the idiot grope at me, and then I let the other one walk in front of me and lift my dress up to my thighs, pushing it and dragging his stinking hands along my skin with a lewd smile as others laugh in the background. Is this what's supposed to be happening? What the hell is he trying to achieve here?

"There's no fucking point in that. He clearly doesn't give a damn about the girl. He'll just watch us fuck her and probably enjoy it," Aiden says as he swipes something off the table beside him. My eyes fly around to the noise and I watch him pound the table in fury. I smile to myself at the fact that he's losing control, and just look back at Alex again as the guy between us disappears again. He's staring nonchalantly over my head again now, more than likely at his father.

"What now, Daddy?" he says with chuckle as I hear the clink of metal against metal. I slide my eyes down to see him moving his hands around a little. Is he trying to get out of those cuffs? Where's Pascal? It's not possible that this is going on without him being involved somehow. He said he'd find me so he must have told Alex about all this in the first place.

"Well, son, I just want my money. It's mine by rights, so if you don't know where it is then perhaps we should ask Elizabeth instead. It's not like I'm stealing it from you," he replies as he walks around in front of me and stands behind Alex with his hands on his shoulders. I stare in horror as I see him flinch. Just the touch of the man is enough to cloud his eyes over with fear. His body may not move, his frame no less bored, but his mind is rolling over every memory he's got, reminding him of every horrific memory and drowning out his future. *I love you. Stay with me.* I'm chanting that at him, hoping he can hear it, hoping he's got enough energy to stop himself falling into the blackness again. He's no fucking use to anybody there. For once I need that animal to come out and play. We both do.

"Elizabeth, do you know where my money is?"

"I... I don't know what you're talking about." I actually don't, unfortunately. If I did, I'd tell him without a second thought, because anything to get us out of this would be good.

"He bought some land in Shanghai, and then when he transferred the money, my special little friend stole it from the account. And now it's gone. Any ideas?" he asks, now rubbing at Alex's shoulders and kneading them as if he has some fucking right to touch him.

"Gone?" I couldn't give a shit. Just get your hands off my man.

"Yes, some other whizz of a computer expert must have stolen it from me." Computer expert? Conner? No, surely Alex would know about that. None of this would be happening if that were the case. He'd have planned it, organised it. I thought Henry was the problem with the Shanghai thing, anyway. What has any of it got to do with this bastard?

"I don't know what you mean," I reply as I scan the room for anything of use. I'm not sure what I expect to do if I find it, but 'planning' Beth has apparently got ideas I'm not privy to just yet. I lock onto my bag in the corner then instantly flick my eyes away from it again, wondering if they've been in it.

"Just leave her out of it. Or fuck her. I don't care, but she doesn't know anything," Alex drawls out as I hear the clink of metal again. I throw my eyes back at him and then back at his bastard of a dad in confusion.

"I think she does, son, and I think if I show her what real pain feels like then she might just remember who the fuck has my money," the bastard says, now rolling his sleeves up and smiling at me. Oh god, that smile. It's so much like Alex's, so much like his sister's. Sister? Evelyn. She knows computers, doesn't she? Maybe she's got something to do with all of this. I never did fucking trust her.

"I don't know anything. I would-" The blow to the side of Alex's head, sending him to the floor, happens so quickly that I hardly have time to blink before the chair is hauled back upright again. Laughter erupts behind me and I just stare in shock as he grunts and shakes his head to right himself again.

"I think you do, and I'm certain you'll remember if you're forced to," Alex's dad says without any trace of emotion. I just gaze into his eyes, looking for anything to work with, but there's nothing. He looks just like Alex in his dark place. Bottomless pools of emptiness stare back at me as he loosens his tie and takes it off. He slowly puts it around Alex's neck and continues his achingly unhurried movements. They're measured and precise as he draws the knot upwards and keeps his eyes on mine. Fear races through me as I try to keep myself together somehow. He's going to strangle him? He can't do that. "I... I don't know anything. I promise. If I knew, I would tell you, but I-"

He pulls it tighter. I get up to stop him but hands slam down on my shoulders to hold me in place. It doesn't matter how much I struggle; there's nothing I can do but watch Alex be strangled by his father in front of me. "STOP! Please... I don't know. It was Henry, wasn't it? I thought Henry De Ville was doing something." The bastard immediately loosens the tie a little and looks back at me with a raised brow.

"Henry DeVille is brainless. Tate has been reasonably useful, but Henry was just a deception. The prat thought he was in control because he knew my son here killed his cousin," he says with an irritated huff and then a deep intake of breath. "Elizabeth, who's got my money?"

"I don't know. I don't know anything about his business." Oh god, I wish I did. I'd give anything to know what the hell the man wants as I watch Alex straining against the tightening tie again. The bastard just keeps pulling it. Why would you do that to your son? Why? I can see the veins rising on his throat as his face turns red, and I watch him gasp for air quietly as if he hasn't got any fight left in him. Enough. I don't care what this ploy is. I can't watch it anymore. I struggle madly against the hands pinning me to the chair, but I still can't get away. "Alex, tell him, please." Nothing comes out of his mouth. He doesn't even seem to be trying anymore. His body is just still as the bastard winds the material around his fist for another pull. His eyes have that glazed appearance, as if he might not even be here anymore. Doesn't he care that he's about to die? "PLEASE, ALEX!"

Fear, panic, rage, they all seem to merge together at the vision in front of me. My man is being strangled, choked, and I have to do something, anything. My arms fight more against the dick holding me down, my legs begin kicking out, sending my heels flying, and my head slams backwards repeatedly in the hope of hitting him, but I can't get him. Nothing is working, and even if I do manage to get to my bag, what good is a knife against guns? Nothing. I can't move. I can't help him. Is this it? Am I going to watch my world being destroyed by the very man that ruined him as a child? No, it's not fucking happening. I heave so hard and fast on my legs that my body slams up into the man behind me and sends us flying backwards. The struggle breaks his hold on me, and within seconds, I'm hurtling towards the bastard trying to kill my man. I can see his eyes widen as I scream at him and launch both sets of nails at his face. I'm scratching and grabbing at his ears, eyes, anything to get him the fuck off Alex. In the midst of my attack, I hear movement of some sort, metal clinking and the rushing of feet maybe, but I don't give a damn who's coming anymore, or what they're holding. I'm in kill mode. Rage is overtaking any sense of logic, and this bastard is going to die for his behaviour. I feel my teeth sink into something and relish the taste. I don't even know what it is, but it's flesh, and the cry of pain that sounds around the room only heightens my need to do it again. So I bite in harder and cling onto the bastard as he tries to prise me off. My legs begin pushing harder beneath me, forcing him into the wall so he can't escape my grip and grabbing at his hair. I'm ripping at it ferociously to try and cause as

411

much damage as possible. Then we're spinning as I climb up onto his frame and hang on tightly. There are other hands pulling at me, yanking at me to try and get me off the fucker. No, this is my chance to show the bastard how much I hate him. I'm like a wild dog, biting and yelling and hitting out to make him feel the hurt he's caused.

A gun fires and I still don't care. What are they going to do? Shoot me while I'm wrapped around the dick? I can't think of anything but destruction, like some sort of motherly instinct has taken me over and is forcing protection mode to kill the threat, or annihilate the possibility of harm.

"Get this fucking whore off me," he yells from beneath me as my arm finds his throat and tightens around it. I can do this – just keep fucking squeezing until the bastard drops to the floor. I'll fucking show him a real monster. It was here in me, lying dormant until he forced it out. He took the most precious thing in my life and tried to kill it in front of me. *Squeeze.* This is what happens when you love someone. You protect them, and you'll give anything to keep them safe. *Tighter.* You offer your life to make sure they're happy, contented and secure. Safe, just keep him safe.

Another shot, rapidly followed by another, brings my head back to the moment a little, and I catch a glimpse of Alex moving with the metal chair in his hand as I spin by. He's swinging it at Aiden's head as I try to hang on and keep squeezing this throat. His body moves fluidly, those muscles working rhythmically as they're supposed to once more. His handcuffs are now dangling from one wrist as he bellows in anger and metal connects with flesh. Aiden crashes to the side of the room at the same time as my back connects with something hard over and over. I want to scream out in agony, but there is no noise, only silence and the sound of Alex thundering around, killing anything that gets in his way, demolishing anything that dares touch him. Vicious, violent strikes and brutal punches as another man comes at him while he tries to get to me. I can see his eyes deadening with every move, as he fights his way to me. I can feel his need to save me overwhelming him as I watch him twist a man's neck so ferociously that he drops to the floor instantly beneath his feet. There's another shot and I gape in horror as blood bursts from the white shirt at his shoulder. He doesn't even flinch, not even a slight recognition of the injury as he storms toward his attacker and launches blow after blow at his head. His legs are just continually spinning and whirling as he keeps raining hell down on the guy so that he can come for me. I watch another man coming up behind him and scream out a warning.

"ALEX, MOVE!" Pain suddenly explodes in the back of my head as it connects with something. It's enough to dislodge my arm a bit, and try as I might to cling on, the need to protect my head consumes me, so I let go and feel myself sliding down towards the floor. My body is hoisted and lifted until I'm in front of the bastard and his hand is around my neck. I kick out for all I'm worth but his grip is too strong, too hard, and I haven't got anything to fight with as my feet scuff the floor in protest. I'm exhausted from trying to hang onto him, and I can feel my body giving up as his fingers tighten around me.

"Whore," he growls as he yanks me around until I'm still in his grasp. I just keep watching Alex demolishing his threats. One of them now lies on the floor, spitting up blood as the other attempts to defend against his oncoming death. I couldn't wish for death more if I tried. It's like some bloodlust frenzy has taken over and all I need is for everyone in this room to be dead except for Alex and me. Just Alex and me, together and safe.

"STOP!" his bastard father roars across the room. Nothing. Alex just keeps going, lost in his own world as he slams another fist in and smiles at the crimson splatter that leaves the guy's face. "Tell him to stop or I'll break your neck," he says to me. He can fuck off if he thinks I'm helping. I'm too consumed by the vision of absolute beauty as Alex primes himself yet again and roars in fury at the room. He's covered in blood, fists closed, with every muscle straining for release as he continues on his darkened path. That's his path. I can see it now. I can see him in his element and revelling in it. I may be his peace from it, but this is as much a part of him as I will ever be, and if I die watching this, if it gives him more chance to survive this fight, then so be it. I couldn't be any fucking happier with the image I'm left with.

Chapter 29

Elizabeth

My feet are dragged across the room as I try to speak. I'm trying to call for Alex, but I can't get any words out because if I do, it'll distract him from his task. I can't put him in any more danger, even if it means I'm taken off somewhere else. I just need to know that he can deal with the men in that room before someone kills him.

"Fucking women," the bastard drawls out in my ear as he yanks me towards the doorway, and I see Aiden haul himself upright and move back into the room to join in. "Leave them, Aiden. We'll deal with this another way. They'll all be dead in ten minutes anyway."

Two turns later and I try to hold on to that vision in my head as we leave the room and I'm heaved across towards a tunnel. I wish I could say I was fighting, but I'm not because there's no fight left. As long as Alex comes out of that room safe, I've done my job. Whatever happens to me isn't relevant anymore. I couldn't care less. I just keep listening to Alex's quietening growls and hear the screams of pain leaving the other men in that room. The bastard's right. He'll kill them all. Guns or not, he won't stop until all of them are on the floor, lifeless and bleeding out their sins. Then he'll come for me. When he's ready, he'll come for me and he'll find me. These two excuses for human life will be killed, regardless of my fate. They must know that. They must know they're not safe anymore. They've taken me from him, and whether I live or die, he won't allow them another breath, will he?

The light from the room starts to dim and I see Aiden point a torch in the direction we're going to brighten the tunnel. I don't know where that is. It certainly isn't the same way we came in. What does it matter anyway? I'm almost amused. If they think they've got any chance of surviving this, they're so wrong.

"You're both going to die," I chuckle out to myself as Aiden grasps my arm and keeps tugging me along. "I hope you think the money was worth your lives, you bloody morons."

"Shut up, bitch," Aiden replies as he backhands my face and grasps on tighter. I've had harder strikes from girls, or maybe I'm just used to the man I love showing me he needs me. He needs me. My smile widens at the thought as I picture him holding me down and fucking me, making love to me in his own particular way as his fingers grip me and push me. Harder, faster, more pain. Pascal was right. There isn't much this body can't take anymore. Or this mind, come to think of it.

"You're both going to die, and I hope it really, really fucking hurts." I can't find a more eloquent way of saying that, and I'm so amused by my response that I burst out laughing in near hysteria. What does any of it matter anymore? I'm a fucking Mafia queen. Feisty Beth is kicking butts all over the place and contemplating murder of her own kind.

"What now?" Aiden says to the bastard. I'm still laughing, now at his utterly moronic question. What now? Get ready to die, you idiot.

"Have you been to church recently?" I don't know where that came from.

"Shut the whore up. I can't think." I'm getting a little irritated with being called a whore by this arsehole, so as Aiden tries to slap a hand over my mouth, I snap out at his fingers until I feel flesh. He grunts in reply and shoves me down to the floor before I know what's happened, then delivers his boot into my stomach. I wheeze out a breath at the impact and pull myself into a ball to defend myself in case another one comes. Pain ricochets around me as he kicks me again in the back and sends my body shooting across the rough ground.

"This isn't fucking playtime. Shut the fuck up when you're told," he snarls above me. I clutch onto my stomach in agony and keep looking at the dirt. The longer I stay down here, the more time is wasted, giving Alex more time.

"Playtime – such a tantalizing word, is it not?" My head snaps up at the sound of Pascal's voice, and I peer down the tunnel in the hope of seeing him. There's nothing there to see, only the echo of his voice and a small light at the far end. "I do hope you were not planning to leave."

Where is he? Aiden's hand is on the back of my neck, dragging me to my feet so sharply I can barely keep them beneath me. I'm

415

promptly placed in front of him as some kind of human shield. "My love, are you injured?"

"Don't answer him," the bastard snarls back to me, quietly, now scanning his options as he looks around to try and pinpoint Pascal. Aiden's hand covers my mouth so I just stay quiet and keep staring forward. I'll hear him before they do. I'll know what I'm supposed to do and when, because either Alex will tell me from behind us, or Pascal will from in front. I'll feel them, won't I? I'll hear them in my thoughts and understand what to do.

"Perhaps it would be wise to enlighten me of her wellbeing. If she is not yet dead, I may not kill you both."

"Can you see anything?" Aiden whispers to the bastard as he switches off the torch.

"No, is there another way out of here? Where is your gun?"

"I shall come and find out for myself, yes?" Pascal says as I hear the crunch of gravel moving towards us. Aiden pulls out a gun from somewhere and points it forward, so I writhe around in his grasp to try and dislodge it, or at the very least, send it off course, when Pascal appears. I scream into his hand to try and send some sort of warning out, but it's too muffled to hear. Whistling comes floating along the tunnel, and I can't quite make out where it's from until the bastard spins and looks behind us. Yes, it's from behind, and then another voice joins it, both whistling the same tune, almost as if they're answering each other.

"Knight to king four," my favourite voice calls up the tunnel. I have no fucking clue what that means, but I'm so happy to hear his velvety voice that I sigh into Aiden in relief. Not that this is over, but he is alive at least.

"That is a terrible move, dear boy. One should use one's rook," Pascal calls back.

"Knight." It's harsh and totally commanding.

"I do so enjoy it when you are irritated. Are you still aroused? I can smell the blood from here. He really is at his finest when he has engaged his savage frivolities, Elizabeth."

I have no idea what the hell to do with that thought.

"Knight to king fucking four." That actually sounded quite pissed off.

"Yes, yes, if I must. Really, I am not dressed for this occasion. Are you ready, Elizabeth?"

Ready for what? I have no idea what I should be ready for. No one is speaking to me. There are no voices floating around. The only thing I'm even vaguely in control of is the gun that's still pointed towards Pascal, or rather the body holding it. Oh, am I supposed to do something with that? I suppose if I was quick enough I could knock him off course, or battle him for it. I just nod into Aiden's hand, as if that's some sort of answer, and hope I know what to do when the time comes.

"Nicholas, I will kill her if you don't let us out," the bastard shouts into the dark, with a slight panicked edge to his voice. I close my eyes for a second and picture Alex. He's probably crouching in the gloom, watching me, waiting. He'll be rubbing his hands into the ground beneath him, getting ready for whatever move is about to unfold. I can see his eyes and his smile at the tone of his father's voice. It's possibly the only time he's had the ability to make him nervous, be in complete control, and he must be laughing at that, enjoying it even.

"Let her go and I'll let you leave," he says from the darkness. It's his calm voice again, the one that tells me he's utterly in control of everything around him. It sends a rush of warmth across my skin, regardless of my current predicament.

"Do you think me a fool, son? I made you. Aiden trained you. There isn't a chance in hell you'll let us leave here."

There's a sudden grunt from behind me, and I'm forced to the floor as the gun fires from Aiden's hand. I wrangle at his arm for control of it, but I can't seem to get any grip, and he's just too strong, too heavy. Something wet begins to pour across my skin as we both lay there fighting in the darkness, and I hear the sound of running coming at me from everywhere. Shoes scuff the earth as I heave on the arm and try to point it towards the bastard, but I can't see him anymore. Aiden tries again to dislodge my arms from his wrist, so I just keep gripping as tight as I can and then try to bang his hand on the stones. Someone flashes in front of me, and then begins grasping at the gun in Aiden's hands. It's three of us now, all roiling around in the dirt for control of the damn thing, and I'm not fucking letting go of it. I have no idea who's who, but I must keep control of this gun, must keep it away from Alex. I can't let anyone but me have this fucking gun.

"Do let go, my dear," Pascal says. Oh, it's him. I instantly release my grip and shove and push until I'm almost clear of the writhing bodies, then stare back into the dark to find Alex. There's nothing there, still only blackness, but I can see the bastard again. He's hovering by the wall, looking around in every direction as I scramble backwards to the side. Pascal is just standing there, still in his full tux, with the gun in his hand as if he's held it a thousand times. His foot is lodged over Aiden's throat. I look down to see that I'm covered in blood and scream in response to it as I check myself for injuries. There isn't any, but I'm still fucking screaming because there's so much of it. It's everywhere and I must be injured if there's this much blood. I brush at it while kicking my feet around in some kind of frenzied attack at it, trying to wipe it off, but it's seeped into the fabric and I'm panicking.

"I'm hurt, Pascal. There's blood, fucking blood everywhere... I'm..." I keep swiping at it and twisting myself to look. It's all over me, covering my skin like some kind of death omen. "Pascal, fuck, I'm dying. Christ... Help me Pascal. I can't. I'm..."

"Perfectly well, my dear. Aiden's blood. He is very nearly extinguished, I think."

I scan the body beneath Pascal's foot and find it also doused in the same substance. His breathing is ragged, and that horrendous gurgling noise keeps popping out of his mouth. "You could always pull it out and put the repulsive inadequacy out of his misery." I stare up at him and then back down to Aiden. Pull what out? I'm not touching anything, certainly nothing that is anywhere near Aiden Phillips. I push myself back into the wall a bit, pull my knees, and the remnants of my halter neck back up and wait for whatever's coming next.

The sound of feet coming along the tunnel has me staring into the murky gloom, searching for him. I just need to see him, to see for myself that he's alive and well. I know I've heard him, but I need to actually see his body, check for myself that his heart is still beating in his chest. There's still nothing as I wait. The crunching seems to go on forever, and I almost jump out of my skin when he suddenly crouches over Aiden's body in front of me. Pascal doesn't flinch, not in the slightest, and I just gaze into blue eyes and smile weakly. He scans me from head to toe as his bloodied fingers brush across my skin to check for damage. There's plenty of it for him to touch, but I can't feel any pain as he wanders his hands over me. All I can feel is his skin on mine again. His touch reminds me that there's a reason for all of this, that I took this pain for him because I love him. His shirt is barely there anymore, and what's left of it is crimson, and his face, oh his beautiful face, is covered in cuts and bruising. He was shot. I saw that. I look at his right shoulder and see the blood still coming out of it. I reach out to touch a split on his lip then rub my palm gently into the rest of his cheek, my cheek, my man. He's alive.

"Are you okay?" I ask quietly. He chuckles, looks down at Aiden, and then with a few quick shoves around, yanks something out of the side of his neck.

"Still trying to protect me?" he says as he holds up my knife and wipes it on his shirt. I flip my eyes down to what's left of Aiden and watch his breathing finally give in as the sound of his last, gurgled breath leaves his body. "You do know you're going to be told off for your heroics, don't you?" he says with a slight smirk.

"I just... I couldn't see a way out, and that bastard was going to..." I can't even say the words as I watch his eyes boring back into mine.

"I told you to stay still."

"I know. I heard you, and I was going to, but..." He stands up mid-sentence with a scowl and turns away from me to look at Pascal, who's still pointing the gun at his father.

"That was not knight to king four."

"No, this is true. However, Elizabeth got in the way. And your aim is pitiable."

"Pitiable?"

"Disgraceful. You are dulled in your retirement, Sir."

"In my defence, I did throw it left handed." Pascal barks out a laugh and nods at the bastard still loitering around near the wall.

"What are we doing with this?"

"Having watched Elizabeth, maybe we should let her at him again," Alex says as he holds a hand out for me. I grab on, and feel myself being pulled up with a quick jerk until I'm by his side. He watched me? As if he could see anything but the six men he was attacking. "Anything hurt?"

419

"Yes, lots of things hurt. But I'm not in pain. You saw me?"

"Mmhmm."

"Did I miss something exquisite?"

"Yes, quite flawless really," Alex replies as he picks up my chin and checks my face again. I stare back at him with a grin and decide to feel reasonably proud of my random attack strategy, given his approval. Although, I still get the feeling I'll be getting a talking to at some point. I step around the lifeless body of Aiden to move closer to Alex and frown at what I'm part of while these pair joke with each other. People have died here. They're dead. Michael included.

"What should your creation do, Daddy?" he says as he takes a step away from me toward the man and lets go of my hand. Pascal lowers the gun and half stands in front of me, so I try to peek around him but he pushes me back again.

"I want to see," I whisper into his shoulder.

"I am positive you do not, my love," he replies as he wraps an arm around my back to hinder me further.

"Now, son, I am still your father," the bastard says. I shove myself away from Pascal and step around him so I can watch the bastard squirm. I need to see it as much as Alex does. I need to be part of this, so I can remember it with him, so I can hold him in his darkest moments and remind him of his power over his nightmares. He flicks my knife around in his hand; over and over it twirls as he approaches the arsehole, as if it's a part of him, like he's spent so much time using it that it's an extension of his arm somehow. It's odd to see him wielding it. I know I just saw him beating men to death, but that was defensive. This isn't. This is threatening, a kind of pure malicious intent as he steps again. Each footfall is now filled with antipathy, or maybe a just a complete lack of that decent emotion I've tried so hard to pull from him.

"What would the man you created do with you? Have you always known? Always watched me? How long have you and Aiden been working together?"

"Son, it's not..." the bastard says, slightly nervously as he tries to back his way along the wall to head up the tunnel towards the light.

"Stop calling me son and answer my fucking questions," Alex cuts in menacingly as he blocks the path and sneers at the man. The bastard retreats a few steps and stares back at him in fear, so I flick my eyes back to Alex again and watch him going quiet. I can see his fury building. I can almost feel it pouring off him as he grows another few inches and tilts his head at his opponent. He's going to kill him, isn't he? He's going to kill his father, and I'm going to have to watch it. Something inside me shakes its head at the thought. It just keeps nagging at me and telling me that this is wrong. Rational Beth is, for some unknown reason, trying to break through all this destruction and bring some sort of calm back. Not that the fucker deserves it, but it's one thing doing all of this when you're under attack, when you have to defend yourself and protect the ones you love, but we're not there now, are we? We're safe now.

"ANSWER ME!" he roars out. I swear the walls tremble around us, and the sound echoes up and down the tunnel so loudly that even Pascal flinches beside me. The bastard just stands there looking sheepish. It's funny really, to see the man who tortured him as a child being scared. It's very nearly enough to shut rational Beth up. I can feel her retreating and feisty Beth yelling at him with every breath she's got in her body. She's still clawing at his face and wanting revenge for all the pain the man caused. But it's wrong, isn't it? Immoral. That's my power in this. That's what he said he'd given me, the moral high ground in this sort of thing.

"I have always watched you," the man eventually says as he dares a step forward. "You are my son, and Aiden has always worked for me."

"What does that mean? Why would he work for you? You're a lawyer," Alex replies, clearly confused as he stares back in astonishment. This seems to give the bastard some kind of authority again because he's suddenly storming over towards Alex, his eyes darkening as he does. Pascal raises the gun again slowly so I stick my hand out in front of it. There will be no more death here.

None.

"Alex, we should leave now," I call over to him, suddenly just wanting to get away from all of this and get home, where it's quiet and safe. He turns his head to me and then quickly back to his father.

"Explain what that means," he says again, now standing two feet from the man.

"Alex, let's just-"

"My empire, my sons," he says slowly as he cuts across me with the most evil smile I have ever seen. My hands shoot to my mouth. Sons? Plural? "One of whom is now dead, thanks to the other."

Alex reels back from the statement, and I watch his feet flounder beneath him as he keeps walking backwards. He looks over at Aiden's body and shakes his head, tilting it as if he can't work out what's going on. His brother? He just killed his brother? Oh god, what must he be thinking? I go to move to him, but Pascal drags me back and pins me against him.

"Leave this for him, my dear," he says into my ear as he tightens his hold.

"But he needs-"

"To find his own peace, his way," he cuts in firmly. So I just watch Alex as he continues backwards, his feet tripping over themselves as they go, stones tumbling and crashing around him as he bumps into them, until he eventually turns, and runs. The dust kicks off his feet, and all I can see is the outline of his form against the light coming from the exit, just his blackened frame powering away from yet another dark nightmare so he can escape it. Oh god. He just killed his brother.

My eyes swing to Aiden's body, and I have no idea what to do with it. I also have no idea what to do with the bastard now chuckling on the other side of the tunnel, but I can feel that fucking rage welling up inside me so quickly I can hardly control it. I wrench myself from Pascal and don't even try to contain myself appropriately.

"Is something funny?" I ask, arms waving and body ready to pounce again at any fucking minute.

"No, my son is dead and the other has just run away from me. You'll forgive me for not knowing the correct response, you fucking whore," he replies, his tone suddenly full of menace and irritation, enough so that I actually stop my waving arms a little and gape. Who the hell does he think he is, calling me a whore, again?

"Well, you just did that, didn't you, you fucking arsehole? What did you expect? I can't believe someone as disgusting as you even exists." Oh, yes. Here it comes. It's going to flow from the depths of me. Arsehole. "I hope you rot in hell for what you've done. Should we kill him, Pascal? What a thought, ridding the planet of such a despicable human being. Or would it be better to just let you live with the fact that you are so despised that your own son runs from you rather than tainting his hands with your blood?"

"I suggest you tone that-"

"You suggest?" I'm actually getting closer to him in my fury, stalking him down, readying myself for the kill as my feet pull me towards him. "You are hardly in any position to suggest anything, are you? You have nothing here, nothing. He's mine now, and if and when I choose to let you explain any further, I'll let him come for you. He's mine. Do you understand that, you waste of a fucking human?"

"He needs to be with his father. He is my son," he shouts as he moves towards me. I hear the foot falls of Pascal getting closer to me, ready to protect me at any given moment, so I continue into him and decide to have another go.

"Oh my god, you are mad, aren't you?" My arms are going again. "Of course you would have to be to have caused such pain to a child, but you really are insane. Do you think you have some rights over him? Some sort of power? You don't. You are worthless to him, and I will spend the rest of my life ensuring he never thinks of you for a second longer than he needs to. He is mine. He is with me. Mine. Just turn around, walk back into that cave, fuck off, and then die somewhere before I let Pascal kill you."

That's it. There is nothing more I have to say to the man. I land my hands on my hips and spit at him in disgust. It lands on his shirt, so I continue to stare him down and prove my utter superiority in all of this, regardless of his increasingly growing stature. He may be evil, dangerous and completely mad, but I have a gun pointed at his head, and a man who's ready to use it. I also need to find the love of my life.

He sneers at me and flicks his eyes over my shoulder. Pascal growls.

"This isn't the last he'll hear from me. There are things he needs to understand," he says as he turns from us, and heads back into the darkness. Yeah, I'm sure it's not, but with any luck, we've just scared him enough to make him piss of for at least a while. "He is his father's son, Elizabeth Scott. You'd do well to remember that," he calls with a chuckle. I scowl at his back and snort in revulsion at his laughter. He is nothing like his father, and he will never hear any words of wisdom that infer anything of the sort. I just continue to snarl at him with my hands on my hips until my fury is enough that I pick up a stone and hurl it at his head to make him move quicker. It more than likely went nowhere near him, but that's not the point. It's the thought that counts. Arsehole.

"My love, you are quite venomous," Pascal says over my shoulder as I follow the retreating figure with my annoyed glare firmly in place. Something crashes into the wall, and I jump in response and turn to search for the threat, my arms out, ready to attack. The gun bounces to the floor near a pile of rocks.

"We might still need that," I snap at Pascal in irritation, still feeling feisty Beth ready to kick some Mafia butt. What's he doing throwing it away?

"Indeed. Regrettably, it is empty."

"Empty?"

"Yes, thoroughly used, useless, quite ineffective. Thankfully, he was not aware of this fact," he replies as he grabs my hand and walks us towards the light rather quickly.

"Oh my god, did you just let me say all that when we had no protection?" He looks down at my feet and then at himself. That bastard could have killed us. He could have had a concealed weapon, or a knife, or he could have just beaten us to death.

"What did I tell you about your shoes? Have you not learnt to run in them yet?"

"I'm sorry. I was in the middle of trying to kill that bastard."

"Look at my suit. It is distressed, as am I. I may need a drink," he says, brushing at it and reaching into his pocket. He pulls out a hipflask and I just stare at it in response as he offers it to me. "Drink, my love. I should carry you, yes?"

Apparently, I don't get a choice in that matter, because the moment I take the flask from him, he scoops me up and begins striding off again. I swig at the liquor inside, not giving a damn what it is, and offer it up to his lips as we move. He drinks liberally and then nods back at me again until we eventually reach the light. Is it daytime? I don't even know what day it is. I have no clue how long we were in there.

"What day is it?" I ask as we reach a black car.

"New Year's Day," he says as he puts me down beside it and checks his watch. "4.30pm to be exact. We should get back. He will be in need of us when he returns."

"He's been shot, Pascal. He has a bullet in his shoulder. What he needs is a hospital and medical care. I know he needed to get away, but you'd think he'd have some sense about his own wellbeing."

Shot. Michael was shot. Oh god, Michael is dead.

"We have to find Michael. His body, I mean. We have to-"

"We have already dealt with that," he says as he waves a hand at the array of other cars near us. All of them have had their boots prised open.

"Was he...?"

"I am afraid so," he says as he looks across the top of the car at me.

I duck my head down with a sigh and slide into the front seat. It seems we haven't all made it out of this alive. A good man died, for me. I look down at the blood-soaked tatters of my dress and try to imagine his face, his smiling face, and then his children's faces assault me, looking at me and condemning me for putting him in any position where that might happen.

"Do you have a jacket or something?" I mumble out. He pulls a long black coat from the back seat and drapes in across me, then starts the engine and reverses out at speed.

"Sleep, my dear. You will need your rest," he says as we drive across some kind of bridge.

I stare out of the window at the quarry we appear to be in and watch the lack of any movement. It's New Year's Day. Happy New Year. What a sodding welcome to it.

Where Alex is, I don't know, and as we pull out onto the road, I wonder how he's feeling, if he's okay. I wish he'd stayed with me, just stayed and held onto me instead of running and letting himself fall into his father's words. I could have helped him, wrapped my arms around him and let him cry, or let him shout at me, or even let him use me if he needed to. I don't know; anything he needed really.

"Are you not tired?" Pascal asks.

"Tired? I'm exhausted. I'm also covered in blood, Michael's dead, I'm thirsty, and concerned about Alex. The last thing I'm going to be able to do is sleep."

"Should I tell you a bedtime story while we drive?"

"I'm hardly a little girl anymore, Pascal. Certainly not now," I snort out in reply as I tuck my legs up beneath the coat and try to cover the sodden dress beneath it. The sight makes me feel sick, so much so that I suddenly throw the coat off and start ripping the fucking thing from my body. Every shred of it is torn and yanked until it's just fragments in my hand. I throw them into the back and pull the coat back over me to cover me up again, although why I care about Pascal seeing me is beyond me. I twist around in the seat to look at him and collapse the side of my face into the headrest. "Do I remember you telling me you loved me?" He raises a brow and keeps his eyes forward.

"Mmhmm, it was a moment of disadvantage. You were distressed," he says, pulling at his bow tie until he can flick the button on his shirt open.

"You mean you don't?"

"Let me tell my dastardly fairytale. My feelings are perhaps better understood that way. You will comprehend my adaptation of love more successfully after it. It is somewhat like your vision of *Dracula*."

I smile weakly at him as he pulls out a bottle of water from somewhere and hands it to me. I sip at it as he begins talking of Counts and castles, and of fathers and young girls. I listen as he tells me of mothers and their limitless power over men of moral obligation, and I nearly weep as he talks of the repercussions of his actions, and the guilt that, even now, continues to wear him down. Only a little, of course.

It's the first time he's ever been so open, so brutally clear about who he is and where he comes from, and I can't help but lap up every word like a puppy learning how to live, how to survive and conquer the world he lives in – that they both appear to live in. His every word is truthful, regardless of whether he believes I want to hear it or not, and he delivers his story with the oratory of a master wordsmith. I cry, I laugh, I swoon and I gasp at his story as he takes me away from Alex for a while and lets me find some sense in his story instead of my own. He just wraps me up in his European accent and allows me a brief respite from everything that's happened so I can breathe and relax. And I couldn't thank him more for it, or his transparency.

We eventually pull to a stop somewhere and I snatch a look out of the window to see the door of Eden looking back at me.

"Why are we here?"

"He will come here," he says in reply as he gazes at me with a small smile. "So, you have my beginning to my present day. There is only one other that knows the entirety, and he made me tell him the moment he collared me."

"Lucinda doesn't know?"

"She knows some, but not all. She is manipulative with her information."

"And Alex isn't?" He chuckles and stares at me as he reaches out a hand for my cheek, then brushes his finger over my lips.

"You are quite extraordinary, Elizabeth. Thank you for allowing this."

"Allowing what?"

"The kiss yesterday. It was unnerving for both of you." I search his eyes for anything to condemn him, or show me a lie or some kind of naughtiness that shouldn't be here in the midst of this honesty, but there's nothing. There's only real love shining back at me from him that I normally see so little of, and for the first time, I think I feel completely comfortable in his presence, as if I could ask him anything and he'd tell me the truth.

"There is nothing unnerving about being in love, Pascal. It is what it is, and will be what it is meant to be. We will find our own comfort in the how's and why's, I'm sure. But I doubt, in all reality, I allowed anything. You know he does what he wants."

"He would not have done this without your permission, Elizabeth. You still do not see that which is obvious, do you?"

"Not really, no. Sometimes I think I do, and maybe one day I will, but I'm still confused most of the time. There's a lot to understand about him, this world and you."

"Hmm," he replies as he stares again and shows me those brightening green eyes with a genuine smile. He eventually opens the door and steps outside, and I watch him stretch his frame out. "Come, my dear," he snaps, in his most Pascal voice, suddenly full of that normal devilish aggression that I adore so much. I giggle at his transformation and shrug myself into the coat to cover my near naked body. It appears his weakened state has disappeared again, and the man I know a little better is back, although, after that story, he'll never be that version again to me. He can't be. I know who he really is now, and I'll never let that image go because that's the only one I want.

He's precious to me.
And it's the one we'll all need to make this work.

Chapter 30

Alexander

Fucking noises. Noises, sounds and voices screamed at him, constantly rattling around and taunting him with their rallying cries of anger, of hate.

Quiet. He needed to find the quiet. Eden. Just get to Eden.

Traffic blocked him and taunted him all the way there. Children hung out of windows, laughing and joking with each other as they celebrated New Year's Day. His own birthday. Sisters, brothers, mothers, fathers, aunts, uncles, all on their special walks to bring in the new year, to make the day unique. He sneered at every single one of them and downed another scotch as the car slowly turned around the corner. He'd made it unique. He'd killed his own flesh and blood.

He still couldn't come to terms with that. *His brother*. It was always possible his dad had had affairs, but Aiden Phillips? They looked nothing like each other. It must be a lie, yet another thing to confuse him, or make the bastard feel like he was in control. What the fuck was Jacobs doing in that room? He was probably still in there, bleeding to death along with the other fucking idiots that tried to hurt his angel, tried to take her from him. He snarled at the thought and brought the bottle up to his lips again. Everything had been a lie. Henry, Jacobs, Aiden. And now Michael was dead, the one man he knew who was a decent father figure. Dead. Gone. Because of him.

Guilt consumed him at the image of the man as he'd hauled him out of the boot and placed him carefully in the car of one of Pascal's colleagues. He'd damn near ripped Pascal's head off when he tried to touch him. He was probably just offering comfort, but it hadn't been what was needed at the time, nor was it now. Not that kind of comfort anyway. That was reserved for his angel, for the woman who held all of him in the palm of her hand. Never had anyone protected him as she did. Never had he witnessed such a blind, vicious attack to protect something that was loved. It was akin to a wolf protecting its cubs, or a lioness her pride. Vicious, hateful, wild and uncontrolled. Beautiful and all-consuming. He'd been so engrossed in her assault for a few seconds that he'd forgotten where he was. He'd just watched her and relished the moment she dug her nails into his father's eyes to cause as much damage as she possibly could. For him. She could have been killed, gang raped, sliced, and yet all she had been bothered about was saving him from another beating, or that fucking tie. He snarled at the image of the bastard touching her, thinking he had some sort of right to ever go near something as precious as her. She was a goddess compared to likes of him, a beacon of heaven shining over the darkness that lived in him, constantly trying to show him the light and prove his worthiness. Even when his father had delivered the information about Aiden, she had still been there, floating around in his head, stopping him from doing the one thing he so desperately needed to do. She probably thought he was scared, confused, but the reality was he needed to kill the man. That's why he'd run. He needed to rip the limbs from his body and then slam his head into the wall repeatedly until his skull crushed in on itself, until the madness in the bastard's mind was nothing more than a slurry of liquid in his hand. He'd run to be decent, to try and give her the emotion she required from him, to prove how much he loved her. He'd run before he killed out of sheer frustration.

He pulled the car up opposite the black door and gazed at it while circling his shoulder around. He could feel the pain twisting inside his flesh, grating and reminding him he wasn't as invincible as he'd previously thought. It was only a flesh wound, painful, but it wouldn't do any real damage. He'd been stabbed more effectively than this, but it still fucking irritated him. Thankfully, the idiot that shot him was probably thinking far worse by now as he was pinned to the floor by a chair leg through his chest. He was another one of Jacob's henchmen, another one that would die for their stupidity, slowly.

The door of the building opened and a couple walked out. She was dressed in a long coat, probably covering what was beneath it, or possibly what wasn't, and the man held her by the back of the neck, gently, protectively. It occurred to him how much decency there was in this lifestyle as he tilted his head at the couple. It would be an odd concept to many, he was sure, but it did have its rules and its obligations. It was essentially built on trust. Yes, there may be a few who walked outside the boundaries, himself included sometimes,

Pascal always so, but the indecent mostly sought each other out for their needs. Most managed to find a pairing that was suitable. It was more realistic than the real world that he was currently sitting in, in reality. More fair, less judgemental. It was a family of sorts, a place to express oneself honestly, openly. That's what Pascal had been teaching him all this time, to let himself go, to be anything he needed to be inside those walls, to give everything he had at those who would accept it, relish it, and worship him for it.

He raised a brow at the thought and wondered if Pascal knew what was coming. He probably did. He'd probably brought Elizabeth here, made her sleep and ready herself. He'd also probably calmed her, maybe given her a little information about himself to help her feel connected to him, safe even. She wasn't, and he could feel that consideration coursing through him as he tapped the steering wheel and stared at the door again. He should leave. He should stop himself right now and just go home. He should call her and tell her to get a taxi back so that they could talk, have a drink, relax and unwind together like normal people did. She would be scared, worried, anxious. She just needed a night's rest and to be held, to be told how precious she was and that he'd never leave her alone again. That's not what he wanted, though. He wanted to sink so far inside her that he'd forget the day and remember only her at the end of it. He wanted to exploit every malicious thought to its full advantage, use her, use Pascal, and bind them all together in a hell that only they could endure. He wanted to hear her scream for him, and he wanted to watch Pascal bleed for him. He could feel his own fingers tightening at the possibility as he scanned the door yet again and tried to push away the image of his father. He just needed to stop the fucking noise. *Brother, empire, worthless, useless.* He couldn't stop them. They kept fucking assaulting him and driving him to just open the door and get out.

After another ten minutes deliberating the idea, he did just that. Got out. He walked across to the door and banged on it so hard it shook. He was going to get her and take her home where she'd be safe. The door opened and another faceless man waved him in, so he walked straight to Pascal's office in the hope they were there. They weren't. There was only a maid who looked shocked at his intrusion as she cleaned the bookcase.

"Where is he?" he asked.

"I think he's in his suite, Sir," she replied efficiently as she curtsied, stared at his bloodstained shirt in horror and then looked at the floor. He shook his head at the dramatics and turned for the corridor again. Why Pascal had to have everyone bowing and scraping was beyond him. Two turns and a staircase later and he was opening the door to the apartment. It was open, unusually. It was a good job, given the fact that he didn't have a key.

"Alex?" her voice asked quietly as her face peeked around from the wingback chair she was sitting in. She smiled and lifted herself from the seat to walk towards him.

"We're going," he said in reply as he scanned her for injury, again. She was wearing a skirt and a top that didn't belong to her, but she seemed unharmed, and clean.

"Okay, you need to see a doctor. We can stop on the way," she said as she made it to him and put those silken fingers on his face again. "Are you okay?" He couldn't stop his lip from curling as she brushed her other hand across his shoulder gently to inspect the damage, increasing his already aggravated state as she did. He snatched at her hand and pushed it away as he tried to tame the inevitable.

"Get your things. We're leaving," he said again, hoping she would do as she was told so he could get her away from the possibility of Pascal tempting him any further.

"Okay," she said as sarcastically as she could manage, as she frowned at his hand and swung her body away from him. "Or how about, *'Are you okay, baby?'* Or, *"Thank you for putting up with my shite, baby.' 'I fucking love you,'* even. How about one of those instead of grunt language?"

He scowled at her temper and stormed across to get her as she turned into Pascal's bedroom. That's the last place he needed her to be. He was hit with the vision of the man himself, reclining on his bed in trousers and a shirt that was undone.

"Sir," he said as he put his hands behind his head and smiled.

"I'm taking Elizabeth home," he replied, watching her like a hawk as she slipped some heels on as seductively as she possibly could and grabbed at a coat of some description. She had no fucking clue what she was asking for.

"It seems Alex is being a dick, Pascal. We'll do this another time, yes?" she said as she purposely pushed her breasts out and wandered over to presumably kiss the man.

"Of course, my love. Whenever he is ready."

Ready? He was more than fucking ready. Ready to cause all sorts of harm to anything that would give him a chance. He screwed his fists tighter at the thought and turned out of the room before the need to fuck her and beat Pascal senseless overwhelmed him.

Nothing happened as he waited for her, nothing, and then she fucking giggled. He turned back to find them kissing, Pascal's fingers twirling her hair as she sat beside him on the bed and he pulled her closer. Then the moaning began, her voice calling him to her, her voice and Pascal's hands, together. There was nothing he could do to stop the rush of adrenalin coursing through him, and there wasn't a thing he wanted to fucking do about it anyway. His could feel his cock hardening beneath him as she kept mewling, and he could sense the need to have all of it plaguing him. He watched the man's hand wander closer to her perfect tits, loosening her top from her skirt and then caressing its way across her skin until it reached its target. Sensitive fingers at first, as always, just to tease him, goad him to ask for more from the man.

"Is this what you want?" he growled at her. She dropped her head onto Pascal's chest. He could feel her questioning herself as she hid her face from him. "Look at me, Elizabeth, and tell me you want what you're offering me." Pascal kept stroking her hair, somewhat protectively. Alex stared at him until he got the message and looked at him.

"I will look after her," he said. "I give you my word." His angel's face peeked up from her hiding place and gazed at him.

"Is this what you need?"

"Yes." There was no point denying it, and for once, the conviction in Pascal's eyes was honest, true. Given what they'd just been through, he hoped it was anyway. He glanced at them both again and waited for her to speak.

"Okay, yes," she said quietly. His body had turned and left the room before his mind was completely convinced about the idea. She'd said yes. That was enough.

"My suite, ten minutes," he shouted back at them as he shut the door behind him and went in search of another man. Any fucking man. Anybody would do, maybe a woman, too. A sudden clatter along the corridor behind him made him spin to find her running at him, and then quite literally launching herself into his arms. He grabbed hold of her weight as she wrapped her body around his and kissed him so fiercely that he struggled for breath. Her teeth nipped delicately and her tongue laved with his until there was no noise, nothing, just the two of them leaning on a wall and finding themselves in a moment of quiet.

"I love you, I love you, I love you," she said between breaths as she pressed her hands into his hair and rained kisses down on his face, then pulled away to look at him. "You stay with me. You remember me when this happens, and prove to me how different this is, okay? I need that from you."

He looked back at her and tried to answer, tried to tell her that he would, that he'd see her face and not just use the lifeless form in front of him, but he couldn't. He couldn't get the words from his throat, and he wasn't going to lie to her, so instead, he pushed her off him slowly and watched her lips tremble. He watched them until his cock was aching to just fuck her here and now, just slam her into the wall and ravage her before the throbbing was too insistent.

"Come with me," he said as he grabbed her hand and led her through into the main room. There was a party in full swing. Pascal had probably ordered the event for New Year's Day, and the noise was excessive. As if he hadn't got enough going on in his own head. He scanned for suitable candidates and caught sight of a man he'd had in the room before. He didn't know his name, didn't fucking care either. He walked over and stared him down until he bowed his head and nodded.

"Now," he said, tilting his head in the direction of his suite.

"I don't want any other... I mean, I'm not doing..." She stuttered from behind him.

"They're not for you," he replied as he raised a brow at two women dressed in leather, who walked by and giggled at him. They'd do as well. He flicked his head at the man who was making his way to the room, and they both trotted over like the good little things they were.

He pushed his way through the crowd until he eventually made it to his suite and pressed his thumb down to gain access. His angel sneered at the other people waiting by the door, probably to prove her superiority. She really didn't need to.

Ripping what was left of his shirt off, he told the three to wait outside and made his way to the bathroom.

"I need cleaning," he snapped at her as she followed him. "And I need you naked. Now." The time for excessive words of love was over. Her face was slightly shocked but she nodded and started to remove her skirt as he turned on the shower and dragged the rest of his clothes off. The water invigorated him to some degree, revitalised his bruised skin and brought back a sense of cleanliness he hadn't felt since they took her from him. But he couldn't get rid of the images still assaulting him: her being held captive, his father trying to kill him, again, and Aiden lying dead in the dirt as he pulled the knife from his body and wiped the blood on his shirt. Over and over again they rolled through him. Murderer – useless and worthless. But he wasn't worthless, was he? He defended her, defended himself even. Nothing was planned. He killed to survive this time, nothing more than that. He killed for her.

A soft brushing across his skin brought him back to the woman in front of him. She was gently swiping at the bloodstains on his body, no doubt trying to remove the image from her own mind as she worked meticulously. He grabbed her chin and kissed her perfect mouth again, kissed it until her hands wrapped around his cock and offered him an instant release. The heat, the smell and the warmth of her had him needing to come almost instantly, so he pushed her down to her knees and rammed himself inside her mouth as deep as he could. His hand braced against the shower wall as he forced her back to it for more leverage. The sound she made as her back hit it was electrifying. He'd hurt her, and the satisfaction that coursed through him at the thought made him fight to stop coming. On and on he drove into her mouth as she squealed and gagged on him. There was nothing soft about his hands as he took the first part of what she was giving him with abandon and reminded himself what he needed from her, from them.

"Does it hurt, Elizabeth?" he asked, pulling out of her and tapping her chin up. She nodded and tried to keep the tears from falling from her beautiful eyes.

"Yes, it hurts, but I want it, I want you," she replied quietly as she stared at him and opened her hungry mouth again. He was so quick to shove himself back in again that she coughed around him, so he got closer and kept still to let the vibration set him off. Her throat constricted and trembled as she tried to move away, but there was nowhere to go, and there never damn well would be. He felt it start in his balls and just let her keep retching. Every nerve pulsed and quivered as her fingers suddenly dug into his calf to ask for mercy. He let go and groaned as he filled the back of her throat, then kept driving in until there was nothing left but a brief silence from the noise in his head. Silence. Her hands slapped at him again, bringing him out of his quiet place so he finally let her breathe again by pulling out.

"Fuck," she muttered as she gasped for air beneath him.

"Not yet," he replied as he pushed his head under the flow of water. He heard the door close in the main room and smiled to himself as he pictured Pascal in there, waiting for him. "Are you ready?" he asked as he stepped from the shower and walked straight out of the bathroom. He couldn't be bothered to dry himself or put clothes back on. What was the fucking point?

Pascal was sitting there in the chair, a smirk adorning his face as he stared at the three imbeciles who'd been invited. The two women were hovering in a corner, one of them looking nervous for a Domme, while the man was smiling at Pascal as he winked back at him.

"None of you touch her unless she asks for it," he said quietly as a naked Elizabeth walked out and crossed the room to Pascal. He'd give her that much before he lost himself. She could make her choices herself if she chose to. "And why are you still dressed?" he continued as he walked to the wall and picked up a whip. Then another. He threw the first one on the bed and nodded at the cross. No one moved.

"Do you want me to make you, Pascal? You're normally so agreeable."

"I do not wish to be tied, Sir," he said as he stood slowly and pushed Elizabeth behind him. Hmm, it was a considered point. He nodded in agreement and looked back at the cross again to wait for him.

"Elizabeth?" he said as he heard the rustling of clothes.

"Yes?" she replied.

"Do I need to strap you down to ensure you don't try to stop this?"

"I..." That wasn't a good enough answer, so he pointed her towards the cross, too. She looked confused for a second but obviously got the message as her perfect arse walked across to it. She wouldn't take the first round; even in his agitated state he knew she couldn't take that, but the safest place for her was by Pascal. He watched her walk and tightened his hold on the whip as the world quietened down. He couldn't hear anything but the dull thud of his own heart and his breath – slow, calm, methodical, like a psychopath readying himself for torture. Nothing was off limits here. He could hurt anything in this room and they would thank him for it, be pleased with the results to their skin as they left the room on their fucking knees and begged for it next time. Pascal eventually walked past him and met his angel over there. She just looked at him and nodded when he pushed her back to the cross. How Pascal knew what he wanted was yet another confusing thing, but at the moment, he couldn't give a damn. He just needed all the noise to stay quiet, and watching them, feeling the atmosphere around him and languishing in it, was keeping it at bay. There was no father here, no brother – just them and their loyalty to him.

Her eyes widened a bit as Pascal pushed his body into hers, covering it, and whispered something into her mouth. Then she looked over at him and smiled nervously. They looked effortless there as Pascal braced her hands out to the side and opened up his back as the target. She just hid behind him and kept her face out of the way. Everything between them was in perfect symmetry, legs spread and arms out wide. He could hardly see her for Pascal's precision as he covered her entirely and just waited for the first strike. But she'd feel this pain. She'd feel every grunt and shout as the man took what he offered and revelled in it. She'd see for the first time the level of damage these hands were capable of, and she'd be part of it.

He watched a breath leave the man's body and flung the whip at him so hard the sound of pain bellowed around the space. The instant raised welt only spurred him on to do it again and again. Different angles, higher, lower, more and more as he heard the man panting and swearing in front of him. Stripes littered his body as he felt his own arm muscles constantly tensing and relaxing. She screamed as savage strikes landed and he saw Pascal's weight suddenly shove into her at the contact. Then she tried to move away, or maybe look at him, but the next strike had her hiding again as the man yanked her back inward to protect her from the pain. *Pain.* He rallied another hit, and then another, and stared at Pascal's body, waiting for him to drop or surrender. He couldn't give a fuck if he did or not, because this couldn't stop. More and more the man had to take. More pain, more agony, more. It had to go on this time until all the fucking noise just gave up taunting him. He had to make it all end so he could give her that peace she was after.

Fathers and brothers were suddenly there again, racing through him and reminding him of himself as he watched blood appear on skin and smiled at it. *Murderer, killer, despised bastard child.* Pascal grunted and fell against her, still trying to hold their weight up as Alex reeled his arm back and threw the whip at them again. He heard a yelp and half halted his swing as her hand wrapped around the man's waist. Was she trying to protect him?

"Move your arm," he managed to say as her face appeared over the man's shoulder. She looked scared, horrified even, and his eyes tried to give a damn but his arm wanted the added expulsion. His own butchering hands and mind needed to see the man on his knees, bleeding, begging, calling out for mercy and howling in pain. She didn't move anything, just kept staring at him and digging her fingers into Pascal's back to help him stand. He swung the whip again with such precision the tail caught her fingers harshly, and he watched her face screw up in agony as she closed her eyes. She still didn't remove her arm, though, just kept it there and then wrapped the other around the man too.

He was still clinging to the top of the cross, still trying to keep himself up for more. That was his fucking job, wasn't it? That's why he'd collared the man, so he could do this, and as he let his arm fly again, the man roared in response and buckled to his knees. She sunk down to the floor with him and wrapped her arms tighter, trying to draw him away from the whip, away from him. He snarled at the image and walked up to them to pull her away. More. There was still so much more hurt to cause. He threw the whip on the floor in disgust at the man's weakness and pushed her off him.

"Move," he snarled out as he grabbed Pascal's arm and began dragging his weight back upwards. He'd strap him on that cross if he couldn't keep his weight up by himself. Fucking useless piece of shit.

"No, Alex, stop. He's had enough. Can't you…"

He couldn't hear a word she was saying as he pushed the weight up and started to clamp wrists into cuffs. More pain, more agony, less fucking noise. Peace, fucking quiet, and no fathers or brothers to criticize his mind with their endless fucking blare of voices constantly violating his harmony. There was no fight in Pascal's body as he hauled it around, just some grunting and groaning as he tightened the cuff and let his body hang in front of him. Stripes and blood and welts decorated his skin, and he chuckled at it as his hand traced the lines by the man's ribs. His fucking marks, left by only him, and more were coming.

"Please," he heard as he walked away to line up again. He turned to find her hovering in front of Pascal, her arms outstretched as she glared at him. She wanted it, too, it seemed.

"Back up," he said as he drew the whip back and flicked it about. "You'll need to lean on him."

There was nothing but figures there now. He could hardly think for the lack of anything coursing through his thoughts. Just a whip and some bodies. Where were the others? They could join in, too. He flicked his eyes behind him to see only the man. He raised a brow and watched the guy bow and back away. He always was a weak fucker, only good for fucking Pascal at the end of it all. But there wasn't going to be an end this time. This would go on and on, until Pascal found some interesting way of using a version of safe words he didn't have. He looked back to find her still standing there, endless legs trying to hide his target from him. Maybe he should fuck her while he did this, or maybe shove his cock down her throat again as she kneeled for him. Then he could hear them both of them begging him, or fucking screaming. Either would be fine, just as long as this fucking noise went away again.

"Alex, I love you. Please stop," she said. He watched the words leave her lips and smiled at them. She loved him. Even in this, she loved him. She wouldn't love him soon enough. She didn't have a clue who she loved, and why should she?

"MOVE!" he roared at her.

He flicked his eyes at the bedpost and remembered her bound to it, screaming as she'd felt only a little of him in flight. Fuck. His already hard cock ached at the thought as he imagined her fighting him, screaming at him and pleading for mercy. Pascal was hardly fighting anymore. The fun in him was almost over. The man just hung there now, ready to take more, but he was intrinsically useless now he wasn't trying to support himself. He was just another body. Still, he could take more, and so he raised the whip and readied himself. If she wasn't going to move then she could feel the brunt of it, too.

She suddenly moved towards him and got in his face, her hands waving around and hair flying brilliant reds at him. He smiled and watched her irritation grow until she eventually pointed at Pascal and said something. He couldn't hear it, wasn't fucking interested. Her body was all that concerned him as she began pushing against him and swearing. He grasped her arm and twisted so hard she screamed and dropped to the floor in front of him. Her face was suddenly nervous and scared again as she gazed up at him and he watched her mouth move again. He just kept staring at those lips saying something, and imagined them with a gag, or another man's cock embedded in them. She was good at that, fucking with her throat. Her perfect throat, his fucking throat. He clamped his hand around it and hauled her to her feet until all he could see was that mouth panting in front of his eyes. Beautiful lips, just trembling and waiting for him to hurt her. Because she wanted that. She must, or she wouldn't be putting herself in the way. He curled his lip at the thought and pulled her across to the bed as she fought him. He could feel her body kicking out at him and her muscles trying to get away, but there was nowhere for her to go. She was just in here, with him, and no one was going to save her from him. No one. She was here to help him forget, to help him lose himself in her and remind himself how indecent he really was. He pushed her to the post and watched her mouth carry on moving as her fists beat at his chest and arms. She really was beautiful, utterly perfect, and as his cock hardened again, he grabbed the whip on the bed and curled it around her arms, binding them together. Her pulse throbbed in his hand along with the beat of his cock as he tied it tighter and pulled her towards a waiting hook. Three turns and she was hanging there for him, just hanging there, waiting to be taken, hurt, bruised. He scanned her body and saw her reaching for the floor with her toes. She could hardly reach it. She was simply trying to take her weight on her bound wrists. Her skin writhed and twisted to get some purchase, and she fought well, but there wasn't a chance she could help herself. He just stood back and watched as he licked his lips and imagined what he could do with her. Maybe he should just watch her hang some more and see how much fight she had left in her. He sneered at the thought, there wasn't much fun in that was there.

Something brought his attention back to her face, and he gazed at her eyes as she kept moving her mouth. Such pretty eyes – angels lived in there, sweet, well-mannered and decent angels. There was nothing angelic happening here. This was where devils played. This was a time for demons and monsters to do their worst, to take that which was offered and rid themselves of some torment for a while. But, as he watched her, he felt those brown eyes trying to tell him something. Maybe they were screaming at the depravity in his soul, asking for more. She could have that. She could have everything from him. It was all for her.

Her mouth moved again as he wandered closer and brushed his fingers across her perfect skin. So milky, so ready to be tainted and torn to shreds. He pinched at her and watched her eyes widen again as her mouth kept moving. Why was it moving? He couldn't hear a fucking word coming out of it as she tried to turn her body away and shuffled her feet toward the bed for support. He grabbed at them and forced them back to hanging, just hanging, dangling by her pretty little wrists. That's all he suddenly wanted, so he could fuck her like that and watch hear her say she loved him, needed him.

Loved him for all of his true self.

Love.

His eyes snapped back up to her face again. Her lips were still animated, still mouthing words at him, and her eyes were still pleading for something as they filled with tears, beautiful tears. But he still couldn't hear the noise she made. It was so quiet in this room, so peaceful, and he could only gaze at them as she wrenched her head about and tried to get to the bed again. Love. Christ, he loved her for giving him this, for allowing it and wanting it with him. And he needed to be inside her now, needed to feel her clamping on him and telling him she loved him, showing him how worthwhile he actually was, or at least could be. He wanted that more than the silence. Or maybe he just needed to create more of it somehow, her version of it, to just revel in her skin and watch it shatter for him, just for him. Her perfect body, it was all for him. She told him that. It was his to own and do with as he saw fit. She offered that, too, didn't she? She said he could take it all from her.

He gasped as a sudden pain tore through the back of his head, and then again, sending him straight to the floor in agony. He tried to turn but another blow hit him from somewhere, and then another. He didn't know what it was, didn't really care either, because as that darkness pulled him under, all he could feel was peace again. Peace and a beautiful quiet. His fingers scratched at the carpet weakly as he gazed up at her legs and saw her hanging on the bedpost.

"Angel," he murmured out, watching the light dancing around her face. Why was she hanging? Had he done that? She looked frightened, scared. Something hit him again, something hard, and everything went black.

Chapter 31

Elizabeth

We've been bobbing around here in the warm Italian water for four days now. Nothing much has been said about what happened. Maybe no one really wants to talk about it, including me. I just want to pretend it didn't happen and try to move on. I don't even know if that's possible really, but as I watch Pascal tying off the main sail and shimmying his way back down towards me, I know there's hope of some sort. He protected me, just like he said he would. Even though he could hardly stand, he somehow managed to get that other chap in the room to uncuff him. He refused to let him help him hit Alex, said it would be rude, so he just did it himself. Typical Pascal, ever the gentleman, even in the most depraved situation. He simply picked up what I now know was a spreader bar, and then hit him with it, repeatedly, until Alex eventually blacked out. At the time, I'd been begging, screaming and shouting all sorts of words at him in the hope he'd stop, but there was no reaction, nothing, just dead eyes and an ever-growing body as he looked towards me with a sneer. I still don't know how I feel about that. I thought he'd hear me, thought our love was enough to pull him out of wherever that dark place is that he goes, but apparently it's not.

"Where is the balm?" Pascal calls as he lands two feet on the deck and smiles at me.

"I've got it," I reply as I dig around under the towels for it. Three times a day, every day, we have to apply it to his back. Not that there's much skin left to apply it to, but he says it'll heal. The skin might, but I have no idea how his mind will.

He wanders over to me in his shorts and shirt, looking every bit the European captain as he skips over the yacht as if he's spent his life on them. Wobbly seas mean nothing to him, it seems. I, on the other hand, am clearly less elegant in my manoeuvring ability on board such a fine vessel as I try to stand.

"Do stay down, my dear. It is quite unbecoming when you attempt movement." I roll my eyes at him and plonk myself back down again. He simply smiles and pulls the shirt from his back so I can smear the balm over his wounds. There are a lot of them, zigzagging and striping his torso to remind me, us both really, what the man we love is capable of.

"How are they today?" I ask as I dig my hand in and slather the oily substance over the crusting surface of what's left of his skin.

"Itching. Where is he?"

"Swimming," I reply with a chuckle as I raise my hand up to shield my eyes from the sun to look for him. He's nowhere to be seen, and if it's anything like the last three days, we won't see him for another two hours or so at least. Apparently it's quiet out there. I suppose it is, given that we're the only ones for miles in an ocean of aquamarine calm waters.

It was his choice to come here. After he came round from his blackout, he just sat there for an hour and looked at us both. He sat stock still in the middle of the room as Pascal and I watched him from the bed, cautiously. Even at that point I was still behind Pascal, I'd been put there before Alex even came round, and told to stay there until he deemed it acceptable. I hadn't argued either. Darkened Alex was a very scary prospect, and it seemed neither of us knew what to expect when he woke up. But after a while, when I saw the look on his face was full of remorse, I couldn't stop myself from going to him. I'd pushed past Pascal and then scrambled down to sit quietly in front of him with my legs crossed, mirroring his position and just gazing into his eyes. He simply stared back with those cool blue eyes and no hint of a smile. He just studied me, occasionally glancing across my body more than likely looking for injury. There wasn't any, Pascal had stopped him before it was too late.

Eventually, the man I love told us we were going to his yacht for some peace. Neither of us questioned it. I'm not sure why. I could have so easily just left at that point, but something told me to trust him, to stay, and I knew Pascal would never leave him regardless of the implications to his body. So we went home and packed our things while Alex made some phone calls, one of which was to Michael's family to tell them the news. He made all the arrangements necessary for the funeral and then quietly packed his things as we waited for him.

"How does he seem this morning?"

"Brighter. He said we should go to the mainland for dinner this evening," I reply as I close the lid on the jar and turn onto to my front in the hope of catching a glimpse of him in the water. There's still nothing to see, just an ocean of blues and greens stretching as far as the eye can see. But as least he is out there somewhere, alive and breathing. Whether he understands what happened in that room or not, I don't know because he just won't speak about it. He won't talk to me about Aiden or his father, either. In fact, he's hardly speaking at all. "Do you think it'll go back to the way it was at some point soon?" I mumble out as I pick up a glass of orange juice and stare into it. Pascal lies down next to me, and looks up to the skies above with a sigh.

"I doubt he will ever go back to where he has come from again, my love. He is perplexed by himself and therefore in need of our patience. We must persist with our perception of love until he realises his potential," he says with a smile wrapped around his very appealing mouth.

"That's your plan, is it? Just let him find his way back on his own terms and damn how we might feel about what happened?"

"How we feel about what happened is not relevant, my love. It is his burden to bear, his cross to carry. You must allow him this time to find himself again. Only then can we find the correct path forward. He will tell us when he finds it."

He twists onto his side and gazes at me as I shake my head at his relaxed posture and try to find his sense of peace in Alex's behaviour. I was so scared at the time, so frightened and horrified at what I was part of. If it hadn't been for the man beside me protecting me, I'm not sure what would have happened. Handle him or not, I was not ready for the nightmare coming at me. I was in no way prepared for the utter look of devastation embedded in his features or the way he didn't seem to see me. He was utterly lost, and there was no coming out of it.

"Why do you trust him, Pascal? Why would you put yourself in the hands of someone who could tear you to shreds without care?"

He turns onto his back again and pulls me into him, so I snuggle into the one man I feel safe with lately and rest my head on his chest.

His heart beats slowly beneath my ear and I smile at the comfort it gives me. Slow and relaxed. Confident in everything he is, does and needs. I've questioned a thousand times if I'm with the right man or not since we got here. It's nearly left my lips twice that he should just take me home and we should leave Alex here. But every time I've seen them together, every time I've watched a single touch delivered to Pascal, with a smile or not, I can see him melting into the man he loves. He'll never leave him again, and he certainly won't at the moment, not when he's needed.

I rub my head into him again and close my eyes as he starts fiddling with my hair and humming some song to himself. I don't know what it is, but it's so gentle, just a caressing mellow tune floating around the air and lulling me to a serene place I haven't been for a while. His ribs reverberate with each breath and cause my cheek to tingle a little, so I giggle at him and let the warm rays keep me calm and safe.

"Do you still love him, Elizabeth?" he says out of nowhere. What a ridiculous question.

"Of course I do," I mumble in reply as I try to keep myself from falling asleep, fail, and snuggle in closer. It's so very warm here, so calming and peaceful. I could stay here forever, and I will, won't I?

I know that to my core. I'll wait for as long as it takes to get my man back. If this is what he needs then I'll stay here with him and wait, hoping for his return, or maybe a new version of him to appear. I don't know, and I'm almost tired of caring.

I came with him when I could have run. I came with no fear of the repercussions because whatever he is, he is mine, and I do love him. And clearly that means I still need something he's offering.

So I'll just wait, and hope he finds his way back to me.

I'll wait with Pascal. We'll wait together.

THE END

Start the Next Journey following this story

The VDB Trilogy continues this saga, and this time it's told from Mr Van Der Braacks POV.

The Parlour (VDB1)

Above all else Pascal Van Der Braak is a gentleman. Devastatingly debonair and seductively charming. Always styled and perfected.
He is also a cad, scoundrel, rouge and kink empire founder.
Tutored in the highest of society, having been born of royalty only to deny it, he found his solace in a world where rules need not apply.
Where he chooses to ensure rules and duty do not apply.
Some call him Sir, others call him master, and no one would dare risk his wrath unless they required the punishment he favourably delivers.
Except one, who has just strapped a collar around his throat. One he asked for. So, now he needs to appropriate his businesses correctly for peace to ensue. He needs to find the correct path forward for everyone concerned, so he can relax, enjoy, and finally hand over the responsibility to someone else.
Simple.
But where comfort and a safety of sorts once dwelled, there is now uncertainty, and a feeling of longing he no longer understands. A need unfulfilled. And as problems arise, and allies scheme, he finds himself searching for answers in the most unlikely of places.

Lilah
It's the same every day. I'd found it odd at first, but I'm used to it now. I was so tired and weak when I got here that it was helpful really. That small woman comes in to help me wash and get dressed. I don't know where the clothes come from, but they're nice enough, and at least they're clean and dry. Not like the rags I arrived in. They were taken from me the moment I took them off to get into the shower, the first shower I'd had in god knows how long. Nearly a year I'd been running

447

the streets, a year without a real bed or a home of any sort. There isn't a long and awful story to tell about an abusive family member, or a broken home. I suppose I just slipped through the cracks and got lost at some point. I lost my job first, and then I couldn't afford the bills on my apartment, so the landlord threw me out. I don't blame him, he did the right thing by himself. And then it was just a long and never-ending road to nothingness.

So now I'm here, wherever here is.

And I don't know why.

This book is followed by

Eden's Gate (VDB2)
And
Serenity's Key (VDB3)

Thus ends the journey of these wonderful characters. Maybe. Until sometime in the future anyway.

Other Works By This Author

Once Upon A (Stained Duet #1)

Alana Williams is three published authors. She has been for years, but now she wants to add another voice to her whirlwind of deadlines and unachievable targets. Trouble is, she knows nothing of her latest literary undertaking – KINK.

Alana

It began as research. Just research. The technical approach. One that delivers the content necessary for a hidden culture to seem plausible, even if it's not. Readers expect perfection from me. They want the experience. They need to be taken on a journey. That's my job as a writer.

Blaine Jacobs is his name. He's my research. A man who seems as logical and focused as me. A man who agrees to help. A man who, regardless of his stature in the community, seems to offer a sense of realism to this strange section of society. And even if he does occasionally interrupt my data with dark brooding eyes and a questionably filthy mouth, what does it matter? It's just research, isn't it? It's not real. None of this is. Nothing will come of it or change my mind.

So why am I confused?
I'm becoming lost.
Falling apart.

And Blaine Jacobs, no matter how calm he might have seemed at first, now appears to linger on the edges of sanity, pushing my boundaries with every whispered word.

18+ ONLY. Intended for mature audiences.

Followed By
The End (Stained Duet #2)

Innocent Eyes (A Cane Novel)
Co-authored with Rachel De Lune
HART DE LUNE

"If he's gross, I'm bailing."
That's what I said to my supposed best friend when she asked me to take her place. A blind date, she said. What harm could it do?
He was charming. Beautiful. God's finest creation. He wined me and dined me. Made me do things I'd never before dreamt of in the bedroom. It was perfect. Dangerous. Arousing.
But Jenny didn't tell me the full story. She didn't tell me about the debt she owed. And now Quinn Cane wants his money's worth, and he's going to make me pay whatever way he can.

"A debt needs to be paid."
The woman who came to meet me didn't owe me money. I could tell by her innocent eyes. Still, the debt will be paid either way.
She was something to play with and use as I saw fit, but something about Emily Brooks made me want to keep her. So she became my dirty girl. Pure. Innocent. Mine.
Then she whispered my damned name and invaded my world, changing its reasoning.
She wasn't meant to break the rules. But she rolled my dice and won.

Shame. Forgiveness. Dark. Erotic. Romance.

This book is intended for mature audiences. 18+ only.

Acknowledgements

There is one person I have to thank for putting up with my constant keyboard tapping every evening and it's my wonderful partner. I love you more than words can say.
Without your support through the last few years, I couldn't have achieved any of this, and you'll never understand how much that means to me. But hopefully, if you look inside the characters, you'll find a bit more of me that you've allowed to open up and free itself from its box.
Me x

To all the blogs that have supported, helped, guided and forged a path for me, I love you all without reservation. However, special mentions go out to:
Leanne Cook, my PA - Love you, honey x
Heather's Red Pen Editing, my rather wonderful editor x
Rachel Brightey - Orchard Book Club.
Rachel Hill - Bound by Books Book Reviews.

And of course, you guys. Anyone who has read the third part of this story and enjoyed it is warmly thanked and acknowledged as super wonderful. I hope you've enjoyed the further journey of my characters and if they've resonated with you in some way, be it small or large, then I've achieved my goal, which was to provoke thought and entertain you.
CEH x

Printed in Great Britain
by Amazon

17465987R00258